MODEL BEHAVIOR

WRECKED ROOMMATES BOOK ONE

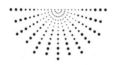

KELSIE RAE

TWISTY PINES PUBLISHING, LLC

Cover Art by Cover My Wagon Dragon Art

Editing by Wickedcoolflight Editing Services

Proofreading by Stephanie Taylor

Published by Twisty Pines Publishing, LLC

March 2021 Edition

Published in the United States of America

❁ Created with Vellum

1

REESE

"**D**on't touch me," I seethe, glaring at my boyfriend's massive hand that's gripping my bicep.

"Babe––"

"Let go of me right now, Ian, or so help me, I will kick you in the balls."

"Reese, baby, come on…" His tone makes my gut tighten. All the moments he's used this voice with me.

Reese, baby.

Come on, baby.

I love you, baby.

I am *not* his baby anymore.

Squeezing my eyes shut, I whisper, "I can't even look at you right now. How the hell do you expect me to stay and talk this out, Ian?"

"Babe…," he tries again.

"Don't call me that. Don't call me anything at all. Will you just let me go?" I tug my arm out of his hold.

"You can't run from me, Reese," he challenges, blocking the front door with his half-naked yet still massive frame. He's always been more of a burly bear than anything else, and it seems he's using it to his advantage against his helpless little girlfriend. *Ex*-girlfriend.

Bastard.

"I'm sorry, okay?" he continues, lacking any real remorse. "It was a mistake. You were never supposed to find out."

I scoff before shaking my head while ignoring the *mistake* who's still hanging out in our freaking apartment. "And that's supposed to make me feel better? Really? That's the apology you want to go with?"

"That came out wrong––"

"No, it didn't. It came out the exact way that it was supposed to."

"Look, if you would just let me explain––"

"Fine." I cross my arms. "Go for it. I want to hear aaalll about the late-night text messages, the canceled dates, the no-shows at work when I had to lie to your brother's face because you were too inconsiderate to show up for your shift. Or maybe you can tell me why I came home to see a girl in our kitchen with wet hair while you were finishing up in the shower with the bathroom door wide open. Would you like me to go on?"

He groans before rubbing his hand across his tired face. "Listen––"

"Nope. I changed my mind. I'm done. Like *done,* done. Now, move out of the way before I really do hit you in the balls like I so desperately want to."

"You won't even let me talk!" he snaps. His anger is finally boiling over, but right now, I don't give a damn.

Going head-to-head with the beast in front of me, I spit, "That's because I don't care what you have to say."

I can see the indecision on his face. The slight twitch of his lip begging to curl in disgust. The tension in his jaw. The iciness in his gaze. Still, I hold strong and refuse to cower. He really is an ass. After another few tense seconds, he caves and moves over a few inches.

"Don't be a bitch, Reese. It's not sexy."

There's a small gap between him and the door, but I know I'll have to touch him if I have any hopes of squeezing through it, which is exactly what he wants. To make me squirm. To make me uncomfortable. To make me feel weak.

How did I not see what a bully he is?

I shift my gaze from the tiny gap and up to his red face. "We both know you've never seen me as sexy, so why should I start caring now? I'm the cute girl, remember? The girl next door. Isn't that what you told me? That I might not be sexy, but I was still fuckable?"

"I said that one time, and I was drunk--"

"You know what, nevermind. I don't care what you think anymore. Tell your brother that I'm sorry, but I quit."

"You can't quit."

"Yes, I most definitely can. Thanks for your input, though," I return sarcastically. "I really appreciate it."

His jaw tightens. "What am I supposed to tell him? He needs you--"

"No offense, but I don't think that's my problem anymore. Maybe you can convince your little friend over there"--I wave my hand toward the skank in the kitchen--"to handle the books while answering the phone like I did for your brother. She seems like quite the thinker."

Ignoring my snide remark, he drops his voice low. "We'll talk later, Reese."

"Like I said. I'm done talking. Goodbye, Ian."

Holding my breath, I continue our little game of chicken and squeeze through the crack between the doorway and his chest. When my butt grazes his towel-covered crotch, my spine straightens.

He used to love makeup sex. Said it was the best part about being in a relationship.

Now, it just makes me wonder why he was in one in the first place if that was the only benefit in his eyes. Although, I'm sure it didn't hurt that I helped his brother with his accounting while we were dating. Maybe that was just an added perk.

Doesn't take the sting away or the fact that I've never felt lower in my entire life. How long has he been juggling multiple women, and why was I stupid enough to believe he actually cared about me?

Because the answer is simple.

He didn't.

WITH MY PHONE PRESSED TO MY EAR, I CURSE UNDER MY breath. "Come on, Milo. Answer your freaking phone."

"This is Milo," the recording starts. "If you're hearing this, then I probably didn't want to pick up the phone. Text me."

Beep.

I don't bother to leave a voicemail because let's be honest, my brother won't listen to it anyway. I've already sent him a dozen text messages, and he hasn't responded to those either. Before I can talk myself out of it, I dial his best friend, Jake.

The damn thing goes straight to voicemail too. Just like Milo's.

With a deep breath, I raise my hand and knock on the door in front of me while praying I'm at the right address.

Please be home, Milo. Please be home.

It took me an hour to get here from Ian's and my apartment. I'd hoped that hour would've been enough time for Milo to call me back. But apparently, fate hates me today, so

I'm not exactly surprised to see an almost-naked stranger on the other side of the door as it squeaks open.

Speechless, I take in the guy from head to toe.

When I catch myself staring at the 'V' on his lower abdomen that I was pretty sure didn't actually exist out in the wild before this exact moment, he clears his throat, and I peek up at him.

With his head cocked to the side and his amusement on full display, the stranger mentions, "Usually, I take the girl out to dinner before I let her imagine me naked like that."

Like a bucket of ice water has been poured over my head, I purse my lips and motion to the guy's muscles and perfectly tanned skin that are on full display. "Well, there's not much left to the imagination, so you'll have to forgive me."

"Who said I was complaining?" He smirks before leaning his broad shoulder against the doorjamb.

How is he so freaking toned?

"Can I help you, sweetheart?" he prods.

"I'm, uh, I'm looking for Milo."

"Milo?" he repeats. I can hear the smile in his voice as I swallow thickly and force myself to hold his hypnotic stare.

I feel like I've fallen into a lion's cage, and the predator is stalking closer, backing me into a corner with nowhere left to run.

"Um…" I shake my head and try to focus. "Yeah. Is he home by chance?"

"Sorry, babe. Milo isn't here."

"Of course, he isn't," I mutter under my breath, shifting my weight between my feet. "How 'bout Jake? Is he home?"

With a crooked yet arrogant-as-hell grin, the bastard chuckles. "Milo *and* Jake? I didn't know *they* were into sharing––"

"Ew. Gross." I shudder. "No, I'm Milo's sister––"

"I'm sure you are. But I have company, and your boys

aren't here. Normally, I'd invite you in, but since I don't do sloppy seconds, and I already have company…"

The wide-open door slowly begins to shut before I slap my hand against it. My palm burns on impact, but I stand my ground.

"No, you don't understand––"

"I understand perfectly. You're a girl who's looking for two different men, neither of which happen to be home at the moment, while simultaneously wasting my time that could be spent buried deep inside my house guest."

My eyes pop. He did *not* just say that to me.

"Babe, what's taking you so long?" A gorgeous blonde appears from the other side of the door. She doesn't even bother to look my way before sliding her hands along his abs and nibbling at the exposed skin along his strong jaw. It's like I'm a ghost with how oblivious she is to my presence. In fact, I'm pretty sure that if I don't let this guy close the door, she'll start dry humping him within seconds. And I can't really blame her. The guy's hot. The problem is that he *knows* it, which is the only reason I'm not dying from insane jealousy as her manicured fingers toy with the hem of his gray basket-ball shorts.

Wait, is she really about to dive into his pants when I'm standing two feet away from her?

Is he really going to let her? I mean, I know she looks like a lingerie model and all, but seriously?

I'm right here!

Thankfully, my brother's roommate can still see me, proving that I am not, in fact, invisible, and decides to throw me a bone. "Try SeaBird down the street. They like to hang out there." Motioning to my hand that's still preventing the door from closing, he adds, "Now, if you'll excuse me, I have some business to attend to."

The door closes despite my feeble attempt to keep it

open, and I'm left alone on the front porch of my brother's house in the middle of a strange city with what little hope I'd been clinging to sliding from my grasp.

I'm so screwed.

A soft moan vibrates through the front door. It's quickly followed by a loud thud that causes the gold knocker attached to it to rattle.

And apparently, I'm not the only one who's getting screwed.

Dropping my head and looking toward the sky, I count to ten, then turn on my heel toward my car that's parked in the driveway.

SeaBird, here I come.

THE PLACE SMELLS LIKE THE BEACH, COMPLETE WITH COCONUT, rum, and a hint of salt. The combination is almost enough to ease the ache in my chest with memories of happier times before my phone buzzes with a text.

Ian: Babe. Come home.

My grip tightens around the screen before I type my response.

Me: We're done, Ian.

I don't know why I'm even bothering to reply. It'll only encourage him to keep sending bullshit apologies.

Oh, wait. That wasn't an apology. It was him being his usual controlling self. How could I forget?

With a huff, I shove my phone into the back pocket of my jeans, march toward the bar, then find an open seat.

"Hey. What can I get ya?" a voice yells over the live band

playing a cover song in the corner. Finding the voice's owner, I'm met with a tattooed Adonis. His arms are etched with ink, stretched on both sides of him as he leans a little closer to hear my order, but I'm too speechless to come up with anything.

Again.

Dude. What is in the water here? And do they bottle it? Because I'm pretty sure I could make a fortune by selling it on the black market.

His straight, white teeth dig into his lower lip in an attempt to keep a teasing smile at bay as he catches me checking him out, but it's pointless. The damn thing still makes an appearance as he prods, "You look like you've had a long day. Are you a whiskey girl?"

"I'm an any-kind-of-alcohol girl when I've had a day like today."

Rapping his knuckles across the polished counter, he replies, "Well, then. First one's on me." He steps away to grab my drink. And boy, do I need it.

What the hell was I thinking? Did I really just throw away my whole life, my future today? Breaking up with Ian is one thing, but he was practically my boss. Now, I'm homeless, and I don't have a job or a future career, for that matter. Hell, I didn't even grab clothes for tomorrow.

I'm an idiot.

An idiot who stayed with the wrong guy for way too long, all because I was afraid to leave him.

But I deserve more than a shitty boyfriend/boss who cheated on me. Don't I?

Where the hell is Milo?

I swivel around on the soft brown barstool and begin my search, but the place is packed for a random Thursday night. Bodies are grinding against each other in perfect rhythm with the base as I hunt for my brother in the crowd.

8

Milo, where are you? I want to yell, but I don't waste my breath.

"Looking for someone?" the bartender calls as the small shot glass clinks against the dark, lacquered counter in front of me.

I nod before picking it up and swallowing the amber liquid in one gulp. The burn is a welcome distraction from the buzzing in my back pocket. Annoyed, I dig the phone out of my pocket and slap it facedown against the counter when I find Ian's name flashing across the screen.

Leave me alone, asshole.

"Who are you looking for?" the hot bartender presses. "Maybe I can help."

"His name is Milo. Milo Anders. Or Jake Jensen. Either of them will work, actually."

As soon as their names roll off my tongue, a spark of recognition flashes in the bartender's eyes that's quickly followed by a quirked brow. "What do you want with them?"

"I'm sorry, is it normal bartender behavior to be so nosy?"

"Maybe. Depends on the day and if I'm serving a *drinks anything* girl or not."

"Oh, so because I'm a little desperate for alcohol and have a vagina, you're allowed to be nosy?"

He laughs, taken aback by my bluntness. "Was it *that* rough of a day, Drinks Anything Girl?"

My expression sours before I nudge the empty shot glass a few inches toward him. "You could say that."

"Wanna talk about it?" He raises a whiskey bottle into the air, then pours a generous amount into the tiny cup that's ten sizes too small.

After throwing it back, I answer, "Oh, you know, just… looking to escape reality, and life, and bad decisions. That kind of thing. And what better place to escape than this bar in search of my big brother who isn't answering my calls?"

Eyes widening, the surprised bartender looks me up and down. "Which means Milo or Jake is your older brother."

I wave my finger through the air like a miniature celebratory flag. "Ding, ding, ding! We have a winner."

"So, you're not sleeping with either of them?" he clarifies, his tone still laced with disbelief.

My face scrunches as I picture either of them touching me in a non-platonic way.

I shiver. "Why does everyone keep jumping to that conclusion?"

"Everyone?" he challenges.

"Hey! I need two rum and Cokes, please," a voice orders from behind me. I turn to see a pair of beautiful girls dressed in tank tops and leather skirts with sky-high heels that make their legs go on for miles.

Day-um. I am so underdressed.

"Yeah, they'll be right up," Hot Bartender answers them before lowering his voice and adding, "I'll be right back."

"Take your time."

The band starts a new song, and I watch the singer hum into the microphone before diving right into the first verse a few counts later. This one is an original, or at least I think it is. It's soft and smooth with a haunting edge that makes me want to give the entire band a giant bear hug. Closing my eyes, I let the harmony wash over me and get lost in its lullaby while feeling more at home in a strange bar than I've felt in my apartment with Ian in a long time.

"All right. Big brother, it is," the bartender announces, shaking me from my reverie while reminding me of our unfinished conversation. "The question is...which one fits the bill?"

"Ooo, I like this game." Apparently, the alcohol's making me way more intrigued in the current conversation than finding my asshole brother who has yet to make an appearance. I rest my elbows on the hard surface and lean closer. "Guess."

Tapping his forefinger against his cleft chin, he considers his options. "Well…you have virgin skin, which immediately puts you in the Jake category, and you're tiny as hell, which would also put you in the Jake category."

I chew the inside of my cheek to keep from cracking up and giving the answer away because he's so freaking far off with his investigative skills.

Detective, you are not, Sexy Bartender.

With a look of triumph, the guy wags his finger at my face. "Aaand there's my answer."

I pull back. "Excuse me?"

"The nervous tick." He motions to me again. "Not only is it exactly like a certain tattoo artist I'm friends with, but the dimple etched into your cheek is a dead giveaway. Sorry, Drinks Anything Girl. But I think you just handed me the key to crack the code without even knowing it. I'm Gibbs, by the way."

"Reese," I return, offering my hand across the bar top for him to take. His calloused grip is warm and strong. But there isn't a zing that I'd initially expected. Probably because my asshole ex has ruined me for all healthy relationships, but what do I know? With our palms still touching, I dip my chin to a freshly-inked skull tattoo along the back of his hand. "So, is that how you know my brother?"

Following my gaze, he inspects the piece of art before shrugging. "Nah. I knew him way before he ever started tattooing. But yeah, this is his work."

"You knew him before he started tattooing?" I ask before ending our handshake to toy with the rim of my empty shot glass. "You sure about that? I feel like I'd remember you."

"I'm not exactly someone you bring home to meet the folks."

I want to laugh at the irony but push it aside as I divulge a family secret that I'm sure he's already privy to if he knows my brother as well as he says he does. "We didn't have folks at our house. We had a pair of alcoholic toddlers who expected us to clean up their vomit."

"Touché." There's an intensity in his hazel eyes as he pins me in place, but I can't quite put my finger on what it means or why I want to lean closer. Sensing my hesitation, he adds, "Maybe it was you he was keeping me from."

A shy smile makes my mouth curve up on one side. "Maybe."

"Hey, asshole. What are you doing talking to my baby sister?" a familiar voice growls from across the bar.

My neck snaps toward the culprit.

Why hello, Milo.

2

REESE

The sea of people part as my big brother stalks closer to me. He's flanked by his friend and exact opposite, Jake Jensen. My pulse spikes. The combination has always reminded me of a pair of overprotective dogs determined to keep me safe. And it seems tonight isn't any different, no matter how unnecessary it is.

Sliding off my stool in an attempt to diffuse the situation, I meet them in the middle of the room before they can get too close to the innocent bartender who has no idea how overbearing they can be. Then, I pull Jake into a quick hug.

"Hey, Jake," I murmur as I peek over his shoulder toward Gibbs. When our gazes connect, he lifts his chin then disappears to help another customer at the opposite end of the bar.

Coincidence that he just ditched me? I think not.

It's not like I blame him, though. Jake's a teddy bear, but Milo's a scary dude. He might not be a massive sledgehammer, but there's always been something simmering just beneath the surface with him. Even in middle school, the kids would give him a wide berth. Like he might go off at any minute. And he *has*––more times than I can count.

He's always been that way, though. But never with me. He loves me too much.

"Hey, Reese," Jake returns before letting me go. "What are you doing here?"

"It's...complicated," I answer vaguely. Tilting my chin up, I look my big brother in the eye then wrap my arms around him in hopes of softening his rigid posture. Unfortunately, it's like hugging a flagpole.

"Hey, Milo," I say, keeping my tone light and easy.

"You," he grits out. "Wait here. I'll be right back."

"Milo––"

Jake wraps his arms around my waist a second time, pinning my back to his front. "You heard your brother. Give him a minute."

Turning around in his arms, I poke Jake in the chest.

"To what?" I accuse. "Rip off an innocent guy's head all because he talked to me? Uh-uh. No deal. I thought we'd moved past the overprotective brother crap––"

"Just give him a second, Reese. You don't want to get in the way of...*that*."

I pause and turn back to watch Milo stalk closer to Gibbs like a man on a mission. "Of *what*, exactly?"

"History," Jake answers with a shrug. "They're friends, though. It'll be fine. Milo just needs to set a few boundaries. That's all."

"He always needs to set a few boundaries," I huff, crossing my arms over my chest. "Maybe he should just tattoo a giant *do not touch* sign on my forehead. Do you think that would keep the boys away? Not like they're interested in *that* kind of way in the first place, but you know what I mean," I mutter under my breath.

Jake's mouth quirks up on one side, but he doesn't comment.

Flustered, I suck my lower lip into my mouth then turn back to the trainwreck that's about to unfold a few feet away from me.

But there isn't one. Gibbs' hands are raised in the air, surrendering before Milo even opens his mouth. My brows pinch in the center as Milo leans forward, placing his hands on the bar top while keeping his voice low. The music is too loud for me to overhear what he's saying, and I kind of want to throw my shoe at the band to get them to stop for two seconds. Unfortunately, I'm not sure it would do me any good anyway.

Nostrils flaring, my brother cocks his head toward me as his lips continue to deliver what I'm sure is an unnecessary threat. Gibbs' gaze snaps to mine. Then he looks back at Milo and raises his chin in a single nod.

Message received.

Satisfied, Milo taps his knuckles against the bar top before he swaggers toward me with the triumph of a gold medalist.

Cocky asshole.

Throwing his arm around my shoulders, he gives me an actual hug. One that's warm and welcoming and is almost enough to make me forget his barbaric behavior from two seconds ago.

Almost.

"Ever heard of answering your phone?" I ask, my tone full of snark. "I've been calling and texting all night."

"You know how much I hate electronics and shit," Milo answers.

With a pointed look at his best friend, I accuse, "And what's your excuse, Jakey Boy?"

ices. "Out of battery. Sorry. What brings you to the woods anyway?"

for my response, both men cross their arms. One set is ██ y and tatted, while the other is a little leaner and ink-free. But they both showcase their muscular biceps and their lack of patience for me showing up unannounced.

This would've been so much easier if either of them had answered their freaking phones.

"I uh…" I gulp, hating the desperation that slips into my response. "I need a place to stay."

Milo quirks his brow. "And why's that?"

Rocking back on my heels, I tuck my thumbs into the back pockets of my ripped jeans while hating Ian more and more by the minute.

"Tell me," Milo demands, his anger simmering just below the surface.

"You were, uh…" A bitter taste floods my mouth as an image of the tall blonde slut in my kitchen rises to the surface. "You were right about Ian."

"What kind of right?" Milo pushes.

Close to tears, I shrug and choke out, "All of it?"

"He cheat on you?"

My face floods with shame as I bite my lip until the sharp tang of blood explodes across my taste buds. Then, I nod.

With a curse under his breath, Jake pulls me into another hug, but it only fans the flames of my imminent breakdown.

How could I have been so stupid?

Resting my head against Jake's chest, I soak up the offered comfort and watch my brother's face turn red with anger.

Three, two, one—

"That sonofabitch," he growls. "I told you he was bad news, Reese. I *told* you. Lying, cheating, motherfu—"

"Hey," Jake barks. "Calm the hell down. She hates it when you get pissed."

16

Milo scrubs his hand across his face before releasing a deep breath. "Sorry."

"It's fine," I whisper, although a small part of me wants to point out that he's already gotten pissed tonight because of me. *Twice.* But it's not entirely his fault that he has a short fuse. It's our dad's. Yet another thing we can thank our crappy parents for.

"You have every right to be pissed," I add, my sadness morphing into frustration. "And to say you told me so."

There's a slight pause before Milo reaches forward and tugs me away from Jake's embrace. When my face smacks against his hard pec, he tightens his arm around me and mutters, "Doesn't make it any better, Reese. I'm sorry I was right, though."

And I know he's sincere because no matter how much fun it is to say, *I told you so*, it's never fun to see your family in pain. And right now? I'm hurting. Bad.

"Me too," I breathe. "He's an ass. I'm just mad that it took me so long to see it."

Milo lets me go. "Don't beat yourself up about it. You can stay with us."

"You sure?"

"Yeah. There's a spare room."

"What about your other roommates? Will they be okay with that?" I press, hating that I even have to ask this of him. But I guess that's what happens when your world revolves around a selfish asshole before it all falls apart because of said asshole.

His chest rumbles with amusement. "I don't give a shit if they're okay with it or not. You're staying. And that's final."

Peeking over at Jake, I ask, "And how 'bout you? Are you okay if I stay for a little while?"

His honey-colored eyes are as warm as I remember as he studies me carefully. But he doesn't answer me. Detecting his hesitation, I open my mouth to retract my request when he cuts me off.

"For however long you need, Reese."

My relief spreads from my chest and out to my limbs like the shot of whiskey I swallowed earlier. Then I release the air I'd been keeping hostage in my lungs.

If he'd said no, I would've understood. I would've probably slept in my car for a few days before coming up with Plan C since, ya know, Plan A was to continue my relationship with an asshole, and Plan B existed because I have an awesome, albeit prickly older brother who is always looking out for me.

But I would've figured out a Plan C if I'd needed to. Besides, I wouldn't blame Jake if he wasn't cool with it. Who wants to live with their best friend's little sister?

"Thank you," I whisper to Jake. It's so loud in here that I doubt he even hears me, but he gives me a single nod in acknowledgment anyway. My hesitant smile turns into a full-bodied yawn in an instant as the last of my adrenaline seeps out of me.

I. Am. Exhausted.

Covering my mouth, I let the yawn take its course before a laugh escapes me. "Wooow. Sorry about that."

"You look like shit," Milo points out with a wry grin. "Come on. We'll take you home."

"No. Stay. Seriously. I don't want to ruin your night out just because I showed up unannounced. I'll go take a quick nap in my car or something until you're ready to––"

"Stop arguing," Milo interrupts. "Did you drive?"

"Yup."

"Then lead the way."

With his arm tossed over my shoulder, Milo guides me back out the front door while Jake trails behind us. As we squeeze through the crowd, I look toward the bar, but Gibbs is nowhere to be found.

Huh.

Shaking off my curiosity, I step outside and breathe deep. The air is cool and calm at this time of night, and I let it wash away my insecurities. Well, some of them anyway. Call it a hunch, but I think the burn from Ian's betrayal won't be going anywhere anytime soon.

Pointing my finger at my dark blue beater car beneath the streetlight parked a few spaces away, I tell them, "My car's over there."

"Where are your keys?" Milo asks.

I raise my hand and jingle them back and forth. "Right here."

He snatches them from my grasp before they fly through the air and land in Jake's palm.

"I rode my bike," Milo explains, motioning to where I assume he'd parked his motorcycle even though I don't see the big black beast anywhere. "Jake will drive you home. I'll meet you there."

"Seriously, Milo. You don't have to––"

"Stop arguing," he orders. Then he jogs around the corner, leaving me alone with his best friend and my pseudo big brother. Smiling shyly, I try to ignore the fact that I just got passed from one guy to another like a bad cold in elementary school.

"I can drive, ya know."

"You heard the boss' orders," Jake quips. "Let's get you home."

Rounding the front of my beat-up Honda, he opens the door for me then helps me inside like I'm a fragile little deer.

Or a weak little girl who just had her heart broken and lost everything.

My annoyance spikes as I collapse into the passenger seat

and cross my arms. "You don't have to open the door for me, Jake. I'm a big girl. I think I can handle it."

"Just because you can doesn't mean you should have to. Besides, my mom raised me to be a gentleman, remember?" His boyish grin flashes back at me before he closes the passenger door, then climbs behind the steering wheel and turns on the ignition.

"Sometimes, I can't believe you and Milo are actually best friends," I admit as I click my seat belt into place.

His chuckle reverberates through the cab of the car. "Yeah, you're not the only person who has a hard time believing that one. He isn't one to open doors, is he?"

"You tell me. He never brings any of his girls around me, so…"

"That's because he doesn't want you to think less of him," he counters, pulling out of the parking spot.

"Why would I think less of him?"

He glances over at me, his eyes crinkling at the corners. "He's kind of a whore, Reese."

"And he thinks I don't know that?" I laugh. "I heard the stories in high school. Hit-It-And-Quit-It Milo Anders. Yeah, I remember those stories quite well. You, on the other hand…"

"Yeah, yeah. I was a reclusive nerd who enjoyed video games and rarely left my room. I remember."

"Unless you were hanging out with Milo," I recall as he turns onto the main road.

"Yeah. I still don't know why he saved my ass from getting beaten every day, but you won't hear me complaining."

"And he graduated because you tutored him, so I'd say it was a pretty even trade."

"The nerd and the asshole. Who'd of thought, right?"

"Mm-hmm," I hum, watching him closely while subtly

scanning him up and down in the glow from the dashboard. He looks good. A little less nerdy than I remember. A little more filled out too.

"Has Milo been forcing you to go to the gym with him again?" I tease.

With a cocky smirk, his grip tightens around the steering wheel and showcases his toned forearms. "You noticed, huh?"

Dude. I'd be blind to not *notice.*

I lick my lips that threaten to pull into another smile. "You look good, Jake. Seriously. If you keep it up and get some ink, you might even *not* stick out like a sore thumb whenever you're hanging out with my brother."

"Yeah, but I will when I'm TA'ing a class," he counters.

"Good point," I concede, pulling my gaze away from his honey-colored eyes to stare out the window. Trees line both sides of the dark street, blurring together as we pass by. "So…how's the master's program going, anyway?"

"It's good. One more semester, and I'll be done."

"Jake!" I squeal before giving him a playful nudge in the shoulder. "That's amazing. Seriously. I'm proud of you."

There's a soft blush that creeps into his cheeks, but he waves me off. "It's not that big of a deal."

"Maybe not in your family, but in the Ander's lineage, it's unheard of. I'm seriously impressed."

"Well…" He glances over at me before turning his attention back to the road. "Thanks. It's not like you wouldn't be capable of it, though. I remember you being a math whiz."

I roll my eyes. "I'd hardly call myself a math whiz."

"Weren't you doing accounting or something for…?" He cringes when he realizes the minefield he just walked into.

"For Ian's family's company?" I finish for him. "Yeah. But it's not like I'll be able to use that on my resume or anything. I didn't go to college, remember? They probably just hired me out of pity in the first place."

"That's bullshit, Reese––"

"Debatable, Jake," I argue with a dry laugh. "Besides, it doesn't matter anyway. Any other company will want a degree, and I don't have the time or money to invest in something like that. I need a new job. Stat. Especially if I'm ever going to be able to afford a place on my own."

"You could take out a student loan––"

"I'm not going to get into debt."

"It's an investment––"

"One I can't afford. Not right now. Not without a job."

"Milo could––"

"I'm gonna stop you right there, Jake. Milo has already done more for me than any brother should ever have to. I'll figure it out, okay? On my own."

His grip tightens around the steering wheel. "You're allowed to rely on your brother, Reese."

"Do you think I would've showed up at SeaBird tonight if I didn't believe that?" I counter. "I know I can rely on him. But it would be nice if I could handle my own shit every once in a while too."

The rev of the engine is the only response he gives me.

With a sigh, I tuck my hair behind my ear. "Speaking of relying on people…thanks for driving me home. And for letting me stay at your place for a little while. I know that Milo likes to pretend he rules the world, but he doesn't, and if you would've said no, he would've supported that. So, thank you. I appreciate it."

His gaze flicks toward me before returning to the road as he flips on the blinker. "No worries, Reese."

More silence.

"So where's your car, anyway?" I ask.

"At home."

"Then how'd you get to the bar in the first place? I mean, if Milo had his bike…?"

"I caught a ride with Sonny," Jake explains before turning onto one of the side roads that lead to their house.

I have no idea who Sonny is, but it seems like Jake isn't feeling very chatty, and I'm not in the mood to dig for answers. Not right now. "Oh. Well, I guess that worked out then."

Giving me the side-eye, he mutters, "Yeah. I guess it did."

The cool glass from the passenger window kisses my forehead as I rest my head against it and let my exhaustion from the day finally catch up to me.

A few minutes later, he pulls into the long driveway of their five-bedroom house and turns off the ignition. "Welcome home."

Home. The word feels foreign. Growing up with alcoholic parents who used all of their money to drown out their problems instead of filling the refrigerator does that to a girl. And moving in with the first boy who ever looked my way, yet treated me like a doormat, never exactly fulfilled the Hallmark version of a home either.

Just a roof over my head.

And now, I wouldn't even have that without Milo.

With my head cocked to one side, I inspect the house looming in front of me. It has two stories with white shutters and dark blue siding, and the grass is freshly mowed with a large tree that reaches for the sky near the white mailbox out front. It's gorgeous. And nothing like the house I was raised in. I hadn't taken the time to study it when I first knocked on the door earlier tonight. I was a little too distracted by nerves and the strange roommate with his houseguest to appreciate the place.

My face pales.

I *cannot* face him again.

"What's wrong?" Jake prods, reading me like a book as he tosses me my keys.

They fall limp in my lap. "Nothing."

"Liar," he teases. "I know you, remember?"

He's right. He does. Or at least, he used to. Then I started dating Ian. And Ian didn't want me to talk to Jake. He insisted it was inappropriate.

Oh, the irony.

Slowly, our daily texting conversations melted away to a meme here or there, then almost nothing at all. And even though I hate to admit it, I miss that friendship. I'm just not sure if Jake's interested in salvaging it now that I don't have an overbearing boyfriend standing in the way.

"Seriously. What's wrong, Reese?" he prods.

Chewing my lower lip, I tear my gaze away from the house and look down at my hands in my lap. "Are you sure it's okay if I stay?"

"We already said yes."

"I know, but…what about everyone else?" I ask. "I don't want to be a burden."

Reaching over the center console, he squeezes my knee. It's innocent. Comforting. And another reminder that he's a rock in my ever-turbulent life. One I'd forgotten I'd had.

His touch eases the ache in my chest, even if it only lasts a second before he releases me and mutters, "Like I said, it's fine. We have an extra room, and the guys are pretty easygoing. Even if they weren't, Milo made up his mind, and we both know how much of an asshole he can be when he doesn't get his way." He laughs dryly. "Seriously, Reese. You can stay as long as you need."

"Are you sure?"

With a groan, he opens the car door and orders, "Stop asking. You're fine. I promise. Now, come on. I'll show you inside."

My knee bounces up and down as I peek back up at the house that's taunting me as an image of the half-naked roommate flashes through my mind. *Again.* I shrug it off and move on autopilot, following Jake's lead as I slide out of the passenger side.

The driver's side door closes with a loud thud before he pops open the trunk and finds it empty.

With a puzzled expression, he turns to me. "Where's your stuff?"

"Oh." I cringe. "I didn't bring anything."

"Why not?"

Wrapping my arms around my torso, I rub my hands up and down my bare arms while hating how vulnerable I'm about to sound. "I, uh…I just had to get out of there."

He slams the trunk closed, then squeezes the back of his neck like he doesn't know what to say. I don't blame him. I don't know what to say either. After a moment of hesitation, he rounds the car and presses his hand to my lower back to usher me inside. "We'll get it later, Reese. Not a big deal."

Oh, it'll be a big deal.

I'm sure of it. Ian is going to be pissed at me for leaving as soon as his guilt wears off. And facing him again won't exactly be a picnic, especially when I know how much his family relies on me to balance their books. Still, it's not like I have much of a choice. I need my stuff. But I guess I'll cross that bridge when I get there.

"Yeah." I gulp. "No big deal."

The rumble from Milo's bike echoes down the quiet street and cuts off Jake's response as we watch him pull up next to my car in the driveway. Flipping down the kickstand, he swings his leg over the side then strides over to us.

"Where's your shit?" he asks, scanning our empty hands.

Jake answers for me. "We're going to go get it later."

His jaw tightens as his gaze bounces between Jake and me, but he doesn't comment on it. "Fine. Let me show you around."

3

REESE

"**G**et your pants on, Riv," Milo yells from the entryway after pushing open the front door. His booming voice makes the walls shake as he adds, "We have company."

The place is decorated with greige paint, warm brown carpet, and sleek chrome accents, all complimented with a few exposed red brick walls. Stairs hug the wall on the left-hand side, while the right is a giant entertainment room complete with a big-screen television, gaming console, and a worn leather couch that currently has a black lacy bra lying on top of it.

Lovely.

And even though it screams bachelor pad--naked chick included--it's relatively clean too. The chestnut-colored hardwood floors beneath my worn Chucks look freshly mopped while the spicy scent of aftershave and--is that cinnamon?--wafts through the air.

"If I need pants around your company, they're obviously the wrong kind," a familiar voice returns from the top of the stairs. Glancing up, I'm gifted with the same set of abs from earlier tonight. Only this time, he's ditched the gray basket-ball shorts for a white terry cloth towel, leaving his muscular chest on full display. Again. My mouth waters as I count his abs before slowly trailing my attention up to his pecs then landing on his amused smirk.

"Hey, sweetheart, long time no see––"

"New rule," Milo barks, cutting him off. "Unless you're walking straight from the bathroom and into your bedroom with a towel covering your junk, pants are required in every room of the house. Understood?"

The roommate scoffs. "I'm sorry. Did I miss your name on the ballot? Since when did you become president?"

"Since my little sister started shacking up with us," Milo returns before he drops his voice and mutters, "Reese, this is River."

What kind of a name is River?

River's brows reach for his hairline before he wrenches his gaze from Milo and over to me.

Unconvinced, he challenges, "So, you really are the little sister?"

"I'm sorry. Why do you still sound surprised?" I demand, unable to hide my irritation. "And why the hell are you more hung up on that little tidbit instead of the bomb he just dropped about me rooming with you?"

Casually, River leans forward to rest his elbows on the iron railing as he studies me closer. His piercing, dark gaze rolls over me, stripping me bare and giving me a taste of my own medicine from when I undressed him with my eyes earlier this evening. My heart picks up its pace, but I try to ignore its frantic rhythm as I wait for him to finish his...perusal.

After a beat of silence, his deep voice breaks the spell he's cast on me as he explains, "Because Milo has failed to mention you. *Ever.*"

Ouch.

I cross my arms over my chest, feeling like a knife's been lodged between my ribs before I whisper to Milo, "You've never mentioned me?"

We're all either of us have. Aren't we?

"He's mentioned Reese before," Jake interjects, his feathers ruffling the longer his roommate's mouth is open. I can't blame him. Seems like River needs a muzzle with how easily he flaps his trap.

River's eyes widen as he registers my name before his boisterous laughter practically shakes the pictures lining the walls.

"*You're* Reese?" he asks in disbelief before another round of laughter hits him.

Confused, I turn back to Jake. "Why is that funny?"

"Because I've known Milo for what, five years?" River butts in from the top of the stairs. "And I'd always assumed Reese was his little brother. Not *sister.*" His Adam's apple bobs up and down as he throws his head back and laughs even harder. "Or maybe I find the situation amusing because not only has he failed to mention you're a chick, but he's never brought you around before either." His hungry eyes scan me up and down. "Yeah. That definitely answers a few questions of mine."

Milo's six-foot-two-inch frame cuts River from my view.

"Careful, River," my brother warns him with a growl. "I heard you have a photoshoot in a few days. Wouldn't want to show up with a black eye, would you?"

Unable to help myself, I shift my weight from one foot to the other and peek around Milo to find River just as amused as before.

He scratches his strong jaw before scolding, "We've talked about this, Milo. No one touches the moneymaker"––he motions to his face––"unless they're willing to suck my balls. You gonna suck my balls, man?"

"You gonna shut the hell up?" My brother takes another step forward, causing my breath to hitch as memories of all the fights he used to get into in high school flash through my mind. He's never been one to back down. Never one to cower. Never one to roll over and take someone else's crap. You'd think his roomie here would know that by now, but apparently, he has a death wish. I reach for Milo's tattooed arm and tug him back.

"He's joking, Milo."

With a wink at my brother, an unflustered River shrugs one of his broad shoulders. "I mean if Milo's offering…"

Jake laughs before he pats Milo on the shoulder. "Come on, man. We both know River's full of shit. He'd be the one on his knees if either of you ever swung for that team."

River joins in, laughing even harder as he points to Jake. "The man's got a point." Then he lifts his chin in my direction and adds, "Nice to meet you, Roomie. You'll have to excuse me. I have no pants on and must follow the new rules set forth by Mr. President over here."

"River, baby," a voice practically moans from the second floor.

She's still *here?*

My lips pull into a thin white line to hide my distaste.

"Coming, darling," River returns while holding my gaze. Then he winks. *Again.* Except this one's directed at me. And it turns my stomach into a knot.

Jake shoves Milo toward the kitchen before he can retaliate. "Come on, man. It's late. Let's show Reese around."

Forcing my feet to move, I trail behind them while silently begging the knot in my stomach to dissipate. Except it doesn't. Like a strange sixth sense, I glance over my shoulder. Those same dark green eyes stare back at me with unrestrained curiosity as River rests his hands on the cold metal railing. He doesn't move a muscle but studies me like a new toy at the toy store. A rush of adrenaline floods my veins while my feet struggle to obey my initial orders of following Milo and Jake to the kitchen. But I can't help it. It's like my body's been injected with liquid magnet and is pulling me toward *him*. The guy on the second floor whom my brother just specifically ordered me to stay away from.

Because you know, that's *healthy.*

"Riverrrrr," his date whines again. The sound is enough to snap us both out of our dazes. Pushing himself away from the railing, he holds my attention for one more second then disappears from my line of sight.

And I hate that I can't help but watch him leave.

4

REESE

"**R**eese, you comin'?" Jake's voice echoes from down the hall.

Tucking my hair behind my ear, I hurry my footsteps and catch up with them. "Yeah, sorry. I was…just admiring how clean the place is," I lie, trying to get a hold of myself. "Who woulda thunk, right?"

Jake rolls his eyes. "Don't sound so surprised."

"Can you blame me? Four guys under one roof? I mean, what else was I supposed to expect?"

An unamused Milo crosses his arms and leans against the granite island in the center of the kitchen. "Do you know me at all?"

"Good point." With a smile, I sing, "Once a caregiver, always a caregiver."

"Damn straight."

Growing up in a shitty trailer park covered in trash will do things to a person. And for Milo, he quickly learned that he loathes clutter and will do anything to keep his living space in tip-top condition.

"Here's the kitchen." Milo motions to the open layout

with a lazy wave of his hand. The white granite countertops are free from crumbs and contrast with the dark cabinets beautifully. A few sleek stainless steel appliances are tucked here and there, and overall, the place is immaculate.

Oblivious to my awe, Milo continues, "Instead of everyone getting their own groceries, we just do a monthly pot for food and take turns picking them up. Jake's our in-house chef unless you're looking for mac and cheese, then I'm your guy. Don't bother asking River to cook. He can't even make a bowl of cereal without forgetting to put the milk away. Although, if you want to piss him off, he keeps his secret stash of Cinnamon Toast Crunch in the cupboard. And Sonny only cooks when he's home at night, which is rare. Any questions so far?"

"Um…how much do I need to put into the pot?"

"Don't worry about it." Milo opens the fridge and grabs the metal water bottle I'd given him for Christmas the previous year.

Twisting the cap, he takes a deep pull of it as I argue, "Milo––"

He swallows and wipes the back of his hand against his mouth. "I gotcha covered, Reese."

A headache threatens to spread from the base of my skull. Whether it's from the long, eventful day or because I know I'm about to go head-to-head with Milo, I'm not sure. It doesn't stop it from pulsing as I argue, "You don't have to take care of me. I can pay for my own food."

"I'm not complaining––"

"I know, but I'm not a little girl, remember? If things with Ian hadn't fallen through––"

"Then you wouldn't have ended up on my doorstep. I get it. Can I tell you how happy I am that you finally left that sonofabitch, though?"

"Don't start––"

"Why? Because he's been messing with your head for years now?"

"Milo––"

"Fine. We'll discuss that later," he concedes grudgingly. "Like you said, you're a big girl, but that doesn't mean I can turn off the big brother attitude either."

"I know that, and you're the best big brother a girl could ever ask for, but I still want to pull my weight around here. I already feel bad enough that I'm bumming a room off you. Please don't make me feel even more guilty by not allowing me to pay for my own food," I beg.

There's a weighted pause as Milo watches me carefully.

Licking my lips, I murmur, "Please?"

"Where you gonna get the money?" he challenges. It's not like I'm stupid enough to keep working for Ian's family. But without them, I'm kind of screwed in the financial department, and it's not like I had a lot of money saved when Ian had a habit of spending his paychecks more often than contributing to our expenses.

I'm such an idiot.

Another sigh escapes me. "I don't know yet. I'm going to go job hunting tomorrow and see what I can find."

"And how long are you planning on staying?"

I shrug. "How long am I welcome?"

"For however long you need me. Just as long as you don't go back to that asshat––"

"I thought we were going to discuss that later," I grit out with a narrowed gaze.

"You were," Jake interjects, reading the situation like a seasoned pro. "Right, Milo?"

Milo stays silent, but his glare is louder than a damn foghorn.

"It's late," Jake points out. "I'm sure she's tired and could use some rest. Let's wrap this up, and we can all get some sleep, okay?"

Finally, Milo nods. "Yeah. Sure."

"Come on. We'll show you upstairs," Jake prods, guiding us back to the front of the house.

The stairs creak slightly from our weight as Jake continues the little tour. When we reach the second floor, he points to the right. "Mine and Milo's rooms are over here." Then he veers left and motions to a shut door. "And this is Sonny's room. You'll rarely see him because he works nights, so he sleeps a lot during the day, and when he isn't sleeping, he's usually writing music and kind of keeps to himself."

"A musician?" I inquire, studying the closed white door curiously.

"Yeah. And the corner bedroom is"––Jake coughs as the familiar sound of moaning seeps beneath the closed door––"River's room. He's uh…"

"Yes! Yes! Right there! Yes!" a girl shouts.

"Kind of a slut," Jake finishes. "If you want to swap rooms so you don't have to listen to this every night, let me know."

My cheeks redden as the girl on the opposite side starts to whimper in rhythm to the bed butting against the wall. It's followed by a low masculine groan that I assume belongs to River.

Clearing my throat while praying Jake and Milo don't notice my bright red face, I reply, "It's totally fine. I'll just buy some noise-canceling headphones or something. And I assume this room's mine?" I motion to the closed door sandwiched between Sonny's and River's rooms on the left while doing my best to ignore the crescendo of a job well done starring one of my new roommates whom I've yet to meet with all his clothes on.

Milo doesn't seem particularly bothered by his friend's sexcapades which only raises more questions for me. Does

River always have girls in his room? And are they always so freaking loud?

"Yeah, this is your room," my brother answers, reminding me of my question from two seconds before. "There's a spare bed in here from when Fender moved out a few months ago to go on tour, so you should be good to go."

"Another musician?"

"Yeah. He's Sonny's brother."

"Half brother," Jake corrects Milo. "You saw him tonight at SeaBird. His band was on the stage."

The haunting melody from earlier echoes through my head before I shake it off. "And he doesn't want to move back in? I don't want to step on anyone's toes––"

"You're not," Jake interrupts. "He's been back for a few weeks and has been sleeping on his buddy's couch. I think living with Sonny was a little much."

"Oh."

"Yeah." Reaching around me, Jake twists the handle then pushes the door open. "Welcome home."

The room is simple, with plain white walls and a bare queen-sized mattress tucked against the back corner. But a hole near the lightswitch is hard to miss. I drag my finger across the cracked sheetrock and mutter, "Why is there a hole in the wall?"

"Fender," Jake answers simply. "We'll get it patched tomorrow."

"I can fix––"

"Not a big deal, Reese. I'll get you taken care of."

I nod, then continue my perusal. There's a window on the opposite side with the blinds pulled closed and a long, waist-high empty dresser beneath it. My guilt rears its ugly head for the thousandth time tonight as I take in Milo's generosity that's laid out before me.

"Are you *sure* you're okay with me staying here?" I grimace.

"Stop asking stupid questions. The bathroom is right here." My brother points to the door opposite mine. "You share it with River and Sonny. Keep it locked when you're in there so no one walks in on you."

Jake adds, "Any questions?"

I scan the empty bedroom another time. "Um...sheets?"

"I'll get them for you," he answers before disappearing to rummage through a hallway closet.

"You're gonna be okay," Milo rumbles. His scruff tickles the top of my head as he pulls me into his chest. "Get some sleep. I'll see you in the morning."

Squeezing him with all my strength, I breathe in deep and soak up his affection like a dry sponge. "Goodnight, Milo. And thanks––"

"Stop thanking me," he orders before letting me go. "We're family. 'Night."

"Goodnight," I repeat.

Satisfied, Milo saunters to the opposite side of the long hallway toward his room as Jake returns with a set of white cotton sheets that smell like laundry detergent.

We make quick work of putting them on the mattress in silence. I think he knows I'm too emotionally drained to make small talk, and he's awesome enough to respect that. After examining our handiwork, Jake tucks his hands into his pockets. "Do you need anything else?"

"I think I'm okay. Thank you, though." I sit on the edge of my freshly-made bed while Jake heads to the hallway, ready to call it a night.

"Anytime," he replies over his shoulder. "See you in the morning."

"Okay."

He disappears from view, following my brother from a

few minutes before until I'm left alone, and the day finally catches up with me.

All I want to do is curl up into a ball and sleep for a week, but I need to wash my face and pee before I can finally give in to my exhaustion. I also need a freaking toothbrush, but that'll have to wait until tomorrow.

Resting my head in my hands, the quiet in the room finally whispers the truth that I've been trying to avoid all day. But it hits me harder than a wrecking ball.

Ian and I are over. We're *really* over. I refuse to go back to him again. Even if he was my first. Even if we've been together so long that I don't remember what it's like to be without him. Even if I know this'll be messy and that Ian won't let me go easily. Not when he needs me.

But I can do this. I can stand on my own.

Can't I?

My body feels heavy as I push myself up from my bed and head to the bathroom. I splash some cool water on my face then cringe as I take in the bags under my eyes in the mirror. I look like crap, and my freckled skin is even paler than usual. Hell, I look like a freaking ghost.

No wonder Ian was screwing other people.

I squeeze my eyes shut and grab the hem of my white T-shirt before remembering that I don't have any pajamas to change into. I didn't bring any.

Well, that's just lovely.

Gritting my teeth, I yank off my bra and weave it through the armhole of my T-shirt.

I should've grabbed a few things before I stormed out of my apartment. That would've made my next twenty-four hours *so* much easier, but apparently, I'm batting a thousand lately.

White bra in hand, I fling the bathroom door open and run into a very hard, very naked, and slightly sweaty chest.

Oomph.

My palms press against it in self-preservation as a gasp escapes me.

"Shit, sorry," River mutters. His hands envelop my biceps, making sure I'm steady while simultaneously putting two feet of distance between us. "You okay?"

Frazzled, I look up at him with wide eyes.

"Uh, yup," I squeak. "Sorry. I was just in my own little world, I guess."

"No worries." A smirk teases his lips as he scans me up and down before dropping his gaze to his bare feet, where my bra is currently residing.

Shit.

Scrambling for it, I squat down to pick up my bra then swallow my tongue as I look back up at a very amused River.

Girl on knees in front of hot guy with no shirt on...now this *is a precarious position.*

I gulp but hold his gaze as my hand mindlessly searches for the lacy fabric that got me into this position in the first place. When my fingers brush against the elastic strap, I fist the material and offer my new roomie a tight smile.

But I don't move another muscle.

I can't.

I'm too frozen with embarrassment, and self-conscious-ness, and awkwardness, and maybe a little curiosity too. Not that I'd actually do anything. Not that he'd even *want* me to. But my brain has been mush since I found Ian and his skank. And for some reason, the heat in River's eyes seems to recharge me instead of siphoning off the last of my energy like everything else in my life.

Or maybe I'm hallucinating from lack of sleep and sheer exhaustion.

His deep chuckle makes my insides tighten as he offers

his hand to help me up while simultaneously breaking the spell he'd cast on me.

Clearing my throat, I take it. His palm is warm and–– despite his pretty-boy eyes that hint he's never worked a day in his life––they're a little calloused, too, which only fuels my curiosity for the enigma in front of me. My forearms pebble with awareness from his touch, but I ignore it and pull myself up.

"Uh, thanks," I mumble under my breath.

"Is that what you're sleeping in?"

Confused, I look down to examine my outfit and find the girls practically playing peek-a-boo through the thin material of my shirt. My face scrunches up in embarrassment.

And it just had *to be white*, I think to myself before folding my arms across my chest.

He smirks. Again. That same arrogance hovers around him like a familiar security blanket that's both annoying and hot as hell. He knows he's attractive. He knows he's making me squirm. He knows that *I know* that he knows.

And he's thriving off it.

With a huff, I explain, "I had to get out of my place in a hurry and forgot to grab a change of clothes. I would ask if you have a T-shirt I could borrow or something, but since I've never actually seen you wearing one, I'm gonna go ahead and assume you're a little behind on your laundry."

He laughs, then steps around me and back into his room without uttering a single word. Baffled and more curious than I'd like to admit, I watch him disappear for maybe three seconds before a cotton missile comes flying through the doorway and hits me in the chest.

I catch it, lifting the T-shirt into the air. The material is gray and looks worn in a way that only the best of shirts are. A University's logo is printed on the front of it. I cock my head to the side and ask, "Do you go to LAU with Jake?"

His mouth quirks up in amusement, but he doesn't answer me as he saunters back into the hallway. "We should probably get some shut-eye. After all, I gotta take care of the moneymaker, and I've heard you had a long day." He tacks on another sexy wink. "Goodnight, Roomie."

My heart flutters in my chest, but I shove the foreign feeling aside. "Goodnight. And thanks for the T-shirt."

Another smirk. Then he steps around me and closes the bathroom door behind him, leaving me alone in the hall as I stare at the solid piece of wood that separates us.

Unable to help myself, I lift River's shirt to my nose and breathe in the unique scent of laundry detergent and Old Spice, then stare at the closed door where he's hiding.

River...who are you?

And why do you smell so freaking good?

5

REESE

With my face pressed against the pillow after a restless night of sleep, I groan. So help me, if that phone vibrates one more time, I'm going to throw it against the wall and break it into a million pieces. I peek one eye open and take in the soft light from the window that casts a cool glow across the room.

It's too early to be awake right now, especially after the day I had yesterday. I squeeze my heavy eyelids closed another time, then pull the pillow on top of my head in hopes of falling back asleep. But my phone vibrates against the nightstand another time.

Cursing under my breath, I mumble, "No, no, no, no. I just want to sleeeep."

It continues buzzing away until I finally chuck my pillow against the opposite wall, then give in and look at the screen.

My teeth grind together as I slide my thumb along the screen to answer the call and seethe, "It's five in the morning, Ian."

"I couldn't sleep."

"Well, I was sleeping like a baby," I lie. "And you woke me up."

"We should talk."

Scoffing, I roll onto my back and stare up at the white ceiling above me. "Of course, you wouldn't apologize for wrecking my beauty sleep. What do you really want, Ian?"

"I already told you. I want to talk."

"You've already said your piece, remember?"

"Yeah, well, I want to say it again."

I squeeze my eyes shut. "And you think five in the morning is the best time to do that? I'm already pissed at you--"

"Listen--"

"No. I'm done listening. I've put up with..." My voice cracks. An image of the blonde bimbo rears its ugly head in the back of my mind.

"Look, I'm sorry, okay? I really am. I'm an asshole, and I deserve being in the doghouse, but you have to forgive me at some point, babe. I made a mistake. It won't happen again."

Licking my lips, I take a deep breath. "I want to break up, Ian."

"No."

It's the way he says it that nearly breaks me.

"Please," I beg. "You don't love me anymore. Just let me go."

"No," he repeats without a shred of sympathy. His stubbornness takes hold until the man I fell in love with is swallowed up by an arrogant asshole who doesn't care about me. Only himself.

A tear slips past my defenses then runs down my temple and into my messy hair as I continue staring at the ceiling above me. "I don't want to be with you anymore, Ian."

"How can you say that? We love each other--"

"If you loved me, you wouldn't have slept with someone else. I just want to pick up my stuff and start over. Please?"

"You know I can't do that, babe. You're my ride or die. I need you. My family needs you."

I squeeze my eyes shut and try to control my breathing, though it's a losing battle. My chest rises and falls in short spurts, my heart beating faster and out of rhythm until I feel like I've run a marathon.

"I don't want to be your ride or die anymore. You screwed that up by sleeping with someone else."

"Where are you?" he demands.

"Doesn't matter."

"Tell me."

"I have to go."

"Reese--"

I hit the end button before I can talk myself out of it, then curl onto my side and pull my knees up to my chest into the fetal position.

I hate him.

I hate him. I hate him. I hate him.

Attempting to stave off a panic attack, I focus on my breathing.

In.

Out.

In.

Out.

It's okay.

It's going to be okay.

He's just a guy. An asshole of a guy that I gave myself to when I was too young to know better. And even though I can't really remember a time without him, I can turn over a new leaf, and I'll be okay. Eventually.

With the knowledge that there's no chance I'm going to be able to fall back asleep after a conversation like that, I head to the bathroom and change into my clothes from yesterday.

The men's large T-shirt mocks me as I fold it carefully while appreciating the soft material between my fingertips. It really is a nice shirt. One with memories attached to it, though I'm not privy to what they are. I can just tell, and I would love to dive into those memories with a bottle of wine instead of drowning in my own that are much less sweet and so much more damaged.

Sighing, I take the shirt back into my room and set it on the edge of the mattress while ignoring my conscience that's telling me to leave it in the hallway by River's closed door. Besides, I might need it another night or two until I can figure out what to do about my stuff, right? I might as well keep it. Then I'll give it back to River later. Not a big deal.

I roll my eyes, hating the need to justify my possessiveness over something that doesn't belong to me while simultaneously hating the possibility of giving it back to its original owner when I haven't slept that well in months.

It's not just the shirt, though, I tell myself. It's the bed. And the room. And the house. And the knowledge that my big, overprotective brother is just down the hall too. He's ready to fight any demons that come knocking at his front door. Including Ian.

The stairs creak as I creep down them as quietly as I can. The sound makes me cringe before I reach the front door and open it carefully. Satisfied I haven't bothered anyone, I tuck my hands into my front pockets then walk down the street. The morning mist brings a chill to my bare arms, but I kind of love how awake it makes me feel. Like a rush of adrenaline is spiking through my veins until my casual walk turns into a full-on sprint down the empty street. Chucks pounding against the concrete. Wind rushing through my messy waves. And a promise that whispers in the gentle breeze.

I'm going to get through this. I have to.

My lungs burn with exhaustion, but the endorphins give me the high I'm desperate for, and I cling to the hope that it's going to be okay.

I'm going to be okay.

I just don't know how yet.

Resting my hands on the top of my head, I catch my breath while eyeing the grocery store across the street. My hand slips into my back pocket and toys with a folded up ten-dollar bill. Now that I've burned off my adrenaline, I'd kill for a coffee. I should probably check to see if they're hiring while I'm here too. Since, ya know, working in a grocery store is exactly what I want to do for the rest of my life. But at least it's *something*.

The road is practically empty, and so is the parking lot. Only a handful of cars are scattered throughout it as I jog casually toward the entrance then head straight for the beverage aisle.

Rocking back on my heels, I peruse the options in search of a bottled iced coffee or something when a vaguely familiar voice interrupts, "Reese?"

I turn and cringe as soon as I recognize the voice's owner. "Gibbs? Uh...hey."

My fingers run through my tangled hair on their own accord, attempting to fix the mess that my run created, but it's hopeless. I'd bet a thousand bucks that I look like a wreck right now, and there's nothing I can do to cover it up.

As if he can read my mind, Gibbs laughs. "Hey. No judgment here. I just got off an eight-hour shift that ended with jello shots and a bachelorette party."

"That sounds promising," I quip before dropping my hands to my sides.

"You have no idea." He shudders.

"So uh…" I cringe, wanting to kick myself for opening my mouth when I know that it's going to come out anyway. "I should probably apologize for my neanderthal brother. I don't know what he said to you, but I can take a guess, and it probably wasn't pretty."

Gibbs chuckles dryly before grabbing the back of his neck and squeezing. "Yeah…I don't think it'd be too far of a stretch for you to figure it out."

"I'm sorry."

"Don't be. Like I said before, Milo and I have known each other for a hell of a long time, but he was right to set a few boundaries. If I had a sister, I sure as hell wouldn't want her talking to a guy like me."

"But that's not my brother's call to make," I argue.

"No, but it *is* mine. So, let's start over, shall we? As friends," he iterates. "I'm Gibson…Gibbs. Nice to meet you."

"Reese," I reply with an accepting smile. Let's be honest. I'm not looking for anything romantic either. But I could definitely use a friend.

"Nice to meet you. Now that we've gotten the pleasantries out of the way, what're you doing here at the asscrack of dawn?"

"Couldn't sleep, so I decided to go for a run."

Scanning me up and down, a teasing smirk slides into place. "In yesterday's outfit? You sure you're not trying to cover up the walk of shame?"

With a gasp, I smack him in the chest. "Excuse me?"

"I'm kidding. There's no way in hell your brother would let you have a one-night stand. Although that doesn't answer the outfit question," he points out.

"It's complicated…"

"The most interesting stories always are."

A ghost of a smile graces my lips at his innocent prodding before I give in and explain, "I just broke up with my ex."

"Oh?"

"Yup. And I left in a hurry, so all my stuff is at our--*his*--place, and I have yet to retrieve any of it." My expression sours at the prospect of actually seeing Ian after everything.

Kill me now.

Sensing my wariness, Gibbs prods, "You don't look too excited about facing him again."

"You have no idea. He's, uh, he's not too excited about the breakup, and I'm afraid it's going to get messy. Especially because I was kind of helping him and his brother with their business, and now I'm...not."

"I don't blame you. Did he screw up?"

"More times than I can count." I laugh even though all I want to do is cry. "But this was the last straw."

Looking remorseful, as if Ian's asshole behavior is his own, Gibbs sighs. "What'd he do?"

My mouth opens like a fish out of water before closing just as quickly. How am I supposed to admit something so vulnerable? To anyone. Let alone a guy I barely know?

My ex cheated on me.

It sounds so simple... But it isn't. His mistake is like a giant spotlight that highlights all of my insecurities, making me question myself, my sexuality, everything. And it sucks. Why wasn't I enough for him? Why did he want to go somewhere else for sex? Am I not good in bed? Am I not pretty enough? Are my boobs too small?

I seriously hate Ian for making me question everything.

Sensing my hesitation, he adds, "You don't have to tell me--"

"He cheated on me," I rush out. "It's fine. Not a big deal, right? The problem is that he's refusing to acknowledge we're over."

The surprise is clear on his face, but he covers it up quickly and replies, "One, that's a very big deal, but I can tell that talking about it makes you uncomfortable, so I'm going to drop it. And two, that sounds like it could be a recipe for disaster. Are you taking your brother with you to grab your stuff?"

"I should," I acknowledge, "but I also don't want to cause a confrontation either. My ex and Milo have never really gotten along. Scratch that. They hate each other. It would be like dousing a bonfire in gasoline while hoping the flames die down."

"Yeah, but if your ex is pissed about the breakup, I don't see him fizzling out anytime soon, regardless of your brother's presence. I think you'd be smart to bring backup."

"You might have a point," I concede. *Especially with our history*, I think to myself before voicing aloud, "Although I don't know how I'm going to bring it up to Milo without him overreacting and threatening to cut off Ian's balls as soon I get them in the same room. So, rock, meet hard place, right?"

"Hmm," he hums, the wheels in his handsome head turning. "We'll figure it out. You ready to head home? Or…?"

My brows wrinkle before I shake my head. "Not yet. I was thinking about an iced coffee, but now that I've cooled off, I think I'm going to grab a croissant and a coffee at the little in-store coffee shop." I point to the black sign at the back of the store that reads *Need Caffeine* in bold yellow letters. "I also need to grab an application and see if they're hiring or something."

Nodding, he pushes his grocery cart holding a couple of frozen pizzas and a canister of protein powder a few inches forward before pulling it back to its original position. "Okay. I'm going to go and catch a few hours of shut-eye, then shower. I'll see you later?"

"Uh…sure?"

"Okay. Take it easy, Reese." Then he pushes past me, and I'm left gawking at his retreating form.

"You, too," I mumble under my breath to no one in particular.

6

REESE

After grabbing an application, I head back to Milo's place. The front door opens with a soft squeak, and I grimace, praying it doesn't wake anyone up. It's still early for a bunch of bachelors, and I have no idea what their schedules are like. I tiptoe into the entryway and take a big whiff of freshly brewed coffee that permeates the air. Apparently, someone's an early riser. Cocking my head to the side, I head into the kitchen to see who's awake.

"Hey," Milo greets me with a coffee cup in his hand as soon as my sneaker-clad feet reach the kitchen floor. He's sitting at the table with an expectant look on his face that makes me feel like a teenager who just got caught sneaking into the house after staying out all night.

I smile, though it feels forced. "Hey."

"We gonna get your shit today?"

Taken aback, I reach for the coffee pot on the counter then realize I don't have a cup to pour it into. My fingers fidget with the black plastic handle for a few seconds before I shove my hands into my back pockets instead.

"Cat got your tongue?" Milo pushes. "Sonny said your ex

isn't too keen on handing it over. Figured you might need backup."

Shaking my head, I ask, "Sonny? I haven't even seen Sonny."

Milo shrugs. "Maybe he overheard you. But is he wrong?"

Damn you, Sonny. Tattling on me even though we haven't met yet, I think to myself.

The chair beneath Milo's massive frame creaks as he leans forward and rests his elbows on the table. "Is he?"

"Nooo," I drag out the word. "But I was just thinking…I mean…what do I really need that's at his place, ya know?"

"Uh, clothes?" Milo offers.

"I could buy new clothes."

With a smirk, he takes another sip of his coffee then sets it back down on the table. "A whole wardrobe?"

"I mean, why not, right?"

"Uh-huh. Sure. And how do you plan on paying for the whole new wardrobe?"

I tap my finger against my chin before offering, "Is prostitution still illegal?"

Quirking his brow, his amusement threatens to evaporate but is still clinging to the bear in front of me with one tiny thread. "Try again."

"I don't know," I whine, dropping my head back while looking up at the ceiling. "I checked with the grocery store. They gave me an application but said they aren't hiring, so I'm not getting my hopes up."

"I can help cover a few outfits, but you're gonna have to face the asshole sooner or later. Might as well rip it off like a Band-Aid. We'll be there to back you up."

"I'm sorry…who's *we*?"

"All of us."

Popping my hip out, I cross my arms and demand, "You're gonna have to give me more than that."

"Me, River, Jake, and Sonny," Milo answers.

The guy acts like this is a normal response when a room-mate breaks up with her boyfriend. I mean, why wouldn't everyone tag along to help me pick up my crap, right? I rub my palm along my face.

This is ridiculous.

"I don't even know Sonny," I protest. "Why would he want to help me?"

Milo waves me off. "Hell if I know. You don't know River, either, but he's adamant on tagging along too."

"How does River even know about this?"

"Sonny's got a big mouth," River offers from the hallway, obviously having overheard our conversation. His long stride quickly eats up the distance between us until he's less than a foot away and reaches into the cabinet behind me to grab a coffee mug. The guy is still shirtless––*shocker*––but smells like heaven as his firm body pins me between himself and the counter behind me. Unsure where to look, my eyes bounce between his tan skin, the scuffed up base-board behind him that's surrounding the kitchen, and my brother shooting daggers at the model who's all up in my grill.

Mug in hand, River steps away to give me some breathing room, then pours himself a steaming cup of coffee before adding a shit-ton of vanilla flavored creamer from the fridge. For some reason, the fact that he has a sweet tooth doesn't surprise me. At. All.

It's actually kind of adorable.

Bringing the coffee to his lips, he inhales deeply then gives me a panty-melting smile. "Ah…that's the stuff. Anyway, Sonny brought me up to speed before hopping in the shower. Which reminds me. You smell. You should grab one before we leave." He hesitates before looking me up and down while sneaking another sip from his steaming cup.

"Nope. I changed my mind. Go exactly like that. Your ex will help you pack up your shit in no time."

"Are you saying that I stink so bad my ex will be glad to get rid of me?"

"That's exactly what I'm saying," he replies shamelessly, oblivious to my brother's glare that I can feel is alternating between River and the side of my head.

I bite the inside of my cheek to keep from egging him on, but I can't help myself.

Who says something like that to someone of the opposite sex that they barely know?

Scratch that. Who says something like that, period?

"Should I be offended?" I challenge.

"Probably. But don't worry, sweetheart. I'll take care of you. We'll just make sure you take a shower *after* we get your shit. See? Simple."

"But I thought it was in the dating handbook to make the ex jealous so you can win the breakup, right?"

"Not when it comes to you and Ian," Milo interrupts, ignoring our banter. "He's been messing with you for too long, Reese."

"Give me a little more credit––"

Milo scoffs. "The guy has you wrapped around his little finger."

"That's not fair," I argue.

"But it's true," Jake interjects from the hallway. He strides toward us with something in his hand and looks beyond pissed, though I have no idea why.

"Ian has *always* been bad news, but you keep going back to him. Tell me, do you like being treated like shit?" The accusation is clear in Jake's voice, but I'm too confused to argue with him until I realize what he's insinuating.

How the hell would he know about all the other crap Ian has put me through? That was between Milo and me.

My rage is almost palpable as it finally clicks into place. I don't need to say a single word as I turn to my brother. My flaring nostrils combined with a glare from Hades is enough to get my point across. Besides, he knows me well enough to read my mind, and I'm sending the signals loud and clear.

What else has he told Jake that was supposed to be between us?

"Don't get pissed at me," Milo volleys back at me. "Jake's been around long enough to piece together your history with Ian."

"Yeah, and I'm sure you were more than happy to fill in all the blanks. Am I right?"

"Am I missing something?" River interjects.

Milo and I continue our little stare-off while Jake jumps right in, more than eager to spill all my dirty laundry. "Ian and Reese go way back. He's been using her like a yo-yo for years." Scowling at me, he continues. "Treating you like shit until you snap and leave his sorry ass. Then he comes back on his knees a few days later after he realizes you're the best he's ever gonna get, and you welcome him back with open arms. Again. And again."

"First, what the hell is your problem?" I snap. "And second, he's never cheated on me before. Or at least, I don't think so?"

He snorts. "*That* sounds promising. I wanna know if it'll be enough to keep you from reviving your dead relationship a week from now, or if you'll remember what a jackass he is this time around?"

"Back up, Jake," Milo orders, his brotherly instincts taking precedence over his annoyance with me. "Reese is right. Why are you so pissed at her right now?"

"Yeah, I've never seen you treat a girl like this," River adds, his earlier amusement evaporating into thin air. With his chest puffed up, he takes a step closer to me. There's a protectiveness in his stance that only digs up more questions.

Have I entered *The Twilight Zone*?

Because Jake is *never* mad at me, and River barely knows me. Why would he be willing to come to the rescue?

Jake scoffs as he takes in River's protective stance. "Shut the hell up, River."

"Excuse me?"

"Milo had one rule, and you broke it in less than twenty-four hours. Although, with your reputation, I don't know why I'm even surprised."

"What the hell are you talking about?" River demands. His muscles are coiled tight like a spring, practically begging Jake to say something wrong so he can finally snap and go after him.

Ignoring him, Jake turns back to me. "And you. Your brother gave you one order to follow if you wanted to stay here. Do you remember what that was?"

Confused, I shake my head back and forth. "What are you talking about, Jake?"

"I found his shirt in your room." He tosses the wadded-up material at me, and I catch it against my chest. "Wanna tell me what it was doing there?"

River laughs out loud, slapping his hand against the granite countertop like this is the most hilarious interaction he's ever had.

"Are you shitting me right now?" he asks. "*That's* why you're pissed?"

Jake's forehead wrinkles in confusion before his spine straightens. "Yeah. *That's* why I'm pissed. Milo told you to keep your hands to yourself––"

"And I have. She doesn't have any clothes, remember? I gave her something to sleep in. That's it."

Jake's jaw tightens, but he doesn't respond. Of course, he wouldn't. There's nothing to say. He just made some huge assumptions with almost no evidence to back any of it up, and it backfired. Bad.

I can't believe he'd think so little of me. That he'd honestly believe I'd betray my brother like that. That he honestly thinks I'd go back to Ian after all he's put me through.

It's like Jake doesn't know me at all anymore.

Chewing on my lower lip, I fight back my disappointment and murmur, "I don't want you to come help me pick up my stuff."

"Reese––"

"Nope. I just got out of a relationship. A pretty painful one, actually, and not only did you just throw it all in my face, but you assumed I'm a girl who would spread her legs for a stranger after she was specifically told not to by her older brother, who happens to be helping her out a lot right now. You came into this kitchen with your ammunition locked and loaded without even bothering to ask questions. I don't want someone who has that much animosity pointed directly at me to pretend they're on my side."

Regret oozes from his pores as he drops his chin to his chest in shame. "Reese––"

"I'm going to go wash up. I'll be back down in a few. Then we can go get my stuff because Ian and I are through"––I glare at Jake––"for good this time. But thank you *so* much for your confidence."

Turning on my heel, I rush down the hall and up the stairs like a demon is chasing me when I know it's my own insecurities that are haunting me more than anything Jake said.

He hit a nerve. And whether I wanted to hear it or not, I can't help the questions that pop into my head as I replay our conversation.

Can I stay strong this time? Will he let me go without a fight?

My head is a hurricane of chaos and self-doubt as I round the corner and crash into a hard, naked chest that's still damp from the shower. As if I've been shocked, my mouth and eyes both open wide, and I freeze in the arms of a man wearing nothing but a towel.

What is it with the men in this house not wearing shirts?!

And why do I keep running into them?

"Shit, Reese, you okay?"

I blink a handful of times, convinced I'm seeing things as I take in the *almost* naked man in front of me. "Gibbs?"

He stares back at me as if I belong in an insane asylum. "Hey."

"What the hell are you doing in my house?"

A low chuckle vibrates from his chest and through my hands that are currently cupping a pair of toned pecs. I pull away but still feel his heated skin against my palms like an aftershock. We're just friends. I mean, he's definitely one of the hottest friends I've ever had, but…

"Shouldn't I be asking you that question?" he counters.

"Huh?"

"This was my house first."

"I think you're mistaken."

His mouth stretches into a grin. "Oh, am I?"

"Yup. This house belongs to Milo, Jake, River, and Sonny. Your name is Gibbs, and as I previously just stated, your name is not on that list."

"To be fair neither is yours," he teases. My eyes transform into tiny slits, daring him to keep up this charade before he explains, "My full name is Gibson. The guys call me Sonny."

"*You're* Sonny?" I balk.

"In the flesh."

"Why didn't you tell me?"

"I thought you knew."

"Bullshit."

"Seriously," he defends himself. "I really did. Why else do you think I asked if you were ready to go home this morning at the grocery store? Did you think it was my not-so-subtle way of asking you to move in or something? I mean, you're hot and all, but, a––we barely know each other, b––your brother would kill me if I touched you, and c––we've agreed to be just friends, remember?"

"Har, har," I return, my face reddening.

When I don't say anything else, he rocks back on his heels and adds, "I'm sorry if you thought I was keeping the truth from you. Should we start over, by chance?"

Staying silent, I peek up at him and shrug one shoulder. Despite my embarrassment over the situation, I think he's telling the truth.

"You mean, start over *again*? Since we've already done this once today?" I ask, unamused.

His smile widens before he extends his right hand for me to take. "Hi. I'm Gibson. My guy friends call me Sonny, but you can call me Gibbs or Gibson." He shrugs. "Or Sonny for all I care. Apparently, we're roommates and will be sharing a bathroom for the foreseeable future. Nice to meet you."

I place my hand in his and shake it once. "I'm Reese, Milo's sister. I'm a bit of a mess and have trust issues with people of the opposite sex." I pause before correcting myself. "Actually, with people in general. Nice to meet you too. Again."

Dipping his chin in acknowledgment, he releases me from his firm grip. "Now that's a proper introduction, *Reese With Trust Issues*. I'm gonna go get dressed. Then we'll get your stuff. Deal?"

I gulp. "You don't need to come. You know that, right? I didn't spill all my problems at the grocery store in hopes of you fixing them."

"I know that. In fact, I'm pretty sure you opened up to me

because you thought I *couldn't* help fix your problems. That being said, we're roommates. When you live under this roof, you have four guys willing to go to bat for you. And that, my friend, is exactly what we're going to do today. Understand?"

Clearing my throat, my eyes gather with tears, but I keep them at bay.

I've never had a group of guys willing to rally behind me before. Well, other than Milo and Jake. But they don't really count because Milo's my brother and Jake is... Well, he's Jake. He's also topping my shit list and is trailing right behind Ian at the moment, which is saying something because Ian is a giant asshole who can go to hell.

Sensing I'm lost in my head, Gibbs prods, "You okay?"

"Uh...yeah. And yeah," I repeat. "I understand. You've got my back, and so does everyone else under this roof."

"Good." He nods. "And don't forget it."

7

REESE

My leg bounces up and down like a jackhammer as I sit between two burly bodies in the back seat of River's truck. Palms slick with sweat, my phone vibrates again with another incoming message.

Everyone in the car is chatting about football season while my anxiety reaches a whole new level. As if I'm a spy, I peek down at my screen. Ian's name flashes across it.

Ian: Hey, baby. You done playing this game yet? Ready to come home?

I swallow the lump in my throat then glance around me at the two guys caging me into the middle seat. Gibbs is on my left while Milo is on my right. Behind the steering wheel, River adjusts his aviator sunglasses before making some smartass comment about Jake's mom. The car rumbles with laughter, but I'm too distracted to follow along.

Taking a deep breath, I debate if I should ask if he's home or not because this will be so much easier if he isn't. He's not stupid, though. He'll know what I'm searching for if I'm not careful, and I honestly don't want to see him again. My teeth dig into my lower lip as I weigh my options before carefully typing out a message.

Me: Sure you should be texting at work? I doubt your brother would appreciate that.

I flip the screen back over and face it toward my lap, hoping that the gesture will keep me from checking for his response every millisecond. And all the while, my leg keeps bouncing up and down in a frantic rhythm. Gibbs places his hand on top of it, surprising me to the point where I literally jump in my seat.

I scowl back at him before smoothing my features. "Can I help you?"

"You okay there?" he returns just as quickly.

"Yup. Just dandy."

My phone vibrates again, but because Gibbs isn't as invested in the conversation humming around us as a minute ago, he notices it this time.

"Is that him?" he asks, dipping his chin at my cell.

The truck goes silent.

I shrug instead of confirming his suspicion when it's just as absolute as my own. I don't need to look at the screen to know the message is from Ian. It's like some sick sixth sense that I've always had with him. I could always tell when he was close. When he was thinking of me. When he was planning something, whether it was with good intentions or not. All of it. I guess that's what happens when you've been with the same person for such a long time.

River pipes in from the front. "Can *I* send him a text?"

A surprised laugh bubbles out of me at his absurd request. "Not a chance in hell would I ever let you touch my phone. That would be a disaster."

Our eyes connect through the rearview mirror as he laughs at my response. His are crinkled in the corner before they slide down to inspect Gibbs' hand that is still resting against my knee. I don't know what it means or why I feel the need to scoot an inch toward my brother beside me, but I do.

Gibson's hand slides back into his lap while River's attention snaps back to the winding road in front of us.

"Come on," he jokes. "I'm a trustworthy guy. Are you hiding nudes on there or something? That why you're so protective of your cell?"

Milo growls beside me. "Please tell me you've never sent a picture of yourself naked to someone."

"Um…" I let my voice trail off before the car erupts with laughter.

With smoke practically coming out of Milo's ears, he shivers in disgust then decides, "You know what? Don't tell me. Keep left at the fork in the road. Let's get this shit over with."

"I thought you'd never met her ex?" Gibbs asks, confused as to how Milo would know where I live.

"Milo helped me move into the complex right before I met Ian," I explain, my earlier amusement dissipating.

"Yeah, which is right around the same time that Reese started bailing anytime we'd try to meet up," Milo growls. "Isn't that right, Reese?"

His accusation makes me flinch before Jake, who's been almost silent during this entire mini road trip, pipes up, "Let it go, man. I think we can all agree Ian is an asshole and wanted to isolate Reese from her friends and family. It's classic abusive behavior."

His face is still turned toward the passenger window, but it's the easy way he said *abusive* that causes my anxiety to spike all over again.

The low and steady hum of the engine mingles with the silence as we digest the heavy accusation while I search for something to say. But there isn't any kind of response that will deny what Jake just tossed into the cab of the truck like a live hand grenade. Maybe if I don't touch it, we might be able to squeak out of here without it detonating.

And I can tell Milo is seconds from exploding.

"It's, uh...it's this building on the left," I mutter to River. His blinker clicks on as he captures my gaze in the rearview mirror a second time. Blinking slowly, he ends our little staring contest then pulls into the parking lot.

River, Jake, and Gibbs open their doors in unison, and I slide a few inches toward the exit Gibbs created when Milo's order makes me freeze.

"Give us a sec."

Jake closes his door first, then it's followed by a heavy slam from River. Gibson doesn't budge.

"You okay in here?" he asks me. I feel like I can't breathe but give him a jerky nod anyway.

Hesitantly, he stands to his full height then closes the back door, leaving Milo and me alone in the cab of River's white truck.

"Tell me the truth," he mutters when I haven't moved a muscle.

"Milo––"

"Tell me the truth, Reese."

"It doesn't matter anymore. I'm done with him. I'm not going back, okay?"

"Am I really that shitty of a brother?"

It's the self-deprecation in his tone that makes me jerk back. "W-what do you mean?"

"That you felt like you couldn't come to me? That you couldn't tell me what the hell was going on?"

Defeated, I rest my head against the leather seat behind me and close my eyes. "It's not like that..."

"Then tell me what it's like."

"Well, for starters, he never hit me. Okay? He was just possessive. And an asshole, which you already know. He would say mean crap, especially when he was drunk, but I never considered him to be abusive until Jake pointed it out two minutes ago."

And now that he has, I feel like I can't breathe.

"I should've recognized the signs," Milo rasps. "Jake did. I'm such an asshole––"

"You're not an asshole, Milo. At all. You're an incredible brother. The best a girl could ever ask for, I promise. I just..."

He scoffs. "You just what, Reese?"

Eyes clouding with tears, I move my head to his strong shoulder, then wrap my arms around his bicep and squeeze it like he's my own personal teddy bear. "I just made a mistake, and I didn't want to make you clean it up for me. Again. Which is exactly what you're doing right now, so that's a lot of fun."

"You know I'm here for you."

"Of course, I know that. You've always been here for me. You've always protected me from assholes. Like Dad. And Mom. You've always been the one to put yourself between the monsters and your baby sister. Not that Ian is a monster. He's just...a mistake that I want to leave in the past. But now I'm starting to wonder if I'm the problem. If I'm just going to attract another rotten apple, ya know? If I'm asking for it."

"Reese––"

"I know. I know that's the wrong mentality. I know that I shouldn't beat myself up, but I can't help it. I'm a big girl, yet I feel like my life is falling apart. And who do I run to? My big brother. You shouldn't have to be the one that rides in on his white horse to save the day. That shouldn't be your job anymore."

"Bullshit, it shouldn't," he argues. I can practically feel his blood boiling beneath his tattooed skin.

"Look," I choke out. "Just because I believe you shouldn't have to be responsible for me anymore doesn't mean I've ever questioned if you'd be there for me if I ever needed you. And yesterday, I needed you. Thank you for letting me stay at your place. Thank you for coming with me to pick up my stuff. Thank you for being the best freaking brother a girl could ever ask for. I'm sorry that I let Ian affect our relationship. That I didn't make it a priority when it's so much more important than the one I had with him."

"I'm gonna kill him."

I laugh in an attempt to diffuse the situation, but I'm not quite sure if he's serious or not. "Milo. You need to promise me that you won't kill Ian."

He doesn't respond, so I lift my head and peek up at him. His strong jaw looks like it's been chiseled from stone.

"Please?" I whisper.

"Is he home?"

If he is, I'm afraid that he's about to get the shit kicked out of him. Sitting up a little straighter in my seat, I scan the parking lot for his polished black muscle car but don't find it.

"Is he?" Milo demands.

"I don't think so."

Grunting, Milo reaches for the door handle, but I stop him from opening it quite yet.

"If he's in there, I'm gonna need you to promise me that you'll keep your head on straight."

"That's bullshit," he scoffs.

"I'm serious, Milo." Grabbing his face, I make him look me straight in the eye. "He isn't worth it."

The wheels are turning in his head. I can practically see

them as he weighs his options, so I do the only thing I can. "If you don't want to make this ugly for me, then you need to keep your cool. Promise me."

He grits his teeth.

"Promise me," I beg.

"Fine." He opens the back door then slips out of the exit. His muscles bunch and pull beneath his black shirt as he marches toward Jake, then cocks his arm back and hits him square in the face.

I gasp.

Jake's head swings to the left, and he stumbles back a few feet while I cover my mouth in shock.

"That's for not speaking up when you thought something was wrong but didn't tell me," Milo spits.

And because he's Jake, he stands to his full height but keeps his arms at his sides. "Then you should probably hit me again."

Milo shakes his head. "No. Because I should've seen it in the first place."

Giving me his back a second time, Milo crosses the empty parking lot toward my old front door without waiting for us to follow.

A hand reaches out from the side of the truck, and I take it before hopping down onto the black asphalt.

"Thanks."

"Don't mention it," Gibbs returns. "Let's go catch up before your brother beats the shit out of anyone else for one day, shall we?"

I laugh dryly and wipe away the excess moisture that's seemed to gather beneath my eyes. "I think that's a good idea."

As we make our way across the open space with parked cars sprinkled throughout the vicinity, I notice Jake still hanging by the carport along the north side of the street.

"Can you give us a minute?" I murmur to Gibbs.

He nods. "Sure thing."

Then he jogs ahead.

Tucking my hands into my back pockets, I ask, "How's your jaw?"

Jake chuckles, but there isn't much humor in it. "Could be worse. Milo was going easy on me."

With a nod, I chew on the inside of my cheek as the street bustles with car engines and birds chirping.

"How did you know?" I rasp.

"I didn't know."

"Well, what tipped you off?"

Running his hand along his bruised jaw, he admits, "You seem more guarded than you used to be."

"I've always been guarded. You've met my parents, remember?"

"Those weren't parents," he corrects me.

"Good point. Still, there had to be something that made you draw that conclusion."

His gaze drops to the dark asphalt beneath our feet. "It was the little things. The missed lunches. The daily texts that turned to weeks, then months. Stuff like that. I had two choices. Either you were tired of my sarcastic memes, or you were moving on and falling in love, too busy to be chatting with your big brother's friend anymore."

"That's not true––"

"It kind of is," he argues with a knowing smile. "But then you showed up at the bar, and I realized there might be a third option. You weren't in love with him. It was just that your self-esteem was so low that you figured no one else would want you *except* him. You've been too afraid to leave his sorry ass because you're terrified of being alone even though he treats you like shit. And you were scared because you didn't know how he would respond to you finally ending things when you've already tried so many times in the past. Combine that with everything else, and I guess I was able to piece it together. I shouldn't have told Milo like that, though. That wasn't fair to him, and that wasn't fair to you either."

"No. It wasn't." Closing the last few feet of distance between us, I wrap my arms around his neck and pull him into a hug. He doesn't hesitate to return the gesture and curls his arms around my waist protectively while resting his chin on the crown of my head.

The seconds seem to slow down as we stand like this, breathing each other in before I whisper, "Thank you for telling him. Honestly, you kind of opened my eyes to the whole thing too. It might not have been the best time, but what's that saying again? Rip it off like a Band-Aid?"

He chuckles softly, his breath tickling the top of my head before he releases me from his grasp. "That's the one. I'm sorry about earlier today too. I shouldn't have assumed you were sleeping with River."

"I'm not that kind of girl, Jake. You should know me better than that."

"I do know you better than that. I don't"--he sighs and lets me go--"I don't know what I was thinking. But I truly am sorry, Reese. I'm an ass."

"Just a little bit," I tease, letting him off the hook. "But I forgive you."

"Thanks. Let's go get your stuff so you can finally move on, okay?"

"Okay."

8

REESE

"**D**o you have your key?" Milo asks as Jake and I approach the second floor where my apartment sits.

"Yeah." I hand it to him. He slides it into the lock, but it doesn't twist.

"What the hell?" I mutter under my breath as Milo continues to jiggle the key.

River watches with his arms crossed over his chest before announcing, "Looks like your loverboy changed the locks."

"Why would he do that?"

Shrugging, River throws out a guess. "Maybe he knows that once you have your stuff, you won't have a reason to ever see him again. Maybe he didn't want you to sneak by and grab it when he isn't home, which is exactly what you were trying to do. Gotta give your boy credit. He's not as dumb as I'd assumed."

"Or maybe he is because now, we get to have an up-close and personal introduction with the guy who cheated on our girl here." Gibbs tosses his arm around my shoulder while River snorts.

"Our girl?"

"Yeah. She's our roommate now––"

"And therefore she's ours? As in, to *share*?" River razzes with a knowing smile.

Face reddening, I pull out my phone and send a text to Ian because I know it'll be pointless to ask the superintendent to let me in. He's just as chauvinistic as Ian.

Me: Funny story. My key doesn't work. Wanna explain that one to me?

My phone rings in less than three seconds.

"Put it on speaker," Milo orders.

Releasing the air in my lungs, I slide my thumb across the screen and answer it.

"Yes?"

"Hey, baby. There's been some break-ins around the neighborhood. Figured I should probably change the locks to keep your stuff from getting stolen while I'm at work."

"Aren't you thoughtful," I grit out. "Any chance you left a spare lying around? I kinda need to grab a few outfits."

"Like that black lacy thong and garter set I bought you a few months ago?" He groans as if he's imagining me in it. "Mmm... Yeah. I like that outfit too."

My gaze darts to the guys around me, who can all clearly hear this conversation. "Or, ya know, a few T-shirts and a pair of jeans."

"Just one?" he inquires, though I know he can see right through me.

I shift from one foot to the other, then pinch the bridge of my nose. "Ian, I need to grab my stuff."

"I think you need to talk to me first."

Raising my hand that isn't holding my cell, I try to keep my own personal bodyguards at bay when they're all chomping at the bit to get their hands on Ian. With a huff, Milo crosses his arms but glares at my phone nonetheless.

"Is there a spare key somewhere?" I press.

"No need. I'm on my way right now."

Then the call goes dead.

Three minutes tick by in silence. We're all too hopped up on adrenaline and anxiety to chit-chat about the weather, but the heavy silence is not exactly helping my nerves.

I check my phone for what feels like the thousandth time and watch the clock change from 12:04 to 12:05 pm. Grabbing my phone from my hand, River slides it into the back pocket of my ripped jeans, then pats the surface with a wry grin as if to say, *calm the hell down, sweetheart.*

"So...how you doin'?" he asks in his best impression of Joey from *Friends*.

I grin, surprising myself with how effortless it feels. "I'm..." My voice trails off as a loud muscle car roars down the road. River follows my gaze, then steps a little closer to my side. Gibson flanks the other while Milo steps in front of me like a terrifying guard dog. Jake's familiar presence greets me from behind as he drops his voice low and murmurs, "Let's just get her stuff, then get out of here, okay?"

"You guys are suffocating me," I huff.

"We're protecting you. There's a difference," River tosses back at me. None of them move an inch. If anything, they squeeze in a little closer, making me feel like a sardine stuffed inside a can of muscles.

"You guys are being ridiculous," I mumble under my breath. Shifting my weight from one leg to the other, I glance around Milo's massive frame. Ian's key fob is in his hand as he presses the button to lock his car then swaggers toward us like a Poodle at a dog show. My palms are sweaty, but I keep them at my sides and watch him approach. He looks good, and I hate that I notice he's wearing the Henley I bought him for Christmas.

"Hey, babe. Wanna call off your guard dogs for a minute so I can get to the door and let you in?" Ian asks in a bored tone.

River's arm snakes around my waist, tugging me into his side with a protectiveness that makes my breath hitch. My gaze drops to his fingers digging into my hip. They're causing little indents on my bare skin from where my shirt has risen up.

But his action doesn't go unnoticed.

I can feel Ian's eyes on me as I inspect River's touch. That same sixth sense tingles with awareness. Holding my breath, I look up to find his heated stare. It pins me in, rendering my muscles useless as he stalks closer.

"So that's how it is, huh? Already moved on? Awfully quick, don't you think?"

"Give me the key and wait outside," Milo practically growls, his fury simmering like a freshly cracked egg in a frying pan.

"And cut our reunion short? I think I'll have to pass. Let me guess. You're Milo." It isn't a question. "I'm Ian. Nice to finally meet you, man."

I snort.

Bullshit, it's nice to finally meet him.

Ian has been putting roadblocks up left and right any time I've tried to bring Milo around. So much so, in fact, that I stopped bothering to introduce them to each other altogether. Who would've thought it was because he was trying to cut all the ties between me and my family in hopes of isolating me until I believed he was the only one I could rely on.

Classic abusive behavior. Jake's right.

"It's probably a good thing we never met," Milo informs

Ian. "If we had, your relationship would've ended a hell of a lot sooner than it did."

"Is that right?" Ian challenges. He might not have ever hit me, but that doesn't mean he isn't a hothead who's always been down for a brawl. Now that I think about it, it was probably only a matter of time before his fist would've found my face in a moment of fury.

They're almost matched for their heights, but Milo is more cut. More muscular. More predatorial. More everything. And I'm so glad he's on my side.

But that doesn't mean I want him to throw the first punch.

Or any punches, for that matter.

River lets go of me, giving me a gentle nudge toward Gibson before he steps forward to break apart the possible fistfight that's seconds from happening. Under normal circumstances, I'd probably give him crap for treating me like a yo-yo, but I bite my tongue and remind myself to thank him later for putting himself in the line of fire.

The vice around my chest begins to ease as River flanks Milo's side then moves between the two stiff bodies.

"Now, now, gentlemen. Let's remember why we're here, shall we?" With his hands raised in defense, he presses his open palm to Ian's chest in a silent warning to take a chill pill. Then River strikes faster than a coiled snake and grabs onto the collar of Ian's shirt with one hand before nailing him in the jaw with his closed fist.

My hands cover my mouth that's wide open in shock as my ex flies backward.

"What the hell?" he screams in outrage. An angry red mark is painted along the side of his face, and I'd bet a thousand bucks he's seeing stars right now. But it only lasts for a second.

Charging toward River like an angry bull, Ian is ready to

73

rip his head off before Milo steps between them and shoves him back a few steps on the concrete outside my apartment door.

"Back the hell up," Milo orders. His face is stone-cold as he dares Ian to disobey him.

Ian's hand flings through the air, motioning to River, whose nostrils are still flaring with adrenaline and frustration.

"That asshole just sucker-punched me on my own property. I could have him arrested for that shit!"

"Look, we just want to grab Reese's stuff," Jake interjects as he steps onto the other side of Milo with his arms crossed over his chest. There's so much testosterone on this porch I'm afraid I might drown in it.

And it's all my fault.

"Then he shouldn't have hit me," Ian growls.

"Then you shouldn't have hurt Reese," River tells him with a casual shrug of his shoulders. "Now, we'd really like to get on with our day, and I'm sure you would too. So if you could be so kind as to open the damn door, then we'll be out of your hair in a jiffy."

"A jiffy?" Ian laughs then turns to me. "Where'd you find this pretty boy?"

River's hand flexes at his side. "This pretty boy is about to--"

"Stop!" I shout, closing the distance between a very pissed-off River and me. My palm brushes against his lower back in hopes of keeping him grounded as I murmur, "I just want to grab my stuff. Ian, will you please let me into the apartment? I'm seriously begging you."

River's jaw tightens as he scowls over at me before returning his attention to my ex. Apparently, he doesn't like the idea of me begging. But he doesn't shrug off my touch. If anything, he leans into it.

Watching our silent exchange, Gibson clears his throat, and I drop my hand back to my side.

"Please, Ian?" I whisper.

Ian dangles his keys like he would a treat for a dog. "Only if you promise that we can talk later."

"That won't be necessary," Milo interjects. He shifts his weight to hide me behind him, and it cuts off my vision until I'm staring at my brother's broad back.

"We just need her stuff, and then we'll be out of your hair," Jake explains in a calm voice, attempting to placate him.

"Promise me," Ian orders while completely ignoring my big brother, who's practically blowing steam from his ears.

Bad idea, Ian.

River's grip returns to my waist, tighter this time, but I pretend that I don't notice his silent warning. He doesn't want me to cave to Ian's demands. Unfortunately, I don't think I have much of a choice.

"Fine," I grit out. "I promise."

Satisfied, Ian announces, "You have five minutes."

Ian walks straight toward Milo. Then, like Moses and the Red Sea, we all separate onto opposite sides. The key slides into the lock with ease before Ian opens the door and ushers us inside.

My feet freeze in place as I take in the apartment. Everything looks exactly the same. I'm not sure why I'm surprised, but it feels like it's been years since I last stepped foot in here when it's only been twenty-four hours or so. A warm hand nudges me forward to keep from blocking the entrance, and I look over my shoulder to find the owner.

With a teasing grin, River prods, "Why don't you show me that bedroom. Maybe I can help pack your panties."

I snort, then smack him on the chest while inside, I'm singing. It feels good to smile.

"Come on, horn dog," I mutter under my breath, finally shaking off my nerves long enough to remember why the hell I'm in Ian's apartment.

It's funny. This was my apartment before he moved in. As I look back at my relationship with Ian, I'm not even sure when he officially moved in and claimed it as his own, but he's smooth like that. Convincing. And with the right dose of confidence, even the craziest ideas can seem sane when delivered with his surety. My fingers graze the white walls lining the hallway as I push aside the memories and approach the bedroom.

Our bedroom.

He wasn't always a complete asshole. In the beginning, he was almost…sweet. Kind. Caring. Made sure I was satisfied. Then things changed. It was all an act. Like the stupid frog in a pot of hot water analogy, only I was the frog. And I was burned alive before I even realized it.

Gibson follows behind River and me as I catch myself staring at the soft, gray comforter strewn across the bed. The one we bought together after I came home from work to see he'd spilled wine on our previous one.

He *never* drinks wine.

My mouth floods with acid. It was probably one of his sluts.

"Come on, River," Gibbs mutters before striding toward the closet and wrenching open the doors. When he finds my gym bag, he tosses it to his friend. "Fill it up with her shit."

Like a pair of bumblebees, the guys buzz around the room, gathering my stuff from the drawers, cabinets, closet. Everything. Until the bedroom is practically empty, and Gibbs takes a final scan of the room.

"Hey, Riv, you got the rest? I'm going to go check the bathroom."

"Yeah. I think we're pretty much done here. We'll meet you in the family room in a sec."

With a final nod, Gibbs disappears into the bathroom and leaves us alone.

I catch River rummaging through my lingerie drawer, but he doesn't comment as his bruised hand grabs a dark red thong before shoving it in the bag with the rest of my stuff.

His knuckles are angry and raw from hitting Ian, and I cringe as I inspect them from afar.

Why would he punch him? The guy barely knows me. If Milo had punched him, I wouldn't have batted an eye. Hell, even Jake throwing a sucker punch would've made more sense than what happened outside, and he's the least combative person I've ever met.

But River? The calm, sarcastic womanizer seems like the prime example of being a lover, not a fighter. But he *did* fight today. For me.

Unable to help myself, I close the short distance between us, then grab his hand and take a closer look. His knuckles are slightly swollen with a few angry red bruises peppered across them.

He must've hit him hard.

"Can I help you?" River asks, his voice thick with sarcasm.

"Sorry. It's just... *Ouch*," I mutter while gently brushing my thumb along the back of his damaged hand.

"Yeah, you're kinda a pain in the ass, Reese."

I'd be offended if it weren't for the crooked grin that's threatening to say hello on his face.

"To be fair, I didn't tell you to hit him," I point out.

"True. But someone had to defend your honor."

"Is that what you were doing?" I laugh as those same stupid butterflies wreak havoc on my insides.

His tongue darts out and slides across his bottom lip as his chest rumbles, "Something like that."

"Hmm...," I hum before realizing how close we're standing. Carefully, I look up at him. "It looks like it hurts a lot."

"Wanna know what would make it feel better?" His question is delivered with a playful bounce of his eyebrows that makes my heart gallop like a freaking racehorse.

How can one man be so damn charismatic?

It isn't fair. Especially when I know he acts this way with everyone yet still manages to make my knees weak anytime he directs it at me.

Knowing I'm going to regret it, I ask, "And what's that?"

His penetrating eyes drop down to my lips. Instead of answering me, he surprises me by asking, "Why'd you jump in when he called me a pretty boy?"

"Because if I didn't, you would've gotten into a fight."

"And? What, you thought I couldn't take him?"

I laugh, even though he looks kind of serious. Like the pretty boy comment bothered him. I don't know why he would be offended by a statement like that. The guy *is* pretty. I mean, he gets paid to be looked at. He's a model, for Pete's sake. A gorgeous model. One that I'm seriously having a hard time staying away from. But it's the vulnerability in his gaze that really does me in. The need to be seen as *more* than a pretty face. Just like how I want to be seen as more than the vulnerable little sister who's managed to screw up her life in ways she never could've imagined.

And right now? I think he might be seeing past my pathetic decisions, catching a glimpse of the real me. Or maybe I'm crazy. Because if my own boyfriend didn't want me, why would the guy in front of me be any different?

"Cat got your tongue?" he teases, that same vulnerability shining just beneath the surface of his dark eyes.

"It's not that I think you couldn't take him," I explain. "I just wouldn't want him touching the moneymaker, right?"

Amused, he replies, "Not unless he got down on his knees first."

"Well, if you had ended up getting hurt, I would've felt like *I* had to be the one to get on my knees." As soon as the statement pops out of my mouth, my face burns with embarrassment, and my eyes widen in shock.

Filter, Reese! Ever heard of one?

River's mouth quirks up in amusement, his thumb brushing against the back of my hand that's still cradling his bruised one.

The innocent touch makes my knees weak as he prods, "So, let me get this straight. If I stormed into the family room right now and picked a fight to defend your honor, you'd--"

"Come on, guys," Jake interrupts from the doorway while simultaneously popping the little bubble I'd found myself surrounded in. "We grabbed everything out here. Are you ready to go?"

River drops his hand back to his side, then zips up the duffle bag with my clothes.

With a subtle shake of my head, I clear my throat and turn to Jake. "Uh, yup. We're ready."

"Good." Jake nods. "Let's get going."

Then he disappears, leaving an awkward silence in his wake as if he knows he just walked in on *something*. I'm not sure what the hell that was, but it was definitely unexpected and...unwanted? I glance over at River, but he's too busy rummaging through the almost empty drawers to notice me.

Apparently, we're done flirting.

Which is a good thing.

So why do I miss it?

Sticking my hands into my back pockets, I turn on my heel and trail behind Jake without bothering to see if River follows me or not. Because I shouldn't want him to. When I reach the family room and kitchen area, my eyes find Ian's without being able to help myself.

"Did you get everything?" he asks, keeping his tone calm and even.

I nod. "Yeah. Thanks."

"Mind if we talk for a second?"

It's like I'm talking to a completely different person than the guy who lost control outside our place less than ten minutes ago, which I guess makes sense when you're dealing with Dr. Jekyll and Mr. Hyde.

Gibbs interjects, "Unfortunately, we have to get going. River has a date tonight and would hate to be late, so…"

I blanch but cover it up with a look of indifference as quickly as I can.

A date?

Jealousy eats at my insides like a crippling stomach bug, though I have no idea why. I'm not jealous. It's River. Womanizing, sarcastic River. Of course, he has a date.

"Please?" Ian begs me. The word is foreign on his lips. "You promised."

Surprised at the gentleness in his voice, I clear my throat as memories from the good moments in our relationship flash in the back of my mind. The thoughts are a welcome respite from the images of River and his revolving door of women he likes to spend his time with, and I grab hold of it with both hands.

"Sonny's right," River interrupts. Sidling up next to me, he presses his hand against my lower back and urges me toward the door. "We gotta get going. Might wanna put some ice on your face, though. Looks like it's swelling a bit."

My feathers ruffle even though I refuse to acknowledge it as I shrug away from his touch and put a few feet of distance between us. Wouldn't want him to be late for his *date*.

"You can go wait in the truck. I'll be out in a minute."

Surprised by my order, he opens his mouth to argue before Jake appears through the front door and interrupts, "Everything's loaded up. Milo just got a call from one of his clients who wants to move up their appointment, so we gotta get going."

"I'll be right out," I reply.

"Let's get going, Reese," Gibbs rumbles.

I shake my head, fighting my annoyance at the fact River has a date tonight, along with the knowledge that every guy in this room wants to control me.

"I said I'll be right out," I repeat without bothering to look at Gibbs. "I promised Ian we'd have a quick chat, remember?"

Jake watches the interaction carefully before motioning to River and Gibbs. "Come on, guys. She's a big girl."

There's a moment of hesitation before a frustrated Gibbs heads out the front door without looking back. The warmth from River's presence behind me disappears a beat later as he follows his friends outside, but he stops at the exit and pushes the door the rest of the way open.

With a pointed stare, he warns, "We'll be right outside." Then he steps across the threshold and leaves me alone with my ex.

A deep, weighted silence envelops the room before I turn to him and lift my chin in defiance.

"I'm giving you two minutes to say your piece. Then we're done."

Tsking, he pushes himself up from the couch and swaggers closer. "Are you sure you want that, babe?"

"Positive."

"And you won't forgive me for this one mistake?"

My breath catches in my throat before my gaze darts to the still-open front door. Thankfully, it's empty, but that doesn't stop the bile from creeping into my throat.

"I've already forgiven you for too many mistakes. I deserve more than that."

He raises his hand and brushes a few strands of hair away from my face with a soft, knowing smile. "Do you? All because those boys out there seem interested in you? Is that why? You think you can just...replace me? What we have?"

"Had," I correct him. My heart is pounding against my rib cage until I'm positive he can hear it.

"Don't do this, Reese. I need you, babe. I don't know why you look so surprised. I told you that we're forever––"

"But you don't even want me anymore, Ian." My desperation slowly seeps into my explanation. "If you did, you wouldn't have cheated on me. This is all about control to you."

"It is," he acknowledges, dragging the back of his fingers along the column of my throat before brushing them along my bare arms in a gentle caress. It leaves my skin crawling. "You've always known how much it drives me crazy to want something I can't have. And you in those tight jeans with the chip on your shoulder?" He chuckles. "It's a heady concoction."

"I'm sure you can find someone else to entertain you––"

"But they won't be *you*. I want you. And we both know that I'm stubborn enough to get what I want. Don't we, Reese? Just like all the times before..."

"It's different this time." I'm not sure who I'm trying to convince. Him. Or me.

Leaning a little closer, his breath fans across my face. "Is it?"

"Yes," I whisper. "I'm not going to let you play with me like your little toy anymore. I deserve more than that."

"Like Pretty Boy? Or maybe it's one of the other guys you're interested in." He pauses, but I don't bother to answer him. There's nothing to say. Regardless, he continues. "It doesn't matter because none of them will ever want you for anything more than a plaything to pass the time. I'm committing to you. I've already committed to you. I can't believe you would throw that back in my face."

"Are you kidding me right now?" I breathe, my tone laced with disbelief. "I'm not the one to throw our commitment away. *You* were the moment you stuck your crooked dick into someone else."

"And what about my brother?"

"What about him?"

"He's your boss."

"He *was* my boss," I remind him. "We've already discussed this. I quit, remember?"

"You can't quit--"

"I most definitely can. I'm sure he can find someone else to balance his books that will accept the shitty pay he's offering, just like I did. Now, if that will be all--"

"I'm not finished--"

"Well, I am," I spit. "Goodbye, Ian. Don't call me anymore."

Then I storm out of his apartment with my head held high even though a little voice is whispering that I just made a giant mistake.

The ride back to the house is pretty quiet other than a few offhand remarks about River's badassery followed by Milo's distaste for not being able to strangle Ian the way he desperately wanted.

When we're only a few minutes away, Milo's massive body leans forward, squishing me against Gibbs on the opposite side of me as he points to a fast-food chain restaurant at the next exit.

"River, when's your date? Think we have time to grab some food first?"

I stare at River through the stupid rearview mirror while practically sitting in Gibbs' lap, but he doesn't bother to look at me before flipping his blinker on.

"We've got time," he answers.

"Thanks," Milo returns. "I'll buy."

"What time do you have to be in to work, Milo?" I ask him.

"In about an hour. I won't be home until late." He settles back into his seat. "You gonna be cool hanging out by yourself?"

"Yes, *Dad*. I'll be just fine without your babysitting for one night, but thanks for your concern."

"What are you gonna do?" he prods.

"Does it matter?"

"Yes. I want to make sure you're taken care of. Do you have a problem with that?"

"Maybe--"

"I was going to work on my thesis," Jake interrupts from the passenger seat. "But if you want, we can watch a movie or something." He tosses a quick look back at me before staring back out the windshield.

"You should work on your thesis," I encourage him. "But maybe after you're finished, we can do a *Lord of the Rings* marathon or something."

Quirking his brow, River glances over at me before returning his attention to the offramp. "*Lord of the Rings?*"

"It's tradition," I offer with a shrug.

"Extended edition or theatrical cut?"

"We both know there's only one correct answer to that question."

"I can take a night off," Jake offers. "Not a big deal."

Distracted by my standoff with River, I correct him, "It *is* a big deal. I've already turned all of your lives upside down. Besides, despite what my brother thinks"--I give him a quick glare--"I don't need a babysitter."

"I know, but--"

"Seriously, Jake. I'll be fine. Work on your thesis for a few hours, then maybe we can watch Netflix or something, okay?"

"Like Netflix and *chill*, perhaps? 'Cause if I knew that was on the menu, I just might find a reason to cancel my date tonight," River jokes, though there's a slight bite to his words that make me pause.

Bristling, I argue, "Sorry, River. Three's a crowd and all

that. Besides, I'm sure you'll be plenty busy with your floozy for the evening, so..."

"Floozy?" He gasps in mock outrage before turning into the drive-thru lane and rolling down the driver's side window. "Who says she's a floozy?"

"Will you two shut up?" Milo groans, only halfway paying attention to our conversation as he pulls out his cell. His fingers begin flying across the screen, so I ignore his request like he didn't say anything at all.

"Just a hunch," I tell River conversationally. "Seems like those are the ones you attract."

His smirk is annoyingly charming as his gaze holds mine in the damn rearview mirror I'm starting to loathe. It's just... too much.

"You calling yourself a floozy, Reese? That's not very nice--"

"Hello, welcome to Burrito Bandito. Can I take your order?" a voice asks through the speaker outside the window.

Jake and Gibbs cut the conversation a little short by throwing their orders at River until I'm sure they're all going to die from heart attacks before they turn thirty. Well, except River, who orders a taco salad. Heaven forbid he lose the 'V' on his abs. The guy is a health nut with a capital H. Although, he *is* pretty to look at, so maybe I shouldn't judge him so harshly.

He's also going on a date with someone else after spending the day taking care of me and making me feel worthy of a person's time. So...there's that.

My annoyance spikes.

"You want anything, Floozy?" River quips with a teasing grin after repeating everyone else's orders.

I glare at him while Jake says, "She wants a shredded beef quesadilla with no sour cream."

Head cocked to one side, River holds my gaze in the

rearview mirror. Like he's daring me to do something. To argue with him. To push him. Hell, to freaking kiss him, for all I know. There are so many options that I'm starting to get dizzy. But it's the intensity that's getting under my skin. Hell, everything that involves River is starting to get under my skin. And that's a problem. Because I don't know how to stop it.

"That right, Floozy?" he asks.

"It's right," Jake answers for me. *Again.* Because he's thoughtful like that and can tell I'm about to stab River if he calls me Floozy one more time.

With pursed lips, River adds my order to the long list of burritos, tacos, queso, and one taco salad, then we pull around to the front and pick up the bags of seasoned goodness. The combination of cumin and chili powder is enough to turn my frown upside down as Jake hands everyone their food. Milo is still nose deep in his phone, so I put his order in his lap then unwrap my quesadilla. My stomach rumbles.

As I take a giant bite and let the flavors melt in my mouth, a soft moan escapes me. "Oh, cheese, how I've missed you." I lick a bit of the buttery seasoning from my thumb and smile in pure bliss. "Like seriously, though."

Four heads swivel in my direction, but the only sound in the cab of the truck is from the rumble of the engine.

With the quesadilla an inch from my mouth, I pause. "What? What is it?"

My brother growls, "Don't ever make a sound like that when I'm around again." He shudders. "Ever."

"A sound like what?" I laugh.

Pointing his index finger an inch from my face, he repeats, "Ever." Then he unwraps his taco and devours it in three bites while I go back to eating my deliciously cheesy quesadilla.

Oh, Milo. So bossy.

REESE

The stairs creak beneath my feet, making me flinch as I sneak down to the kitchen. With the entire house painted in darkness, I cling to the banister then breathe a sigh of relief when I reach the main floor without waking anyone up.

I can't sleep, and I blame my stupid attraction for a stupid roommate for keeping me up. I could've sworn I heard moaning. But maybe I'm imagining things.

Please say I'm imagining things.

And why do I even care in the first place? It's not like anything can ever happen between us. I would never betray Milo like that. And I don't think River would cross that line either, no matter how much he likes to flirt with me.

It can't happen.

Ever.

So, why do I care that he took someone else on a date tonight? Someone who wasn't me. Why does it feel like a slap in the face after we spent the day together? He doesn't owe me anything. At all.

So, why. Do. I. Care?

Desperate for some tea, I open the cupboards and begin my search, but it's too freaking dark in this place. I blindly search for a switch on the wall and flip it on. The light above the sink isn't very bright, but it does the job. There's coffee, protein powder, and a few boxes of kid cereal. No tea.

Lovely.

My shoulders hunch in defeat before I flick off the light when the stairs squeak quietly in the otherwise silent house. My head snaps in its direction. I tiptoe toward the hall to investigate, but when a soft giggle breaks the silence near the entryway, I freeze.

Shit.

With barely-restrained curiosity, I squint my eyes and make out two bodies near the front door. It's a different girl from earlier. But the guy pressing her against the wall doesn't have a shirt on, so it doesn't take a genius to figure out who he is.

Taking care of the moneymaker, River? Really? With what? Orgasms?

I roll my eyes and try to ignore the sharp pain in my chest. He grabs the door handle and ushers his new guest outside. When the front door closes, he turns and faces me before his heavy steps echo down the hall toward the kitchen.

My heartbeat freaking skyrockets, but my feet stay planted in place.

Why do I feel like I just got caught doing something I shouldn't?

Needing to disappear, I look around the kitchen for a hiding spot, but it's too late.

"Hey, Roomie," River calls, keeping his voice low.

With an awkward wave and the knowledge I've been caught spying, I shove my jealousy aside and mutter, "Hi."

"You look good in my T-shirt."

The hem of his shirt barely reaches my mid-thigh. I tug at

it before giving up. "If I'd known it was your last one, I would've just borrowed one of Jake's."

"Bet he would've loved that," he mumbles under his breath before flipping on the light switch.

"Excuse me?"

He ignores my comment. "I'm wearing pants, so I'm abiding by Milo's rules, unlike someone I know." His pointed stare makes me squirm before he adds, "But shirts are still optional, Lil' Miss Rule Follower, and I reserve my right to go without. You're welcome to do the same if you feel so inclined, by the way." His teasing makes my stomach tighten before he changes the subject, practically giving me whiplash. "Were you looking for something?"

"Oh." I shrug and scan the dark cabinets that failed me. "Couldn't sleep. I was just looking for tea or something."

"Was I keeping you up?" His concern is like another knife to the chest, but I keep my poker face in place.

"With your sexcapades? Nope. Didn't hear a thing," I lie. "Although I'm impressed with your endurance. Sounded like quite the crescendo around 2 am. Bravo, Roomie. Not too shabby."

"Happy to oblige. Hell, I might've invited you to participate. Ya know, if you weren't Milo's little sister."

"Not interested."

"You sure about that, Floozy?"

I gulp. "Positive."

His crooked smirk almost does me in as he inches closer. Like a deer in the headlights, I freeze before my backside hits the counter behind me. He crowds me against it then pulls out a pair of mugs, setting them beside my hip on the swirling granite.

As his scent tickles my nostrils, my mouth waters. The guy smells like sex and bad decisions.

Very bad decisions.

And *very* good sex.

He steps back to give me some space and warms some water in a tea kettle on the stove.

Desperate for air, I take a deep breath, praying the oxygen will wake me up from this encounter, and I'll be tucked in bed and away from the smell of sex and bad decisions.

"Darn genetics," I quip, forcing myself to focus on anything but his abs and the way they flex with his every move. I shouldn't be noticing them. My fingers shouldn't be itching to touch them. My mouth shouldn't be craving his taste even though I've never sampled his lips before. Especially when they were pressed against someone who wasn't me earlier tonight.

What is wrong with me?

"Darn genetics." He laughs. "So, how was *Lord of the Rings?*"

"Fine. How was your floozy?"

His gaze heats as he glances over at me with a smirk. "Distracting."

My brows furrow. "What's that supposed to mean?"

"Do you like honey or sugar in your tea?" He pulls open a drawer near the stove and pulls out two tea bags.

"Honey, please," I answer, making a mental note as to where the tea is kept while brushing off the way he ignored my question. Then again, I'm not sure I want to know what he meant about his floozy in the first place.

As he pours the hot liquid over the tea bags in our mugs, I ask, "Is it caffeine-free?"

That same crooked smirk greets me as he answers, "I might look like a god, Reese, but I'm still very human and need my sleep after a night like tonight."

"Which means...?"

"It's caffeine-free."

"You could've just said it's caffeine-free without adding the whole *look like a god* comment."

"And miss your disgusted expression? Where's the fun in that?"

Shaking my head, I attempt to hide my annoyance by talking, but it's no use. "Are you always this cocky with the ladies?"

"I'm *more* cock-y," he emphasizes, "with *all* the ladies. This is me toning it down." He adds a drizzle of honey into the steaming tea and sets a mug in front of me. "You're welcome, by the way."

"For toning down your cockiness?"

He lifts his chin toward the mug in front of me. "I meant for making you tea. But sure, you can thank me for toning it down too. Goodnight, Roomie."

"Goodnight."

Giving me his back, he moseys down the hall and up the stairs with his own cup in hand while I watch him with barely-restrained curiosity before he disappears from view.

River, who the hell are you?

And why am I still thinking about your stupid floozy?

REESE

Chewing on my lower lip, I look up at the vintage tattoo sign hanging on the rough brick building. With a deep breath, I grab the door handle and swing it open. After filling out a dozen applications on barely three hours of sleep, I'm beat and am missing Milo like crazy. The scent of cleaning products and cigarette smoke burns my nostrils but makes me smile as I soak it up like a dry sponge. This. This is where Milo has always belonged. And I'm happy he finally found it.

The front area is scattered with chairs, magazines, and art books for clients to peruse while waiting for their turn. But there isn't anyone to greet me. A giant *Help Wanted* sign is taped to the front of the receptionist's desk in lieu of said receptionist. My head tilts to the side as I step closer to it.

What the hell?

I run my fingers along the thick block letters before my nails dig into my palm. Pissed, I scan the large open room that's broken up with half-wall cubicles in search of my big brother. Tucked in the corner of the room sits the lying asshole of the hour, chatting with his client like he doesn't have a care in the world.

Looks like he's in for a rude awakening.

My worn Chucks scuff against the linoleum floor as I close the distance between us.

"Hey, Milo," I greet him, my voice sickly sweet.

The buzzing from his tattoo gun ceases as he looks up at me. "What are you doing here?"

"What? I can't stop by and say hello to my big brother?" I ask.

"What's wrong?"

"Nothing," I lie before waving a brown paper sack back and forth through the air. "I just bought burgers. Figured you might be hungry. But it looks like you're busy. I would leave it with the receptionist, but apparently, you don't have one."

With a sigh, he sets his gun on the countertop behind him and mutters to his olive-skinned client, "I'll be right back, Lou." Motioning to a doorway near the back, he adds, "Let's go."

I shove the brown sack into his chest, then march into the break room that's just as pristine as the kitchen at home. Pacing the freshly swept floor, I fold my arms and bite out, "Why didn't you tell me?"

"About what, Reese?"

"Don't lie to me." I stomp toward him and jab my finger into his chest. "You know exactly what I'm talking about, Milo. I asked you if this place had any openings. I asked you, and you said no. Why? Why did you say no? Would it be that terrible if we worked together?"

His jaw tightens, but he doesn't answer me.

My nostrils flare. "You *know* I'm desperate, Milo. You *know* how guilty I feel about sleeping in that house without being able to contribute to living there. This"--I wave my hands around——"would help me contribute. Seriously, am I that bad? Would it be that terrible to work together?"

He scratches his jaw but stays silent. *Again.*

"Answer me, Milo," I growl. "Why did you lie about the job?"

"Because you hate being a receptionist."

"So? It pays the bills and is the only thing on my resume other than being a freaking grocery worker. I'll even do accounting if you need me to——"

"You hate accounting."

"So?" I repeat. "I'm desperate, Milo——"

"Which is why I didn't tell you about the job."

I jerk away from him. "But...why?"

"Sit down, Reese."

"No. I want to know——"

"Will you just sit your ass down?" he barks. "Please?"

The chair scrapes against the ground as I untuck it from the large rectangle table placed in the center of the room. The sound echoes throughout the otherwise silent area before I collapse into it.

Then I sniffle and cross my arms. "There. Happy now?"

Satisfied, Milo takes the seat across from me before pulling out our burgers. He sets one in front of me. The white wrapper is stained with grease, but I don't bother to peel it away from my lunch. I'm too hurt to enjoy it anyway.

"Tell me," I beg.

"There's nothing wrong with being a receptionist."

"I know that——"

"Or an accountant. Or a grocery worker," he continues before taking a giant-ass bite of burger. I watch him chew with his mouth closed, anxiety eating away at my nerves until he swallows. "But there *is* something wrong with being stuck doing something you don't want to do."

"It pays the bills——"

"It makes you miserable."

"Sometimes we have to do things we don't want to do."

"And sometimes we *don't* have to do those things, but we're too stubborn to think any differently."

"What's that supposed to mean?" I ask.

"It means that you hated your past job, Reese. You hated filing paperwork. You hated the monotony. And I hated seeing you miserable. This time, I want you to take your time. I want you to really think about shit. About what you want. Without the pressure of needing to make ends meet."

"But I *do* need to make ends meet," I argue.

"I'll cover you until you figure it out."

"I can't ask that of you."

"You're not asking. I'm offering."

I roll my eyes. "You know what I mean. Why didn't you tell me? Why did you lie?" I whisper. "We don't keep secrets from each other, remember?"

Setting down his half-eaten burger, he grabs a napkin and rolls it between his fingers, watching me with that same sharp gaze that I grew up with.

"Tell me," I beg.

He sighs. "I didn't tell you because I knew you'd take it. For once in your life, will you be selfish? Will you allow yourself to *want* something? If you won't do it for you, then do it for me."

I open my mouth to argue that doing it for him would kind of defeat the point of being selfish, but he beats me to it.

"Don't be a smartass. You know what I mean. Take some time to think about what you want. *You.* Not anyone else. And if, for some messed-up reason, you come back to the idea that being a receptionist, or accountant, or *whatever* is your dream job, then the position is yours. Deal?"

"You promise?"

"Yeah," he grumbles.

I stand up and wrap my arms around his neck. "Deal."

"Thanks for the burgers," he mumbles.

"You're welcome. Thanks for letting me barge in on your day."

"You're welcome."

"I love you," I add.

He shoves another bite of burger into his mouth. "Yeah, yeah. Love you too."

And I know he does. And that it might not be conventional, but it's the best brotherly love a girl could ask for. Even if he's shitty at showing it sometimes.

"So, what are your plans for tonight?" I ask.

"Work. You?"

"I dunno. Probably just Netflix again. Jake has his thesis, and he already dropped everything to watch *Lord of the Rings* with me the other night, so I'll probably let him off the hook this time. Maybe Gibbs or River is free."

"Sonny's working, and River has a date."

"Another one?"

Milo pauses and gives me a weird look. "Is there something I should be worried about, Reese?"

"No…I just…am surprised, I guess." I shrug one shoulder. "I mean, he's good-looking and all, but he isn't that great."

With a snort, Milo shakes his head. "Pretty sure you're the first girl River's ever met who hasn't worshipped the ground he walks on."

"You're joking, right?"

"Nope." Crunching the paper wrapper into a ball, he tosses it toward the large black garbage can in the corner of the break room. As it swishes, he drops his chin toward my untouched burger lying on the table. "You gonna eat yours?"

"I think I'll take it home and eat there. I'm sorry I just dropped in--"

"Don't apologize. But I do need to finish Lou's piece. We'll talk later, okay?"

"Okay. Love you, Milo."

"You too."

I n a pair of yoga pants and a tank top, I lounge on the
leather sofa in the family room with a remote in hand
while surfing through the choices good ol' Netflix has
to offer. My controller hovers over *The Office* before River
comes down the stairs looking like sex on a stick.

*How the hell does he make a casual T-shirt and dark jeans look
so drool-worthy?*

With a scowl, I push the down button a few times,
searching for a solid serial killer documentary. Maybe if I
ignore him, he'll go on his merry way, and I can stop
thinking about him for two freaking minutes.

Not that it'll help. Especially if he brings his date back to
his room tonight, and I have to listen to them going at it like
rabbits, but...

Yup. I'm definitely in the mood for a stabby documentary.
With a bit more force than necessary, I jab at the buttons like
my life depends on it. I can feel his eyes on the side of my
face, tickling my senses with awareness, but I ignore them
and click on something about Ted Bundy.

River clears his throat.

I ignore that too.

"You good in here?" His voice is a little rusty from lack of use.

Sighing, I purse my lips and pretend to give him half my attention when, in reality, he's owned all of it since he hit Ian square in the jaw.

"Yup," I answer, popping the 'p' at the end to emphasize my point while refusing to look at him.

"You ignoring me?"

Squeezing the remote in my hand, I force myself to face him and smile tightly.

"Nope."

My eyes peruse his muscular frame like a buffet before I can stop myself, but my nose scrunches up as soon as I realize what I'm doing.

Come on, Reese. Keep it in your pants, ya floozy, I berate myself.

"So, uh, can I ask you something?"

"What?"

"Would you hire me for my bod?" he asks with a knowing smirk. But it feels forced. Like a façade.

My jaw drops. "I'm sorry...what was that?"

"I mean, you might as well help a guy out while you're here. How do I look?" He motions to his simple black T-shirt that hugs every freaking muscle in his shoulders and biceps. The ones that I'm having very dirty, very inappropriate thoughts about that I've already committed to memory.

"So?" he prods, snapping me back to reality.

After a slow, deliberate blink, I wipe my sweaty palm on my yoga pants as discreetly as I can then wave him off. "Meh. I think your head is big enough already."

His expression brightens as if I've given him the response he was looking for.

Greeeaaat.

"You should see what else is big," he teases.

I snort, then turn back to the television. "You're ridiculous."

"I'm charming."

"You're something," I mutter, still pretending to ignore him.

"I'll take the red cheeks as a yes, I look good enough to eat, which is exactly the look I'm going for tonight. So thanks, Floozy. I appreciate the input."

"Don't mention it. Good luck on your date tonight."

"Uh, thanks." He squeezes the back of his neck, making his biceps bulge as he studies me carefully. "I'll see ya later, yeah?"

I nod, then push play on the Ted Bundy documentary. "Yup. Sure thing."

From the corner of my eye, I watch the front door open then close, leaving me alone.

Oh. So. Alone.

I should be used to the feeling. Ian and I rarely spent our nights together, and I never cared. Hell, I savored the respite. But River's absence? Especially when I barely know the guy?

What is wrong with me?

I guess I miss his snark. His comments. His smirk.

Man, I'm pathetic.

With a sigh, I grab the nearest pillow and hug it to my chest as the images blur together on the screen.

A few minutes later, the stairs rattle in rhythm with Gibbs' footsteps.

"Hey. I'm about to head to work. You good here?"

"You're the second person to ask me that," I growl. "And, yes. I'm fine."

"You sure about that?"

"Mm-hmm," I hum.

As if he's a mind reader, Gibbs strides over to me and sits on the armrest of the couch before inspecting me closer.

I scowl back at him. "What do you want?"

"Go get dressed."

With a huff, I hit pause then turn to him. "I'm sorry, what?"

"Go get dressed."

"I've had a long day."

"I can see that. Now, go get dressed."

"Why?"

"Because you've had a long day and could use a drink, Drinks Anything Girl." He nudges me playfully. "Besides, I like hanging out with you. You can entertain me during the lulls at work."

I hesitate, chewing on the inside of my cheek as I check his expression for sincerity and find it in spades.

"Fiiiine," I drag out before pushing myself up from the couch. "Give me five. I'll be right down."

"No worries. I'll be out in my car and can drive you home after my shift. Or if you decide you want to call it a night before then, I'm sure Jake will pick you up."

"You don't have to do that, and neither does he. I'm a big girl, remember?"

"Yeah, but we're both happy to help out, Reese. You should start taking advantage from time to time."

"Oh, you mean like how you helped me get my stuff back from my ex? Like that kind of advantage?" I quip.

"If I hadn't promised your brother that I'd keep my hands to myself, I'd tell you." He winks.

"Now, hurry up. Clock's ticking." His forefinger taps his wrist that's lacking a wristwatch for good measure. Then he claps his hands when I still haven't moved. "Chop, chop, Reese's Pieces. Haven't got all day."

"Reese's Pieces?"

"It's better than Floozy, isn't it?" he returns with a smirk.

I roll my eyes before bitterly conceding. "Good point."

Seven minutes later––so sue me––we're on our way to SeaBird, where the promise of a stiff drink is enough to erase any remaining nerves and confusion from the knowledge that River is out. With a floozy. That isn't me.

∾

"ANOTHER ONE!" I SHOUT AT A DECIBEL THAT WOULD BE impolite if it weren't for the bass thumping from the corner of the bar.

Gibbs laughs, pouring another shot of whiskey in a fresh glass.

"Milady." He sets it in front of me but loses his playfulness as something behind me catches his eye.

Curious, I turn around and scan the dance floor. My face sours.

Sonofabitch.

I grab my glass and shoot the liquor down my throat.

"Another," I repeat with less bravado than before. My words slur as I hunch on my barstool.

Gibbs cringes. "Give it a sec."

"Come on…" I pout. "Like you said, I've had a long day. Help a Reese's Pieces out, would ya?"

Tilting his head, he reaches for another glass but fills this one with water before setting it in front of me. "I'll make you a deal. Drink this whole thing. Then I'll give you another shot. Okay?"

"You and Milo," I grumble as I toy with the glass. "So bossy."

"You have no idea." He lifts his chin at the water. "Now, drink up. I gotta make sure you're staying hydrated, or else your hangover tomorrow is gonna be a bitch."

"My hangover is gonna be a bitch regardless of my hydration level," I argue, but I gulp down the entire glass anyway. Satisfied, he pours me another small tumbler of whiskey then disappears to help a customer. Leaving me alone. With my whiskey. And my stupid jealousy that flares the moment my curiosity gets the best of me. My attention wanders back to the dance floor, but River isn't there anymore. As my body starts to swell with panic at his absence, I sit a little taller and search for the big-headed model who enjoys driving me crazy.

Tucked away in one of the back booths, I find him. The stupid, charismatic, egotistical, yet somehow charming roommate who hit my ex in the jaw. The same roommate that made me tea and let me borrow his shirt. The same roommate who's managed to sneak under my skin without any regard as to what that means to a girl like me.

And yet, he managed to do it so effortlessly.

How the hell did he pull that off?

And why am I letting him?

But he isn't alone.

Of course, he isn't.

My gut tightens as I take him in. With his elbows resting on the small table between him and his date, he leans closer to her. Holding her gaze. His expression painted with interest.

I feel like I'm intruding. Like I should look away and give the bastard some privacy while he casts his spell on his unsuspecting date the same way he cast it on me. But I can't. Because he *has* cast that spell on me. And I can't do anything about it.

I wipe my sweaty palms on my thighs and hold my breath. That same cocky smile makes itself known from across the room as he hands her his phone. His date takes it before examining whatever is shining on the screen, her grin widening with intrigue.

My nose wrinkles in distaste.

It's probably a dick pic or something.

Hey, wanna see how big my other head is?

Gross.

"You doin' okay?" Gibbs asks, making me jump in surprise.

I gulp. "Oh. Uh. Yup."

"You sure about that?" he presses with a concerned wrinkle in his brow.

I peek back at the booth before groaning and giving them my back. "Does River always have a date?"

Drying a glass with a white towel, Gibbs answers, "Pretty much."

"That's a different girl than the one he had moaning last night," I point out like that's a rebuttal worth mentioning.

"So?"

Annoyed, I huff out, "What do you mean, *so?*"

"He's a slut, Reese."

It's the way he says it that pisses me off. Like it's obvious. And the really annoying part is that he's right. River's man-whoring ways are *definitely* obvious. Hell, I could probably look the definition up in a dictionary, and his cocky face would stare right back at me. But I'm too dense to acknowledge it or any of the glaring signs of his other womanizing ways whenever he looks at me.

My heart twinges in pain.

I really am desperate. And hurting. And lonely. And every other emotion in the book. I really shouldn't be out tonight, yet here I am. With front row seats to my crush who's about to get laid.

My face scrunches with determination as I shake my head and attempt to focus on the conversation instead of the asshole across the bar. "Jake said the same thing about Milo, and I've seen you flirting it up with a bunch of the girls at the bar tonight. Are any of you *not* manwhores?"

He laughs. "Pretty sure it was part of the roommate agreement. Must be a manwhore to apply," he adds in a deep, authoritative voice.

A Cheshire grin spreads across my face. "Oh, really? Does that mean I need to pop my whore cherry and sleep with a stranger tonight?" I bounce my eyebrows up and down mischievously, even though I'm sure I look like a lunatic. There's just too much booze thrumming through my veins for me to care.

Gibson starts pouring a concoction of beverages into the clean glass for someone else, multitasking like a champ as he argues, "I think there's a clause in the agreement somewhere that lets you off the hook."

Pouting, I cross my arms. "That's not fair. What about equal rights and all that jazz?"

"I'll have to check the rulebook, but I think Milo would kill me if I let you go home with a stranger."

"Yet there's River, prepping the girl to spread her legs in ten minutes or less," I mutter under my breath.

Following my gaze, Gibson sighs. "River's a good guy, but he has the attention span of a toddler. He treats every shiny new toy like it's the greatest thing ever invented, then plays with it for a few minutes before getting bored and moving on to the next one. Trust me, Reese's Pieces. You don't want to get mixed up with that. You deserve better."

"Like you?"

He laughs. "Hell, no. I'm even worse than River. Besides, your brother and I go way back, and I promised him that I wouldn't cross that line with you even if it's tempting. I'm not going to mess with our friendship again because of a girl."

"Again?" I ask, tilting my head to the side. My intrigue seems to drown out my jealousy, and I'm grateful for the respite.

He doesn't clarify but starts shaking a martini, so I press, "What's your story, Gibbs?"

"Not sure it's tailored for Milo's little sister."

"Come on, Gibbs. I'd like to think I'm more than Milo's little sister. Maybe you could look at me like your friend once in a while too. Ever consider that one, buddy?"

Glancing over at me, he exhales.

"Go on," I press. I'll take anything that doesn't involve stupid River and his stupid spells.

"Well, Milo and I..." Gibbs hesitates before setting the shaker aside and squeezing the back of his neck.

"You...what?"

I swear I'm not usually this nosy, I want to add, but I bite my tongue because he looks close to breaking, and I'm dying to hear this story.

Carefully, he holds my gaze but stays silent. I can almost hear him weighing his options to see how he can get out of this, but I've got to know.

"Tell me," I laugh. He's kind of cute when he's nervous. "I can handle it."

With a shrug, he gives in. "We... We have the same taste." Then the shaker is back in his hand as he mixes up another drink, and I'm left wanting. Hard.

"And?" I prod.

"And we used to..." He rims a martini glass with lime, then shifts his gaze to mine. "Share."

Jerking back, I freeze, afraid he's a skittish squirrel, and I'll scare him if I overwhelm him with too many questions.

"Oh?" I offer, because really? What the hell am I supposed to say to that?

He chuckles before giving the briefest explanation I've

ever heard. "He fell for the girl, but I thought we were all just having fun. Things got messy. She disappeared. And we agreed to never let a girl affect our relationship again, which is why you and I will always be just friends."

Friends.

I smile. "I'm good with that."

"Me too. Now, I gotta go deliver these, so I'll leave you to continue drooling over a guy that doesn't deserve it."

"Wait!" I call as he turns to deliver the drinks.

"I want one more shot."

Shaking his head, he sets the beverages down and fills an empty shot glass with more whiskey before putting it in front of me. "You're going to be puking tomorrow."

My face scrunches as I let the amber liquid slide down my throat. After swallowing, I retort, "If I have to watch Manwhore get it on in the middle of my bar, it'll be worth it."

"*Your* bar?" He laughs.

"Damn straight. Now, get to work, Gibbs. Stop slacking."

Shaking his head with a smile etched onto his face, he picks up the freshly made drinks and disappears to deliver them as I swivel around on my barstool to assess my nemesis. And just like that, my earlier amusement from only seconds ago disappears.

She's pretty. Soft blonde hair. A little older than I'd expect someone like River to be dating, but hey, who am I to judge? She's dressed in tight, black leather pants and a black crop top that makes her look like she could star in that old movie, *Grease.*

Throwing her head back, she laughs at something River says before she keeps scrolling her long, blood-red nails through the pictures on his phone.

Gag.

How many dick pics can you take, River? You disgust me.

"Hey, there," a deep voice surprises me from my right.

Jumping as if I've been caught doing something I shouldn't––which is quite accurate because River does not deserve an ounce of my time––I swivel in the owner's direction, causing the room to spin. Clutching the counter, I find my balance and inspect the guy beside me. The voice's owner is sporting a soft white Nirvana T-shirt and a pair of dark jeans and has long, curly hair that looks like it belongs to the guy from *Outlander*. Vision blurry, I squint back at him before registering that he's the singer from the band.

Whoa. When did they stop playing?

I turn to the vacant stage, then cock my head and listen carefully. Oh. Wait. Music's still playing. It just isn't the band anymore. It's one of this year's big hits that Ian loves. I groan before remembering that I haven't acknowledged the guy beside me yet.

Whoops. There go my manners.

"Are you…?" my voice trails off because I have no idea who he is. "The band guy?" I offer with a wrinkled forehead.

He laughs. "Fender. Nice to meet you."

"Mm-hmm… Hi."

"And you are?" he prods, clearly amused if the soft dimple etched into his cheek is anything to go by. Hesitating, I inspect it closer before noticing the deep cleft in his chin.

Why does that look so familiar?

He clears his throat before his amusement spreads into a wide, shameless grin.

My attention slides up to his navy blue eyes. "Oh. I'm Reese. Hi."

"Aw, so you're Reese. Nice to meet you."

"Mm-hmm," I repeat, my head swiveling back to River as if it has a mind of its own.

"Want to dance?" Band Guy asks.

My brows furrow before turning back to the hottie band guy. "Pardon?"

"Dance. You. Me. Want to?" Sliding off the barstool next to me, he raises his hand and waits for me to take it. And because I'm a glutton for punishment, I do.

My legs feel like noodles as––*what was his name again?*–– walks me toward the dance floor.

The buzz from the whiskey turns my muscles into liquid as I sway my hips with the beat of the song and close my eyes to get lost in it. But it does nothing to erase the image of River laughing with his date. His gorgeous date, who probably thinks he really likes her when he's only looking to get laid. Or at least, I *think* that's all he wants. But what if he actually does like her? What if he's looking for more than an easy lay? What if she's the girl to finally change his man-whoring ways?

Whoa there, Reese. Now you're just being ridiculous, a voice whispers in my head. A leopard doesn't change his spots, remember? Or is it a tiger who doesn't change his stripes? What's the saying again? And haven't I already played this game? I tried to change Ian. I believed he could be someone other than an absolute asshole. And I got burned because of it. *Bad.*

I shake my head, losing the beat for a split second until a set of hands rests against my hips. Band Guy finds his own rhythm behind me, guiding me while giving me the freedom to stay lost in the music. And I kind of love the freedom. Raising my hands into the air, I let go of everything and just *feel* without dissecting the why behind those emotions.

For the first time in a long time, I accept the elusive freedom that always seems to slip through my fingers, grabbing hold of it while ignoring my spidey sense that says someone's watching me. Squeezing my lids closed even tighter, I spin in Band Guy's arms, then wrap my hands around his neck and smile. He smells good. Different. A little woodsy with a hint of citrus. But good. Leaning a little closer, I take a big whiff, then turn away and shimmy out of his grip and straight into a hard chest.

Ouch.

My eyes pop open, and I raise my hands in defense, my heart pounding a million beats a minute as I look up at the angriest set of green eyes I've ever seen. Unable to help myself, I peek around him to the table he had been sitting at, but it's empty.

"She left," River growls before sending a glare over the top of my head to my dance partner. "Hey, Fen."

It doesn't sound like much of a greeting to me, but what do I know?

"Hey," Fender returns.

"Shouldn't you be on the stage right about now?"

"We took a break," he offers.

"Looks like it's over."

Fender stays silent, analyzing the situation for...*something.* Although, if he can figure out why River's over here instead of naked in the bathroom with his date, I'd love for him to fill me in.

"Never took you for the possessive type," Fender announces casually after coming to some kind of conclusion.

"She just got out of a bad relationship. She doesn't need to start another one," River grits out.

"Or maybe she doesn't need a relationship at all right now. Maybe she just needs to get laid."

Blinking rapidly, I try to register what he just said, convincing myself that I've heard him wrong, and the alcohol is making me hear things. Honestly, with how much is thrumming through my veins right now, it's definitely possible.

River turns back to me. "Is that what it is, Reese? You just wanna get laid?"

"H-he asked me to dance," I stammer.

"Hear that, Fen? She signed up for a dance, not dry humping."

I snort, and River glares down at me.

"Sorry," I quip, "But I'd hardly call what we were doing dry humping. Fen"--*I'm so glad River reminded me of his name*--"has been a complete gentleman, thank you very much."

The bastard's jaw tightens, but he doesn't move a muscle. He looks like he belongs at the Met. Every muscle in his body is so tense with frustration that he could be a freaking statue.

"I'm sure he has," he mutters after a beat of silence. "But he needs to get back to work now. I'll drive you home."

"Maybe I'm not ready to go home," I argue. "Maybe Fender's right. Maybe I do wanna get laid. Maybe I wanna pop my whore cherry--"

"I'm sorry, what the hell did you just say?" River bursts out. I can practically see the steam coming from his ears.

My hand slaps over my mouth as my eyes dart over to Gibbs. He's too busy with a group of girls celebrating to help dig me out of the hole I just made for myself.

"We're going," River announces, grabbing my forearm with a gentle but firm grip. I shake out of it.

"Nope. I'm good here."

"Bullshit. Your *whore cherry?*" he spits. "Not a chance in hell am I letting you out of my sight."

"Then I guess you can watch me and Fender dry hump some more," I return with a cocky smirk.

Turning around, I find Fender with his hands raised in surrender. "Sorry, Reese. But this is a whole new side of River, which makes him unpredictable as hell. I'm not gonna step into"--he waves his hands between us--"that. However, when River gets bored, you should come find me." Raising his chin to River, he adds, "Good luck, man. She seems feisty." Then he heads back to the stage. Leaving me

alone. With a manwhore who, for some reason I can't iden-
tify, has cockblocked me.

Asshole.

"You're annoying," I declare with a scowl.

His mouth twitches. "Ditto. Let's go home."

The warmth of his hand seeps through my shirt as he
places it against my lower back, but I don't move an inch. "I
need to tell Gibbs where I'm going. He was going to drive me
home at the end of his shift."

With a jerky nod, a frustrated River rocks back on his
heels. "I'll be at the front door."

Fender's gritty voice flows through the speakers as he
announces the next set of songs they'll be playing while I
walk a not-so-straight line back to the bar and flag Gibson
down.

"Hey, bartender! I need to talk to you!"

Raising his finger for me to give him a second, he finishes
chatting with a big guy in a dark suit then answers me. "I'm
not giving you any more whiskey."

"You're no fun," I pout.

"Someone's gotta take care of you."

"Pretty sure that job has already been filled for the night
by your party pooper roommate."

"*Our* party pooper roommate," he corrects me. "I didn't
see Jake walk in, though."

Confused, I replay our conversation before snorting. "No,
not *that* party pooper roommate. The other one." I hook my
thumb over my shoulder toward the front door where River
promised he'd be waiting for me.

Eyes bulging, Gibson's spine straightens before he turns
back to me and drops his voice low. "Shit."

"What's wrong?"

"Looks like you're the shiny new toy despite Milo's
warning."

"What warning?" I slur.

"Nothing." He curses under his breath before sighing. "Be careful, Reese. Like I said, River's a good guy. I just don't want you to get hurt."

"I'll be fine, Gibbs. He's just giving me a ride."

"That's what I'm afraid of," he mutters.

"Huh?"

"That he'll give you a...*ride*," he emphasizes the word, "but that's it."

My mouth quirks up, showcasing my dimple at the fun little pun before I sober at Gibson's concern. "I meant in the car. But I'll be fine, Gibbs. I'll see you at home?"

"Be careful, yeah?"

"Mm-hmm," I hum, ignoring the way he's kinda, sorta, spinning. "I'll be careful."

He sets a bottle of water in front of me. "And take this with you."

"Yes, sir." I salute him before grabbing the water and walking back to River at the front door.

"You ready?" he asks gruffly.

"Yup."

"Good." He opens the door, but my foot snags on the lip of the threshold as I attempt to step over it. Preparing myself for a nasty fall, my arms straighten in front of me before a hand wraps around my waist and catches me.

"Come on, Reese," River mutters under his breath. But he keeps his arm wrapped around me as he guides me.

Giving in, I rest my head against his shoulder and close my eyes, soaking up the stolen moment that I know is a mistake. I just don't care. I can hide behind the excuse that it's okay to do this because I'm inebriated and don't know what I'm doing. I can hide behind the lie that I'd be leaning against anyone right now, ignoring the truth that I kind of like when I'm with him. Even though he annoys me like no one else on the planet. Even though my brother told me he's off-limits. And even though I just got out of a shitty relationship that basically put my life on hold.

River's crawled under my skin in such a short amount of time that it scares me, and the only thing that seems to soothe the ache is *him*. His touch. His annoyed sighs. His snarky remarks.

All of it.

Maybe Jake's right. Maybe I don't know how to stand on my own. Maybe I really do search for my self-worth in guys and the attention they're willing to toss my way. Maybe Ian is right too. Maybe he's the only guy who could ever want me like that. Maybe I'm imagining the chemistry between River and me.

And maybe I'm too drunk to be thinking at all right now.

I don't know how long I'm lost in my thoughts, but I do know that River hasn't pushed me away.

Yet.

13

REESE

"You still awake, Floozy?" River asks, his warm breath tickling the top of my head.

I laugh dryly and lift my head. It feels like it weighs a thousand pounds. We're standing next to his truck, and I have no idea when we stopped moving or how long I've been leaning on him, but he certainly gets points for his patience.

"I'm awake. Sorry."

"Don't apologize." Cautiously, he scans my face before brushing my mussed-up hair behind my ear. "I'm sorry I was an ass inside. Let's get you home."

With his help, I climb into his lifted truck, then rest my head against the leather headrest and close my eyes as River rounds the front of his vehicle and gets behind the wheel.

"I'm sorry I made you leave your date," I whisper.

He turns on the ignition, and the rumble from the engine is all I get in reply.

Defeated, I squeeze my eyes shut and release a shaky breath.

I don't feel so good.

"It wasn't a date," he mutters, pulling onto the road.

I glance over at him, but he doesn't meet my gaze.

"You said it was a date."

"Well, I lied."

"Oh."

More silence.

Then I add, "It looked like a date."

"She's not my type," he divulges under his breath.

"I heard you weren't too picky."

He breathes out a deep laugh. "Where'd you hear that from?"

Shrugging, I dodge his question and follow it up with one of my own. "If it wasn't a date, then what was it?"

He cracks his neck from left to right before rolling his shoulders.

"You don't have to tell me," I clarify, though I'm dying to know.

Glancing my way, his forearms tighten as he squeezes the steering wheel. If there were such a thing as arm porn, he'd be able to make bank. Actually, he'd probably be able to make bank at real porn, too, but...

"She's my agent," he answers me tightly.

"Oh?"

"Yeah. I know. You don't usually meet agents at a bar unless it's for porn or something."

Dude. Can he read minds?

"But," he continues, "an opportunity popped up, and we wanted to go over the game plan."

"What kind of opportunity?"

"She was able to get me in for a photoshoot with a pretty big-named photographer who happens to know a guy that's looking for a fresh face for one of the last movies that he plans on directing."

Wait. A movie? Like a legit one?

I shake my head in an attempt to focus before acknowl-edging that Gibson was right. I'm going to be so sick tomor-row--scratch that. I might be sick in five minutes.

"T-that's...big, right?" I stutter. "I mean, I know I'm drunk, but that sounds like a pretty huge deal. Is that a huge deal?"

That same deep laugh puts my mind at ease as he glances at me with a wry grin. "Yeah, Reese. It's a pretty big deal, but I didn't want to jinx it or anything by telling the guys yet."

"So, how did it go? The whole game plan," I clarify.

"It went very well. She thinks I have a shot at the part as long as the photoshoot goes well with the photographer. He's known for hooking up his models by helping them shoot a quick audi-tion tape to send to his friends in the film industry if he thinks they have potential. It's...complicated and pretty unheard of, but he's done it at least a dozen times. And, if the photoshoot goes well, and I can bring the heat"--he winks--"then he'll pitch me to the director for one of the leading roles."

Bring the heat? Yeah. Call it a hunch, but I don't think that's going to be an issue.

"That's amazing, River. Want to know a secret?"

He glances over at me. "What's that?"

"When I was a little girl, I wanted to be an actress." I laugh. "The movie stars all looked so happy, ya know? And I loved pretending to be anyone who wasn't me. Someone who didn't have alcoholic parents. Someone who people wanted to be around. Someone who could be whoever they wanted without anyone else to tell them they couldn't. But that's a pipe dream, ya know? And yet...here you are. You're actually pulling it off. I'm seriously proud of you, Riv."

His smile is shy and totally adorable as he meets my gaze. "Don't be too proud yet. And don't tell anyone, okay? I need to make sure my mom keeps her nose out of it, or else I'll walk away from the project. I swear she has eyes and ears everywhere, so keeping this on the down-low is going to be impossible."

"Your mom?" I ask.

There's something about the way he mentions her, with a hint of disgust and animosity that would break a woman's heart.

"Yeah." His jaw tightens, but he doesn't give me any other explanation.

"Who's your mom?" I press. I blame the liquid courage but don't back down.

Clearing his throat, he pulls into the driveway and turns off the car, but he doesn't open his door, which gives me hope that he won't end the conversation when I'm dying for a few more details.

Still, my stupid mouth feels the need to backpedal. "You don't have to tell me--"

"Monet Cavier. That's my mom."

Jerking back, I hit my head on the passenger window and rub the sore spot with my fingers. "Ouch," I mumble before adding, "Like...*the* Monet Cavier?"

He nods. "That's the one."

"Like...*award-winning* Monet Cavier?" I press.

"Yeah."

"Holy shit, River. That's insane!"

His giant hand rubs his tired face roughly. "It's not that big of a deal."

"Uh, I mean... It's *kind of* a big deal."

He rolls his eyes, though there's a genuine smile threatening to break through his annoyance, so I'm going to say that's progress.

"Can I ask you something, Riv?"

"What's that?"

"Actually," I correct myself. "Can I ask you two somethings?"

He chuckles. "Go ahead. Apparently, when I'm around you, I'm an open book."

"One." I raise my index finger. "Why do I get the feeling you hate your mom? And two..."--I lift my middle finger to join my other one in the air--"Why do you live with three other guys when your family's loaded? Oh! I take it back. I have three questions. Question number three. What's your last name? 'Cause I could've sworn it isn't Cavier."

"One. My childhood was hell whenever my self-centered mother was in town. She didn't even want me around growing up. In fact, she didn't want me, *period*. As soon as she found out she was pregnant, she wanted an abortion, but my dad convinced her to keep me around. Not sure how he pulled that one off, but...yeah. I guess he had a convincing argument to justify a few stretch marks that she could pay to have fixed once I was born."

Ouch. If I thought I sensed a bit of animosity before, now, I'm drowning it.

"Are they still together?" I ask.

"My parents?"

"Yeah."

He scoffs. "They were never together. They hooked up for like three months when my mom was in a rebellious stage even though my dad was in love with her. Anyway, since I was such a...," he pauses to search for the right word before giving me a wry grin, "*pretty* kid, she started to show interest when I was three or so and would make me prance around like a prized pony at all the celebrity parties. My dad couldn't handle seeing me used as a pawn, so he got a lawyer and took full custody."

"And she lost?"

"She didn't have a leg to stand on. She was always knee-deep in drugs and orgies." That same venomous tone snakes itself through every word. "She let me go before my fourth birthday and only checks on me when it's convenient for her or when she's searching for a new publicity stunt and is hoping I'll step into the limelight to help make her relevant again."

"That must be hard. To feel used like that."

"The lady's a washed-up actor who can't accept it," he admits. "She tries to throw money at me every once in a while in hopes of getting me on her side, but I refuse to take it. Well, except for this house anyway."

Digging my teeth into my lower lip, I ask, "What got you into modeling then? Sounds like you would want to stay away from all of that."

"I dunno. Maybe I got my work ethic from her," he quips, his voice dripping with sarcasm. "But modeling is easy, and it pays well. Besides, might as well milk my good looks for as long as I can, right? Once they're gone...that's it. I'm not going to chase the newest aging serum or spend my days cheating wrinkles with Botox and shit like my mom does."

"And what about acting?" I press. "Do you honestly think you can hide your identity from all the paparazzi and stuff?"

He shrugs. "In the long run? Probably not, but I want to make it on my *own* in this industry if I make it at all. I don't want to piggyback off her success, especially when I'm pretty sure she slept her way to the top. I've been able to keep my identity hidden for this long in the industry, which means that if I get this part, it's because of me and my hard work. My natural talent. My good looks. Although, I guess I can't take full credit for that last one," he clarifies with a smirk. "Good genes and all that shit. Still. It's my sweat in the gym every morning. It's my self-discipline at the restaurants that keep me in shape. *Me.* It has nothing to do with my mom or how many awards she's earned or what kind of strings she could pull."

The passion in his voice is hypnotic, almost lulling me to sleep if I weren't so invested in his words.

"I get it. I would want to look back at my success, whatever success that might be, and claim it as my own too," I admit. "I wouldn't ever want to question if the only reason I found success is because someone handed it to me."

"Then, I guess I shouldn't suggest hooking you up with my agent, huh?"

I laugh. "And why would you do that?"

"You mentioned that you wanted to be an actress, remember?"

"Not for real, though," I hedge. "I mean, come on, right? I'm a nobody, trailer trash, tossed aside girl with no degree. No talents. And no future. I'm not exactly someone you'd want to place your bet on, ya know?"

His eyes widen in surprise. "Whoa there. This conversation just took a dark turn."

The glass from the passenger window is cool as I rest my head against it in defeat. "Sorry."

"Don't apologize. But I do feel the need to correct you on a few things. First, I'd bet my entire life savings on you if it would prove to you that you're amazing. You're not a nobody. You're Reese Anders. Gorgeous. Smart. Sassy. The whole nine yards, babe. And trailer trash? Everyone has their pasts. Do you think I enjoy telling people that my mom tried to get me to snort coke at an afterparty as some kind of messed up party trick before a real adult intervened and called my dad?"

I gasp.

He shakes his head and squeezes my knee. "We all have our shit, Reese. But it's our choice whether or not we let it hold us back. And don't get me started on the fact that your asshole ex didn't see what he had in front of him. Any guy would be lucky to have you. And trust me...I'm not just saying that." He leans closer, making sure he has my full attention and reiterates, "I'm *not*. But that's not the point. My point is that if you want to be an actress, be an actress. If you want to be a clown and join the circus, then be a freaking clown. I guarantee that Milo, Jake, Sonny, and I will buy front row tickets to cheer you on. Just...be you. And own that shit."

Digging my teeth into my bottom lip, I stare blankly at my hands, unsure what to say.

"So, tell me," River prods. "If you don't want to be an actress, then what *is* your dream? Jake mentioned you want to be an accountant?"

"Just because I'm good with numbers doesn't mean I like them," I clarify. "And I definitely don't want to drown myself in debt by going to college for something I hate."

"Then what do you like? What do you want?"

Wringing my hands in my lap, I peek over at him. "Honestly?"

"Yeah."

"I don't think I know what I want. And it's terrifying. In high school, I was so desperate to get away from my parents that I grabbed on to the first guy who gave me attention after I graduated."

"Ian?"

"Yeah. And then, I guess I was so used to being treated like crap that I didn't even care about how he treated me as long as he said he still wanted me. Even when they were just words and his actions proved the opposite," I ramble. "I bent over backward for him. I built my life around him. And now that it's all fallen apart, I'm expected to pick up the pieces. Alone. But I couldn't even do that. I had to run to my big brother to save me. I don't know how to stand on my own. I don't know how to stand up for myself. I feel like I don't know how to do *anything*."

River's warm hand tightens his hold on my knee, grounding me in the moment when I'm so close to getting lost in my guilt and regret.

"Tell me something, Reese. If Milo was ever in trouble, would you stand up for him and give him everything you have if it would help his situation?"

"Of course, I would––"

"And would you look at him as weak for asking for your help?"

"I know where you're going with this––"

"Then you know that I'm right. Learning to accept help when you need it isn't a weakness. It's a strength. Give yourself a little more credit. The fact that you realized you deserve better in a relationship and in your own personal life, that you're willing to fight for those things...*that's* success."

I open my mouth to argue, but it snaps closed just as quickly. Maybe he's right. Maybe all those self-deprecating thoughts were planted by Ian, and I need to tell them to shut the heck up. Maybe I need to recognize my own strengths instead of focusing on my weaknesses even when I feel like I'm drowning from them.

"Now, where was I?" he quips, letting go of my knee. "Oh. Right. As for question number three, I took my dad's last name as soon as I turned eighteen and could legally change it without my mom's signature on the certificate. I doubt it'll be enough to hide my true identity from the paparazzi, but it's worth a shot, right? And question number two was...?"

"Why do you have three roommates?" I ask, grateful he changed the subject. "You said you've never taken anything from your mom except the house, which means you probably don't need to live with anyone to help cover rent, right?"

"I did take the house." His attention shifts to the two-story home in front of us as his fingers wrap back around the steering wheel, making his bruised knuckles turn white from the pressure of his tight grip. "She gave it to me for my eighteenth birthday. I guess that I kind of figured she owed me, so I accepted it. I knew it wouldn't even put a dent in her bank account, but I still wanted to see her pay for being a shitty mom."

With all his defensive layers pulled back, I'm finally given a glimpse of the real River. And it's one of the most captivating sights I've ever seen. Like a powerful ocean with high and low tides. Easy waves but also raging storms. Sure, he might go with the flow most of the time, but there's an underlying current beneath his easygoing demeanor. One that I could get swept away in if I'm not careful.

"I'm sorry, River," I whisper. There's an electric current that pulses between us as I reach closer and rest my hand against his forearm that's still braced against the steering wheel like he's preparing for impact.

As if in slow motion, River's intense gaze slides from my hand clutching his arm to my eyes, but I don't let him go.

"I know it's not the same––and that we've kinda, sorta already covered this topic––but I can relate to the whole shitty parents thing. I get it. But I want you to know you've turned out to be a pretty great guy in spite of a crappy mom."

"I had my dad to rely on."

"And I had an older brother who looked out for me," I reply with a smile. "Without him, I probably would've ended up on a milk carton. Milo took care of me and made sure I was okay."

Eyes shining with mirth, he teases, "Yeah, I may have seen his papa bear attributes once or twice in regards to you."

I cringe. "I kind of figured. I'm pretty sure everyone has seen those papa bear attributes a time or two."

"Does it bother you? Having him breathing down your neck for everything?"

I shake my head. "Not really. I've never had great luck at making my own decisions, as we've also previously discussed." I laugh. "But I can usually trust Milo's gut about things."

"Usually?" he prods.

I'm not sure when I scooted toward the center console or how I ended up practically laying on it to get nearer to River, but I catch myself inching closer like an addict looking for her next fix.

I lick my lips and open my mouth to reply when the rumble of an engine cuts me off. Turning toward the sound, my brother's bike pulls up the driveway before he kicks down the stand and swings his leg over the seat.

Speak of the devil.

As if he has some crazy sixth sense, he approaches the truck instead of heading inside after a long night at work. When he sees me up front, Milo opens the passenger door and helps me out of it without asking.

As soon as my feet hit the ground, he shoves me behind him and turns to River. "How'd your date go?"

It's a pointed question like he's poking holes in River's response before he's even uttered it.

"Fine," River answers carefully.

"Funny. If it went well, I would've thought she'd be in your front seat instead of my baby sister, who"--his nose wrinkles--"reeks of alcohol, by the way. You get her drunk?"

"Milo--" I start, but he holds up his hand to silence me.

Raising his chin in my direction, a prickly River reveals, "She got herself drunk and needed a ride home. Sonny doesn't get off work for another three hours. I was doing her a favor." The driver's side door groans in protest as River opens it with a little more force than necessary. "I was doing you *both* a favor. You're welcome."

Then he slams it closed and strides to the front door, leaving Milo and me in his dust.

Ignoring him, Milo turns around to face me, then demands, "He touch you?"

"What? No--"

"You sure about that?" There's a tick in his jaw as he stares down at me, waiting for me to break under his scrutiny. But it's not the first time I've had to go head-to-head with him, and it won't be the last.

Even though the street is spinning, I cross my arms and spit, "Why the hell would River touch me?"

"Because he's an asshole who doesn't follow rules. I see the way he looks at you, Reese--"

"And how does he look at me, Milo? Huh?"

"Like he wants to fuck you."

I flinch back, sobering at the sharpness in his voice. "Excuse me?"

"You heard me. I have rules, Reese. And I'm gonna need you to follow them, especially when I can't trust River to listen to a damn word I say."

"Milo," I sigh. "You know I love the crap out of you, but--"

"Promise me, Reese. Right now, or I'll take you to a hotel and pay the bill until you can find a different place to stay."

"Milo--"

"Promise me," he repeats. "I have my rules for a reason. I need to protect you from getting hurt again."

Squeezing my eyes shut, I let the memories from our childhood wash over me. The screaming. The broken dishes. The smell of vomit on the kitchen floor. The sound of Milo's whimpers when our dad would hit him before Milo was strong enough to stand up to our asshole father. The nights when Milo would order me to run to my room and lock the door. When he would make me promise to keep it closed until the next morning. I remember all of it.

"I know, Milo. I know. You've *always* had rules. And have I ever broken any of them?"

"Just once," he answers coolly. "And we both know how that turned out."

Ian.

He told me Ian was bad news. He told me not to date him. He told me to stay away. But I didn't listen.

And he's right. We both know how that turned out.

Swallowing thickly, I nod my head up and down before he tosses his arm around my shoulders and guides me inside.

"Let's get some more water in you, then get you to bed, sis. Come on."

"Okay."

14

REESE

M y stomach rumbles its protest as I roll onto my side and shove a pillow over my head.

Who the hell would play music right now?

It feels like it's five in the morning. With a groan, I blindly search for my cell phone on the nightstand beside me before prying one eyelid open to peek at the time.

It's almost noon. Sticking out my lower lip, I wallow in self-pity for a solid three Mississippis, then pad down the hall and scowl at Gibson's cracked door. The noisy musician stumbles on a chord but doesn't see me as he curses under his breath and tweaks the progression another time.

Kar-ma, I sing to myself before continuing toward the kitchen in search of something greasy to settle my stomach.

The eggs are cracked, and the bacon is sizzling in no time. Then the quest to find painkillers begins when a deep, familiar voice catches my attention.

Turning down the heat on the stove, I try to look busy by turning my over-easy eggs into scrambled with the spatula while shamelessly eavesdropping on the tail end of River's phone conversation as he paces near the entryway.

"You spoke with him? Brett Carter? What did he say?"

A pause.

"Seriously?"

Pause.

"That's awesome. Thanks again for showing him my portfolio."

Pause.

"So, I'm officially on his books? Do you know who he wants me to do the shoot with?"

Man, I'd give anything to hear the other end of this conversation.

"Seriously? Olivia Porter?" River asks in disbelief.

My stomach drops. Olivia Porter is freaking gorgeous. She models for almost every major designer in the industry and has been crowned the sexiest woman alive by multiple magazines.

"You've already set it up? It's official?" River prods.

Pause.

"Yeah. Of course. I'll do whatever it takes. Let's just make sure to keep this quiet for now, okay? I don't want anything to get out before they officially make any announcements. And that's if they pick me at all."

I glance over my shoulder. River is still busy pacing in dark jeans and socks without a shirt on. *Shocker.* For some reason, the socks make me smile. He just looks so...casual without shoes on. Human, maybe? Instead of the put-together Adonis I've grown accustomed to having around. Yet somehow, he still manages to look damn near lickable.

Attractive bastard.

And he's going to be doing a photoshoot with freaking Olivia Porter?

Why, hello, insecurities. Nice to see you again.

The girl is so hot that even *I* have a crush on her, and I'm straight. There's not a chance in hell I could compete with a girl like that. Not that I'm trying to compete, but...

River's gaze catches mine, and he cocks his head to the side.

Dammit! I've been caught!

Turning back to my botched eggs, I frown. They're going to taste like rubber. I guess I deserve it for eavesdropping on a conversation that doesn't involve me. But it's River. He's always been good at piquing my curiosity. However, there's a saying that I'm pretty sure I should have tattooed across my forearm. Curiosity killed the cat. And I don't feel like being roadkill. The salvageable bacon is shoved into my mouth before I dump the eggs in the sink and start over.

"Yeah, Gina. See you then. And thanks again for this. I know you didn't have to--"

His voice trails off for a few seconds, then his footsteps fade away and are replaced by a pair of heavy black boots pounding against the staircase.

"Hey, whatcha makin'?" Gibson asks as he enters the kitchen.

My gaze narrows as I turn to the culprit. "You're in the doghouse this morning."

"I am?"

"Yup. You woke me up."

His concern transforms into relief as he strides closer and glances into the frying pan. "Eggs? For lunch?"

"Hey, it's only lunch if you've had breakfast already. This"--I point the spatula at the freshly cracked egg that's bubbling in the bacon grease--"is breakfast because *someone* woke me up this morning."

"You mean they woke you up this afternoon," he corrects me. "And I'm glad I was finally able to confirm you're still alive and didn't die from alcohol poisoning last night. Milo was pissed at me this morning when I saw him. Said I should've cut you off earlier."

"You know Milo, always looking out for his little sister," I quip while sprinkling a little salt and pepper on my freshly cracked egg.

"I can see that," he notes before grabbing my wrist and twisting me until we're face to face and he has my full attention. "I need to ask you something."

"What is it?"

"And I want you to tell me the truth," he adds.

"Okay, shoot."

"With your parents' history, are you okay voicing your own limits, or do I need to keep an eye on you at SeaBird?"

My parents' *history*. Yeah, I remember their history. Empty beer bottles scattered along the floor. Soiled carpet beneath my bare feet. The stench of vomit and piss permeating the air. Milo's bruised face when our dad was feeling particularly angry for no reason at all. It's funny how something like alcohol can be so addicting for one person yet doesn't affect someone else to the same degree.

Sobering slightly, I murmur, "I know my own limits. Thank you for asking, though."

He raises his chin in acknowledgment then lets me go. "Don't mention it. Speaking of SeaBird…"

"Yeah? What about it?" I ask, dishing up my breakfast onto a white ceramic plate.

"They're hiring."

My jaw hangs on its hinges, and the fork in my hand clatters on the plate. "I'm sorry…what was that?"

Don't get your hopes up, Reese. Don't you dare get your hopes up.

"SeaBird's hiring," Gibbs repeats. "Would you be interested? I know you were looking for a job––"

With my breakfast and headache forgotten, I jump into

Gibson's arms and give him the biggest bear hug I can muster.

"Yes! Yes! Yes!" I chant. "You are the best person ever, Gibbs! Seriously. You have no idea how much it would mean to me if I could find a freaking job."

A throat clears near the entryway and breaks up our little celebration. As soon as my bare feet touch the cool hard-wood floors, Gibson's grasp disappears. I tug my sleepshirt down and awkwardly wave my hand at the latest visitors for the day. Jake and Milo. They're each sporting a pair of basketball shorts and white T-shirts with their hair slightly mussed from their workout. And even with all their similari-ties, they still manage to be total opposites like the yin and yang of an unbreakable friendship.

And right now, they're looking at me like they just caught me with my pants down when I was simply chanting *yes* and hugging my roommate. Totally typical behavior for a Saturday afternoon.

"Oh. Hi," I greet them. My smile is tight, though I have no idea why.

"Don't mind us." Milo's tone is snarky as hell with a silent challenge on his tongue. "Please. Continue."

"I was just telling her about an opening at SeaBird," Gibson explains like he's used to Milo's tantrums. "Do you want a water?"

"I'll take one, Sonny," Jake pipes up before striding toward the kitchen island. Gibson opens the fridge and tosses him a reusable bottle filled with ice-cold water they keep stocked in the fridge. Untwisting the cap, Jake takes a swig then he asks me, "How are you feeling? I heard you had quite the evening last night."

"And which little bird told you that?"

His mouth quirks up, but he doesn't answer me.

"Ya know," I continue, "if I'd known I was moving in with

a bunch of mother hens, I might've reconsidered my options."

With a deep chuckle, Jake defends, "I'm just checking up on you. Did you find the Advil I set on the bathroom counter?"

Damn you, Jake. Making me feel guilty for your thoughtfulness.

And stupid. I should've gone to the bathroom first. That would've saved me a world of headache. Literally.

"I may have missed it," I admit with a grudging frown before plopping down onto one of the barstools tucked beneath the center island.

He laughs. "I'll go get it for you. Be right back."

"Thank you!" I call out to his retreating form. His back muscles and triceps flex and pull as he jogs away and disappears up the stairs.

Seriously, when did Jake get ripped?

"So tell us more about this job," Milo demands, distracting me from appreciating his best friend's backside.

Shrugging, Gibson plops down onto the barstool next to me. "It's pretty simple. She'll just be running drinks, cleaning up tables here and there, and possibly get behind the bar to learn a few simple cocktails on the nights when it's chaos, and I need the help. Would you be interested, Reese?"

My anticipation is buzzing, but I try to keep my excitement in check. "Why, yes. Yes, I would. It sounds different but...fun. Do you think you could set up an interview for me?"

"No need. There's two spots available, and Chuck trusts me, so when I mentioned your name, he asked if I would hire you, I said yes, then he told me to relay the news. You're good to go."

"You serious?" I hold my breath.

"Yeah, of course."

With a squeal, I wrap my arms around his neck and pull him into an awkward side hug thing since we're both still seated at the counter, but I don't really care if I'm making a fool out of myself because I have a freaking job!

Striding over to the fridge, Milo grabs a protein shake as he interjects, "When does she start?"

"Oh, so you're okay with this?" I challenge. "You know, since you like to pretend you have a say in what I do with my life and all."

Milo's mouth twitches, but he doesn't take the bait. "It's something different," he offers. "And you need *different*."

"Hmm," I hum, still unconvinced.

"So, when does she start?" Milo repeats.

"Tonight, if she's ready." Gibbs turns to me and raises his brows.

With a deep breath, I nod. "I'll be ready."

"And your hangover will be taken care of?" Milo pushes.

"Yup. I'll rest up and drink lots of water, Papa Bear. But thank you for your concern."

Grumbling *smartass* under his breath, he rounds the corner and drops a quick kiss to the crown of my head. "You're gonna rock it." Then he turns to Gibson. "Thanks, man. Keep an eye on her, yeah?"

"Sure thing. And don't worry. I remember the rules."

Nodding, Milo twists off the cap from his protein shake, downs the whole thing, then bellows, "Yo, Jake! Where's my sister's Advil? She's got shit to do!"

Ya know, the man's got a point.

"I should probably get going too," Gibson adds as he checks the time on his cell. "But be ready by five, and we can ride together, okay?"

"Sounds good."

As Gibson exits the kitchen, Jake returns and offers me a couple of painkillers. "Here ya go."

"Thanks."

Popping them into my mouth, I take a quick swallow of juice to wash them down, then sigh in relief. "You're the bomb dot com, my friend."

With a grin, he takes a seat next to me. "I got your back."

"Always have and always will. Right, Jakey boy?"

"Always," he returns. His grin softens as he takes me in. "So, how have you been acclimating so far?"

"To living here?" I shrug. "Good, I guess. Gibbs got me a job, so there's that."

"Yeah, he may have mentioned that earlier this morning to me before you graced us with your presence. I think you'll do great."

"You've always been my biggest cheerleader," I point out with a cheeky smile.

"And I always will be. I'm sorry I've been absent so much lately––"

"Don't apologize."

"I want to. You deserve more from me––"

"You owe me nothing," I argue.

"I know, but since you've been living here, we haven't really had a chance to hang out other than our *Lord of the Rings* marathon. We haven't even been texting. We used to always text, Reese." The regret laced with anxiety in his voice makes me pause as I consider him.

He's right. We used to always text. Especially before Ian and I started dating. It was almost daily that I'd wake up with a message from him. Sometimes it was a simple, *Hey, what are you up to?* And other times, it was nothing but a funny meme, but they made my day every time.

Then Ian started to give me crap for texting another guy, so the messages slowly started to dissipate until they were nothing but a once-a-week reminder that the world didn't revolve around Ian. That I had other people who cared about me too. And if I'm being honest with myself, they were what gave me the courage to finally walk away from my toxic relationship because I was reminded that I mattered. To Jake. And to Milo.

Sighing, I push the eggs around my plate. "I know. Ian has been texting me a lot, so I've kind of been ignoring my phone."

"Do you know how to block him?" Jake returns with a serious expression.

"I *have* blocked him, but he keeps finding new ways to contact me. Whether it's with one of his friend's phones or changing his own number, I don't know, but it's been...a little off-putting."

He scoffs. "I'd say so. How about I take you to the store to change your number so he can't contact you anymore?"

"I've had this number for forever. I don't want to give it up just because my ex won't leave me alone. Besides, I'm sure he'll get bored and move on sooner or later."

"Yeah, but if he's making you miserable––"

"He's not. I'm just learning not to be too attached to my phone, that's all. Honestly, it's probably a good thing, but I'm sorry if I've missed any of your texts."

"Don't worry about it. I should probably close the books every once in a while and come check on you physically instead of relying on text messages anyway. I've missed you, Reese. It's good to have you here, even if I've done a shitty job of showing it."

"I've missed you, too, Jake. But don't feel bad about focusing on your thesis right now. Seriously. I support you. You're gonna do great things. And don't worry. I know how to be a patient girl while waiting for a guy's affections," I quip, batting my lashes at him.

He laughs and steals a bite of my bacon. "Careful with those things, Reese. They're dangerous."

"What, these ol' things?" I bat them a second time, grinning from ear to ear.

"Yeah. Even without mascara and shit, they could still knock a guy on his ass."

"Says the guy who's been locked up in his room or stuck at the library twenty-four-seven. Maybe you just need to get out more if my raccoon eyes are threatening to knock you on your ass."

With another dark laugh, he reaches for my cup of juice and chugs half the damn thing before setting it next to my plate. "Trust me. I've tried that already. Didn't take."

"Liar." Shoving him in the shoulder, I roll my eyes then finish off my juice before he can steal the rest of it.

And even though most of our conversations are filled with meaningless banter, I've missed it. I've missed him. But I'm not going to be a distraction for the guy when he's meant for so much more.

Even if he's practically begging me to be.

Nope. He deserves more than that.

15

REESE

A few hours later, my blood is thrumming through my veins as Gibson pulls up to SeaBird and parks near the back entrance.

"You ready?" he asks. The car's engine stops rumbling as he takes out the key.

"I think so?" Fidgeting with my slicked-back high ponytail, I glance in the side mirror then brush back a few of my flyaways.

"You'll do great. And you look fine, by the way. Stop stressing. The people who work here are a good bunch. Well, other than TJ, but I doubt you'll have to worry about him. He's terrified of Milo, so you should be in the clear."

"Everyone's terrified of Milo," I point out with a laugh.

"And they have every reason to be. Now, let's get going, Reese's Pieces. You don't want to be late on your first day."

Wiping my sweaty palms along my black jeans, I open the passenger door, and we make our way inside.

The place is already crowded, and it's not even six o'clock yet. Gibson leads me down the dark hall and to the back room, weaving in between the people waiting in line for the bathrooms like a champ.

"Is it always this crazy?" I ask.

"You've seen the place."

"Well, yeah, but I've never been here before nine."

"The band usually plays their own stuff in their first set, and the second set is usually covers of other artists," he explains while pointing out the olive green lockers at the back of the small, square break room. "This one's yours, by the way."

"Thanks." Once my purse is safely tucked away, I turn back to him. "So what you're telling me is that the band is pretty good."

He laughs. "Meh. They're all right."

"Mm-hmm. And do people know you're the genius behind the music?"

Narrowing his eyes, he scans the empty break room. "Not exactly, and I'd prefer we keep it that way."

"Why?"

"Because I'm not one for the limelight."

"Is there a reason for that?" I prod.

Something else grabs his attention behind me, and he grins like the Cheshire cat. "Oh, look at that...a pretty new girl who's lost." He winks at me, then calls out, "Hey, can I help you?"

The blonde reminds me of a mouse as she skids to a halt in the doorway and smiles shyly back at us. "Um, hi. I'm looking for Ashton or..."––she checks her phone––"Gibbs? Gibson?"

"Are you the other new girl?" Gibbs questions, his earlier interest morphing into...annoyance?

Her brows pinch––probably because she can feel the same shift I can––before she nods. "Yes, that's me."

Striding toward her, he offers his hand. "I'm Gibbs."

She tucks a gossip magazine with Monet Cavier's face printed on the cover and the title *Washed Up and Wanting* beneath her arm, then takes his hand. "Hi. I'm Dove."

"Dove? Like the bird?"

Her cheeks heat. "Um, yes?"

"Huh." He cocks his head to the side and scans her up and down. "I'm sorry. Have we met before?"

As her gaze drops to the ground, she tucks her white-blonde hair behind her ear. "I don't think so. I've only been here once, and that was for my interview with Chuck, so…"

"Huh," he grunts again. "Interesting. You must just have one of those average faces."

She peeks up at him with crystal blue eyes that are unique, and gorgeous, and definitely *not* average.

"Uh…thank you?" she returns, clearly just as confused as I am.

Realizing the backhanded compliment he just dished out, Gibson clears his throat but doesn't correct himself. "Your locker's over here." He motions to the bottom locker next to mine.

Uh, why is Gibson being a jerk?

Hell, she caught Gibson's attention with a single glance, and the guy could have any girl he wants. She definitely pulls off the whole innocent girl next door vibe, though I doubt she knows it. Which makes me like her instantly.

"I'm Reese, by the way," I introduce myself to her in an attempt to salvage the uncomfortable situation as she carefully sets her things into the open locker.

Peeking up at me, that same white smile nearly splits her face in two.

"Dove. Hi," she returns with a small wave.

Damn, she's adorable.

Like a little puppy you want to pat on the head and take home with you. I've never really gotten along with girls. I've just never been one for drama, but I might be willing to make an exception for this one.

"Hi," I repeat. "So, Monet Cavier's washed up and wanting, huh?" I dip my chin toward her magazine.

"What? Oh. I have no idea." She grimaces, then explains, "It's my sister's magazine. She left it in my car, and I'm not a clutter person, so in the garbage, it shall go." She demonstrates by tossing the magazine in the garbage can next to the set of lockers.

"Wanna come clean my car out?" I quip. "'Cause, it could use a little extra love."

"I mean if you need help––"

"I'm kidding."

"Oh. Yeah. Of course. Sorry, I guess I'm just a little nervous."

"Same," I admit. "It's my first day too."

Her light blue eyes light up like a Christmas tree. "Oh, so you're the other new girl?"

"Yup. That's me. I've heard we'll be training together. Have you ever worked at a bar before?"

She shakes her head. "Nope. This is definitely a first for me."

"Me too. The closest experience I have is when I waitressed at a diner, and that was for like two weeks before a different job landed in my lap."

"All right, ladies," Gibson interrupts. "I gotta get to work. Follow me out to the bar, and I'll pass you off to Ashton, who will show you the ropes. But if you have any questions, come find me. I'll help you out."

"Okay," Dove murmurs, her pale complexion burning from Gibbs' offer.

I think someone has an admirer.

"Yo, Gibbs!" a voice yells as a familiar head pops through the doorway from the hall. He's one of the members from

Broken Vows, Fender's and Gibson's band. The drummer, I think? With long, curly red hair and a big, bushy beard, he reminds me of a Viking more than a rock star, but his eyes are kind, and his usual smile is contagious, yet somehow absent as his gaze finds Gibbs'.

"Yeah?" Gibbs answers.

"Fender didn't make it to practice earlier today. Thought you should know."

"Shit," he mutters under his breath. Then he checks his pockets and pulls out his cell.

"There a problem?" I ask.

"I gotta find Fen."

"Is something wrong?"

"Nothing out of the ordinary," he mutters, his eyes glued to his phone as his fingers type furiously. "He's either strung out, passed out, or needs me to bail him out of prison."

Ouch.

Dove and I exchange worried glances before I offer, "Anything we can do?"

"I got this. Tell Ashton I'll be back in a bit."

I nod. "Okay."

"Thanks." Then he turns to the drummer. "Hey, Phoenix, is Sammie here?"

"Yeah, she's setting up."

"Good. Tell her to cover for me, all right?"

"Yeah, man. I'll tell her."

"Thanks." Then Gibbs rushes out the door.

"Who's Sammie?" I ask, unable to help myself.

"The other bartender," Phoenix replies. "She's hit or miss because of school, but Chuck's her dad, so she makes her own hours."

"Cool."

"She's gonna love you two," he adds, his eyes rolling over each of us with an amused smirk etched into his cheeks.

A confused Dove turns to me as if I have all the answers.

I shrug at her then ask, "And why's that?"

"'Cause, she's sick of being the only hot girl who works here." His laugh is light and jovial as he hooks his thumb over his shoulder toward the main area of the bar. "Come on. I'll hand you off to Ashton."

shton is nice and knows Milo from the tattoo shop. Apparently, my brother is the only guy he trusts with a needle, and I don't blame him. Milo is freaking talented. I can still see him as a kid as we'd walk home from school, a notebook tucked beneath his arm since we didn't own backpacks. Usually, we'd just use a plastic sack from the grocery store, but Milo didn't want his art notebooks to warp, so he'd hold them instead. They were always brimming with beautiful drawings. Some of his works were colorful, others were etched with pencil, and they varied from a piece of fruit to the entire valley.

When he told me he wanted to become an apprentice at a tattoo shop, I wasn't surprised. He was made for it. And I'm glad that I'm not the only one who's noticed.

"All right, ladies. I want each of you to get comfortable on the floor and collect empty glasses, greet the customers, wipe down any tables, that kind of thing. If you have any questions, flag me down or ask Gibbs when he gets back from rounding up Fen. Oh, and if any customers give you trouble, let me know. Usually, they're pretty respectful, but sometimes they like to test the boundaries when we hire new girls. Any questions?"

Dove and I look at each other before shaking our heads.

"Nope. I think we're good," I reply.

"Good. I'll check on you in a few."

Then he's off, leaving us on our own, and I do my best to stay busy and not embarrass Gibson by completely failing on my first day.

The next few hours go by in a blur of, *Can I get you anything else,* and, *Would you like a refill,* until I catch a certain new girl staring at a certain bartender with big goo-goo eyes. He made it back about thirty minutes ago with a very tense half-brother in tow who's standing on the stage singing his lungs out.

My gaze follows Dove's. Gibson is currently starring in every woman's fantasy as he flips bottles and serves alcohol to the long line of customers with a seductive wink and a sexy smirk. And even though Dove isn't the only one drooling, I sneak up behind her, then slap my hand against the table at her side.

After jumping a mile into the air, she turns around with wide eyes and an apology on the tip of her tongue as though she just got caught with her hand in the proverbial cookie jar.

Then she sees the culprit and screeches, "Reese! You scared the crap out of me!"

"Sorry." *I'm not sorry.* "You just looked a little preoccupied, so, ya know, I figured I'd help a sister out and make you get back to work."

"You're right. I'm so sorry––"

"I'm totally kidding. And I think it's kind of cute."

"What's kind of cute?"

"That you kinda, sorta, *might* have a thing for Mr. Gibbs over there."

146

Her gaze darts toward said bartender before returning to me. "Um, no."

"You sure about that?"

"Yes."

"Positive?" I tease.

She folds her arms, then mutters, "Fine. I'm just curious what I did to make him dislike me so quickly."

"He doesn't dislike you. He was just anxious to get to work."

"Hmm," she hums, unconvinced.

"I'm serious. You should've seen the way he was looking at you before he found out you're the other new girl. Maybe you two could hit it off?"

Dove scoffs. "With a guy who thinks I have an *average* face? No, thank you. Besides, I'm not looking for anything like that."

"Like what? Like a date?" I prod.

"Yeah."

"Why not?"

Chewing on her lower lip, she glances over at Gibbs then stares down at the tall table in front of us that needs to be wiped down. "Just...bad timing, I guess. Besides"--she peeks over at him again--"do you see all the girls drooling over him right now? There's just no way."

"No way that he could have a thing for you? Bullshit. No offense, Dove, but you're gorgeous. Like I said, you should've seen the way he was looking at you before he found out you're the other new girl."

"And you're being too nice," she counters, wiping the crumbs onto the floor with a damp washcloth.

"I'm really not--"

I hear his laugh before I see him. My stomach clenches with anticipation, and my skin prickles with awareness as the atmosphere charges around me. Scanning the bar, I find

River leaning against the bartop chatting with Gibbs. Milo and Jake flank his sides as they each order a drink. Apparently, it's *take your friends to work day* for good ol' Gibson.

Not that I mind.

And I doubt I'm the only one who felt the testosterone ratchet up a few clicks as soon as they walked into the place, not to mention the view of four sexy friends as the guys settle in for drinks.

"Ohhh." Dove drags out the word, and I snap my attention back to her. Her eyebrows bounce up and down a few times. "Gotcha. Which one's yours?"

I clear my throat and point to the behemoth of the group. "That's Milo. My brother. I met Gibson because of him."

"Interesting," she notes, "but I meant from a boyfriend standpoint, 'cause I totally just caught you drooling."

"I was not drooling."

"Oh, okay. Is that how we're going to play it? Denial? Gotcha."

"I'm not in denial."

"And I'm not an innocent lil' Plain Jane who's being way too obsessive over the jerk bartender over there. See? Two can play that game, my friend."

Friend.

The term's fitting.

Sticking my tongue out at her, I ask, "Would you like me to introduce you to them?"

She blanches. "Oh. No, no, no, no––"

River's deep, booming voice echoes above the sound pouring from the speakers. "Found her. Hey, Floozy! What's up?"

My jaw drops.

He did not just call me that.

Dove snorts, then she whispers, "Did he just call you Floozy?"

"Yup. He's a shitty nicknamer."

"Or he's like a little kid in elementary school who's currently tugging on your pigtails. I mean, that never happened to *me*, but I'm just sayin'."

I bite my tongue to keep from arguing with her since the whole gang is currently sauntering over to us. And I definitely don't want them to overhear our conversation or the fact that they're the topic of it.

"Uh, hey, guys," I greet them.

Tossing his arm over my shoulder, Jake pulls me into a quick hug before I get passed around like a bottle of rum from one guy to the next. When my face is shoved against River's chest, I want to melt into him and take a big fat whiff of his mouth-watering scent, but I restrain myself.

Nope. Not happening.

Milo yanks me out of River's grasp and into his before rumbling, "Hey. How's your first day going?"

I give him a quick squeeze then step back to make sure Dove's included in our little gathering. "It's good. This is Dove."

She gives another small wave identical to the one she gifted me with in the break room when we first met. "Hi."

"Dove, this is Milo, Jake, and River." Like a conductor, I point to each of them, and they take turns raising their chins in greeting.

"Hey."

"Nice to meet you guys," she replies, her voice quiet and shy. "Do any of you want a drink or anything?"

"We already put our orders in," Jake tells her. "Thanks, though."

"Okay." Tucking her thumbs into the back pockets of her skinny jeans, she rocks back on her heels. "Well––"

"Have I ever given you a tattoo?" Milo interrupts, cocking his head to the side as he studies her. "You look familiar."

With a shrug, she raises her bare arms from her sides to showcase her ink-free skin. "Nope. Sorry."

"Huh," Milo grunts, unconvinced.

"That's a pretty cool profession, though," she offers, battling the awkward silence from her dismissal. "Do you like it?"

Milo shrugs. "It pays the bills."

"He's being modest," I interject. "He's an awesome tattoo artist, and he loves what he does. If you ever decide you want one, he's the guy to make it happen."

A shy smile threatens to slip past her nerves as she answers, "I'll keep that in mind."

"I hope you do," Milo rumbles.

My eyes nearly pop out of my head as my attention shifts from Milo to Dove and back again.

Well, this just got interesting.

Dove tucks her pale hair behind her ear and drops her gaze to the ground, practically screaming innocence from every single one of her pores. "I should probably get back to work. Um." She peeks back up at Milo, then scans the rest of the crowd. "If you guys need anything, don't be afraid to holler."

Dirty dishtowel in hand, Dove weaves between the growing crowd as I add, "I should probably get back to work too. But it's good to see you guys. And like Dove said, if you need anything, just let me know."

"Anything?" River asks. His deep, gritty voice is laced with a magnetic confidence that makes me squirm. When I work up the courage to hold his intense stare, he winks.

"Ignore him," Jake orders, snapping me out of the spell River had cast on me. "Good luck tonight."

"Oh. Thanks."

"Yeah. Good luck tonight, Floozy." My heart picks up its pace as I register the nickname again. And even though I hate it, I can't deny the way my entire body responds whenever it slips past River's lips. His hand brushes against my hip, though it's nothing but a whisper of a touch, as he leans closer to me and drops his voice low, "And if I need *anything*, I'll definitely let you know."

My gaze darts over to Milo, but he isn't watching our exchange. He's too consumed by the conversation at the bar where a certain new waitress is chatting with a certain bartender who happens to be our roommate too.

Hmm.

The warmth from River's touch disappears as Jake slaps him on the shoulder with a little more force than necessary and shoves him toward the booths in the back of the dimly lit room.

"Come on. Let's grab a seat," Jake orders.

Milo and River head to the booth, but Jake hangs back and rubs the palm of his hand roughly over his face before giving me *the look*.

"Is there a problem?" I ask.

He blows out the oxygen from his lungs and drops his arms to his sides in defeat. "Just…be careful, Reese."

"Of what?"

"Of thinking River's really interested in you."

Ouch.

Covering my hurt with amusement, I cross my arms and reply, "I'm not stupid, Jake. He's a flirt. But an innocent one. He wouldn't screw up his friendship with Milo just to get laid. Trust me. He doesn't need to. I've heard plenty of first-hand accounts on that front."

"Good."

"Good," I mimic. "Anything else?"

"No. Well. Just--"

"Spit it out, Jake," I joke.

"If his *teasing* bothers you, let me know, okay?"

I smile and tug on the hem of his grey T-shirt. "I'm a big girl, remember?"

"Yeah. I know."

"Then you know I can take care of myself."

"I know. But maybe…" His honey-colored eyes capture my full attention as the toes of his shoes kiss mine on the dark floor before his lips pull into a thin, white line. Like he's holding back. I just don't know why.

"Maybe *what*, Jake?" I ask.

"Maybe one day you won't have to take care of yourself." He clears his throat and steps away from me. "I'm gonna go get my drink."

"I work here, remember? Go take a seat. I'll bring some drinks over in a few."

"We already put our order in with Sonny," he reminds me.

"Then I'll bring them right over."

"Thanks, Reese."

"You're welcome. And thanks for keeping an eye out for me. You're a good friend."

"Yeah." His jaw tightens. "*Friend*. I know."

REESE

The steam from the shower swirls through the air and clings to the mirror as I wrap the gray terry cloth towel around me. With a brush, I comb the tangles from my wet hair, then tuck the corner of my towel between my breasts. I unlock the bathroom door and jerk back a few inches when I find River on the other side of it. With his hand raised in the air like he was about to knock, he freezes.

"Shit," I breathe, clutching at my chest. "Riv, you scared me."

"Sorry." His eyes lazily scan me up and down, though I'm not even sure he's aware he's doing it. We've been playing this cat and mouse game for so long that I'm almost used to his attention by now. *Almost.*

Slowly, he lowers his hand back down to his side, though his eyes keep roaming my exposed skin like it's an exhibition of art. But that's as far as it'll go.

Looking.

No touching.

No mercy.

Only his heated gaze and all of the possibilities that will always be just out of reach.

If I didn't crave his attention so much, I'd call him out for it. But I won't.

Besides, it's harmless.

Like Jake said, Riv would never be interested in me. He's a flirt. And I'm his live-in entertainment.

"Can I help you?" I tease in hopes of breaking the electric current pulsing through the cramped hall. I can only take so much torture in one day.

He doesn't step away, leaving less than a foot of space between us. My body hums with awareness of our proximity before I fold my arms, using them as an impromptu barrier between me and the man who enjoys toying with my libido.

When his eyes finally meet mine, he tells me, "Your phone's been ringing off the hook for twenty minutes. I just wanted to make sure you were okay in here."

"My phone?"

"Yeah."

Who the hell would be calling me?

Sure enough, the familiar tune of "She Hates Me" by Puddle of Mudd filters from my bedroom. My expression hardens before I raise one finger in the air as a silent request for him to give me a second. Then I rush to my room. I can feel River watching me from the doorway as I fumble with the silence button on my cell, but I'm too annoyed to care.

"There. Sorry about that."

"Who is it?" River demands, his earlier amusement evaporating into thin air.

"No one," I mutter under my breath while trying to keep my lady bits covered with my towel in front of the guy I'm totally crushing on.

"Does he still call you often?"

"Only when he's drunk or high."

Hovering near the entrance of my room, River weighs his options before giving in and striding over to me.

"Could he be dangerous?" he demands.

I scoff. "No, of course not."

Unconvinced, River's eyes narrow into tiny slits. "Look, I know you don't want to hear this, but we've already established he was emotionally abusive. I need to know if that could ever cross into physical."

"What? No, of course not," I repeat. "Besides, it was just a phone call, Riv."

"You sure about that?" He crowds my space a little more until I can barely think straight as his familiar scent washes over me.

Damn, he smells good. Why does he smell so amazing?

"Answer the question, Reese."

I squeeze my eyes shut to concentrate, but it doesn't work. He isn't playing fair. Looks I can handle. But smells? Especially when I'm pretty sure I could bottle his scent and make millions? A girl can only take so much.

What's next? Touch? Taste? Does he want *to kill me?*

With an exasperated sigh, I look up at him when my phone starts to buzz in my hand.

Dammit, Ian!

"Give me the phone, Reese," River demands.

"No."

"Give me the phone, so I can tell him to leave you the hell alone."

"I'll take care of it."

"You've had plenty of time to take care of it, and apparently, he isn't getting the hint. Give me the phone." River raises his hand with the palm facing up, but my phone stops buzzing at the same moment.

"No need." I lift my cell and wiggle it back and forth to

155

display the dark screen, but the damn thing lights right back up again.

As River lunges for it, I twist my arm behind my back but find myself in a bear hug of muscle and testosterone when he continues his pursuit of my stupid cell. With my breasts smashed against his broad chest, his strong arms envelop me until all I can see, feel, and smell is *him*.

"Give me the damn phone, Reese," he growls. The sound vibrates through me, shining a light on our precarious position like a damn strobe light.

I freeze.

Me. In nothing but a towel and a stubborn attitude that could rival a bull's.

And him. In a T-shirt and dark jeans, looking good enough to lick.

Literally.

With our chests pressed together and his arms wrapped around my waist, my breath hitches. This is new. And it's too much. Too much temptation. Too much lust. Too much curiosity for my own good. Then I peek up at him and regret it instantly. Looking is one thing, but with his cool minty breath fanning across my cheeks...*shit.*

That same electric current pulses, promising a spark that could easily turn into an inferno. I feel his fingers dig into the gray terry cloth along the curve of my lower back before the bruising pressure disappears just as quickly. Like I'm dangerous. Like I'm a ticking time bomb that could detonate at any second. And we'd both be obliterated, causing irreparable damage in the blink of an eye before either of us could help it.

But man, what a way to go.

Stepping away from me, River motions to the phone in my hand as it lights up again.

"If you don't take care of that, I will," he threatens.

Then he's gone, leaving me alone and more confused and sexually frustrated than I've been in a *long* time.

My palms are sweaty as I give in and finally answer the stupid call. "What do you want, Ian?"

"You know what I want," he answers nonchalantly like he hasn't been blowing up my phone for a solid thirty minutes.

Pinching the bridge of my nose, I tell him, "Listen. I called the landlord a couple of weeks ago. He was generous enough to take my name off the lease. You can keep the security deposit to help cover rent for the next month or whatever, but you might want to contact him if you plan on moving out."

"You serious?" His voice is dripping with disbelief, and I want to laugh when I realize he's actually surprised I haven't run back to him yet.

"We're through, Ian," I remind him.

"Bullshit. You know I can't let you go. You know--"

"Stop calling me, okay? Goodbye."

Then I push the little red button to end the call and release the tension I'd been holding from the moment I answered.

He's right, though. I know how possessive he can be. I know how much he loves a challenge. And I know that he won't leave me alone until he finds a new girl to play with, which is ironic because that's what pushed me to end things in the first place.

Asshole.

C losing my bedroom door, I get dressed quickly, then skip down the stairs in search of food in hopes of it erasing the bitter taste my conversation with Ian left in my mouth.

My feet dig into the hardwood floor at the base of the steps when River's voice filters through the air from the kitchen.

"Appendicitis? Are you serious?"

Silence.

"Then what the hell am I supposed to do? It's not my fault that I can't show Brett my potential when the girl I was supposed to do the photoshoot with is getting her appendix removed."

Inching forward, I sneak a peek around the corner. River's pacing back and forth in the kitchen. His hair is a mess, as if he's been running his fingers through it in frustration. The question is, is it from our encounter in my room? Or is it from his phone call?

He pauses then barks out, "I can't miss out on this opportunity just because Olivia won't be able to make it."

Scratch that. It's definitely because of the phone call.

"I need--" His eyes catch mine before his eyebrows wrinkle with concentration. I don't think I could move even if I wanted to, regardless of how guilty I feel for being caught eavesdropping.

"Sorry," I mouth, inching back to the stairs, but he holds up his palm and mouths, "Stop."

I freeze.

"I think I found a solution," River murmurs into the speaker. "Tell Brett to keep me on the schedule and that I'll see him at the session this afternoon."

Silence.

"I'll take care of it." After ending the call, he sets his phone down on the counter then gives me his full attention. "Hello again, Roomie."

I roll my eyes and enter the kitchen fully. "Why, hello, Manwhore. Sorry if I interrupted something."

He waves me off. "Not at all. Have you eaten breakfast yet?"

"Not yet."

"Can I make you something?"

"I heard you don't cook."

"I make a mean bowl of cereal."

I laugh. "You? Cereal?"

"It's my only weakness."

"Your only one, huh?"

His mouth quirks, but he doesn't comment.

"What kind of cereal?" I ask. "'Cause if it's Wheaties or something that isn't covered in sugar, then I'm gonna have to pass."

"You're in luck. I just replenished my secret stash." With a wink, he rummages in the back of the cupboard and retrieves an unopened box of Reese's Puffs cereal.

"That's not where we keep the cereal," I point out while

ignoring the way his muscles bunch and flex beneath his T-shirt as he finds a bowl and spoon. A small part of me wishes we could go back to the no-clothes way of living that disappeared the moment I moved in, and Milo set a new batch of rules.

Party pooper.

"That's not where we keep the *boring* cereal," he clarifies before setting a bowl and spoon down at the center island. "And like I said, it's my *secret* stash. I expect you to keep it that way."

"If it's so secretive, then why'd you show me?" I ask as if I didn't already know where it was.

Sweet, naive River.

"Because I need your help with something," he admits.

I quirk my brow. "Oh? And you think you can buy me off with cereal?"

"A guy can dream, can't he?"

With a grin, I sit down on a barstool in front of River's freshly prepared breakfast while he steps away to grab the gallon of milk from the fridge.

"Thank you," I tell him as he pours the perfect amount into my bowl.

"You're welcome."

I can feel him watching me as I take a big bite of peanut-buttery goodness, but I try to ignore it as I chew and swallow. "So, what do you need help with?"

"Remember the night I brought you home from SeaBird wasted? And you told me about your dreams of becoming an actor?"

"*Childhood* dreams," I clarify. "But go on."

He smirks. "Well, do you remember that photoshoot I told you about? The one that could land me the role in a big movie production?"

Taking another bite, I nod and watch as he rounds the corner and sits down on the barstool beside me.

"Olivia had to cancel at the last minute, and without a woman to take the pictures with, then the *couple's* photoshoot won't be a *couple's* photoshoot, and I won't be able to show off my skills to the photographer, which means the director will go with someone else for the part."

I grimace. "That sucks, Riv. I'm sorry."

"I haven't gotten to the favor part…"

Setting my spoon down on the counter, I tilt my head and ask, "And?"

"And I'm curious if you'd like to earn a few bucks by helping me out with something. Who knows? It might even look good on your resume."

Even though I know where he *might* be going with this, I purse my lips. "Spit it out, River."

"Will you come to the photoshoot with me? It's in an hour, and there's not enough time for me to find another suitable replacement."

My heart leaps in my chest. Convinced I've heard him wrong, I ask, "A photoshoot?"

"Yeah."

"With me?"

"Yeah. I need you to take a few pictures with me and possibly run some lines if the photographer offers to record an audition tape for me."

He can't be serious.

I shake my head. "River. I'm not a model. And I'm definitely not an actress despite my drunken rambling that night."

"You don't need to be either of those things. If anything, your lack of talent will help mine shine."

"Gee. Thanks."

He laughs. "That's not what I meant. I'm just saying that

you don't need to be a famous model or actress to help me out today. You just need to show up, trust me, and do what the photographer says."

Sighing, I rub my hand over my face and weigh my options. I could use the money, especially since I won't be getting my deposit back on the apartment. And it would help River out too. I know him. He wouldn't be asking for my help if he didn't really need it. He's too prideful for that. Plus, it could be fun.

Right?

"Please?" he murmurs in a quiet voice.

My teeth dig into the inside of my cheek before I hedge, "I'm not sure this is a good idea."

"But it's the only choice I've got."

Those damn pleading eyes are what finally do me in. I give him a jerky nod. "Fine. I'll do it."

His stupidly-perfect smile widens, causing my heart to gallop in my chest. "Seriously?"

No.

"Yes," I grudgingly confirm.

"Thank you, Reese."

"You're welcome," I whisper. My anxiety spikes at the prospect of actually going through with this, but I try to ignore it and take another bite of my now soggy cereal.

"Do you think you can be ready to leave in thirty?"

"I guess?" I look down at my red crew neck and jean shorts. "What am I supposed to wear?"

"They'll have clothes for you at the place," he returns like it isn't a big deal.

My eyes widen. "Whose clothes?"

"The designer's."

Designer? What designer?

I feel so far out of my league right now it's not even funny. My damp hair hangs around my shoulders, and I toy with the ends before asking, "And what am I supposed to do with my hair?"

"There's a stylist that'll help you when we get there. Don't worry about doing your makeup or anything either. She'll take care of all of that."

I gulp. "I'm not sure this is a good idea, River."

"Why not?"

"Because I'm not...model material. And no matter how good of an actor you are, you can't make up for my short-comings in front of the camera. I'm not Olivia. I'm not as thin as her. I'm not as tall. I'm not as pretty. I'm *nothing* like her. And no, this isn't me begging for a compliment or anything. I'm just trying to be honest here, and I don't want to disappoint you." I take a deep breath to stop myself from rambling, then wait for him to say something.

But he doesn't.

He's silent.

Then he narrows his gaze.

Like I've somehow pissed him off, though I have no idea what I did. The intensity radiates off him in waves as he analyzes me from head to toe. I tuck a few strands of hair behind my ear, then drop my gaze to my cereal bowl and nudge a few of the last pieces around in the milk. I can feel him assessing me. Taking me in. Every flaw. Every insecurity. Until I'm left bare.

"Want to know another secret, Reese?" he murmurs in a low voice, finally putting me out of my misery as he breaks the silence and leans closer to me.

I stay quiet but look over at him through my upper lashes.

"There are a lot of different kinds of beauty in the world. From what's on the inside to outward appearances. From girl-next-door cute to Victoria's Secret model sexy and everything in between. And no matter how much society is trying to erase those labels, I've seen how difficult it can be--especially for women--to remember their worth. It destroyed my mom and turned her into a shell of a human being, all because she wasn't comfortable in her own skin. And if I'm being honest, those same labels have screwed with me too."

"How?" I breathe out.

He's gorgeous.

"They've left me terrified of what my future could be if I ever skipped a day at the gym and ate a dozen pizzas instead. I'm far from perfect, and I have my own shit to sort through, but I can tell you right now that you're fucking gorgeous, Reese Anders."

My lips part as a quiet gasp escapes me. His attention drops down to my mouth. But he doesn't move a muscle. With a simple look, he presses against my own little personal bubble until I'm positive it's going to pop. And the scary part is that I'd be okay if it did. Because whenever I'm around him, I can't seem to get close enough. Even after our little incident in my bedroom earlier, I can't help it. I want to get under his skin the same way he's managed to sneak under mine.

Oblivious to my desires, his deep, gritty voice wreaks havoc on my insides as he adds, "You need to stop comparing yourself to Olivia Porter or any other woman you classify as beautiful. Because they don't hold a candle compared to you."

"River…"

"I'm serious, Reese. Want to know why?"

Licking my lips, I whisper, "Why?"

"Because they aren't you. *You're* you. And I can guarantee that when you find a guy who's worth your time, he'll be the luckiest bastard in the world."

"Then why did Ian cheat on me?" I challenge, finally facing my deepest failure and fears head-on. "If he was the luckiest bastard in the world, then why wasn't I enough?"

"Because he wasn't worth your time, yet you still gave it to him even though he didn't deserve it."

"And how will I know when someone *is* worth my time?"

He doesn't answer me, but his breath fans across my cheeks as we both stay frozen in the silence.

Swallowing, I stare at his mouth that's only a few inches from mine before he pushes himself off the counter to give me some space. Space that I'm not sure I want, though I don't point it out.

"I'm going to grab my keys and put on some shoes," he mutters, standing up. "I'll meet you at the car in a few."

"O-okay."

I don't watch him leave, but the wood creaks under his weight down the hall, then up the stairs as I'm left reeling at our little conversation. Maybe he's right. Maybe I should stop comparing myself to others. Maybe I should stop blaming myself for Ian cheating on me.

And maybe I should figure out if River's worth my time or not because I'm afraid I'm already giving him too much of it if he doesn't feel the same way.

19

REESE

"Hey, man. Thanks for still doing this," River says as he shakes hands with an attractive guy whom I assume is the photographer. "I'm River. Nice to officially meet you."

With a camera strapped around his neck, a black Beatles T-shirt, and dark jeans, it makes sense. We're at a small warehouse about an hour away from the house, but the time flew by as we got lost in the music blaring through the speakers. We didn't talk much because enough was said during breakfast. Or maybe he could tell I wasn't in the mood to chat after he peeled back a few of my layers to reveal a very insecure girl with trust issues.

And now we're here, and I'm being scrutinized up and down by River's friend.

"This is Reese, by the way," Riv introduces me.

I step forward and take the photographer's offered hand while my nerves buzz inside of me like bees in a hive.

I cannot believe I'm actually doing this.

"Nice to meet you," he returns. "I'm Brett."

"Hi."

Releasing his grasp on my hand, his reluctant gaze bounces between us. "Look, I'm going to be honest with both of you right now. There's a very big chance that nothing will come out of today. I'm doing you a favor by even bothering to take the pictures after Olivia bailed. To be honest, if I didn't have a good relationship with Gina, I wouldn't even waste our time."

"I know, man," River returns, "and I can't tell you how much I appreciate your help."

"Don't mention it. I've seen your work, and I think you'll do well for this project." He turns to me. "Do you have any modeling experience?"

"Uh…" I look at River and shrug.

"Just some small stuff," River jumps in. "But she has a heart of gold and is willing to help me out today."

"Are you guys sleeping together?" Brett asks point-blank.

Eyes bugging out of my head, I choke out, "Excuse me?"

"Are you, or have you ever in the past, slept with River?"

"What? No. Of course not––"

His mouth ticks up in a half-smile. "Are you okay if he touches you during the photoshoot?"

"T-touches me?"

"Nothing inappropriate. Like your hip, your cheek, your back, that kind of thing. This is a lingerie shoot. We want it to be sexy. Intimate. But it'll still be tasteful."

"Oh." My eyes dart over to Riv. The pleading in his gaze is enough to push over a damn Redwood tree. With a gulp, I mutter, "Uh, yeah. Sure. I mean, whatever you think."

And why does it feel like I'm about to film my first porno?

"You sure?" Brett prods.

"I'll do whatever it takes to help out a friend."

"Friend." That same knowing smirk graces Brett's lips. "Noted. Trish is in the back room, and she'll take care of your makeup and hair. Once you're finished, she'll give you a few outfits to change into. Then we'll get started. Any questions?"

I shrug but stay quiet.

With an amused chuckle, Brett motions to the back room. "Then, off you go."

~

As I stare at myself in the full-length mirror, a single thought comes to mind.

This is a terrible idea.

"Girl, you look hot!" announces Trisha, admiring her work. The girl's either a miracle worker or made a deal with the devil for her expertise. I haven't quite decided which one fits the bill.

Brushing a perfectly curled strand of hair away from my face, I inspect myself closer and gulp. Hard.

I *do* look hot. That's the problem. Not because I don't want to look attractive but because I don't feel like me. Maybe that's a good thing, though. Maybe if I don't look like me, I can pretend I'm whoever the stranger is staring back at me in the mirror. Still, the white lacy lingerie-style dress that I would never in a million years wear in public makes the top of my small breasts play peek-a-boo with any spectator within a two-block radius.

Okay, maybe I'm being a little ridiculous.

I turn to the side and take in my silhouette.

Nope. Not being ridiculous.

I didn't even know I had a body like this. I've always been a hoodie and shorts kind of girl. This? It's like a second skin, accentuating my tiny curves in a way I didn't even think was possible. I'm finally, kinda, sorta pulling off the whole sexy vibe, and I didn't even know I was capable of it. With another deep breath, I smooth down the lacy material across my abdomen, then turn around and look at my butt. The thing is so short I'm not even sure it fully covers it. If I bend down, I'm screwed.

"Stop questioning it," Trisha orders. "I already told you that you look hot. Embrace it, girl. And lick River for me, would ya? You have no idea how jealous all the girls are that you're actually doing a session with him."

"What do you mean?"

She shrugs. "I dunno. He's always insisted on doing singles versus couples. Personally, I think it's because he likes the spotlight, but what do I know? He's doing this with you, right? You're a lucky girl."

"Lucky, my ass. I'm just helping the guy out. He owes me big time for this."

Trisha's light laughter turns wicked as she leans forward and whispers, "I'm sure he could think of a way or two to pay you back. A big cock for a big favor sounds like a pretty even trade to me."

My cheeks redden. "No, thank you. I've never really had a thing for manwhores."

"At least you know what you're getting into with a manwhore," she argues. "I used to only date stand-up guys. You know, the ones that seemed like they wanted to settle down and commit to a girl instead of sleeping their way through half the state?"

An image of Jake pops into my head before I catch myself nodding. "I know the type."

"Yeah, well, once upon a time, I was seriously dating one of them when he yelled out another girl's name while we were having sex. After that, I ditched the prince charmings and decided to stick with manwhores. My heart's safer that way, and the orgasms are an added bonus."

"I'll keep that in mind," I mutter.

My breathing quickens when River's deep voice echoes

through the closed door and cuts our conversation short. "Hey, are you guys ready? Brett's getting anxious."

The stylist nudges me toward the exit. "She's coming!"

I can hear his retreating footsteps as I turn back to Trisha. "Thanks. For..."–– I motion to my body––"this."

"Don't mention it. Now, go get 'em, tiger. We can chat more during your next outfit change."

I look down at the tiny piece of material covering my body that barely passes for a dress. "Are you sure I should wear this?"

She grins. "Yup. This is just round one, girl. What else did you think you'd be wearing?"

"I don't know? A pair of jeans would be nice."

"Jeans? Honey, this is a lingerie shoot. But don't worry. You'll get used to it. And once you're in front of the camera, Brett has a way of making you feel comfortable in your own skin. Now, go! We don't want to keep either of them waiting."

With a final glance in the mirror, I take a deep breath then head out the door.

River is helping Brett with the lighting equipment as they set up the first shot. Obviously, he isn't wearing a shirt because why the hell would he? The guy was made to be naked, and it's easy to see he's comfortable in his skin. If only I could manage to channel his confidence and make it my own.

My mouth waters at the view while I mentally curse Milo for his stupid clothes rule. I could stare at this all day long. I probably wouldn't get much work done, but it'd be worth it. Tearing my gaze away from the Greek god in front of me, I take in the rest of his ensemble before realizing he doesn't look much different than usual. The dark red waistband of his boxers plays peek-a-boo an inch or two above a pair of dark jeans that hang low on his hips. So low that I can see the damn 'V' that leads to his––

I clear my throat, then focus on the cement ground beneath my crimson, sky-high stilettos.

How the hell am I supposed to walk in these things?

On shaky legs, I make my way toward them, then cross my arms as I wait for further instruction. I've never felt so out of my element in my entire life. My hair even has hairspray in it, for Pete's sake, and my lips are lacquered with gloss that tastes like cotton candy. I feel like a damn barbie. My nose wrinkles before I wring my hands in front of me in hopes of hiding their shaking.

"Perfect, you're here," Brett greets me when he catches me out of the corner of his eye. "Come stand right here." He points to the ground where River is standing, then turns to him. "All right, man. I'm not going to give you a ton of direction unless you look lost. The only thing we're trying to sell today is chemistry, and if you can make your clothes look good while doing it, then that means we're successful. Because your counterpart had to bail at the last minute, you're basically carrying this. Any questions?"

"Um…I have one," I pipe in. Two sets of eyes turn to me. "What do you want me to do?"

"I want you to act natural, ignore the camera, and pretend you want to have sex with River. Anything else?"

I gulp but stay silent.

Pretend I want to have sex with River?

Did he really just say that to me? I'm *so* not cut out for this.

Brett smirks, taking in my ashen complexion, but he doesn't comment on it. "Let's get this started."

My heels click against the cement as I close the rest of the distance between Riv and me while Brett grabs his camera and starts adjusting a few settings. With wide eyes and a slack jaw, I ignore Riv and watch Brett fiddle with a few buttons, unsure what the hell *act natural* even means.

"How you doin'?" River murmurs, demanding my attention.

I clear my throat and glance over at him. "Fine. Just dandy, actually. Did I mention how much you're going to owe me after this?"

His chest rumbles with amusement before River raises his hand and drags his fingers along the lace at my shoulder. "The dress looks nice on you, though."

"It's hardly a dress."

"It's sexy as hell." My pulse quickens at the way he says it. Like it's a fact, and I'd be a fool to disagree with him. And I don't disagree. It makes my girl-next-door cute look like a damn sex kitten or something.

Whatever a sex kitten is.

Still, when the compliment slips from his lips, it means more to me than a regular Joe on the street though I refuse to acknowledge why.

Toying with the neckline above my breasts, River gives the camera his back while practically swallowing me whole with his commanding presence. I hold my breath and peek up at him. "I might have to convince Brett to let you keep it," he continues as if we're having a conversation at a coffee shop when his hands are only a few centimeters away from my freaking boobs.

My heart is pounding a million beats per minute as I scramble to reply.

Wait, what are we talking about? Oh. *The dress.*

"And why would you do that?" I murmur. "It's not like I'd actually wear this thing in public. Don't get me wrong. It's gorgeous, but…"

My voice trails off as the sound of the camera clicking distracts me. I look over River's shoulder and find Brett's camera pointed directly at us while snapping a billion more pictures.

I probably look ridiculous. Like a first-time hooker. Or a deer in the headlights with––

"But what?" River prods, demanding my attention. Again.

I try to focus, then peer up into his eyes. They're gorgeous. Like moss with little flecks of gold around the iris. How the hell does he have such pretty eyes? And his lashes? Don't even get me started on those bad boys. Long and dark, with just enough curl to frame his eyes without looking feminine. It's the perfect balance.

His mouth quirks in the corner as if he's making fun of me, and it's enough to bring me back to the present instead of the daydream I could easily get lost in. You know the one where he bends me over backward and kisses the shit out of me.

I clear my throat. "But if I'm not sleeping with anyone, and since I wouldn't wear the dress in public, then what's the point of taking it home? Does it classify as loungewear? Do you think Milo would be cool if I was just hanging out in the family room while watching Netflix in this thing?"

His breath of laughter fans across my cheeks before a bright flash makes me flinch.

"Sh…," he whispers. "Ignore it. It's just you and me." He grabs my waist and pulls me against him. With a soft gasp, I press my hands against his naked chest. I'm in desperate need of a little space, yet I'm craving the closeness more than my next breath. It's a heady––and confusing––concoction.

"That's easier said than done," I point out as my fingers flex against his muscular pecs. He's so warm and hard, yet silky too. I feel like I could curl into him and sleep for days.

His grip tightens around my waist before he presses his groin to my lower belly. Sliding his hand across my spine and up my bare back, he tangles his fingers in my messy waves at the base of my skull. The slight sting from his punishing grip has my knees buckling with need.

"Maybe I'm just not distracting you enough," he murmurs.

I lick my lips, then drop my eyes back to where my hands are practically clinging to him. "I think you're doing just fine."

My pale skin contrasts with the sun-kissed flesh stretched across his taut muscles like the yin to his yang.

We couldn't be more different. Both physically and personally, but there's something about him that makes me curious. About what life could be like if our paths crossed in a different way. About what Milo would do if I gave in to my curiosity and kissed River. About what River would do if I gave in and kissed him. Yeah. I'm curious about a lot of things. Things that I should definitely never act on but aren't exactly torture to think about.

Or maybe it *is* torture. But I like getting lost in the fantasy that will never be my reality.

A few more clicks combined with the bright light from the flash make me squeeze my eyes shut as reality comes crashing back to the surface. River's hand at the base of my skull disappears, and he cups my cheek, leaning closer as if he's going to kiss me.

"W-wait. What are you doing?" My eyes slip to his mouth.

"Chemistry, remember? Don't worry. I won't kiss you unless you beg for it. Besides, it's the almost-kiss that's torture anyway. And we want to torture the audience if I have any hope of getting this role."

The *audience*. Right.

I practically deflate in his arms as reality hits me square in the chest. Again. Somehow it's so easy to get lost in him when it's apparent that I'm just his plaything. His means to an end. Forget about torturing *me* during this entire thing because we mustn't forget about the audience.

Sensing my melancholy shift, he runs his nose against the bridge of mine before teasing, "Loosen up, Roomie. You were doing good. Don't bail on me now."

You know what? No. No deal. I'm not his plaything. Besides, Trisha said I look hot. Even River admitted it. So why am I so insecure? Why am I so positive that River couldn't want me the way I want him? I'm done being a pawn. Now, it's time to prove it.

"You think I would beg for your kiss?" I whisper, pushing up onto my tiptoes until I can practically feel the heat from his lips against mine. "That I can't bring chemistry? That you're the only one who knows how to tease?"

A flash of a smile stretches across his face before he challenges, "You tell me."

Cocking my head to the side, I drag my fingers down his chest and over his abs before toying with the hem of his boxers. But I keep my eyes on his the whole time until I see the familiar heat start to sizzle below the surface.

"By the time I'm through with you, you'll be the one begging for a taste, River. And so will the *audience.*"

"Is this a game of chicken, Reese? Because we both know I won't lose." His voice sounds like he's gargled broken glass, but it only spurs me on.

Pressing my chest against his, I weave my hands through his short hair and give it a soft tug. "This is me proving that you're not a gift from God and that you're not the only one who knows how to play this game."

His mouth quirks up on one side before his other hand cups my ass, and he pulls me into his very hard, very ready––

"This is great!" Brett announces. "Let's do a few with Reese facing me, and River, I want you at her back."

Releasing me, River brings his chest to my back, and I

glance over my shoulder at him. His chiseled jaw looks good enough to eat as his hand spreads against my lower stomach. Arching my back into him, I gasp when I feel *him* against me.

"Careful, Reese. I know you mentioned that you felt like this was your first porno, but we wouldn't want to make it one, now would we?" he tsks against my ear. The sound races down my spine, hitting every nerve with precision before I glance up at him and bite my lower lip. That same heat returns to his gaze, penetrating me as he leans forward and presses an open-mouthed kiss to my throat. I moan softly at the contact and close my eyes to savor the heat from his lips as it brands my sensitive skin.

Holy freaking shit.

I've never been more turned on in my entire life. The lightboxes directed at us continue to flash while Brett snaps away in the background. But I'm grateful for the annoyingly bright light. It reminds me that none of this is real, even though it's starting to feel like it might be. Even though I'm starting to feel like I want it to be. Because with his heated gaze and his demanding touch, I feel empowered. I feel beautiful. I feel like I could conquer the freaking world if I wanted to.

Raising my arms, I lace my fingers through the back of River's hair, then twist in his grasp and press back onto my tiptoes to close the distance between us. The shift is enough to turn predator into prey, and a small part of me ignites when I see the intrigue shining back at me. I never really thought I'd be the one to take the lead during this whole shindig, but my body has other ideas. And I'm done fighting it.

With my head tilted to the perfect angle, I lick my lips then whisper, "You going to beg me yet, Riv?"

The heat in his gaze is scorching as he dips down a few

more inches until I can taste his breath on my tongue. It's minty and sweet, taunting me to––

"That's perfect!" Brett interrupts. It's followed by applause that acts like a wet blanket on my libido. "Go change into your next outfits. Then we'll do it again."

Untangling myself, I clear my throat and tuck my hair behind my ear before bolting toward the back room in search of sanctuary.

Because whatever the hell that was? Well, it was too close.

"All right, that's a wrap. I think we'll have plenty to work with, which is saying something considering the fact that Olivia's appendix almost burst this morning. River, would you be interested in auditioning for the role Gina mentioned? I think Henderson would be interested in seeing whatcha got."

I hold my breath and wait on pins and needles for River's response. This is the moment he's been waiting for. And it worked. The freaking impromptu modeling session hooked Brett.

Riv did it. He knocked Brett's socks off.

I bite my lip to contain my squeal and turn to River.

Covering his surprise with a look of confidence, he rocks back on his heels and nods. "Yeah, man. That'd be great. I really appreciate the opportunity."

"And I appreciate your dedication to the photoshoot today and for thinking outside of the box by bringing a...*friend*. I'm going to be honest with you, River. I think you've got a shot with Henderson if you can nail this audition. You up for it?"

"Yeah, of course." River is practically buzzing with excitement, and it's kind of adorable to witness.

"Good." Brett turns to me. "Reese, do you mind helping him read a few lines for an audition tape?"

"But I'm not an actress," I argue, stating the obvious even though River had warned me about this possibility.

"You weren't a model before today either," he points out dryly, calling our bluff. "And yet you knocked it out of the park. Besides, people run lines all the time. It'll be easy. Let me give you a quick CliffsNotes version of the story, so you'll be caught up. You'll be reading the lines of Kristine, and River is going to be Jon. You were childhood sweethearts, then Jon moved away, became a rockstar, fell into drug addiction, and came back to your hometown to recover and write a new album with the intention of moving back to the big city after it's all said and done. This is the scene where Kristine finds out Jon's leaving again and confronts him. Any questions?"

I raise my hand like a kid in grade school. "What am I supposed to *do*?"

With the patience of a saint, Brett strides toward me and hands over a piece of paper. "Here's the script. This is a very emotional scene, but we aren't expecting you to show any of that because, like you said, you're not an actress. Just do your best, and it'll be plenty. Basically, just read the lines and imagine how you'd feel if you were Kristine. River, as we both know, you were supposed to be doing this scene with Olivia, but obviously, she isn't here. Just do the best you can, and we'll see how it goes, okay?"

We both nod before I start scanning the script while mentally trying to pump myself up.

I can do this.

I can totally do this.

And, bonus points, I'm even wearing jeans.

"Are you guys ready?" Brett inquires as he adjusts the camera.

Turning my pleading gaze to River, I shake my head, but the bastard only laughs in response.

"Yeah. We're ready," he answers for us.

"All right. Action."

The words blur together on the page as I stare at them before River prods, "You're up, Floozy."

I roll my eyes then attempt to focus on the script in my shaking hands. "A-anything you want to say to me?"

"Kristine…" His voice trails off, and I realize I'm supposed to have cut him off.

Oops.

I fumble with the script and find my next part.

"Don't, Jon. Don't lie to me, okay? You"--I clear my throat--"You promised me you were through with the lies."

"Do you think I want to go?" The bite in River's voice makes me pause and look up at him. "I have obligations, Kristine. Obligations that you made me promise to keep because that's what an honest man does. Isn't that right?"

I swallow and look back down at the paper in my hands, surprised to find them still shaking. Only this time, it isn't from my nerves. It's from witnessing River's passion. The animosity in his voice. The anger and defeat he feels. It's almost palpable.

Just read the damn page, Reese.

"Don't put this on me," I whisper, peeking back up at him.

He scoffs, then starts to pace back and forth like a caged lion on the brink of attack. He runs his fingers through his hair, tugging roughly at the roots until I have to fight the urge to stop him from hurting himself.

"Do you think I want to go back to that life?" he demands. "Do you think I want to be followed by paparazzi? Do you think I want them to document every single fucking mistake in my life? That I want them to air out my dirty laundry, my regrets, my missed opportunities? Every little detail until there's nothing left that's mine? I've given up everything for my career, but it's the only way I know how to live."

My heart starts to pound in rhythm to his heavy footsteps as I find myself just as invested in the conversation as he is.

"Then what do you want?" I beg, my voice cracking as I lose myself in the moment that feels more real than anything I've felt in a long time. "It's not like anyone is chasing you out of this town, Jon. They didn't the first time you left, and they sure as hell aren't chasing you out of town this time, either. This is on *you*."

"Is that right, Kristine? You're asking me what I want? Fine." He storms toward me, but I keep my feet planted in place and hold my breath as he gets up in my face. Crowding me. Making me feel small. Almost hated. Like I'm his weakness. His kryptonite. But precious. Desirable. And cherished too.

His energy is so electric that the only thing I can see or smell or hear is *him*.

Not River.

Jon.

And in this moment, I'm not Reese anymore. I'm Kristine. Wounded. Broken. And terrified of losing the only person that matters to me yet too stubborn to admit it.

He grabs my chin, forcing me to look up at him as I forget about the damn sheet of paper in my hand and drop it to my side.

"I want a reason to stay, Kristine," he growls, his breath fanning across my cheeks. "Did you ever think of that? I want a reason to put roots down."

My lower lip quivers, but I stay silent.

"I want the white picket fence that you're adamant I can't

give to you no matter how hard I've tried to prove you wrong."

I squeeze my eyes shut and swallow back tears.

"I'm not perfect, babe," he continues, his voice raw with emotion that washes over me like a damn hurricane. "You know that better than anyone. But instead of convincing yourself that I'm going to leave again, why the hell don't you ask me to stay?"

Caught up in the moment, I grab his wrist that's still holding me in place. My tears fall freely as I look up at him and hold his heated stare. Because I've been where Kristine is. I've felt like the backup plan before. I've felt like the girl who couldn't ever be enough to hold a man's interest. To be the most important thing in his life.

But she deserves her happiness.

She deserves the strength to ask for what she wants instead of hiding behind her fears.

The same way I deserve to get what I want. To grab onto what I deserve despite what others believe. What others feel is best for me.

So I give in and find the courage Kristine needs to ask for what she wants.

What she *needs*.

To be loved.

To be cherished.

To be put first for once in her life.

Isn't that what we all want?

Another tear rolls down my cheek. I lick my lips.

"What. Do. You. Want?" he growls.

"Stay."

His mouth crashes onto mine, his fingers weaving into my hair to hold me in place as his tongue pushes into my mouth. The kiss is laced with an urgency that's so damn potent I'm afraid that if I don't give myself to him, then we'll both suffocate.

It's ridiculous. I know that. But in this moment, when I'm not Reese, I can set aside my own reservations and insecurities. I can be Kristine. The girl who's brave enough to finally admit what she wants. *Who* she wants. And it's Jon...the man who's currently delivering a toe-curling kiss that's ruined her for all other kisses. And I'm jealous. Because I'm not brave like she is.

I'm weak.

Too weak to fight for what I want.

Too weak to admit that I want a man who's off-limits. Who would never settle down. Who looks at girls like they're playthings. Or at least, I thought he did. But when he looks at me, it's different.

Isn't it?

Or maybe I'm wrong.

Is that all I am to him? A plaything?

My insecurities battle for the spotlight when River's punishing grip tightens in my hair before softening.

Like he's giving in to what he truly wants. To let down his walls. To let me in.

To let *Kristine* in.

My chest heaves as I let Kristine take over and reciprocate the only way I know how by pressing my chest against him and opening my mouth to let him in too.

Because Kristine? She needs to let him in. She needs to let herself be loved. She deserves it. And she deserves the wounded rockstar with a shitty past.

A soft moan escapes me as I cling to his bicep and slip my tongue into his hungry mouth when––

"And that's a wrap," Brett calls out.

I freeze in River's grasp and peek up at him with tear-stained cheeks before letting my heels touch the ground.

Whoa.

His eyes are dark yet filled with a lust that's so thick I can almost taste it. Slamming his mouth against mine a second time, Jon disappears, replaced by River. The *real* River. Not the actor. And he sure as hell isn't kissing Kristine. He's kissing me. Lil' ol' me. The girl who isn't an actress or a model. She's just a regular girl next door who is being consumed by the sexiest man she's ever met.

And I let him. I siphon a bit of Kristine's courage and wield it like a weapon. Piercing through River's barriers the same way he's managed to wreck mine. Weaving my fingers into his hair, I rise onto my tiptoes again and glide the tip of my tongue along his, tasting his minty flavor while committing it to memory. Because I have no idea if I'll ever have the courage to kiss him after this moment.

Not like this.

Not without the sorry excuse that we're pretending. That this is all for a stupid audition tape when we both know it's more than that.

At least it is to me.

"I said, that's a wrap," Brett orders, more amused than anything else.

Panting, I pull away from River and try to catch my breath. The intensity in his eyes makes it damn near impossible. He clears his throat, lets me go, and steps back to give me some space.

Space I'm not sure I even want anymore.

What. The. Hell just happened?

Wiping the back of my hand against my swollen lips, my cheeks flushed, I release another unsteady breath. My mind and body are still stuck in the emotional mess from five minutes ago, and I'm left feeling...helpless. I need to know what happens to Jon and Kristine. I need to know if he leaves. I need to know if the kiss I just shared with River was real or if I imagined the whole thing. And I need my heart to stop galloping in my chest so I can catch my breath and act natural when all I want to do is grab River's face and kiss him again.

Which would be *so* wrong.

"You guys went off-script," Brett notes, "but I think the director will appreciate it. Do you want to shoot it again?"

"I think we're good," I squeak. "I'm just gonna go…" Hooking my thumb over my shoulder toward the dressing room, I turn on my heel without waiting for their approval. As I retreat to the only space where I can get a minute of privacy, I keep my pace steady and my head held high.

Nope.

That was plenty of acting for one day.

REESE

The energy in the truck is humming with anticipation as we drive home like *our* kiss never happened. Just Jon and Kristine's.

River's hands tap against the steering wheel in rhythm to the song on the radio while my knee bounces just as chaotically.

Tap. Tappity-tap-tap. Tap. Tap. Tappity-tap-tap. Tap.

"So that was…interesting," River mentions.

"Brett sounded optimistic, don't you think?"

"Yeah."

Tap. Tappity-tap-tap. Tap. Tap. Tappity-tap-tap. Tap.

"Do you think you'll get the part?" I ask.

He glances over at me. "No idea. But I think we put on a hell of an audition. And I have you to thank you for that."

"I didn't do much," I hedge, my cheeks heating.

"Bullshit. You rocked it in there, Reese. No offense, but when you said you dreamed of being an actor as a kid, I didn't think you had the talent to back it up."

"Gee, thanks," I mutter.

He laughs. "Seriously, I couldn't have asked for a better

partner. If I get the role, then it's because you helped me get it. Even going off-script played to our advantage. And the kiss? Damn, Reese. The director's gonna eat that shit up."

The kiss.

My gaze drops down to his mouth before I tear it away and stare out the windshield.

I liked the kiss. Loved it, actually. I loved that it made me feel alive. That it came from River. That I felt desirable. Wanted. All of it. But he's right. It was for the director. It wasn't for me.

It was *acting*.

Chewing on my thumbnail, I recount the moment for a few seconds, then wipe my fingers against my lips in hopes of dispelling the feel of his mouth pressed against mine.

It doesn't work.

Desperate for a distraction, I ask, "So, why does this role mean so much to you, anyway? You said you've never really been interested in acting, but this opportunity kind of fell into your lap."

The tapping on his steering wheel ceases, and he glances over at me again. "B.T. Henderson. Ever heard of him?"

"The director? Wait––*that's* the director for the film?" My eyes pop with disbelief.

"That's the one."

"He's huge, River."

"Yeah. He's considered one of the pioneers in the business. He's also one of the most critical directors and snubbed my mom when she was at the peak of her career."

I catch myself leaning closer to him, enraptured with the story as well as the man telling it. Realizing my behavior, I sit up a little straighter in the leather seat. "So, what happened?"

"When she was flying high with offer after offer, her agent put her up for *The Stars in Our Eyes*."

"The one that won all those awards forever ago?"

"That's the one. It got leaked that she was going after the part, and she was confident she'd get it. Personally, I think her publicist started the rumor, but what do I know? Then good ol' Henderson responded to the rumors that he'd rather use a mannequin to star in his film than hire the infamous Monet Cavier because not only was she impossible to work with, she had less talent than a...I believe the word he used was..."––he tilts his head to the side––"a gnat?"

Jaw dropping, I cover my mouth and try not to laugh. "Are you serious?"

"Yeah. My mom was pissed. Actually, pissed is an understatement. After that, the jobs that were once flooding in dried up overnight. She had to claw tooth and nail, sleeping with who knows how many directors to steal a few roles. But she was never the same."

"And yet you may or may not end up starring in one of the last films of his career," I point out.

His eyes dart over to me, holding so much restrained hope and ambition that I want to offer him the role right here and right now just to see him smile. If only I could.

"I guess we'll just have to wait and see," he murmurs, turning his attention back to the road.

"You know your mom will find out, though, right? There's no way she doesn't keep an eye on those kinds of things. Especially when it's in regards to her nemesis."

He laughs. "Nemesis. I like that. And it won't matter as long as she doesn't find out before B.T. Henderson watches that audition."

"But if she finds out first..." My voice trails off, and I wait for him to fill in the blank.

"Then she'll do what she does best and will meddle with the whole thing until Henderson probably won't watch the audition at all regardless of Brett's recommendation. If Henderson finds out I'm related to Monet Cavier before he officially offers me the role, then I can kiss the part goodbye. It's that simple."

"But...why?" I prod. "So, you're related to Monet Cavier. It's not *that* big of a deal, right?"

"Like I said, Reese. There's a reason I've tried to bury all my connections with her. She accused Henderson of slandering her name and even tried to sue him for it. Thankfully, the judge dismissed the case, but it still pissed off Henderson and basically blacklisted my mom from every project worth having. Then it was just a downward spiral from there." His knuckles turn white around the steering wheel before he adds, "She's...she's not a good person, Reese."

Hesitantly, I reach out and squeeze his knee. I don't know what makes me do it. Whether it's the insecure little boy that peeks through anytime he talks about his mom or if it's the big, strong man who has a habit of letting his guard down around me. Regardless, I like this side of him. The one that he hides from most people but lets *me* see. It makes me feel important. Needed. And maybe even special.

I've *never* felt special.

Or important.

Or needed.

Until him.

"I'm sorry, Riv," I murmur over the rumbling engine.

He shrugs. "Don't be. We all have our baggage, right? It's too bad we can't pick our families the way we can pick our friends."

"Maybe not by blood, but I'm pretty sure Milo looks at you and the rest of his guys like his family."

"Good point." He pauses as if considering my comment before looking down at my hand that's still touching his thigh. "He's my family too."

"Which means he can't know about the kiss." I lift my hand and place it back in my lap, hating the way my stomach tightens from the loss. But I'll never forgive myself if I get between them. And there's no way Milo would ever be okay if I kissed any of his friends. Even if it was for an audition tape.

River's aviators cover his eyes as he looks at me again. But I'd give anything to see them just so that I could have a hint about what he's thinking as he scans me up and down.

After a moment, he shrugs then turns his attention back to the highway. "We were acting, Reese. Not a big deal."

Right.

Acting.

Then why did it feel so right?

Silence encompasses the cab for the next thirty minutes before River pulls up the driveway and parks his truck. "So what're you doing tonight? Want to go out and celebrate with a few drinks for a successful photoshoot?"

I hesitate. This is *not* a good idea. I need space if I'm going to get my head on straight. But the chance to hang out with a guy I'm totally crushing on is almost impossible to pass up even though I know it's a terrible idea.

Maybe I really am weak.

"You don't have to," he adds with a laugh. "I can call Melanie or Steph––"

"No, no, no. I want to. It sounds fun."

The idea of waking up in the middle of the night to him humping away in the next room––again––is unbearable. Especially after our kiss. Even if it was meaningless for him, it stings just to hear him mention another woman's name. I can't imagine how awful it would feel to see him with one firsthand now.

No, thank you.

"Okay. Let me shower and see if any of the guys want to come. Then we'll go. Sound good?" he asks.

"Sure."

It would probably be a good thing if I wasn't alone with him right now, even if I *did* just agree to hang out with him so that I won't have to listen to a girl moaning all night. My emotions are already a frazzled mess, and if alcohol was added to my bloodstream, I'm afraid it would only be worse.

Besides, friends go out for celebratory drinks, right?

Right.

2 2

REESE

"Hey," Jake greets me from the doorway of my room. Sitting on the edge of my bed, I massage my sore feet from the stilettos at the photoshoot, then slip on my favorite pair of worn Chucks for the night.

"Hey," I return with a smile before pulling the heel of the shoe into place.

"I heard the photoshoot went well."

"It did."

Leaning against the doorframe, he adds, "That was nice of you to help River out."

"Oh. Thanks." I drop my gaze down to my lap and brush off a bit of nonexistent lint as memories of him accusing me that I slept with River my first night here filter through my mind.

"He said you did a great job."

"I didn't do much." I shove aside the image of River's mouth on mine as my guilt threatens to slip to the surface.

"And I beg to differ. River doesn't ask for help often. None of us do. But he said that you helped him out of a bind, and I want to let you know that I think that's great. I know

I've jumped down your throat more than once because of him, and I'm sorry."

"Seriously, Jake. It's not that big of a deal."

"It is," he corrects me, squeezing the back of his neck. "I know I've been an overbearing ass since you got here, but I'm proud of you for making friends with Sonny and River. You're growing up and can make your own decisions. I guess it just took me a little while to recognize it. I'm glad you're here."

"Thanks, Jake," I murmur before standing up and grabbing my purse. "That means a lot to me."

With a relieved sigh, he slips his hands into his front pockets and adds, "River mentioned you're going out for drinks..."

"Yeah, are you coming?"

His weight shifts between his feet before he mutters, "I can't tonight. I'm tutoring someone."

"Oh. Well, that's good. You're staying busy."

"Too busy lately," he admits before pulling his gaze from the ground and back to me. "Once things calm down a bit, I'd love to start hanging out more. Catch up, maybe?"

"Yeah, for sure. I've missed you, Jake."

"Missed you too."

He smiles shyly, and it reminds me of the old Jake I knew from high school. The insecure little nerd who couldn't even look at a girl without blushing, let alone kiss one. Sometimes, I forget he's still in there, especially now that he's a total stud. It's kind of adorable, actually. I still don't see him with women much, though. He's probably just too occupied with school. However, when he graduates, I'm going to have to find him a lady friend or two.

"Don't have too much fun without me, okay, Reese?"

"I wouldn't dare," I quip with a grin.

23

REESE

"So, has Ian still been calling you?" River asks before tipping back a shot of whiskey.

Milo had to work tonight, and Jake's tutoring someone from his class, which left River, Gibbs, and me. Sitting on the barstools with Gibbs' band playing in the background, I soak up the ambiance and try to ignore Gibson's frown as he registers River's comment.

"He's still calling you?" Gibbs demands.

I glare at River while twirling the straw in my fruity yet dangerously potent drink.

"Answer me," Gibbs orders.

"Sometimes…"

"He needs to leave you alone, or you need to get a restraining order. Right now, those are the only two options I can see," Gibbs announces.

Rolling my eyes, I take another sip of my cranberry vodka. "You're both being overly dramatic. It's fine. I know how to ignore a phone call."

"I think we should change her number," River mentions to Gibson. He presses his back against the chair to get comfortable, completely ignoring my presence. "Or we should go visit him again."

With a narrowed gaze, I mutter, "That won't be necessary."

"Won't it?" He locks me in his intense stare. "The guy won't leave you alone. Pretty sure that if he knew where we lived, he'd even be dumb enough to try knocking down your door."

"Then I guess it's a good thing he doesn't know where we live, huh? Speaking of people who won't leave other people alone...has anyone else noticed the table of girls over there?" I lift my chin to one of the booths in the back corner.

Gibson laughs but doesn't comment, while River doesn't even bother to look in their direction.

The combination piques my curiosity. "Do you guys know them?"

Another laugh.

"You could say that," Gibson confirms.

My face wrinkles in disgust. "Oh. You *know* them. Gotcha."

"Don't look so grossed out. I warned you that your room-mates have voracious appetites."

"I remember you mentioning your slutty ways. And believe me when I say I've heard them sneaking out in the middle of the night. But that doesn't mean I need to see your leftovers giving you guys googly eyes in the light of day."

"Who said they're leftovers?" Gibson challenges with a knowing grin before he stands and knocks his knuckles against the lacquered countertop. "I'll see you guys later. And congrats on the photoshoot. Riv, do you want me to save one for you?"

I almost gag but swallow it down as I wait for River's answer.

I shouldn't care.

I *know* I shouldn't care.

Hell, I'm going to wind up pissed regardless of whether or not he stays. Because if he does stick around, then that means he *knows* that I care, and that's even more annoying.

I don't want your pity, River.

"You should go and do…whatever the hell mansluts do on a Saturday night." I wave my hand through the air. "Don't mind me. I'll just be over here getting lost in my vodka cranberry."

Or maybe I can sneak a bottle of whiskey from behind the counter and can drown my sorrows in it.

Glancing over at me, River lifts his drink and takes a calm and collected sip before waving Gibbs off. "Nah. I'm tired tonight."

"Tired? Since when are you too tired to get laid?"

"Since tonight." He shrugs.

Gibson's gaze bounces between River and me before he throws a silent warning my way. I hear it loud and clear.

Be careful.

Ignoring him, I raise my glass in a silent toast before tipping the whole thing back. The indecision painted across his face is easy to read before Gibbs shakes his head and mutters, "See you guys later."

"Bye," I reply as he saunters off, leaving me alone with a River who––for once in his lifetime––is too tired for sex.

Yeah. I don't believe him either.

The question is, *why?*

"No sex?" The alcohol makes my tongue loose.

"Not in the mood," he grumbles in return.

I scoff. "Says the guy with the revolving door of women in his room."

"So you noticed?"

"It's hard to block out all the moaning," I answer in a syrupy sweet voice.

Resting his elbows on the counter, he leans closer. "Is someone jealous?"

"Of the girls moaning in your room?" I bristle. "Of course not."

"You sure about that?"

"Positive."

"Then why are you flushed right now by just thinking about it?"

Another scoff escapes me. "I am *not* flushed."

"Just like you're not jealous," he notes. "You're a terrible liar. You know that, right?"

"You wanna discuss lying?" I swivel on my chair and face him fully. "Okay. Let's discuss it. Tell me the truth. Since when are you *not* in the mood for sex? You can ask any of your roommates, and they'll call you out point-blank for being the biggest whore of the group. And that includes my brother, who likes to share women with Gibson, by the way. And what about that kiss, huh? The one between Jon and Kristine," I spit their names like a curse. "Because that was just acting, right? Or maybe we should mention the one that happened *after* Brett announced that he'd stopped recording the audition. What about that one, huh?"

My nostrils flare as the memories of his lips pressed against mine threaten to consume me.

"You want to discuss a fucking kiss, Reese? What are you, twelve?" River spits.

I flinch back and try to get a handle on my outrage when I know it's a losing battle.

Why can't you see *me*? Look at *me*? Want *me*?

"Twelve? Wow, River. Real smooth there. Tell me, was your cock rubbing against my ass during the photoshoot part of your *acting* too?"

Now, it's his turn to jerk away from me. "I'm sorry. Are

you pissed at me right now all because my dick got hard around you while you were rubbing up against me?"

"Oh, so it's my fault that I turned you on? Is that it? Oh, wait. What am I thinking? I didn't turn you on. It was all for show, wasn't it? Heaven forbid you'd actually be attracted to a girl like me when you could have anyone you wanted, right?"

I keep my hands clenched around my empty glass instead of rubbing away the phantom pain that's rooted in my chest at the idea of him wanting someone who isn't me.

Because *no one* wants me. Especially a guy like River.

"What the hell is your problem, Reese?" he growls.

Honestly, I don't even know. I'm being completely irrational right now, but I don't really give a shit. I *am* jealous. And I'm frustrated that I'm caught up in a guy that doesn't look at me the way I look at him. A guy who, under different circumstances, would be swaggering over to that group of girls right now with the intention of sleeping with one or two or hell, maybe even three of them. Yet here he is, hanging out with lil' ol' me, his best friend's baby sister. The thought burns. I need to get away from him before I start to spew more bullcrap that I know I'll regret in the morning.

Grabbing my purse from the counter, I slide off the barstool and fold my arms. "You know what? Forget I said anything. Go have fun getting laid or whatever it is you want to do tonight. I'm going home."

I march toward the back exit and pull out my phone to call Jake or Milo or a freaking Uber, for all I care. I just need to get out of here.

As the outside air kisses my cheeks, I try to clear my head and control my breathing when a pair of hands grab me from behind. Clawing at the stranger's grasp, my adrenaline spikes before my gaze lands on the culprit.

"What do you want from me, River?" I seethe.

The rough brick of the building bites into my back as River pushes me against it. But he doesn't answer me.

Nope. Instead, I'm gifted with a glare that nearly sets me on fire.

Crowding me with his massive frame, he drops his voice low and bites out, "You wanna talk about my cock, Reese?" He grinds against me. "About the way it gets hard anytime you walk into the room? Is that what you want to talk about? Should we dive into that kiss that's been consuming my thoughts since the moment it happened? Or maybe we should talk about the fact that I've been friends with your brother for years, and he warned me to stay away from you. Should we talk about that?" Again, he grinds against me. The back of my shirt inches up, causing that same cool brick to claw at my skin, but I welcome the slight sting of pain. It's a stark reminder that our actions have consequences. And this one's a doozy.

"Do you think he'd approve of my cock rubbing against you right now, Reese?" he rasps into my ear. "Do you think he'd appreciate the mornings I've spent in the shower jerking off while envisioning you on your knees in front of me?"

I whimper in response, squeezing my eyes shut in an attempt to block out the way his face is so close to mine. The way the streetlight bounces off his strong jaw and his heated gaze. The way I'd give anything to wrap my legs around him and soothe the ache pulsing at my core.

I've never wanted something so much in my entire life.

"Tell me, Reese. What the hell do you think we should talk about?" he demands. The heat from his breath is laced with alcohol but only adds fuel to the flames licking inside of me.

Pressing my back into the rough exterior, I turn my head away from him. "You're right. Go inside, River. Go work off your frustration with some other girl."

He slams his hand against the building, keeping me pinned between it and himself before he runs his nose along the column of my throat, breathing me in.

And I love it.

The push.

The pull.

The need.

I'm seconds from exploding, and he hasn't even kissed me.

When he reaches the shell of my ear, he growls, "Tried that already. Didn't take. Any other suggestions?"

I gasp as he continues his slow torture and brushes his lips against my skin before sucking a piece of the flesh into his mouth. My breathing quickens, but I can't think straight. Not when he's doing that. I'm going to end up with a freaking hickey on my neck if he doesn't stop this, but it'll be worth it if he just keeps--

"Answer me, Reese," River demands between sucking and biting. Fingers tangling in my hair, he tugs my head to the side, making my scalp tingle from his punishing grip. But he doesn't stop his delicious torture.

"U-unfortunately, I don't have the answers to all of your problems," I tell him with a moan.

Please, don't stop.

"You're right. You *are* the problem," he announces. "And I'm done playing games with you."

What? No!

I freeze as he stands to his full height and looks down at me with an expression that's a mixture of lust and disgust. I'm just not sure if he's sickened by me or if it's our actions that he finds so deplorable. Or maybe it's our betrayal against one of his best friends and *my* older brother if we let this go any further.

And I want it to go further. I *need* it to.

Still, the sting from his comment makes me pause, my forehead wrinkling in confusion. "You're done playing games with me? What the hell is that supposed to mean?"

"It means I'm taking you home, and I'm going to put us both out of our misery."

Oh.

24

REESE

ulling out his cell, River checks something on the screen before pressing his large, calloused palm against my lower back. I follow without protest as he guides me around the front of the building.

My anticipation rises with each passing second. Like I'm climbing to the top of a giant hill on a rollercoaster. And there's no escape. My only option is to just let go and enjoy the ride.

But I've never been very good at letting go.

"Where are you taking me?" I whisper.

"I already told you."

"Your truck is over there." I point in the opposite direction of where he's leading us.

"I'm not sober enough to drive, and the Uber is out front. Any more questions, Nancy Drew?"

A smile tugs at the corner of my lips before I bite my cheek to keep it at bay.

After checking the license plate on a dark blue sedan parked on the side of the street, River ushers me into the back of it. Then he slides in beside me and closes the door.

My pulse jumps as the jarring sound scatters the haze of lust and bad decisions I'd had wrapped around me.

This is a terrible idea. What are we thinking? Milo will kill me when he finds out. *If* he finds out.

I peek over at Riv, then stare at the unvacuumed carpet beneath my worn Chucks and tuck my hands under my thighs.

It's just one night. I can hide one night. We can pretend it never happened. My brother doesn't have to know. And we can finally give in to what we've both wanted for far too long.

Since the moment we met, I've been curious. I've wanted him. And what started as purely physical has transformed into...something else that I can't quite put my finger on. Which is ridiculous because I know River. For him, everything is just physical. There is no depth. No emotion. River doesn't *do* feelings.

And I don't do one-night stands.

So, where does that leave us? And why am I overthinking things?

It's just one night.

This is too real. Too much. We barely know each other. But in a way, he knows me better than I know myself, even though he's been fighting the pull between us as much as I have. He lets me feel free and supports me, pushing me to do absolutely ludicrous things that I would never do without him by my side. Like a photoshoot. And an audition tape. And climbing into the back of an Uber with the intention of having very hot, very sweaty sex with a guy who has zero intentions of ever committing to an actual relationship.

But none of that matters anyway. Anything more than a one-night-stand would never work. Milo would kill us.

Which means he can't find out. *Ever.*

River's heavy hand lands on my knee before he squeezes my thigh.

"You okay there?" River teases, his voice raw and gritty.

Looking down at where he's touching me, I realize I've been bouncing my leg up and down like a freaking jack-hammer as my anxiety started to eat me alive.

"Sorry," I mutter.

"Don't be."

If I didn't know any better, I'd say he can read minds and could tell I was seconds from having a mental breakdown. Yet, with a simple touch, every doubt is replaced with that same thick haze of curiosity. Want. *Need*. All of it seems to drive me insane anytime he's around.

With a thick swallow, my gaze finds his again, and my breathing turns shallow. His earlier resignation is gone, but his determination is so palpable I can hardly think straight. And by some miracle, it makes my own reservations disappear.

I want him. Not just physically. But emotionally too. I was wrong in the bar earlier tonight.

He *does* see me.

And no one has ever seen me before. Not really. Not without my layers pulled back to reveal the real me that I keep tucked away for safe-keeping.

And I'm tired of playing it safe. If a one-night-stand is all I can have, then I'm going to grab hold of it with both hands, and no one can stop me.

The car is silent other than the rev from the engine as River inches closer to me in the back seat.

With bated breath, I wait. Daring him to give in. To kiss me again. To push us both toward the inevitable fallout that will occur as soon as our lips touch another time.

And he *is* going to. I can feel it. I can see it. Hell, I can practically taste it. I lick my lips and close my eyes as my anticipation consumes me, that same insane roller coaster guiding me to the inevitable fall that has my stomach in the best kind of knots.

No wonder the ladies are always moaning in the room next to mine. This isn't his first rodeo. It isn't mine, either, but that doesn't stop my insecurities from roaring their loudest. It *is* my first one-night stand. And to him, I'm afraid that I'm just another faceless floozy in a long list of no-strings-attached sexual encounters.

Which is all I will ever be to him.

The thought makes me pause before I shake it off and lift my chin, giving him silent permission to kiss me.

In the back of a freaking Uber.

Because I'm *that* desperate to see if I imagined his addictive taste earlier today.

Please say I imagined it.

"Here we are," the driver comments, breaking the silence as he pulls up next to the curb in front of the house. Brows furrowed, I tear my attention away from River and search for the familiar voice's owner.

My jaw drops before I scramble to cover it with indifference.

No. No, no, no. Please don't recognize me. Please *don't recognize me.*

I chant the same thought over and over inside my head as I untuck my hair in hopes of hiding part of my face from our Uber driver.

River murmurs something to him, but the blood rushing through my ears drowns it out. I'm too distracted by the fact that one of Ian's best friends is currently behind the wheel of the car that just dropped us off at my brother's house. Which means that if he recognizes me, then Ian is going to know where I've been hiding.

River slides out of the seat, and I follow him carefully,

feeling like all the oxygen has been sucked out of the vehicle. If I can just get out of the damn car, then I'll be able to breathe again. And everything will be okay.

"Nice to see you again, Reese," the driver murmurs from the front seat. "I'll make sure to tell Ian you said hi."

Shit!

REESE

M y attention darts over to a very confused, very tense River outside the car. I'm not sure if he's going to yank me out of it or slam the door in my face and call it a night. With my luck, it'd be the latter. And I wouldn't blame him.

River clamps his jaw shut and crosses his arms but stays quiet to see how I'll react. Unfortunately, I feel just as helpless as he does.

Play it cool, Reese.

"Oh. Hey, Rocky. Long time, no see." I keep my tone light and casual. "I wouldn't bother telling Ian anything, though. He and I broke up."

"Does he know that?" the driver challenges with an arrogant smirk.

I force myself to my feet. Then I bend at the waist and hold the asshole's stare through the backseat of his sedan. "Yup. Thanks for the ride, Rocky. Good to see you again."

"You too," he replies, his tone thick with amusement as I close the door behind me.

Shit. Shit. Shit.

I watch his taillights disappear around the corner of our street, then wait for River's inevitable interrogation.

"Rocky, huh?" he grits out a few seconds later.

"Uh, yeah," I mutter. "He's an old...acquaintance."

"An old acquaintance that you met through an ex-boyfriend by chance?"

It isn't a question, but I answer him anyway, waving my finger through the air like a white flag. "Ding, ding, ding. We have a winner."

"Which means Ian is going to know where you live."

"Not if Rocky keeps his mouth shut."

"And how likely is that, Reese?"

Shrugging, I run my hands along my bare arms. "No idea. Rocky moved out here about six months ago. I don't know how well they keep in contact, but it doesn't matter because Ian and I are through. And that isn't going to change even if he's stupid enough to show up here."

I take a step toward the porch, desperate to end the conversation when River grabs my bicep and holds me in place. "If he shows up here, he's going to get his ass kicked. You know that, right? Whether it's me, Milo, Sonny, or even Jake, it'll happen."

"Jake?" My mouth curves up on one side, showcasing my dimple. "Jake's a lover, not a fighter."

"Says the girl he's in love with," River counters.

Convinced I heard him wrong, my smile slips off my face, and I cock my head to the side. "What are you talking about?"

"You didn't know?" River laughs, but it's laced with something I can't quite put my finger on.

Jealousy, maybe?

No. I don't think that's possible. A guy like River doesn't get jealous. Not when he can have any girl he wants.

"Jake doesn't love me," I argue.

"Bullshit."

"He doesn't."

"Are you really that blind, Floozy?"

As if I've been slapped, I jerk away from him. "Excuse me?"

Jaw tight, River rubs his hand across his face, then mutters, "Sorry. You're not blind. You're just...infuriating."

I scoff. "Oh, and that's more palatable? No offense, Riv, but if I didn't know any better, I'd say you were jealous."

"I don't get jealous."

"I know, which is why I'm so confused right now."

Tongue in cheek, he scratches his jaw and scans me up and down. And I can *feel* it. From the top of my head to the tip of my toes. I can *feel* his gaze in the moonlight. Like a caress. A whisper of a touch. A promise of what's to come if we walk through the front door and have sex the way we'd initially planned.

But still, he doesn't say a damn word.

Feeling exposed, I drop my gaze to the ground. "W-why are you looking at me like that?"

"You have no idea, do you?" he rasps.

"About what?"

"About how dangerous you are."

"Dangerous?" I throw my head back and laugh. "Hardly."

"You *are* dangerous," he reiterates, stepping closer until the toe of his shoe brushes against mine on the driveway that's still warm from today's sunshine. "For a guy like Jake." He tucks my hair behind my ear, then forces me to look at him. "For a guy like me."

"You're being ridiculous," I deflect.

"I'm being honest, though I doubt it'll get me anywhere. You're as stubborn as your brother. You know that, right?"

"I may have been told that a time or two. Speaking of Milo...we should go inside in case he comes home." I glance down the dark street and swallow hard. If my brother catches us, I'll never forgive myself. Hell, if Jake catches us, I'll never forgive myself.

But I don't want my––whatever this is––with River to end quite yet, either. I want to finish what we started in the alley. I need to.

River's hand drags down my bare arm before he tangles our fingers together and tugs me toward the porch. "Come on."

I follow without argument, though my brain feels like it's about to explode from so much overthinking. Why should I feel guilty for wanting someone that wants me too? This is so messed up. And I know I could back out, and River wouldn't hold it against me, but how is that fair?

Aren't I allowed to want something?

Aren't I allowed to live? And to be crazy? And to have fun?

Damn you, Milo.

Leading me to the front door, River pulls out his keys and unlocks it before asking, "What's wrong?"

I shake my head and step inside the dark house. "Nothing."

"Liar. I freaked you out, didn't I?"

It isn't a question.

"No. You didn't freak me out. I just…I wish this wasn't complicated," I admit. "You don't do complicated––"

"We all have our shit, Reese."

"And?" I press.

"And you're right. I don't do complicated."

Ouch.

Shaking off my hurt, I reply, "Exactly––"

"But I'm willing to do it with you."

"Because you want to sleep with me," I finish for him.

"Yeah, I wanna sleep with you, but not if it freaks you out."

"The repercussions--"

"Are worth it for me," he answers simply.

My breath hitches as he closes the door quietly behind us before he steps in front of me and runs the tip of his finger across the back of my hand lying limply at my side. His touch is soft. Gentle. Hell, it's nothing but a ghost of a touch that I would've missed if every single nerve in my body hadn't been on full alert since the photoshoot earlier today.

His chest rumbles, "But if the repercussions aren't worth it for you…"

I grab the collar of his dark T-shirt and pull him into me as I push aside the regret. The guilt. The unanswered questions that will still be there in the morning. I've had enough talking for one day. Enough overthinking. Enough stupid voices inside my head telling me what to do. What to want. What's enough. What isn't. Who I am. Who I should be. All of it.

Right now, I just want to feel.

I want to feel wanted.

I want to feel sexy.

I want to feel cared for.

I want to feel alive.

I want to let go and be free.

I want to feel River's mouth against mine.

I want to feel him moving inside of me.

No. I *need* it.

Not wasting any more time, River closes the last inch of distance between our lips, and I sigh at the contact.

This. This is exactly what I need.

And I'm done fighting it.

It's just one night.

26

REESE

The warmth from his kiss spreads like wildfire, burning me from the inside out. I tangle my fingers in his T-shirt, fumbling with the cotton fabric as if my life depends on it. I need to feel his bare skin against mine more than I've ever needed anything in my entire life.

He laughs and––much more eloquently––rips my shirt off before dropping it next to our feet. With his help, his shirt joins mine, and I grin as I take in his mussed-up hair before tugging him back to me so that I can taste him again. The kiss is hard. And messy. And mixed with a depth that I've never felt before.

Grabbing onto his shoulders, I jump and hook my ankles around his hips, then dive right back into his mouth. His kiss makes me feel like I'm baring my soul to him. Exposing all my flaws. My wants. My needs.

It's just a kiss, I remind myself.

Then why do I feel like I need it more than my next breath?

I almost whimper when his tongue dances with mine. He tastes like whiskey and dark chocolate. The combination makes my head spin as his fingers dig into my ass, pulling me closer.

Then he squats down, and I squeal, clinging onto him like a little monkey.

"What are you doing?" I whisper-shout even though I'm fairly certain we're the only people in the house.

"Grab our shirts," he orders against my lips.

Keeping one hand planted against his shoulder for balance, I squeeze my thighs, arch my back, and reach for the clothes scattered along the floor. River leans forward and presses a quick kiss between my breasts as if he can't help himself.

And I love it.

His need. His desperation. A small blossom of hope swells inside of me. That maybe we can figure this out. Maybe he really is willing to do *complicated*.

But where will that take us? I still have an older brother who would never approve of this moment.

It's just one night.

I shake myself back to the present then grab our shirts from the floor. With the fabric dangling from my fingertips, I do a half sit-up and wrap my arms around his neck.

"Got 'em," I whisper. Then I kiss him again, rubbing myself against his bare abs like a cat in heat.

Desperate much, Reese?

I can't get close enough.

River takes the stairs two at a time. His bruising grip beneath my butt only spurs me on until I'm a squirming mess in his arms. Licking. Biting. Sucking. Every inch of skin I can get my mouth on.

Again, that dark laugh greets my ears as he pauses in the doorway. "Your room or mine?"

"Mine," I answer.

He twists the handle then tosses me onto the bed like I

weigh nothing more than a feather. And I love that too. That he looks at me like I'm more than a damaged damsel in need of saving. That I can handle whatever he throws at me. That I'm not made of glass. And I love that even more. That I can feel delicate yet invincible whenever he's around.

He snakes his arms around my back and makes short work of my black lacy bra. When his large hands practically engulf my small breasts, my nipples pebble at the contact of his calloused palms.

Ian used to hate how small my breasts were. Always gave me shit for it, even though it's not like the size of my boobs is exactly within my control. But River's eyes are brimming with lust, and it's enough to dissipate the last of my insecurities.

I feel sexy.

Desirable.

Wanted.

Throwing my head back, I whimper and squeeze my eyes shut as he massages my aching breasts. How can he make something so simple feel so freaking good? I feel like every nerve in my body is humming with anticipation and longing. To be closer. To feel him inside of me. To be filled, both physically and emotionally, in a way that only he's capable of.

It's just one night.

Then his warm mouth replaces his left hand before he goes to work on the button of my jeans.

"Shit, Riv," I breathe, my voice nothing but a whisper. Fingers tangling with his hair, I hold him against me and curse under my breath like a damn sailor.

"You like that?" he teases, his whiskey-laced breath dancing along my sensitive skin.

Duh.

I don't bother to answer him as I slip my hand between us

and squeeze his hard length through his jeans in hopes of giving him a taste of his own medicine.

The groan that vibrates through his chest is like music to my ears.

"You like that?" I return with a coy smile before I let him go, then follow his lead and unbutton his pants.

Chuckling, he grabs the waistband of my jeans and tugs them off with one swift pull, leaving me in nothing but a pair of cotton red and white polka-dot boyshorts. Not exactly what I'd wear if I knew someone else was going to see them, but there's no use worrying about that now.

"Smartass," River murmurs, distracting me from my poor fashion choice. Cupping my cheeks with his rough hands, he cages me against the bed and kisses me again. It's probably in an attempt to keep me from replying with another snarky comment, but I'm not about to complain. Instead, I let our tongues duel it out, savoring every brush. Every flick. And every teasing taste that has me seconds away from begging him to put me out of my misery.

Because this? This is torture.

And I couldn't think of a better way to go.

Slowly, River makes his way to my neck and peppers a few more open-mouthed kisses along the column of my throat just like he did outside of SeaBird. Then he moves to my breasts again, lavishing each of them for a few seconds before continuing south. The cool air against my damp skin shocks my system, magnifying every single movement River makes.

His fingers dance along my inner thighs, turning my muscles into a puddle of need under his expert touch as he runs his nose along my entrance and breathes deep.

My hips buck off the mattress.

Shit.

I gasp and fist the cotton sheets in my hands, searching

for an ounce of control against this man's ministrations, but it's useless.

He freaking owns me.

His eyes connect with mine as he pulls off my underwear to reveal the most intimate part of me. A part that only one person has ever touched, let alone come face-to-face with. I'm not scared. *I'm terrified.* But some of the best things are on the other side of fear. And I'm sure as hell not going to turn back now.

This might be a terrible idea, but I can't blame this moment on alcohol. I'm as sober as a nun. And if River keeps looking at me like *that*, I think I just found my new religion.

"Riv––"

"Sh…"

With a cocky grin, he dives right in, lapping at my folds as his fingers rim my entrance before slowly slipping inside of me.

My jaw drops, and my hands squeeze the sheets until my knuckles turn white. Ian didn't do this. Not after the first few times we were intimate, anyway. Sure, blow jobs were great, grand, and wonderful, but returning the favor wasn't exactly part of his repertoire. Honestly, I didn't think I was missing much. Obviously, I was wrong about that one.

"Shit, Riv," I breathe out.

I can feel his smile against me, but he doesn't stop. If anything, my curse only spurs him on, and it doesn't take long for a scream to slip past my lips.

It's official. The guy has a magic mouth. One that is currently torturing me in a way that I've never experienced in my entire life. As my heels dig into his shoulders for leverage, my back arches off the mattress, and I shamelessly press myself against him, desperate for the final push that'll bring me to oblivion.

"Right"––I gasp––"*there.*"

My skin feels too tight. My breath feels too forced. As if I need to fall apart, but I don't know how.

"River——"

Like waves against a rocky cliff, my orgasm crashes into me. And he lets me ride out the moment as if he has all the time in the world. Licking. Biting. Sucking. Pumping his fingers in and out of me until I can't take it anymore. I push him away and let my legs open limply. I'm too sensitive. Too drained. Yet on cloud freaking nine and desperate for more.

It's just one night.

Without a word, he climbs on top of me, pushes his boxers off, and lines himself up with my entrance.

"You ready?" he murmurs against my heated skin.

A dry laugh escapes me. "Stick a fork in me, Riv. I'm done."

"I'd rather stick a cock in you if you don't mind," he jokes, rubbing the head of his erection along my damp slit. All the blood in my body rushes low, prepping me for round two in record time. And despite my over-sensitized flesh, I'm *so* ready for round two.

"I mean, if you insist," I tease.

"I'm clean. Are you on the pill?"

"Yes," I whisper.

His smile is tight before he pushes into me in one long thrust.

Shiiiit.

Jaw slack, I dig my fingers into his back and attempt to catch my breath.

The guy isn't small, and my muscles tense at the foreign intrusion because, let's be real, Ian doesn't compare to the man inside of me.

"Wait," I whimper, blowing out the oxygen from my lungs.

"Sh…" He kisses my forehead softly before placing

another one against my lips. And in this moment, I feel cherished. Seen. And like I'm more than a one-night stand.

But maybe that's why he's so good at them. He makes all of his floozies feel special. Important. Like more than just an easy lay. And if that's the case, then we should hand this guy an Academy Award. Because that's exactly what he's doing to me.

It's just one night, I remind myself for what feels like the thousandth time. I should enjoy it instead of comparing myself to his previous conquests. Right now, he's with me. He *chose* me. And I'm going to soak up every second of it.

After a moment, I relax and give him a nod.

"You okay?" His gaze is filled with an intensity that I can't quite put my finger on as it bounces around my face to assess my sincerity.

Again, I nod as an amused smile takes over my expression. "Yeah. You're kinda cute when you're concerned, though."

"Is that right?"

"Mm-hmm," I hum before wrapping my arms around his neck and pulling him closer. This. This closeness. This longing finally being placated. It's exactly what I never knew I needed.

With another soft kiss against him, I add, "Seriously. I'm good. You can uh…move now."

"You sure?"

"Duh."

Hooking my legs around his hips, I swivel mine in hopes of encouraging him to get to work. It seems to do the trick. His back muscles ripple beneath my fingertips as he thrusts into me slowly at first before picking up speed when I don't protest.

It doesn't take long for that sweet ache to build inside of

me again as I match River's rhythm and scrape my nails along his bare back.

Yes. Yes. Yes.

His skin is slick with sweat, and I sneak a taste of the salty moisture along his neck before biting down roughly.

It's never been like this before.

Ever.

And I had no idea what I was missing out on until now.

Good job, Riv. You've officially ruined me.

With a low, guttural groan, he picks up his pace and pushes me over the edge a second time. Then he tumbles right after me. Chest heaving, I try to catch my breath as he collapses on top of me and attempts to do the same. His massive frame isn't suffocating, though. It's...comforting somehow. And I'd give anything to do this again. And again.

But we *can't.*

It would kill my brother. And after everything he's done for me, I could never betray him like that.

But I can pretend. Even if it's just for one night.

A few seconds later, River rolls onto his side then pulls me against him. I tuck myself into his chest and listen as his galloping heart slowly steadies into a slow, content rhythm that seems to match my own.

The silence surrounding us is comfortable. Peaceful, maybe. And I soak it up as he drags his fingers through my messy hair, sending tingles dancing along my scalp.

I grin against his chest and savor the feeling, wishing I could bottle it up and save it for a rainy day.

He laughs. "Didn't know you were a cat."

"Huh?"

"You're practically purring."

"Well, I'm feeling pretty good right about now," I admit with a sheepish grin. But I don't dare to look up at him. If I do, he might see how happy I am now that my walls are down. How happy he makes me. And that's dangerous. It makes me feel vulnerable. And if I've learned anything from my past, it's that vulnerability isn't exactly a strength.

"What are you thinking about?" he asks.

"Just that..."--I swirl my finger around his tight little man nipple--"I guess I can see what all the fuss is about."

His chest rumbles with amusement. "Glad I can be of service, Floozy."

That same sheepish grin nearly splits my face in two as I work up the nerve to rest my chin against him so that we're eye to eye. "Is that all I am to you? Your floozy?"

Gaze softening, he brushes a few strands of hair off my forehead then runs his thumb along my flushed cheeks. "Would it freak you out if I said yes and claimed you for myself?"

My chest tightens. "Would you want to?"

A ghost of a smile flashes across his face before disappearing just as quickly. "Ladies first. Didn't I already prove that once tonight?"

I laugh. "Always the gentleman."

"You know me."

My amusement fades slightly as I consider his question. "We can't."

"Why not?"

"You don't do relationships, remember?"

"I've never done them in the *past*," he clarifies. "That doesn't mean I don't want to try it with you. You're more than a casual lay, Reese. If you weren't, I wouldn't have jeopardized my friendship with your brother."

My brother.

How can two simple words be so sobering?

"Riv...I don't want you to jeopardize your friendship with Milo."

"I won't."

"You don't know that," I argue, chewing on my thumbnail. "Milo is…"

"Overprotective. I get it."

"You don't, though. We've always *only* had each other. Hell, you didn't even know I was a girl when I first showed up. That's how overprotective he is. He was the only one who cared about me growing up, you know? And the last time I ignored his advice, I ended up in a really bad relationship––"

"And you think a relationship with me would be bad too?" he challenges.

"No. That's not what I meant. I just…"

"Just what, Reese?"

"Look, can we just…stop talking for tonight? And enjoy this moment? Because I was feeling pretty good two seconds ago, and I'd like to keep it going for a little longer before reality catches up to us. I like you, okay? And I don't usually do one-night stands. If I did, I would've picked up a random guy at a bar instead of my roommate. But I didn't do that, obviously, because I'm not that kind of girl. I've only ever been with one other person, River. Sex is…it's an emotional thing for me, okay? I don't do it just to get off. I can take care of that on my own."

Those same green eyes darken with lust, and I smack him in the chest. "Oh, come on, ya big horndog," I tell him in hopes of lightening the mood. "I'm just saying that I like you, okay? And not just because you delivered the best freaking orgasms I've ever experienced."

"Best orgasms, eh?"

My cheeks are starting to hurt from smiling so hard, but I seem to do that a lot when I'm around him. And even though we're discussing some heavy shit, I like how light he still manages to make me feel. "You're ridiculous."

"I am," he acknowledges before pulling me back into him.

"But I wasn't kidding when I said I liked you and that I'd like to give this thing a real shot. Just say the word, and I'm in. I'm *all* in."

"And if I say yes? What then? What about Milo? What about Gibson and Jake? What do we do? What do we say? I just...I don't know! This is so far out of my element that I have no idea how to handle this situation."

"Neither do I, but we'll figure it out."

"You make it sound so easy."

"Easy is overrated. And I'm not the only here who likes it"--he lifts his hips to showcase his swelling erection--"hard."

Rolling my eyes, I swing my leg over his hips and get ready for the next round because he's right. I've never been one to take the easy road. And in this case, I definitely like it *hard*.

Crap.

I really am his Floozy.

At least for tonight.

27

REESE

roggily, I wake up to my phone vibrating in the pocket of my jeans that are still scattered along the ground from yesterday. With absolutely zero desire to answer it, I shove my pillow over my head and squeeze my eyes shut as if that'll make the damn thing stop.

Shocker.

It doesn't.

"You gonna get that, Floozy?" a deep voice mumbles beside me.

My heart leaps in my chest before my brain catches up and places the familiar voice.

River.

In my bed.

Naked.

I'll take it.

With a soft smile, I nuzzle into his warm chest. "Morning."

"Morning," he returns in that same gritty voice. "You gonna answer your phone?"

"It can go to voicemail."

"It's already gone to voicemail."

My head is too fuzzy for riddles, so I mumble, "Huh?"

"It's been buzzing for the past fifteen minutes."

I groan and burrow a little closer to him, making sure the sheets keep us covered as I get lost in his heat. There's something comforting about morning snuggles. They scream security and bliss. Two things I wasn't exactly raised with, and therefore, two things I crave more than anything else in the world. I want to soak up as much of it as I can before reality hits, and I have to pretend that River and I are just friends. Or face the repercussions that we're more than that, and neither option sounds very appealing.

"Come on, Floozy. The damn thing is giving me a headache, and you don't want to know what'll happen if I get up to turn it off and I see your ex's name flashing across the screen."

"To be fair, I changed his name to Dickwad, so you wouldn't see his real name."

"That's a small technicality. You sure you wanna toy with that idea?"

"No," I grumble, throwing off the sheets. "Besides. Like I said, I blocked his number so it wouldn't pull up by his name, anyway." The cold from the floor seeps into my bare feet as I pad across it in search of my blasted phone. When I find it, my expression falls.

"It's him, isn't it?" River murmurs.

Technically, I don't know for sure since it's a random number, but my look says enough.

"Let me answer it, Reese."

With a jerky shake of my head, I mumble, "I'll take care of it." Then I slide my thumb along the screen and lift the phone to my ear.

"What do you want?"

"Hey, baby."

I glance over at River. "I'm not your baby anymore, Ian. Why are you calling me?"

"Because I heard you *think* you're not my baby anymore," he spits, his anger slowly rising with every passing second. "Which one is he, huh? Is it the pretty boy? The one who sucker-punched me? Did you fuck him yet? I bet you did, didn't you? You're such a fucking slut. You know it was a pity fuck, right? Something to pass the time. You're not pretty enough to be actual girlfriend material for anyone but me, remember? Do you understand that, baby?"

There isn't anything for me to say, but I still search for a way to make him understand we're not together anymore. Why does he act like he still cares about me? Why does he think he wants me when he's never wanted me before? And why would River be interested in a girl like me when I have baggage like Ian, who won't leave me alone?

"Answer me!" Ian barks like a rabid dog.

I cringe at the familiar tone and squeeze my eyes shut to push away the memories. The moments when his spit would fly through the air and sprinkle down on me as he yelled at me for another stupid situation that was out of my control. Yet here I am, dealing with it all over again.

A set of strong arms snake around my waist as River pulls me against him. I curl into his touch. Carefully, he takes the phone out of my grasp and puts it to his own ear.

"Hey, man. I'm gonna need you to calm down," River consoles, keeping his tone calm.

"Hey, motherfu--"

"I'm gonna stop you right there." Looking down at me, his jaw clenches before he continues. "You do not own Reese. She is not an object. She is a person. And while I agree that you lost the best thing that ever happened to you because you couldn't keep it in your pants, it's over. You don't get to dictate when someone falls in or out of love with you. She's made it very clear she isn't interested anymore. You need to let her go, and you need to stop calling her. If that is too difficult for you, then I'll have to intervene and trust me when I say that you really don't want me to have to do that. Understand?"

So this is what it's like. To have someone calm and level-headed who cares about you. If he weren't my brother's best friend, I could get used to it. Burrowing a little deeper against him while simultaneously pushing away reality, I feel River's steady heart against my ear as we wait for Ian's response.

The silence, however, is unbearable. I just want him to leave me alone. Is that too much to ask?

"You'll be through with her by the end of the week," Ian growls.

Click.

The call disconnects, and River drops his arm to his side.

"That could've gone worse," he offers dryly.

With a breath of laughter, I squeeze him a little tighter, then press a kiss against his bare pec. "I think you did the best that you could. Although I'm not sure how well he'll take the thinly veiled threat you tacked on at the end. He's always been a sucker for a pissing match."

"He needs to understand that he can't bully you anymore. You're not alone. And even if last night had never happened, you would still have me, Sonny, Jake, and Milo to rely on."

"You guys are too good to me."

"Nah. You're just not used to being treated like a real human being. Don't worry, though." His arms tighten around me. "We'll warm you up to the idea. Does Milo know Ian's still bothering you?"

"It's fine––"

"I'll take that as a no."

Biting the inside of my cheek, I admit, "Not gonna lie. It's worked out quite nicely that Jake's been busy with his thesis and tutoring and that Milo's been working his butt off to earn enough money to buy his boss' shop off him. If either of them found out Ian is still trying to contact me, it wouldn't be pretty."

"It still isn't pretty, Reese."

"I know," I whisper, the weight from his phone call catching up to me. "I just don't get it."

"Don't get what?"

"Why won't he leave me alone. Why does he even care that we're over? Is he really that possessive of me? I'm not that special––"

"Bullshit," River growls.

"You know what I mean. I just...I don't get it. We didn't even have a good relationship. He pushed me around and made me feel like shit. Oh. And I helped his brother do his accounting, but that's about it. Why won't he let me move on?"

"Because he doesn't care about what you want, Reese. He looks at you like you're an object. A thing to own. He doesn't care about your wants or your needs. He only cares about what *he* wants. And right now, he still wants you."

"Which is ridiculous––"

"I don't want you going anywhere alone," River decides. "I have a feeling his little Uber buddy told him where you live, and I wouldn't be surprised if he showed up here to confront you."

Opening my mouth to argue, I slam it closed just as quickly and bite my tongue as my fear threatens to claw its way up my throat.

He's right.

I never thought Ian was *that* crazy, but he's shown his true colors since the breakup. I'm not entirely sure what he's capable of anymore. And that's what's so scary about the whole thing.

Another buzzing sounds throughout the room, but it isn't my cell this time.

"Where's your phone?" I ask.

He shrugs before rummaging through his clothes. When he finds it, the screen lights up before his annoyance spikes.

"What's wrong?" I ask.

"Nothing."

"You can tell me."

With a sigh, he rolls his shoulders then tosses his cell behind him onto my unkempt bed. "My mom. She's been calling."

"Why?"

"I dunno."

"I thought you guys weren't talking."

"We're not," he answers.

"So…are you gonna call her back?"

"And ruin my entire day? No, thank you."

With a frown, I inch closer to him and rest my hand on his forearm. "Is it that bad?"

"She either forgets I exist or calls over and over again until I answer, and she gives me her latest sob story. She's a wreck, Reese."

"Speaking of wrecks and sob stories, I may have seen her face on a gossip magazine the other day."

"The one where it says she's a washed-up actress with too much plastic surgery?"

Grimacing, I mutter, "That's the one."

"Yeah. I saw it. Usually, she spirals after something like that, gets desperate for good publicity, and thinks I'm her golden ticket. Hell, she's been begging me for years to do a PR stunt with her in hopes of gaining a few brownie points with moms and shit, but I've always refused. As far as everyone knows, her son disappeared twenty years ago, and I plan on keeping it that way for as long as possible."

"Won't she just keep calling?"

"Probably." He snorts. "I've even had my number changed in the past when it gets particularly bad, but she always manages to find my new one, so I've learned it's a waste of effort."

"Are you sure––"

"Hey, Reese?" a voice interrupts from the opposite side of my closed door.

My eyes widen in fear of being caught naked with River, and I shove him away from me. The bastard barely moves an inch and shrugs his shoulders as if to say, *what do you want me to do right now?*

I mouth, *Hide!*

Rolling his eyes, he grabs his discarded jeans from the floor before ducking into the closet. Then he closes the door as quietly as he can, but it still causes a soft creak to echo throughout the otherwise silent room.

"Reese?" the voice calls again.

"Just a second!"

Fumbling for the nearest shirt I can find, I slip it over my head before realizing it's the same one River wore yesterday.

Motherfu––

"Reese? You okay in there?"

"Yup!" I squeak, bouncing up and down on the balls of my feet like the little Energizer Bunny while having a complete mental breakdown. There's no time to change. He's going to know. I'm going to get caught. And I'm not one hundred percent sure which bruting roommate is on the other side of the door. I'm so freaking royally screwed that it's not even funny.

The sweet ache between my legs pulls a pathetic, whim-

229

pery laugh out of me as I realize that I have, indeed, been royally screwed recently.

Damn it, River!

This. This is why it'll never work between River and me. I can't do this. I can't hide him away in a closet. I can't pretend everything is hunky-dory and that I didn't stab my brother in the back last night while his best friend stabbed me with his monster cock.

My face scrunches at the imagery.

Ew.

"Can I come in?" that same voice asks through the door.

Welp, I guess that crosses off Milo as the culprit. The bastard would've just barged right through.

"I'm coming!" I return.

Hopping over to the door, I open it a crack, then peek my head through to find Gibson on the other side.

"Hi," I greet him with a forced smile.

"Hey. You okay there?" An amused grin graces his lips as he looks me up and down, taking in my disheveled appearance.

"Yup. How can I help you?"

"I just wanted to make sure you got home okay."

"Yup. All safe and sound."

"Have you seen River? His truck isn't out front, and he isn't answering his cell."

"Oh." *Shit.* "He, uh, he got me an Uber, then sent me home a few minutes after you left to hang out with those...*ladies.* I'm not sure where he went after that."

"I thought I heard him with a"––he clears his throat––"*guest* last night, but then I didn't see his car this morning, so maybe I imagined it. Did you hear anything?"

Feeling like my face is on fire, I shrug and try to cover up my embarrassment with an awkward laugh, but he sees right through it.

"You sure you're okay?" he prods.

"Yup. And yes, I heard it too. He was up all night humping a floozy, so, ya know, that's a lot of fun."

Gibson's amusement falls. "Shit, Reese. I didn't think about how that would make you uncomfortable since you like him."

"I don't like him," I scoff while hating the fact that a certain someone is hiding in my closet and is hearing first-hand about my crush on him. It doesn't matter that we've just slept together. Right now, I feel like a teenager who just got caught drooling over the popular guy in school. The popular guy who could have any girl he wants but is slumming it with me for the time being.

Great.

Gibbs smirks before pointing out, "You're wearing his shirt."

I look down at the dark fabric that practically swallows me whole, then fist the fabric in my sweaty palms at my sides. "T-that's because he loaned it to me on my first night, and it's comfortable. It has nothing to do with the manwhore who owns it, okay?" I cross my arms and lean against the door jamb, daring him to argue.

Because he has an ounce of self-preservation, he drops it. "Oookay, then. If you want me to talk to him and ask that he goes over to his floozy's place instead of inviting them over here for a little while, just let me know. I can blame it on my muse or something. But trust me, you need to keep this as an unrequited love kind of relationship. If you pursue something with him, you're going to wind up getting hurt, and Milo will never forgive River for that."

Sobering, I release a shaky breath and drop my gaze to my bare feet before whispering, "I know, Gibbs."

"If you hear from him, let me know, okay?"

"I will."

Turning on his heel, Gibson walks back into his room and leaves me alone with way too many *what if's* before my morning coffee. I close the door, then sit on the edge of my bed, resting my head in my hands as the closet opens and River unfolds himself from the tiny space. Striding over to me, he sits down and pulls me into his side.

"Hey. You okay?"

I shake my head back and forth. "Not really."

"He's wrong, Reese."

"Is he, though?" I argue, peeking up at him with red-rimmed eyes. "'Cause I think he has a pretty valid point."

"That's bullshit, and you know it. I told you last night that I want you."

"Yeah, but for how long, Riv? I'm just a shiny new toy who happens to be your best friend's little sister. It's not like a girl like me would ever hold your interest."

"You think I would risk my friendship with Milo for a shiny new toy? Bullshit," he spits, his spine straightening. "You mean more to me than a one-night stand, Reese."

"I can't betray my brother like that——"

"You've already betrayed your brother. We had sex, Reese. And despite how shitty you perceive me, it meant something to me."

"It meant something to me too," I whisper.

That same penetrating gaze pins me in place as he cups my cheek, rubbing away a bit of yesterday's mascara while managing to still make me feel beautiful. And I hate it. That I crave his touch. His smiles. The confidence he gives me. All of it.

"I like you, Reese," he murmurs.

"I like you too, Riv."

"I want to give this a shot." He gives me a defeated smile. "I want the damn label."

Biting my lower lip, I close my eyes and lean into the palm of his hand. "I don't think I can give you that--"

"Why not?"

"Because as soon as you have it, you'll get bored of me," I whisper, hating the way my voice cracks at the end. "You'll be ready to move on before Milo even has time to wrap his head around the idea that I'm dating one of his best friends. And where does that leave us, huh? I'm just a shiny new toy to you--"

"Bullshit, Reese." The warmth from his touch disappears before he shoves himself to his feet and paces back and forth in my room. Running his fingers through his mussed-up hair, he tugs on the roots and seethes, "Do you really think I'm that shallow? That I would risk my friendship with your brother over a shiny toy?"

"Do you blame me? That's your MO."

"Bullshit," he repeats.

"It's not bullshit," I argue, my sadness morphing into something sharp and bitter. "You don't do relationships--"

"But I would for you."

"Don't lie to me--"

"I'm not the one lying, Reese. You told me last night that you can't do sex without emotions." He waves his hand at me. "Yet, look at you now. I tell you I want the real deal, and you won't even let me prove myself. That's bullshit, and you know it."

"My brother," I choke out. "My brother would never forgive me."

"That's bullshit too. Your brother and I are friends, Reese. He knows me. He knows that I don't do anything half-assed. He knows that I would treat you like gold if I told him I was all in."

My pulse races as I cover my quivering lips. "River, don't--"

"Don't what?" he growls. "Don't tell him?"

"Please," I whisper, tears streaming down my face. "I can't let him know that I betrayed him. It was just one night––"

"To you," he finishes for me. "To you, it was just one night. To me, it was more than that."

He storms toward the door before squeezing the handle so tight I'm surprised it doesn't break off.

"River––"

"Don't worry. I won't say anything."

Then he's gone. And I feel more broken than ever before.

28

REESE

"Hey, Oscar," Dove teases as I wipe down one of the tables.

With my head cocked to the side, I mutter, "Oscar?"

"As in, the grouch. Oscar the Grouch. Why so glum, chum?"

Mouth curved in amusement, I scan the crowded bar before admitting, "I had a shitty morning."

"What kind?"

"The worst kind."

"Can I help?" she asks.

"I don't know. I'm in a conundrum, and I don't know what to do about it."

"What kind of conundrum?"

"One that's…complicated."

"Trust me. I know *complicated.* Maybe not personally, since my own life is the most boring thing on the planet, but I'm a great listening ear to my older sister who's entire life is the definition of complicated. I'd be happy to play the part for you, too, if you want."

"You don't have to do that," I hedge, though a tiny voice inside of me is screaming at me to spit it out. Am I being ridiculous? Should I give River and me a real shot? Would that ruin everything if I did?

Things would be so much easier if I could examine my situation from a bird's eye view. Right now, I know I'm too close to everything. Too attached. Too helpless to listen to logic. I'm too freaking caught up in my emotions and the potential fallouts that are leaving me paralyzed to fight for what I want.

I do want River.

I just don't know how to *keep* him. And if, by some miracle, I manage to, how can I keep my brother's trust? It feels impossible.

Dove slips the rag from my hands, then sets it against the table and offers, "You can talk to me, you know. I know we don't know each other very well, but I'm not exactly a gossip kind of girl, and I promise to never repeat anything you tell me in confidence. And…call it a hunch, but you look like you could use someone to open up to."

"Is it that obvious?"

"Maybe a little."

I puff out my cheeks before letting it bubble out of me in a not-so-steady breath. "Fiiiine. I met someone. And he's awesome. And he says he wants to be with me. But he's also a manwhore who doesn't exactly do relationships, which is terrifying because I'm not all that great, you know? Why would he want to stick around for me? And then, as a nice little cherry on top, he's friends with my brother, who's adamantly against us dating, which means I'm screwed. I don't want to stand in the way of their friendship, but I don't want my brother to stand in the way of our potential relationship, either. And that sucks because my brother is literally the only person in my life who's ever really cared about me," I ramble. "The thought of him not approving of my relationship with his friend…it really sucks, Dove."

"Hmm," she hums, tapping her trimmed fingernail against her chin. "That *is* quite the conundrum."

"I know."

"Okay. First of all, you're amazing, and gorgeous, and nice, and you need to give yourself more credit. He'd be a fool not to want you, so if he's willing to try a relationship with you, and that's what you want, then you can't let your insecurities hold you back. As for the brother predicament, how long have you liked his friend? Is it like a spur of the moment kind of deal, or have you felt something for him for a while now and are just now considering acting on it?"

"*Considering?*" I grimace.

She gasps before giving me a surprised grin. "Dang, girl. I'm jealous. Okay, so *something* has already happened. The question is, what is it, how are you handling it, and how are you and Mystery Boy going to move forward?"

"Ladies!" Ashton calls while weaving in between tables with a tray in his hands. "Less chatting, more cleaning."

"Sorry!" we both return in unison.

My damp rag is still resting on top of the table, and I pick it up before turning back to Dove. "We should have a girls' night or something. Then I can maybe pick your brain a bit more."

"Okay." She smiles shyly and decides, "I like that idea. Are you free tomorrow?"

"Yeah. Then I can give you all the gory details about epic sex and my messy love life."

Her cheeks heat. "Sounds like a plan since epic sex and a messy love life are about as foreign to me as walking on the moon."

"Wait, you've never had sex?" I ask.

"Um…nope."

"Seriously?"

Dove shakes her head. "My parents are super old and super religious. I was their golden child before moving in with my sister, who was disowned after she came home and told us she was pregnant. So, nope. No sex for this girl."

"That's…" I pause, praying I haven't offended her. "That's cool?"

"No, it's depressing," she corrects me with another shy smile.

"It's not depressing––"

"It totally is, but it's okay. Honestly, it's probably a good thing. The idea of being the center of a guy's attention is full-blown terrifying to me. And the idea of disappointing my parents after the way my sister broke their hearts? Well… that's also terrifying. Anyway. Yes. I'm free tomorrow and would love to have a girls' night if I didn't scare you off with my unconventional past. What time works for you?"

"Um…maybe sometime after seven?" I offer.

"Okay, perfect. Do you mind if we go somewhere cheap, though? I know that sounds super trailer trashy, but because my sister's pregnant and the guy was a jerk who left her high and dry, I've been saving every single penny to pay for diapers once Baby comes."

Damn. That sounds rough. My life might be a mess right now, but at least I'm not pregnant with some asshole's baby. Sounds like a piece of work to me.

"Sure thing," I answer her. "Why don't you just come over to my place tomorrow night, and we can watch Netflix and binge ice cream while I tell you all my woes?"

"Sounds like perfection to me. Can I bring anything?"

"Nope. We have a bunch of junk food in the fridge that no one touches but me, and I need help getting rid of it. Let me text you my address, and you can meet me there."

"Okay, thanks. And I look forward to getting all the dirty

details later so I can live vicariously through you." She bounces her eyebrows up and down.

"Glad I can be of service," I return, feeling lighter than I have since the moment River stormed out of my room. My life might still be a shitshow, but at least I can share it with someone.

"As for your problems and what little information I have so far, the only advice I can offer is to think about the way Mystery Man makes you feel. If you feel better and happier when you're around him, then I think that's all your brother really wants. Even if he never expected his friend to be the one to help you find that happiness."

Well, shit.

When she puts it like that, the answer seems obvious. But it can't be that easy. Not when Milo is involved. Not when River is known for having a short attention span. Still. He does make me happy. Really happy. Maybe Dove has a point.

"That's...deep," I mutter, the wheels in my head still churning a million miles a minute.

Dove's laugh is light and bubbly and snaps me out of my chaotic thoughts. "See? I told ya that I'm a good listening ear. Now, I gotta get back to work because Ashton is giving me the evil eye, and my people-pleasing heart is not liking it. Will you handle Gibson's orders tonight, and I'll deal with Sammie?"

"Again?" I ask. She's been avoiding Gibson since her first day and only stares at him from afar. I just wish I knew why.

"It's not a big deal," she mutters. "Sammie's just...nicer. We'll chat later, okay?"

"Sounds good. See ya."

The next thirty minutes go by in a blur as SeaBird continues to fill with more customers.

After cleaning a few more tables, I head to the bar to grab another tray that needs to be delivered.

"Hey, will you take this to your brother's table?" Gibson yells over the music.

I glance behind me and scan the crowded area. "Milo's here?"

"Yeah. Corner booth with Jake," he tells me before setting a pitcher on my tray with a few clean glasses.

So, no River.

Noted.

My relief that he isn't with Milo and Jake is quickly replaced with disappointment.

I miss him. Especially after the way we left things. I just want to apologize. I want to make everything better. I want to go back to last night and savor his taste a little longer. I just want him.

And I hate it.

"So, you gonna deliver this or...?" Gibbs asks.

"Yup. I got it," I answer him. "Quick question, though."

"Yeah?"

"Why have you been such a jerk to Dove?"

"I haven't been a jerk."

"Seriously? You've been super cold with her since her first day. It's to the point where she only deals with Sammie for drinks and makes me come to your surly ass every night. I wanna know why."

He squeezes the back of his neck as his attention shoots to where Dove is taking a group of frat boys' orders.

"Tell me," I push.

"There's nothing to tell. I'm this way with most of the girls who work here."

"It's true," Sammie, the other bartender, interrupts. "He was an ass to me for six months until he found out I wasn't attracted to *asshole*."

"What's that supposed to mean?" I ask.

"It means that being an ass is how he keeps employee fraternization down. Am I right, Gibbsy?" she teases, turning to him.

"Get back to work, Sam," he grunts.

"Wait," I interrupt. "So, because she's an attractive coworker who, under normal circumstances, you'd want to have sex with, you've decided it's okay to be a jerk to her?"

His expression sours. "I don't shit where I eat."

"What does that even mean?"

"It means that even though he'd like to get in Dove's pants, he makes sure to keep his charisma turned down *extra* low so that she doesn't get the wrong idea and try to jump his bones," Sammie interjects.

"You're insane," I point out to Gibson.

"And you're supposed to be working," he returns, dipping his chin to the brimming pitcher and glasses on the tray in front of me.

I glare back at him, then pick it up. My balance isn't anything to write home about, so I grab the tray with both hands and rest it against my hip as I bob and weave between patrons and tables.

"Hey, guys. Fancy seeing you here," I greet them, avoiding Jake's gaze. After River's little declaration the day before, no matter how inaccurate it is, I feel uncomfortable. Which is ridiculous. It's Jake. My Jake.

Get a grip, Reese.

Shaking it off, I hand each of them a glass, then set the giant pitcher in the center of the table.

"Fancy seeing you at all," Milo counters as he slips out of the booth and pulls me into a bear hug.

"So, how's work been going?" I ask. "I feel like I haven't had a chance to catch up with you lately."

"Fine," he grumbles before surprising me when he adds, "I'm beat."

Leaning into him, I give him another quick squeeze. "With good reason. They've been working you to death."

"Nah, it's just that time of year."

"Are you at least making some good money?" I ask as he slides back into the booth. "Enough to cover the cost of the shop when the owner decides to finally sell it?"

"Yeah. It'll be fine."

"Good. I'm glad. And if you need anything, you know you can rely on me, right?"

He smirks. "I know, sis. I got this, though. Stop worrying."

"I can't help it. You're my big brother."

"Which means I've got it taken care of," he reminds me. "When's your next break?"

"Not for a while. Are you guys going to be here long?"

"For a little while. River's supposed to be joining us."

"Oh." I hesitate, praying he doesn't hear the way my breath hitches at the sound of his friend's name. "Okay."

"Everything all right?" Milo demands with a narrowed gaze. The guy should be a detective.

"Yup."

"You sure about that?"

"Stop interrogating her," Jake reprimands. "Give her a break. She's probably just sick of the guy since they spent all day together with the photoshoot and everything."

"Photoshoot?" Milo repeats. "What photoshoot?"

"Uh…" My eyes bounce between both of them in hopes of Jake stepping in, but he finishes pouring beer into their glasses, leans back in the booth, and smirks at me.

Bastard.

"What photoshoot?" Milo demands, his tone brooking no argument.

"Riv didn't tell you?"

"Tell me what?"

"Um. There was a cancellation? River asked if I would help him out."

"What kind of photoshoot, Reese?"

"Clothing?" I answer, though it comes out as more of a question than anything else.

Why the hell do I feel guilty right now?

It was a photoshoot. A completely respectable, non-porno photoshoot. Besides, Milo is the one who encouraged me to find something I love to do. And it turns out that I kind of loved modeling yesterday. So, sue me.

Milo doesn't look any more convinced at the validity of the shoot than he did before he knew what kind of session it was, but he stays quiet, studying me carefully. As long as he never sees the pictures or how the *clothing* was more like lingerie than a hoodie and jeans, I think I'll be safe.

And so will River.

"Why didn't you tell me?" he demands.

Helpless, I mutter, "I kinda thought you knew."

"River said the photoshoot was scheduled with some other model," Jake interjects, throwing me a bone. "But she had to cancel, so he asked Reese to tag along and help him impress some big-time photographer or something. He said she did good."

Almost instantly, Milo relaxes and asks me, "Did you get paid for helping him out?"

"Yup."

In cash. And *orgasms.*

So, ya know, win-win, right?

Satisfied, Milo nods. "Good. Did you have fun?"

"Actually, yeah," I admit. "The photoshoot was a lot of fun."

"And Riv?"

Shrugging one shoulder, I rock back on my heels and hug the empty tray to my chest. "Was his usual...*self.*"

"Hmm," he hums, but he doesn't press the topic as he picks up his drink and brings it to his lips. After a quick gulp of beer, he sets it back down and tells me, "When you get a break, you should come hang out with us."

"Sure thing. For now, is there anything else I can get you guys?"

"We're good. Thanks, sis."

"You're welcome."

I turn to Jake, shoving aside the last of my reservations after everything River told me about his potential...feelings. That same familiar warmth shines in his eyes as he holds my gaze. But there isn't any heat or longing. Just kindness. Patience. And a sense of camaraderie after everything we've been through together.

Just like always.

River's wrong.

Jake doesn't love me. Not like that, at least. We're *friends*, and I wouldn't jeopardize it for the world.

"How 'bout you, Jakey Boy?" I ask. "Can I get you anything?"

"I think we're good. Thanks, though, Reese."

"Okay. I'll be back in a few."

With an empty tray in hand, I head back to the bar before veering toward the front door when I see a very attractive River scanning the premises. He hasn't spotted me yet, leaving me the chance to admire him from afar.

Why would a guy like that be interested in a girl like me?

I still don't get it. It's like I keep waiting for the other shoe to drop. But it hasn't. And ever since he stormed out of my room, I've felt empty. Lonely. Even though I'm the one who told him that I needed time to think about things.

Because that makes perfect *sense.*

I roll my eyes before my attention catches on a few tables near the entrance. They're filled with women who are busy checking River out like he's a damn library book. Just like I was before my own insecurities got the best of me.

I'd promised myself I would ignore him tonight so that I wouldn't raise any more suspicion, but my jealousy flares, and I can't tamp it down no matter how hard I try. Each of them is gorgeous. Each of them resembles the girls I've seen sneaking out of River's room in the past. Like a single carbon copy made for wet dreams. Long straight hair that looks thoroughly teased. Dark lined eyes brimming with interest. Pouty red lips smirking in appreciation.

And they all want River.

But River's had women like that. Probably more times than he can count. He's never wanted any of them for more than one night.

But he still wants me.

Or at least he said he did.

With a deep breath, I glance behind me where Milo and Jake are chatting, completely oblivious to River's presence. Then I saunter toward him.

REESE

"Hey," I greet River, my smile tight.

"Hey," he returns cooly, though his gaze doesn't meet mine.

I look back at my brother's booth. They're still in their own little world.

Stepping closer, I lick my lips, then reach for his hand and brush my pinky along his clenched fist hanging at his side. "Can we…?" I sigh. "Can we talk?"

"Not sure that now's a good time."

"Oh." The empty tray nearly slips from my grasp before I clutch it to my chest, my shoulders rolling forward. "I guess I should just, uh…" My voice trails off, and my body temperature rises from his not-so-subtle brush-off.

Cocking his head to the side, he studies me carefully with a tight jaw, though I have no idea what he's searching for.

"How 'bout tomorrow night?" he offers.

My eyes widen in surprise. "A-are you asking me out?"

"You said you wanted to talk."

"I do," I rush out. Then my face scrunches with regret. "But I have plans tomorrow night."

"You told me you weren't working--"

"I'm not. I have a girls' night planned."

"Girls' night? With who?"

"Dove?" I offer.

"Who's Dove?"

I point to her across the bar as she wipes down a table near the stage. Her white-blonde hair almost glows like a halo from the purple lighting and makes her stick out like a sore thumb. How she wound up working at a bar with her upbringing is beyond me. I'll have to pry it out of her during our girls' night.

"Oh, yeah, the hot new waitress," River confirms.

My face falls.

"Sonny's words, not mine," he clarifies. "Don't get me wrong. She's cute and all, but--"

"You should stop while you're ahead," I mutter, slightly offended.

"You didn't let me finish." He laughs. The sound makes my stomach tighten. "*But...*I have my sights set on the other hot new waitress. Unfortunately, she keeps turning me down when I ask her on a date."

"Keeps?" I quirk my brow and cross my arms. "You've asked me once."

"Which is exactly one more time than I've ever asked a girl out in my entire life," he retorts.

I flinch back slightly, attempting to hide my surprise, though I doubt I'm successful. "Really? You've never taken a girl out before?"

"Not with the intention of actually *dating* her. Just you."

Digging my teeth into my lip, I try to keep from grinning like a loon, but it's a losing battle.

"Let me take you out," he presses, inching closer to me.

"I'll have to check my schedule."

"Playing hard to get?"

"I thought you liked it *hard*," I quip.

His deep chuckle sends tingles racing down my spine as he leans forward and whispers in my ear. "You're making me hard right now, Reese, and I'm about to have drinks with your brother. Do you think he'll notice that I'll be undressing you with my eyes the entire time? That I'll be imagining you straddling me, your tits bouncing up and down as you ride me like you did last night?"

I gulp but stay silent.

"Let me take you out," he murmurs.

My voice catches in my throat as I reply, "Let me think about it."

His heated gaze rolls over me like warm honey. "Not exactly the answer I was hoping for."

"I just——"

"Need some convincing. I get it. Have you heard from Ian at all since this morning?"

I shake my head, ignoring the whiplash I feel that he just brought up my ex after asking me out on a date.

With a frown, he says, "I think we should tell Sonny about Ian so he can keep an eye on you when you're at work."

"That isn't necessary."

"And I think it is," he answers, looking more determined than ever.

"Even if he shows up here, what's the worst he can do, River?" I ask. "Cause a scene? Been there, done that. The bouncers will throw him out, and the night will go on like it never happened."

Inching forward, he brushes his fingertips against my hip, then drops his hand back to his side. "I don't trust the guy. I just want to make sure you're okay, but I'm not trying to control you, all right?"

The sincerity in his tone melts a bit of my reservations.

Licking my lips, I whisper, "Thank you. For looking out

for me. And for being patient. I'm sorry about this morning. After Gibson's little words of wisdom, I've been...scared? Confused? Honestly, I don't even know anymore, but I hate how we left things."

"I don't blame you." He reaches up and cups my cheek as if I'm a fragile doll, but I don't shy away from his touch. Instead, I lean into it, savoring the warmth and slight scratch from his calloused palm as if my life depends on it. Even though I know it isn't the smart thing to do. Even though I know my brother could see us, and it would ruin everything. Even when I know River has the power to ruin me.

When I'm with him, all of that bullshit seems to fade away.

And it's going to bite us in the ass one day.

"He gave us both a lot to think about, Reese. I know that things are a little...precarious?"

A breath of laughter escapes me. "You could call it that."

"But I can't stop thinking about you." He drops his hand to his side as if it pains him to have so much distance between us. The same way it pains me. "Let me take you out on a real date. I promise we won't be seen, and your brother will never know about it, but I want you to give us a real shot before you make any decisions. Do you think you can do that?"

A lump of emotions gets lodged in my throat as I take in his sincerity. Then I nod.

"Good girl." He steps around me and walks over to my brother's booth in the back of the bar while I'm left checking out his butt in his jeans as his praise runs through my mind over and over again.

I'm in trouble.

With a wistful sigh, I shake myself out of the lust-induced haze that seems to cripple me anytime River's around and get back to work when a very uncomfortable Dove catches my attention. Her face is pale, and she seems frozen in place as a large figure towers over her and whispers something in her ear.

Cautious, I close the distance between us. She doesn't even look at me. She's too shaken.

"Hey, Dove!" I greet her, my tone extra chipper. "Everything okay here?"

She gulps, then glances up at the mystery man who can't be more than five years older than me and screams, *pretty boy with a dark past.*

"No problem," the stranger answers for her. "Right, *Dove?*" He emphasizes her name. "I was just leaving."

He steps around her but uses his menacing frame to make her feel small and insignificant. Just like how Ian used to do to me. My upper lip curls in disgust. I follow his every movement with my gaze, my muscles and lungs poised and ready for action if he doesn't leave peacefully right now. It's funny how much easier it is to stand up for someone else than it is myself. Thankfully, he heads out the exit without causing a scene but gifts Dove one more knowing look before he walks out the door.

I breathe out all the oxygen I'd been holding hostage, then turn to Dove. "You okay?"

She pauses and licks her lips, blinking slowly as if she's just woken from a strange dream. "Uh, yes. Yes, I'm fine."

"What was that about?"

"Nothing."

"You sure?"

With a jerky nod, she wrings the rag that's used to wipe down tables between her hands. "Yes. Yes, I'm fine."

"You don't look fine. What happened, Dove? Who was that?"

"I-I don't know. He was looking for Fender."

"And?"

"And I told him that I didn't know where he was."

"Okay? Is that it?" I ask carefully.

It isn't exactly out of the ordinary for people to ask about where Fender is. He's the face of a huge up-and-coming band. It doesn't make sense that Dove would look like she's seen a ghost if a simple question like that is what brought it on.

She shakes her head. "No. Then he started asking me how long I'd worked here and if I'd be interested in..."--she clears her throat--"in hooking up later."

I grimace but stay silent.

"I lied and told him I had a boyfriend, thinking maybe that would get him to back off."

"That's a good idea, actually--"

"It didn't work. So, I told him that Gibson was my boyfriend and that he'd be back any minute and wouldn't appreciate him talking to me. I know it's the furthest thing from the truth and that Gibson hates me, but it just popped into my head, and--"

"Seriously, Dove." I grab her wrist to keep it from shaking. "I think that was a brilliant idea."

Again, she shakes her head. "He knows him. Gibson. Supposedly, anyway."

"Oh."

She smiles tightly, but it looks forced. "Yeah. That's not the weird part, though."

"What do you mean?"

She hesitates as if replaying the conversation in her head before voicing aloud, "He said that if Gibson and I were a thing, then I must be having...relations with his friend Milo too."

"Oh." My lips purse. "Yeah...I heard they're into sharing."

"That's a thing?"

With an awkward laugh, I shrug. "Supposedly. Is that why

you're spooked? With your history and all, I'd get it. That probably sounds terrible. For two guys to--"

"That wasn't it," she clarifies, stopping me from making a fool of myself as I attempt to explain the birds and the bees to a girl who's still a sheltered virgin. "I mean, it sounded weird, but who am I to judge? No. He..." She hesitates and glances toward the bar where a very oblivious Gibson is mixing drinks. "H-he warned me about something."

"Huh?" I ask, confused. This conversation doesn't make any sense.

"He just said that if I was smart, I'd stay away from Gibbs. And Milo."

"Why?" I press.

"Because their last girlfriend disappeared after they broke up, and it would be a shame if the same thing happened to me."

"He said *what?*"

"I know," she rushes out. "It sounds crazy, right?"

"Definitely crazy. I know Gibson, Dove. And I know Milo. Whatever bullshit that guy was spewing, it was exactly that. *Bullshit.*"

"You're right. You're right," she repeats, though she still looks spooked. "It was just the way he said it, ya know? Like he knew something. But you're right. He was probably just being a jerk."

"I'm sure that's exactly what he was being--"

"Do you know anyone named Em? Emma? Emily? Something like that?"

I search my memory, then shake my head. "Sorry. I don't. But if it'll make you feel better, you could always ask Gibbs."

With a dry laugh, she rolls her eyes and tucks her hair behind her ear. "No, thank you. That would be...weird. He hates me, remember? But you're right. It doesn't matter. We aren't even dating. He's my coworker. I just made that up to get the guy to leave me alone. It's fine. Everything's fine."

"You sure?" I ask.

She nods. "Yes. Definitely."

"Okay. We still on for tomorrow night?"

"Yes. Definitely," she repeats. "Let's get back to work before we get yelled at again. And thanks for saving me."

"Anytime."

REESE

"**S**hit," I mutter under my breath in the otherwise silent kitchen. "Why isn't this working?" The acrid smell of burnt sugar stings my nostrils as I assess the damage.

"Need any help?" a deep voice offers from the hall.

I glance behind me, then glare at River. "From the house's worst cook? I think not."

He lifts his chin toward the burnt goo that was supposed to be a good distraction from him before I got lost on my head and ruined it.

"If you keep this up, you might steal the title from me, Floozy. What are you making?"

The pot hisses as I put it in the sink and fill it with tap water. "I'm trying to make caramel popcorn."

"Why?"

"Because it's a must for our girls' night. The instructions online made it look easy."

"Never trust the internet, Floozy. That was your first mistake."

"Oh, so your mom *isn't* spiraling from another big movie

rejection?" I quip before pulling out the last clean pot from the cupboard.

"Nah. That one's probably true."

"You still haven't talked to her?" I ask as I scoop some butter, sugar, and corn syrup into the pot before setting it on the stove. Then I crank up the heat to medium-high––just like the stupid video told me to––and start stirring.

"Nope. And I don't plan to." An innocent River peeks over my shoulder like a seasoned chef inspecting my third attempt at making the damn candy as if he has all the time in the world when a little bird told me the opposite.

My stirring stops and I look up at him as my frustration gets the best of me.

"Am I distracting you?" he rumbles, that same cocky smirk painted across his lips.

Stupid. Sexy. Arrogant asshole.

My head snaps back to the stove.

"Nope. So..." I give the mixture another half-assed stir and take a deep breath. "Where are you going tonight?"

"Nowhere."

"Then why are you dressed like that?" I wave my hand toward him as if he's an annoying fly that won't leave me alone.

He looks down at his dark, fitted T-shirt and worn jeans that hang low on his hips. "Dressed like what?"

Annoyed, I drop the spoon in the pot and twist around to face him. "You're wearing a shirt, which in *River terms* means you're going out."

Throwing his head back, he laughs. Hard. "Oh, so because I'm wearing clothes, that means I have plans?"

"You tell me."

"Is somebody jealous?"

"What? No––"

A quiet knock at the front door cuts me off. I wipe my

hands on the yellow hand towel hanging next to the sink, then take a step toward the entryway. "Dove's here."

His warm hand envelops my bicep and holds me in place. "Milo's home. He'll get it."

My gaze drops down to his steely grip before I find the courage to look back up at him.

How can one man knock me on my ass so freaking quickly?

With a simple touch, a simple look, a simple smirk, I'm a goner.

"You never answered me yesterday," he murmurs.

"About what?"

"About whether or not you'll let me take you on a date."

I lick my lips. He's close. Too close. We shouldn't be standing like this. Not when my brother's still home. But the idea of putting some much-needed distance between us is crippling.

I peek back up at him. "Riv…"

"Let me take you out."

"I don't––"

"Crap," a familiar soft voice mutters from the hall. "Sorry. I'll just––"

Our heads snap toward the culprit in unison before I wiggle out of River's grasp as if he has the plague.

Shit.

"Hey, Dove," I squeak. My face feels like it's on fire.

"Hi." She waves awkwardly, pretending she didn't just catch us in a precarious position before her button nose scrunches in distaste. "What's that smell?"

I sniff.

"Dammit, River!" Rushing to the stove, I grab the hot pad and throttle the pot's handle until my knuckles turn white.

Stupid TikTok and their stupid thirty-second recipes.

"I burnt the caramel again," I announce with more venom than a damn rattlesnake.

"Caramel?" Striding over to the stove, Dove assesses the black sludge at the bottom of the pot. "*That's* supposed to be caramel?"

"Well, it *was*," I defend.

"And how 'bout those over there?" She points to the two other pots in the sink.

River chuckles under his breath. "Told ya, Floozy. Have fun on your girls' night."

"And where are you going?" I ask––again––trying to keep my tone light and airy. But it comes out with an edge that screams jealousy no matter how much I try to hide it.

Because I *am* jealous.

Where is he going? And why won't he tell me?

"I already told you," River answers me. "Out."

"You told Milo you have a date." The truth slips out of me before I have a chance to stop it. I hate how vulnerable I sound, but I can't help it. The idea of River going out with someone who isn't me... It guts me.

"Where's the bathroom?" Dove interrupts, desperate to give us an ounce of privacy. Clearly, I'm doing a bang-up job of hiding my feelings for my roommate. Lovely. At least Milo isn't here to witness it.

I clear my throat. "The one on this floor is clogged, and they're all waiting for someone else to fix it like a bunch of pansies. But if you go to the top of the stairs and turn left, it'll be the first door on your right."

"Left and then a right. Got it."

"Yup."

Her sock-clad feet turn her into a silent ninja as she rushes out of sight, leaving me alone with a guy I'm not too happy with.

"Did she take off her shoes?" River asks, his gaze still glued to the gorgeous waitress from the bar who happens to be turning into one of my good friends.

257

My stupid jealousy flares all over again as I give him my back and mutter, "Apparently."

"That's...nice of her?" he offers.

"I guess."

Shoving the third pot of charred sugar into the sink, I turn the water on full blast and watch the clear liquid swirl into a dark, opaque sludge. Just like my jealousy.

"Hey," River murmurs, crowding me against the sink. The warmth from his chest heats my back, though I refuse to lean into him. If I do, I'm afraid I'll crumble.

"What do you want from me?" I whisper.

"I want you to say yes and go on a date with me."

"Why would I do that? It seems you already have one."

His hands skim along my hips, but he doesn't touch me. And it's his lack of touch that really does me in. Like I'm some forbidden treasure when he's the one who always feels just out of reach.

He bows his head forward. "I'm sorry, Reese."

"For going on a date tonight?" I choke out.

"No. For making you even question whether or not I'd betray you like that."

I dig my teeth into my lower lip, my eyes glazing with unshed tears as the dirty water spills over the pot's edge.

"I lied to Milo," he reveals. "The only girl I want to go out with tonight has plans with a coworker. If she didn't, I'd be bending her over backward to convince her to give me a chance."

"I believe the correct term is bending over backward. Not bending *her* over backward," I correct him, my voice nothing but a whisper. The vice around my chest slowly eases with each passing second as I register his statement.

He doesn't have a date tonight.

He still wants me.

He still wants *us*.

River's palm spreads across my lower belly before he pulls me into him, pressing my back to his front, where I feel a very thick, very hard erection.

I gasp and squeeze my eyes shut as my stomach tightens with anticipation.

"Pretty sure I had it right the first time," he growls against the shell of my ear. "Say you'll go out with me."

"Riv…"

"Say it. It doesn't have to be tomorrow or even next week. I can be patient," he promises me. "But I need an answer."

"Okay," I breathe. "I'll go out with you."

"Good girl. Have fun on your girls' night. And don't make any more caramel."

His touch disappears, followed by his heat at my back. The combination leaves me cold, turned on, and even more frustrated than before.

And he still didn't tell me where he was going tonight.

Sneaky bastard.

"Where are you going?" I call out to his retreating form.

"Out."

The front door closes behind him, but it doesn't stop me from glaring at it.

Cocky asshole.

"**D**ude, what took you so long?" I ask as I grudgingly pop a non-caramel-covered kernel of popcorn into my mouth. I'd finally given up after River ditched me in the kitchen, but I didn't expect Dove to spend twenty minutes in the bathroom.

Come on, girl.

Television remote in hand, I open up Netflix and start scrolling as Dove plops down next to me.

"Sorry," she apologizes. "I got…distracted."

I quirk my brow. "Candy Crush get ya again?"

"Uh, yup. That's the one." Her gaze darts toward the second floor before she snuggles further into the couch cushion.

"You okay over there?" I ask, taking in her flushed cheeks.

"Yup."

"Did something happen in the bathroom? 'Cause if you clogged the toilet or something, it's not a big deal or anything."

Her button nose scrunches. "Ew. No. Nothing like that."

"Then what is it?"

"You didn't tell me that one of your roommates is Gibson," she rushes out. Her gaze darts over to mine for an instant before returning to the television screen in front of us.

"Oh." I pause and pop another kernel into my mouth. "I thought you knew."

"Nope. Definitely didn't know that little tidbit."

"Oh," I repeat, trying to read the girl beside me though I can't quite put my finger on what she's feeling right now. Embarrassed, maybe?

"Well, Gibson is one of my roommates," I tell her.

"Gee. Thanks for the heads-up."

I snort. "Sorry. Did you run into him or something?"

"You could say that," she returns cryptically.

"And?"

"And nothing," she decides, but I'm not sure who she's trying to convince. "So..." She drops her voice to a whisper. "Is Lover Boy still here?"

"Nope. He went out."

"Out?"

"Yup." I glare at the bowl of popcorn in my lap before shoving another small handful into my mouth.

"You don't sound too thrilled about that," she points out.

"He wouldn't tell me where he was going, so he's kind of on my shit list."

Treading carefully, she murmurs, "Are you worried he's on a date or something? In the kitchen, it sounded like that might be something you were a little nervous about."

"We're not exclusive," I admit with a frown. "But that doesn't mean it feels good to hear from my brother that he has a date tonight, regardless of whether or not it's true."

"So, it isn't true then?"

"He says it isn't," I tell her. "He said he would wait until I was ready to actually date him."

261

"He said he would wait?" A soft smile stretches across Dove's face. "That's...that's like the sweetest thing ever."

Chewing on the pad of my thumb, I try to keep my hope in check, but it's useless. I drop my hand back to my lap and push the bowl a few inches toward her. "Every once in a while, he gives me glimpses of his awesome boyfriend material. But then I hear my brother and his friends joke about how River's the biggest manwhore in the world. It doesn't exactly give me warm fuzzies."

"Maybe he just needed the right girl to tie him down," she offers with a shrug before reaching into the popcorn bowl to grab a small handful.

"And maybe I'm naive to think that I could be the one to do it."

Popping a few pieces into her mouth, she chews them slowly while considering my counterargument. After she swallows, a hum escapes her. "Hmm."

"Hmm?"

"Let me ask you this," she continues. "The last time we talked, I asked how he makes you feel when he's around. Remember?"

"Yeah."

"And did you figure out your answer?"

"It's complicated," I hedge.

Her laugh reminds me of a fairy as she tucks her white-blonde hair behind her ear. "A potential relationship might be complicated, but my question isn't. How do you feel when you're around him, Reese?"

Excited. Turned on. Happy. Content. Desperate. Frustrated. Comfortable but on edge that my brother will find out. And pretty much every other emotion in the book. I rub my hand over my make-up-free face, grateful none of it will smear into a mess as I pinch the bridge of my nose and swipe at my closed eyelids.

"That's a loaded question," I mutter under my breath after a few seconds of silence.

Again, she laughs. "Then tell me the first feeling that comes to mind."

"I feel good," I admit, holding her curious stare. "Happy."

"And isn't that all we really want in a relationship? Or in life in general? To be happy?"

"Yeah, but if I pursue something with River, then I'll have to tell Milo, and he'll be pissed, which'll put a damper on said *happiness* big time. So will I *truly* be happy if I go down that road? Especially when I know Milo will never forgive River, and I'll lose his trust forever? Debatable, my friend. Very debatable."

"Yeah, but if you *don't* go down that road and give your relationship with River a real shot, then you *know* you won't be happy. Period. Just sayin'."

Forehead wrinkled, I throw a popcorn kernel at her, then shove a handful of it into my mouth. It turns to sawdust as soon as it hits my tongue.

She's got a point. The idea of not pursuing a relationship with River only to be given front row seats to all of his conquests after me is less than appealing.

It's pretty freaking terrible. My erratic heart rate spikes at the thought before I take a deep breath, forcing myself to calm down.

The question is, how do I tell Milo that I like his friend without him turning into the Hulk?

A satisfied Dove picks up the kernel I'd thrown at her from her shirt then tosses it into her mouth. "Told ya I was a good listener. Now, stop overthinking things. Just take it a day at a time and soak up that happiness, Reese. It's not easy to come by."

I pause and tilt my head to one side. "That's a cryptic comment."

She shrugs. "What's a cryptic comment?"

"That happiness isn't easy to come by. Are you happy, Dove?"

"In general?" She shrugs one shoulder--again--but avoids my gaze. "Sure."

"That doesn't sound very convincing."

"Sorry. My life is just pretty boring in comparison."

"I dunno about that. Tell me about yourself."

"There isn't much to tell."

"Liar," I tease. "You've fascinated plenty of gentlemen at the bar so far."

Her jaw drops. "I have not."

"Oh, my dear friend, you most certainly have." I almost bring up the creepy stranger from the night before but bite my tongue before asking, "What's your story? I know you gave me the CliffsNotes version at the bar the other day, but I want all the gory details."

"About my past?"

"Yeah. Who is Dove..." I pause. "What's your last name again?"

She smiles. "Walker. My name is Dove Elizabeth Walker."

"All right. Who is Dove Elizabeth Walker?" I press. "And how did she end up working at SeaBird?"

She hesitates. "It's...complicated."

I laugh. "Says the girl who made my life sound so easy. You don't like to have the spotlight on you, do you?"

Grimacing, she wrings her hands in her lap as a slight blush spreads throughout her cheeks. "Is it that obvious?"

"Maybe a little. When we're talking about me, you're all about asking for details and giving your advice, but as soon as I changed the subject to you, you went quiet."

"Sorry," she apologizes. "But you're right. I'm not good at being the center of attention."

"Why not?"

"I don't know?" She bites her lip and peeks over at me. "My sister, Madelyn, was kind of a troublemaker growing up, so she always managed to steal the spotlight in our house, ya know? I guess I just got used to it. Then she moved out, and I stayed with my parents to look after them. Which is kind of ridiculous when I say that out loud," she admits. "It's not like they're old and decrepit or anything. I just felt like that's where I belonged. I was their perfect little daughter who kept to herself and didn't really do anything. Like a trophy daughter or something. The one who stuck around after their oldest decided to disappear into thin air. Not that my parents bothered to look for her. They basically disowned her as soon as they found alcohol hidden in her closet."

My eyes pop. Talk about polar opposites. I would've been raised with alcohol in my baby bottle if Milo hadn't stepped in when we were little, yet Dove's sister was ostracized for having it in their house. My parents were so hands-off that I'm surprised I didn't wind up in the system, while Dove's were so overbearing that she was practically suffocating. Yet neither childhood sounds like a positive environment to be raised in. How's that for irony?

I nudge Dove's shoulder with mine. "Damn, Dove."

"Yeah."

"So, then what happened? How did you end up here?" I can't help but ask.

She laughs. "Well, my sister came back home when she found out she was pregnant, and there was a huge blowup."

"Why? I mean, I get that a pregnant daughter doesn't exactly sound like a walk in the park, but it isn't the end of the world. There are options––"

"Sex before marriage in my house is a huge deal, Reese. It made the alcohol in her room look like a walk in the park. It's not just frowned upon. It's *strongly* prohibited. When my parents found out, they disowned her and told her they weren't going to help with the baby. My sister stormed out of the house, promising to never come back. And I chased after her."

"Why?" I whisper. Suddenly, my drama doesn't seem so bad. At least my brother would never disown me.

"Because my parents were wrong," Dove explains. "And I was tired of sacrificing my relationship with my sister and my future niece or nephew because of them. So, I chased after her. I forced her to see that I wasn't going to be judgmental or awful like my parents were, even though she still looked at me like the perfect, butt-kissing little sister I was known to be. She kept telling me to go home, you know? But I refused to listen. I followed her home to her crappy apartment that's about twenty minutes away from SeaBird. I left with nothing but the clothes on my back and the determination of a workhorse, despite how sheltered I grew up."

"That's crazy, Dove. Is your sister still mad at you?"

"Depends on the day." She smiles tightly. "I'm not sure if she fully trusts me yet, but we've worked out a plan for when Baby gets here, which is why I work at SeaBird. My sister can work during the day, and I can be at home with Baby, then I'll go to work in the evening, and she can watch Baby and have a normal routine at night. This way, we won't have to hire a babysitter to make ends meet, ya know?"

"That's amazing, Dove."

"It isn't that big of a deal."

"Uh, yeah, it is."

She rolls her eyes but doesn't bother to argue with me. "I'm just excited to help my sister get back on her feet even though she hates relying on me to make it happen. Then again, when the sperm donor is an asshole who refuses to help her, I guess she doesn't have much of a choice."

"Do you know who the father is?" I ask carefully.

"Nope. We weren't close before she wound up pregnant.

Honestly, we're not particularly close now, either, but it takes time to heal wounds, so…"

"Yeah. I get that."

She nudges her shoulder into mine, mimicking my movement from minutes before. "See? You're not the only one with family drama. But we got this."

"Yeah," I decide with a definitive nod. If she can handle leaving the only life she's ever known to become a badass sister who works at a bar, I can handle facing my fears and fighting for what I want.

Right?

"Good," Dove returns. "Now, let's watch a show. Something with lots of explosions."

"Deal."

About halfway through the movie, the front door opens, and I look over to find River with a brown paper bag in his arms.

"Ladies," he greets us before striding closer to me. He hands me the sack.

Curious, I peek inside and snort. "Caramel popcorn?"

"Someone told me it was a must for girls' nights, and I ruined your batch. Just one, I'd like to point out. The others were on you, but I'll still take the blame if you need me to."

"That's…" I bite my lip to keep from grinning back at him as the sugary goodness makes my mouth water.

Or maybe it's the man in front of me.

"Thoughtful?" Dove offers beside me.

Pointing at her, River tells me, "I like her. Have fun, ladies!"

Then he heads back to the front door, and I call out, "Where are you going?"

"Out!"

The door closes. *Again.* But it isn't followed by my usual

frustration. Just a longing that's so deep and so sharp that it feels hard to breathe.

"He's a keeper," Dove decides before reaching her hand into the paper bag that's still in my lap.

That's the problem, though.

I think she's right.

After the first two *Matrix* movies, which dear sweet Dovey had never seen before, we call it a night with the promise to finish the third one soon. My stomach has officially been stuffed to the brim with popcorn and ice cream. With a groan, I waddle up to my room in the dark while loathing that last pint of Ben & Jerry's.

The boys made it home throughout the evening and are in their rooms, including the elusive River, who has yet to admit where the heck he went tonight. And even though Keanu was a pretty good distraction, I couldn't stop thinking about him. I blame the few popcorn kernels stuck in my teeth that kept annoying me all night. They're all his fault.

Him and his thoughtfulness.

Damn him.

Dove's right. If I don't pursue this thing with River, I'll regret it. Now, I just need to figure out how to keep it quiet until River and I are both ready to confront Milo.

Which, if we knew what was good for us, would be *never*.

The floor creaks beneath my feet as I hesitate outside River's room before reaching for the handle, twisting it, and peeking my head through the doorway.

It's dark. Quiet. And obvious he must be passed out beneath his tangled, navy blue comforter lying on the mattress. Which is so…human. Not that he isn't human. It's just that sometimes, he seems like he's larger than life. Like he's living it to the fullest and is soaking up every moment. But right now, he's catching up on some much-needed rest. And it's kind of adorable. Especially now that I've decided to pursue something with him.

Damn caramel popcorn.

Fighting off the urge to sneak into his bed and snuggle, I close the door again then head to my room.

My brows furrow as I reach the closed door.

I could've sworn I'd left it open.

Who's been in my room?

With my head cocked to one side, I cautiously push the bedroom door open and find a shadowed figure on my bed. My heart leaps in my throat as a scream threatens to spill out of me, but I hold it back. With my feet planted in place, I squint and let my eyes adjust to the dimness. The light from his cell shines on the shadowed figure's face before he sets it down on his bare chest, blanketing the room in darkness again.

"Took you long enough," River murmurs.

A sigh of relief whooshes out of me before I step into my room and softly close the door behind me. "I'm sorry. I wasn't aware you'd be waiting up for me."

"Did you have a good time?"

"Yes."

"And did you like the popcorn?"

With an amused chuckle, I repeat, "Yes."

"And did you make a decision?" There's an edge of hope in his tone that makes my stomach swell with butterflies.

Or maybe it's the damn popcorn.

"About what?" I ask, feigning ignorance as I inch closer

and turn on my bedside lamp. A gentle glow of warmth spreads throughout the small room.

Like a cobra, River's arm darts out and grabs my wrist before he tugs me into his lap.

"Answer the question, Floozy," he orders in a deep, sexy voice.

"Ya know, Riv, if I'm gonna be your girlfriend, I think we should probably discuss alternative pet names."

His grin lights up the room as he presses a quick kiss to my mouth before squeezing me tighter against him. "I dunno. I kinda like Floozy."

"Of course, you do."

"I do," he reiterates, not even bothering to hide his grin. "But I think you're right. I definitely need a pet name if we're going to give this relationship a real shot. What do you think about calling me, *daddy*?" Bouncing his eyebrows up and down, his hand slides down to my butt, and he grabs a handful.

"You better be joking, or I might have to reconsider the whole girlfriend thing."

Rolling me onto my back, River cages me in on both sides, then settles between my thighs. "I bet I could convince you otherwise."

"Not if *daddy*'s on the table," I quip, fighting the urge to close my eyes and savor the feel of his heavy frame pressing me into the mattress.

His chest rumbles with amusement as he plants a lazy kiss against my lips before grinding against me. "Even though I'm pretty sure I could make you cave, I'll let you win since I was joking, and the idea of you *actually* calling me daddy gives me the shivers."

"Oh, really?" I breathe out, my stomach tightening with anticipation as the outline of his long, hard erection presses against my core.

"Yeah. Call me crazy, but I'd rather you work with Sex God/Master of Orgasms or something classy like that."

"That's classy?" I'm grinning like a loon, but I catch myself doing that a lot when I'm around him.

"Sex God/Master of Orgasms?" He turns serious and contemplates the pet name before giving me a definitive nod. "Yes. That's the definition of class, Floozy. Get with the times."

"Sex God/Master of Orgasms," I repeat. "It's a bit of a mouthful, don't you think?"

"I could always fill your mouth with something else if you'd prefer." His mock innocence is overshadowed by the knowing smirk painted across his face. He knows exactly what imagery just popped into my head, and he doesn't regret it in the least.

Innocent, my ass.

With a very unladylike snort, I push against his chest and roll him onto his back. Then I take control like a good little floozy. Using the hair tie around my wrist, I put my hair in a ponytail and watch his face transform from amused to impatient.

And I kind of love it.

Licking my lips, I inch down his toned frame but keep my eyes locked on his as I murmur, "Well, if you insist."

33

REESE

The room is painted with a soft white glow as the morning light peeks through the window.

A yawn slips out of me as I burrow under the covers and into River's side. With the scent of musk and sex still lingering in the air, I drag my nose along his warm skin and breathe him in.

How can he smell so good?

"Morning," Riv grumbles.

"Morning."

"I fell asleep."

"You did," I confirm with a smile even though he can't see it.

"I missed the gym."

I pat his bare chest before swirling the tip of my finger around his tiny man nipple. "I think your muscles can survive a day without working out."

"Debatable," he mutters under his breath.

"And why's that?" I laugh.

"A model is only as good as his looks, Reese. If I want to

keep working––and keep the attention of a certain floozy–– then I need to take care of it."

"Did you just imply that I'm only with you for your bod?" I question, pushing myself up to meet his gaze.

"Are you trying to imply that you'd still be with me if I had a beer belly?" he counters.

Pursing my lips, I throw my leg over his waist and straddle him. The bastard's eyes heat, but his somber expression stays firmly in place. As I lean closer, my hair falls over one shoulder, and I press a soft kiss to his frown, but it doesn't disappear.

"I like you for you, Riv."

"You like me for me as long as I look like this," he challenges. His muscles flex beneath me and turn him into stone. Like a gorgeous statue carved by Michaelangelo, yet just as wounded and tortured too.

Damn you, Monet Cavier.

She has no idea how much she's screwed up her son, though I'm not about to point it out to him. Although, the fact that he can't see himself the way I see him nearly breaks me.

"Don't get me wrong, Riv. I definitely appreciate the effort you've put into this bad boy." I run my hands up and down his pecs. "But even if you had a beer belly and didn't work out a day in your life, I'm attracted to what's up here." I tap my finger against his temple.

He scoffs.

"I like you for you," I whisper. "I promise."

"We'll see."

"What's that supposed to mean?"

"Nothing," he lies as his fingers dig into my thighs on both sides of his waist.

"Tell me."

"It's nothing, Reese."

I bite my tongue to keep from calling him out, though the irony isn't lost on me. The guy is so far out of my league that it isn't even funny, yet he's terrified I won't be attracted to his mind when I'm afraid that's the *only* thing he's attracted to when it comes to me.

"What are you thinking about?" he asks, dragging his fingers along my sensitive skin.

"Just that it's ironic."

"What is?"

"That you question whether or not I'm attracted to your mind, while I can't help but wonder what you see when it comes to me physically. I've seen your other conquests, Riv--"

"Don't--"

"How can't I? That's a little pot calling the kettle black, isn't it?"

"You're beautiful, Reese. I've told you this--"

"Where did you go last night?" I demand. "And you better not say *out*, or I'm going to give you a turkey on your chest."

"You're feisty this morning," he notes.

"I'm feisty every morning. Now, answer the question. I know we aren't officially together, but--"

"I'm gonna stop you right there, Reese." His strength makes me gasp as he lifts me off him and sets me on the mattress like I weigh about as much as a gallon of milk. Then he rolls out of bed and pads across the floor in his birthday suit while I'm left drooling as I take in the view of his chiseled backside.

Day-um.

A few seconds later, he returns with a white envelope in his hands and offers it to me.

"This was my backup plan in case you still weren't sure if you wanted to give us a real shot."

"What is it?" I ask as I cautiously open the crisp envelope.

He doesn't answer me, but I can feel his gaze bouncing around my face, anxious to see my reaction.

Curious, I slide out the contents, then gasp.

"Are these…?"

"They're from the photoshoot. Gina sent me a few of the digitals for my portfolio, but I thought they might sway you to give us a chance if you saw them. That's where I was last night. I printed them out as a last-ditch effort in hopes they'd convince you. And even though it didn't end up being necessary, I still thought you might like to see them."

My gaze meets his before dropping back down to the 4x6 photos. They're gorgeous. Every one of them holds so much emotion that I'm left breathless. Part of me wants to deny that the woman in the images looks like me, but they do. I don't look overly photoshopped or fake. I look beautiful. I look like a girl who might even deserve River. And the look on his face in these pictures proves that he thinks the exact same thing.

"Gina said she was blown away by the chemistry in the pictures. She said we were gonna light the lingerie catalog on fire." He chuckles before gripping the back of his neck and examining the pictures with me.

He's right. These things are hot.

And now, I'm terrified for them to be printed anywhere that Milo might see them because if he managed to stumble upon these, River would be dead, and I'd never be forgiven.

I need to tell him. I just don't know how.

"What are you thinking about?" River asks gently.

I peek up at him. "Is there any chance Milo could stumble upon these?"

He shakes his head. "Not unless he snoops in your room."

"He would never do that."

"Then it'll be fine. Most likely, we won't see them, either.

Well, outside of the ones Gina sent me, anyway. It's for a foreign designer."

Letting go of the oxygen in my lungs, I go back to looking them over.

"You rocked the whole modeling gig," I admit as I take in his abs in the photograph. The fact that I get to touch, kiss, and lick these things in real life is mind-blowing. I run my fingers along the photograph before my stupid insecurities rear their stupid heads.

He's just so…pretty.

Why the hell would he want to be tied down in a relationship?

Yes, I look good in these pictures, but I'm all dolled up. It's not like I look like that every day of the week. In fact, I'm not even the one who did my hair or makeup. I barely even wear the stuff on a regular basis.

Like right now, for example. My hair is a messy rat's nest, I'm bloated from ice cream and popcorn last night, and I haven't brushed my teeth in almost twenty-four hours.

I cover my mouth with my hand and glance over at him with shame.

"Reese." Reading my mind, he cups my cheeks and forces me to look at him. "Your reaction is the opposite of what I was looking for when I printed these off to show you. What's wrong?"

I shrug.

"Tell me," he pleads.

I swallow thickly. "I don't always look like this."

"So?"

"Was this just a job to you? And I don't mean that negatively, or like I'm accusing you of doing anything wrong. I just want to know. If Olivia didn't have her appendix nearly burst, would we still be here? In this room? Would we still have slept together? Or would it be her bed that you woke up in instead of mine?"

"Now look who's calling the kettle black," he points out.

I bite my lip but don't reply.

"You don't get it, Reese." His thumb runs along my jaw, but his grip stays firm. "It didn't feel like work with you. It *wasn't* work with you," he corrects himself. "If anything, I finally got to let down those walls and show my real feelings around you. Feelings that have been dying to come out for months. I've wanted you since the moment you showed up on our doorstep and announced you were looking for Milo and Jake. I didn't know you were Milo's sister back then. I was jealous as hell that their names were the ones that slipped past your lips instead of mine. If it were Olivia, it would've been another job, and I wouldn't have jacked off to the pictures when Gina sent them to my phone for my portfolio. It's you. It's always been you."

"It's always been you for me too," I breathe out before slapping my hand over my mouth again because ew... morning breath.

"Good. Now move your damn hand out of the way so I can kiss you."

"I haven't brushed my teeth." The words are slightly muffled since I refuse to drop my hand.

Shaking his head, he answers, "And I don't give a shit." Then he engulfs my wrist with his long fingers and twists my arm behind me before bending me back and kissing me until my toes curl.

And I kind of love this part too.

"**Y**ou know what they say about guys with lifted trucks, right?" I ask as I clamor into River's giant white baby in immaculate condition. We've been sneaking around for weeks, but this is the first time I've been able to be with him in the light of the day, and I couldn't be more excited.

After rounding the front of the truck, he gets behind the wheel, then slides his sunglasses on and reaches for my hand. "What's that?"

Batting my lashes at him, I try to keep from swooning at our laced fingers as I quip, "That they're compensating for something."

He laughs. "Well, you've seen my junk, Reese. Tell me, am I compensating for something?"

Tapping my trimmed fingernail on my opposite hand against my chin, I make him sweat for a second.

"Floozy?" He drags out the nickname with a stern expression that promises a solid spanking if I don't give in and admit the truth.

And no matter how tempting it is to push him a little

harder, I put him out of his misery. "Nooo… But that's just what they say."

"Who's they, anyway?"

I shrug. "I dunno. The population? The experts? The guys with tiny penises?"

"Or maybe it's the girls who can't get with the guys who own lifted trucks. Ever think of that one, Floozy?"

"Floozy." I purse my lips and quirk my brow. "Never gonna let me live that one down now, are ya?"

"Don't count on it, sweetheart." He lets go of my hand to put the truck in reverse and backs out of the driveway before squeezing my knee. "I do think you're adorable when you pout, though. However, today is not the day for pouting."

"And why not?"

"'Cause, you're with me. The guy with the sexy, lifted truck who's *not* compensating for something."

"Mm-hmm. So, tell me. Where does one go when they're asked on a secret date where no one can recognize them in case said witnesses have any connection to a certain older brother who's yet to know about said relationship?"

"So many questions," he tsks.

"And so few answers."

"Don't worry. I've got it all covered."

"Can I have a hint?"

"I've already given you a hint."

"When?"

"The other day."

"You're gonna have to be more specific," I prod. "It's been weeks since you asked me out at SeaBird, remember?"

"I'm talking about when I told you to wear comfortable shoes and asked if you were allergic to bug spray."

My eyes transform into tiny slits as the sun threatens to slip beneath the horizon. "But when I asked if I needed a jacket, you said no."

"And?"

"And that makes me question whether we'll really be outside or if you were just messing with me about the whole bug spray thing."

With a grin, he points out, "You're cute when you're annoyed too."

"I hate surprises, ya know," I huff.

"That's because they've always let you down. Don't worry, babe. The Sex God/Master of Orgasms is going to blow your socks off on one condition."

"Nice caveat," I quip. "What's your condition?"

"That you don't compare Date Number Two with Date Number One 'cause I'm not sure if I can top this."

His insecurities are adorable and kinda make me want to jump his bones, but I resist since, ya know, car accidents and stuff.

Poking the bear a little more, I challenge, "You're positive you'll be able to squeeze a second date out of me?"

He grins and squeezes my knee. "If I'm lucky enough. And if your brother doesn't kill me first."

"Har, har. We've been sneaky so far, haven't we?"

"Your brother's not stupid, Reese," he reminds me.

"I didn't say he was stupid. I was complimenting our sneakiness--"

"Our *luck*," he corrects me. "The fact he hasn't caught me sneaking out of your room yet--"

"The fact he hasn't *heard* me yet," I clarify.

"Oh. He's heard you. He just assumes I'm still a manwhore who likes to bring home random women. But if you aren't ready to tell him--"

"I'm not."

"Then we wait until you are."

Sucking my lips between my teeth, I study the man beside me who's risking so much more than anyone should have to just to be with me. We've been dating for weeks now behind everyone's backs. And it's been…rough. Having to hide an innocent touch in our own home. Having to steal a tender moment while no one's looking. Having to lie, making up excuses about where we're going or who we'll be with. The whole thing is so damn frustrating that I'm ready to pull my hair out. But I'm too much of a coward to put us out of our misery, which leads us to three reschedules for a first date and an oblivious brother who thinks I'm having a girls' night with a coworker and River is meeting with Gina for an update on a new photoshoot.

And it's all bullshit. If it weren't for the man beside me, I'd question my sanity and end the entire ruse right now. But it's River. My River. And I'll claim him for as long as he'll have me.

"Thank you," I breathe out before shoving aside way too much emotion for a first date. "So, about this date…"

With a smirk, he barks, "Stop asking questions. I don't want you to ruin the surprise. You like road trips, right?"

"Road trips?"

"It's about an hour's drive."

Scrunching up my face, I demand, "Where are you taking me?"

"You're cute when you're bossy too. And that's saying something." His grasp disappears from my leg before he digs his cell out of his front pocket, types in the passcode, then hands it to me. "Pick some music, Reese. I've got the rest covered."

The bastard's confidence is sexy as hell as he adjusts his sunglasses and grips the steering wheel. His forearm muscles are on full display, leading up to his bicep and muscular shoulder, and even though I'm blatantly checking him out, he's too focused on the road to notice.

Or maybe he's too used to it to care.

Before I can second guess myself, I lean across the center console and kiss his stubbled cheek. Because I can. Because I'm his girlfriend. And because, even though he seems so unattainable, he's agreed to be mine. And I'm going to take full advantage for as long as he'll let me.

As I sit back in the passenger seat, he glances over at me with the softest of smiles. "What was that for?"

I shrug. "Just because I could."

The cab of his truck is still quiet as I pick up his phone to choose some music, but the screen is dark, and when I turn it on, it asks for a passcode.

"Crap. Could you...?" I offer it to him.

"It's 4-5-7-2-0-0," he answers without batting an eye.

"Your passcode?"

"Yeah."

"You just told me your passcode," I point out, stating the obvious.

He glances over at me. "So?"

"So, no one's ever done that before."

"Given you their passcode?"

"Nope."

His brows peek up above the rim of his sunglasses. "Not even you and Ian?"

I scoff. "Definitely not me and Ian. Trust was not a component to our relationship."

"That's..." His knuckles turn white around the steering wheel. "Rough."

"Not when you don't know any better."

The cab stays quiet for a minute as I stare out the windshield, trying to push aside all the crappy memories with my ex. There were so many signs. How did I miss them all?

River's low voice cuts through my self-deprecation like a hot knife through butter. "I want this relationship to have trust, Reese."

"So do I."

"If you ever think I'm keeping anything from you, just ask me. I promise I'll tell you the truth."

"Same. I have nothing to hide."

Except, you know, our entire relationship.

The thought leaves a bitter taste in my mouth, but I ignore it and punch River's passcode into his phone before choosing the first playlist I can find in his Spotify app.

But I don't hear a thing because my guilt drowns it out. We need to tell Milo. I just don't know how.

"Sooo...are you planning on killing and burying me out here?" My sarcasm is thick, but my excitement is over-whelming.

Where the hell is he taking me?

The area is pitch black except for our headlights as the truck climbs the dirt hill with ease. We turned off the main road about twenty minutes ago and have been weaving through dirt paths and rolling hills ever since.

"Damn it, I forgot my shovel," River returns just as quickly.

"Rookie."

"I believe you mean Sex God/Master of Orgasms," he corrects me with a wink. "Besides, why dig a hole when the coyotes can do the work for me?"

"River!" I shriek, smacking his arm.

"I'm kidding!" He laughs. "We're almost there. It's just around that bend in the road."

"You call this a road?"

Chuckling, he squeezes my knee, then turns the corner and pulls off to the side.

"Wait here," he orders. Hopping out of the truck, River

rounds the front of it, then opens my door like a gentleman and helps me out until my feet are on firm, albeit rocky ground.

"Where the hell are we?" I ask while scanning the darkness for clues. It's official. I'm lost. And if I didn't trust him completely, I'd be terrified out of my mind. There's no way I'd get cell service out here.

Riv pecks me on the forehead then tangles our fingers together. "Trust, remember?"

Digging my teeth into my lip, I peek up at him and breathe, "I do trust you. It's the coyotes I'm worried about."

"That's my girl." He bends closer to me and closes the gap between our mouths like mine is a homing beacon. Sliding his tongue along the seam of my lips, I open up to him and smile when a hint of peppermint teases my tastebuds.

I'm falling.

Hard.

"Come on," he orders after standing to his full height.

There's a set of camping chairs surrounding a makeshift fire pit, and he guides me to it. "Take a seat, milady. I'll be right back."

The air is cool at this time of night, and I rub my hands along my bare arms as my skin begins to pebble. When he returns, he tosses an oversized hoodie at me then winks. "You liked my sleeping shirt so much that I figured you might appreciate my sweatshirt too."

"Speaking of my sleepshirt––"

"*Your* sleepshirt?"

"I mean, obviously, I'm not giving it back since it was a gift, and it would be rude not to accept it."

That same familiar smirk is etched into his handsome features as he waves his hand in acceptance. "Obviously. Go on."

"So my question is, why does it have LAU's logo on it? You never told me."

He shrugs. "I was enrolled for a couple of years. Wanted to be a teacher, actually. Then the whole modeling gig got started, and I figured I might as well milk that career while I can, then I'll go back and finish my degree once I get bored of it or become a washed-up model. Now, put on the hoodie. You look like you're freezing."

My heart melts as I lift it to my nose and breathe deep.

How the hell does he smell so freaking good?

"Thank you," I murmur before pulling it over my head. The warmth envelops me almost instantly, making me feel like I'm wrapped in one of his warm hugs. "This is perfect."

"This is just the beginning."

With a duffle bag in hand, he begins to pull out roasting sticks, a small Bluetooth speaker for music, a couple of extra blankets, and hand sanitizer.

Yes, hand sanitizer. Because the guy is a genius.

Before long, a fire is blazing, and a cooler filled with hot dogs, condiments, sliced fruit, s'mores supplies, and a case of cold beer is at our feet.

It's the most perfect date idea in the history of man, but I bite my tongue to keep from pointing it out. No need to make River's head any bigger, right?

My belly is full with a roasted hot dog as I stick a marshmallow on the end of my roasting stick and twist it slowly over the fire to make sure I have an even toast when I catch River watching me.

"What? Do I have ketchup on my face?"

He shakes his head. "No."

"Then why are you staring?" I laugh to cover my embarrassment while squirming in my camping chair.

Shrugging, he grabs the arm of my chair and drags it

closer to him before planting a quick kiss to my forehead. "You're just adorable when you roast marshmallows too."

"I didn't know someone could make roasting marshmallows adorable."

"Neither did I, but you've managed to pull it off."

"And how exactly am I doing that?"

"I dunno?" Looking me up and down, he decides, "You're so determined not to let it catch on fire, and your eyebrows are pinched in concentration." His thumb brushes between my furrowed brows. "You also get this little pursed-lip thing going that's sexy as hell." Dragging his thumb along my lips, he smiles then drops his hand. "It makes your dimple stand out more than usual."

"That's a lot of things going on with my face. I'm surprised you've caught it all."

"A normal man wouldn't. But I'm the Sex God/Master of Orgasms, remember?" He winks.

"How could I forget?"

"The trick is to watch your partner's face so you can remember every tiny detail. That way, you can catch any little differences from one moment to the next." The fire's reflection dances in his glassy eyes, making them heat until I'm sure my entire body is going to ignite. "Wanna know why?"

I gulp but can't find the discipline to turn away.

"Why?" I whisper, hating how breathless I sound.

"Because they're the ones that speak louder than words."

Tapping his forefinger against my nose, he breaks the spell in an instant and turns back to the fire that's licking at my blackened mallow.

Dammit.

I scrape it against one of the rocks, then grab another one from the bag and stick it on the tip of the roasting stick.

Focus, Reese.

"Seems like caramel and marshmallows don't like you," a very amused River points out as I rotate the stick in my hands.

With a huff, I demand, "Did you just relate my s'mores face to my sex face a second ago?"

His deep chuckle makes my stomach tighten as he shakes his head. "That's not exactly where I was going with it, but I'll let you know when I watch you lick some melted marshmallow off your fingers. If, ya know, you don't burn this one too."

My cheeks heat, but I pray he can't see it from the light of the fire. "Gee, thanks. Any chance you'd be willing to open up the chocolate and set it on a graham cracker for me? Usually, I'm more prepared, but I got a little excited when you pulled out the big guns."

"I bet you did." With another wink, he unwraps the chocolate and sets two small squares onto half a graham cracker sheet.

Smartass.

"So…" I motion around the dark forest with my stick before setting it back over the orange flames. "How did you find this place?"

"I may have stretched the truth about my whereabouts the other night. I did go get those pictures printed, but I also came out here to search for a good spot for our date."

"Which is when you set up the camping chairs, I assume?"

He nods.

"And they've been sitting out here for weeks?"

"Why do you think I was so anxious to take you out?" he jokes.

"Man, you're brave."

"I wasn't too worried about it. And on the off chance that any of it had been stolen, I brought some backups in the truck."

I glance over at the white behemoth parked a few yards away. "Like what?"

"Like more blankets and chairs in the back. Nothing too crazy. Do you like it, though?"

Dropping my head back, I look up at the dark sky sprinkled with stars and release a contented sigh as an Ed Sheeran song filters through the speaker he'd set up near the cooler.

"Yeah," I admit. "I kinda do."

"Kinda?"

I grin. "Kinda. I'm not used to thoughtful guys, though. You'll have to give me a little time to get acclimated to the idea that someone actually cares about me and is willing to put effort into a date instead of expecting me to pick up dinner on the way home before a quick screw. Not that there's anything wrong with that on occasion, but––"

"I get it," he interrupts, prickling at the idea of me screwing someone that isn't him. "Trust me."

"I do trust you."

The smell of burnt sugar distracts me from his warm gaze. Marshmallow flaming, I curse under my breath, then pull it from the fire and blow on it.

My lower lip sticks out as I inspect it to see if I can salvage the gooey goodness. Unfortunately, the charred dessert is pathetic at best.

River's laughter pulls me from my self-pity party as he grabs another marshmallow, spears it on his stick, then puts it over the fire. "Ya know, I was kidding before when I mentioned the caramel. But the other night, you blamed the mess on me and said I was too much of a distraction. Now, this? I'm beginning to think you're the common denominator here, not me."

"You were there for both burnings, so I stand by my initial argument."

"Don't worry. It'll be our little secret," he teases, multitasking like a champ as he keeps the stick turning at an even pace.

With a half-assed glare, I settle back into my camping chair and tuck my knees to my chest, soaking up the ambiance like a dry sponge. It really is gorgeous here.

The marshmallow slowly browns to golden perfection before River offers it to me a few minutes later.

"For me?" I ask, pointing to my chest.

"Don't say I never gave you anything."

Smashing the marshmallow between two graham squares, I let it start to gush out the sides, then wiggle it between us. "Only if you promise to share it with me. I mean, I know it's not Reese's Puffs or one of your other sugary cereals, but some moments are worth celebrating with gooey desserts and empty calories. What do ya say?"

"I haven't had a s'more in at least a decade."

"Then it's time we remind you how amazing they are."

"Ladies first," he prods. His eyes are crinkled in the corners, and my cheeks pinch from smiling so much. But I better get used to it because I'm pretty sure I've never been happier.

With a light laugh, I take a bite then moan as the warm, melty goodness oozes into my mouth.

"Dish ish sho good," I mumble through my mouthful of food. I can feel his eyes on me as I chew it before licking my fingers to get rid of the stickiness.

"I called it," he announces before grabbing my wrist and shoving the rest of the s'more into his mouth.

"Called what?"

Pointing at me, he waves his finger around before swallowing his bite and answering me. "Sex face. And the moaning? Come on, Floozy. How come you never sound like that when we're together?"

"Because I have to be quiet when we're together."

His gaze darkens. "You don't have to be quiet out here."

I look around the empty forest. There isn't a soul for miles in any direction.

With a nod, I announce, "You make a pretty sound argument."

"And now, I'm going to make you scream." Like a damn lion, he pounces on me, muffling my laughter with loud-mouthed kisses that are playful, and fun, and make me feel happier than I've ever felt in my entire life.

I don't *do* playful.

I don't *do* fun.

And I'm not sure I ever really felt happy and carefree before this very moment, either. I smile against his mouth as his tongue grazes my lips before he pulls away and mutters, "You taste like marshmallows."

Then he dives right back in, cupping my breast through the thick, worn hoodie he'd given to me earlier as he continues to devour me like a damn s'more. And suddenly, it's not enough. I need more. Pressing my thighs together, I squirm against him, desperate for more friction the same way I'm desperate for Riv. The air is cool, but the heat from the fire combined with the fervor in his kiss makes the hoodie that's swallowing me whole feel like a straight jacket. I tug at the hem of it while keeping my mouth on his as that same familiar sense of desperation settles into my bones.

To be closer to Riv.

To connect with him.

To feel him inside of me.

Over and over again.

I'd been naive to think that one night would be enough together. And even after all these weeks of sneaking around, I'm afraid I've only grown more attached. Needier. More desperate. And for the first time since we've gotten together,

I can officially show him how I feel without fear of my brother catching us together.

With my hand pressed to his chest, I push him away, then pull off my hoodie and breathe a sigh of relief when the cool air kisses my bare shoulders.

"You. Sit back," I order, brushing my hair away from my face.

I wish I had a damn elastic.

"Someone's bossy." He grins back at me as he settles into his dark red camping chair and lets his thighs hang open. Tempting me. Taunting me. Daring me to make my next move.

A thick bulge greets me through his dark jeans, and I lick my lips before sliding onto my knees in the dirt in front of him. "Are you complaining that I'm bossy?"

"Only if you tell me I can't touch you."

The thought of his hands not tangling into my hair as I push him to the edge makes me pause. I peek up at him and ask, "Will you think I'm clingy if I tell you that I always want you to touch me?"

The fire reflects in his soft gaze as he looks down at me and smiles. "No. I'd think you were perfect."

"You're just saying that 'cause you want me to suck on your dick," I tease.

Throwing his head back, he laughs. And it's loud. And playful. And makes me feel lighter than air. "I didn't say it because of that, but now that you mention it, you *are* rather chatty right now. I think we can find better things to do with that mouth, don't you?"

He runs his thumb along my cheekbone then presses the pad against my lips, making them part. Greedily, I suck his finger into my mouth and swirl my tongue along the tip. His eyes darken with each passing second, transforming his earlier amusement into full-on need.

"Still thinking about marshmallows?" he challenges, his voice raw and gritty.

I bite his thumb, then pull away and tilt my head to one side, dragging my hands from his knees to his front pockets before massaging his cock through the fabric. "Do I look like I'm thinking about marshmallows?"

"You look like you're thinking about something."

Laughing, I unbutton his jeans, then carefully slide the zipper down and pull out his erection through the gap in his boxers. A drop of precum drips from the slit as I lazily rub my hand up and down his length. Like I have all the time in the world. Like I'm not dying with anticipation. Like this isn't turning me on in a way that I've only ever felt with him.

I lean closer and drag my tongue along the head, lapping at him like he's a damn ice cream cone while savoring the way his breath hitches and his fingers drag along my sensitive scalp.

Peeking up at him, I smile when I see his head thrown back and his Adam's apple bobbing up and down as he tries to catch his breath.

"Shit, Reese. Stop. Stop." He cups my face, pulling me off him with a slight pop before dragging me up his body. "I thought I was the one who's supposed to make you scream," he growls.

"I'm sorry. Are you complaining?" I quip. I'd be offended if it weren't for his staggered breathing and the lust reflecting in his eyes.

"Hell, no. But I want to be inside you."

My core clenches with need. "I mean…if you insist."

Another laugh escapes him before he pulls me to my feet then stands to his full height. "I insist."

Then he guides me to the bed of his truck and kisses me again as his fingers make short work of my jeans. With a swift pull, they're tossed aside, and his mouth is busy sucking on the column of my throat.

"Riv," I moan.

"Come on, babe." His fingers dig into my bare thighs before he lifts me and sets me on the edge of the tailgate that's littered with blankets. Then his mouth is on mine again. Biting. Kissing. Sucking. Filling me to the brim with a longing so deep that I'm afraid I'll never feel complete until he's inside of me.

"River," I whimper. "I need you."

Without a word, he kicks his pants and boxers off and climbs into the bed of the truck. The stars above us are brighter and more breathtaking than I've ever seen, but they don't hold a candle to the man on top of me.

"Do you want me to torture you or put us both out of our misery?" he asks between kisses.

I hook my ankles around him and lick my lips. "No more torture. I don't think I can wait any longer."

"Good girl." He lines himself up with my entrance and pushes into me. Stretching me. Making my toes curl and my back arch as he grabs my waist to keep me in place.

With a gasp, I dig my nails into his back and hold on for dear life.

His movements are slow and steady, giving me time to adjust until I'm matching his pace and urging him on.

"You're still quiet," he points out, his voice stilted with every thrust.

"What? You thought I'd give my scream to you?" I challenge with a quirked brow.

His smile is wicked before he leans down and bites my neck. Hard. My mouth opens, and a silent scream escapes me, but it only spurs him on. Shifting his weight, he snakes his hand between us, then rubs at the apex of my thighs in rhythm with his punishing movements.

Then a real scream claws its way up my throat, and I chant his name over and over again.

So. Close.

Right. There.

Don't. Stop.

It doesn't take long before my entire body is vibrating with energy, and an orgasm rushes through me.

Like I'm on fire.

And then I'm floating.

His grunts pick up their pace before he collapses onto me. The weight of his massive frame isn't suffocating. It's comforting somehow. I feel protected. Safe. And maybe even a little cherished too.

"That was…" My voice trails off.

He rolls off me and stares up at the gorgeous stars above us.

"Better than a s'more?" he offers.

"Definitely better," I agree with a big, dopey grin plastered on my face, still trying to catch my breath.

He settles back between my bare thighs, resting on his forearms to keep from suffocating me with his weight, and pushes my hair away from my forehead. His calloused fingers scratch my skin but make my heart flutter as he brushes his mouth just above my eyebrows.

"I could live here, you know," he murmurs against my dewy skin.

"Between my thighs?"

He grinds against me. "Yeah. Here too. But I meant away from it all. Out here, we can be together without having to hide shit. We can just…be."

He's right. It feels nice to have those barriers down. To live in the moment without stressing over who could walk in on us or if our alibis will check out on the off chance someone bothers to call us. Sneaking around isn't fun. But facing the truth doesn't exactly sound like a picnic, either.

"I could live here too," I murmur, dragging my fingers along his bare skin.

And I really could.

The moment is sweet. Tender. It'll be etched into my memory until the day I die.

He was right. There's no way he's going to beat Date Number One.

35

REESE

I didn't expect us to fall asleep in the bed of his truck while looking up at the stars. But sometimes, the unexpected moments are the sweetest.

When my stomach grumbles for something other than hot dogs and s'mores, River throws everything into the back of his truck, then we make our way down the dirt road in comfortable silence.

But as soon as our cells have service, the messages start pouring in.

"Six missed calls from Milo and a dozen texts," I mutter. "Did he message you too?"

"Yeah. Three texts from him and nine calls from mommy dearest. Which is a record, even for her. Any chance we could turn back around and disappear into the wilderness?"

"I'm not sure Milo would let me." I grimace and turn back to scanning the demanding messages that could make a grown man cower in fear. "What do I say to him?"

After squeezing the back of his neck, River sets his phone down in the cup holder, then focuses on the road. "We gotta tell him, Reese."

"Yeah, but I don't know *how*," I whine, sticking out my lower lip.

"Neither do I, but we'll do it together, okay?"

"He'll kill you." Though my tone is light, there's an underlying severity that's loud and clear.

River's laugh is dry as hell. "He won't kill me. He'll probably hit me. And I'll likely have to see a dentist and-or plastic surgeon afterward, but it'll be fine, Reese. The sting is going to come from us hiding it from him more than us having feelings for each other. The sooner we tell him, the better he'll handle it."

"W-what if you ask his permission or something? We can say we haven't done anything yet––"

Knuckles white, a frustrated River sighs. "He's not stupid, Reese. We both disappeared last night. He can put two and two together. He probably already has."

My phone vibrates with another incoming text from Milo.

Milo: Gibson said he heard you in your room last night, so I must've missed you. I'm on my way to work but call me when you get a sec. Want to make sure you're okay.

"What is it?" River prods as he watches me from the corner of his eye.

I read the message a few more times before answering, "H-he said Gibson heard me in my room last night."

"But you weren't in your room."

"Obviously."

"Which means he's hearing things, or he covered for us," River finishes.

Considering the options, I nod. "Yeah. I guess he did."

"We still need to tell Milo."

With another nod, my heart aches. "I know."

"It'll be okay, Reese." He squeezes my knee, but it does nothing to ease the pain in my chest.

That's the problem. I don't know if it will be.

We sit in silence, lost in our thoughts, when River's phone starts blaring.

My breath hitches as I turn to him and grimace. "Is it Milo?"

"Gina," he answers with furrowed brows before accepting the call. "Hello?"

Her voice filters through the Bluetooth speakers and allows me to hear both ends of the conversation. "Hey, you. How are you doing?"

"I'm fine." He smirks, glancing over at me. "How are you?"

"Amazing. I tried calling last night, but it went straight to voicemail."

"Yeah, sorry. I was out of cell range. What's up?"

"I got a call yesterday…"

"And?" he prods.

"And it was from a certain casting director."

I gasp and cover my mouth as excitement threatens to bubble out of me.

River's gaze darts to mine as he fights his own elation before replying as cool as a cucumber, "And?"

"And they want you. We're discussing terms and dates right now. But if everything lines up, they'll be sending over the contract later this week."

With a soft squeal, I dive right into my happy dance in the passenger seat of River's truck while completely freaking out inside.

He did it! He freaking did it!

His stunned expression is priceless, and if I weren't so invested in the conversation, I'd snap a picture for a keepsake. Slowly, he blinks, barely registering her words as if he's still in shock.

"River? Are you still there?" Gina's voice crackles through the speakers.

"Yeah." He clears his throat. "I'm here."

"You should be proud of yourself."

Looking over at me, his numb expression morphs into a giant grin. It's so wide, and boyish, and almost giddy that I want to jump up and down, screaming from the rooftops that he did it! But I keep my mouth shut as he answers, "I am, Gina. Thanks. Uh, keep me updated, I guess?"

"Will do. Congrats, River. This is a huge opportunity."

He tosses me another glance. "I know."

"I'll talk to you later, okay? There's something else I want to discuss."

"Sounds good. Just let me know when you want to meet."

"I will."

"Thanks again, Gina."

"You're welcome. See ya."

As soon as the call disconnects, I grab Riv's arm and shake him back and forth. "You did it!" I scream. "You freaking did it!"

His laughter is loud and carefree, laced with childish disbelief that's contagious. Then he releases a loud *whoop* and pumps his fist into the air. Rolling down the windows, we blast some upbeat music and get lost in the euphoria from Gina's call.

And just like that, the heavy melancholy from minutes ago has evaporated into thin air, replaced with an electric buzz of enthusiasm thrumming through our veins.

Because he did it.

He really did.

And I couldn't be more proud.

36

REESE

As we pull up to the house, I scan the driveway with my heart in my throat. Milo's motorcycle is missing. River squeezes my knee as that same depressing funk returns to the cab of his truck.

"Come on," he urges.

With my chin to my chest, I follow him inside. The place is quiet, and I assume we're alone until the faint sound of a guitar whispers through the house.

The stairs creak beneath our weight as we make our way to Gibson's room. His door is cracked open, but I knock anyway.

"Hey, Gibbs?" I call out.

"Reese?"

"Yeah, it's me." Pushing the door open a little further, I smile when I find him sitting cross-legged on the ground with his guitar in his lap.

"What's up?" His lazy smile tenses when he zeroes in on my hand laced with River's.

"I... We"––I correct myself––"wanted to thank you for covering for us last night."

He shakes his head. "I didn't cover for you."

"You said you heard Reese in her room last night," River interjects.

"I *did* hear Reese in her room last night."

"What?" I whisper, my mind desperate to find a solution as to why he would've heard someone in my room when I clearly wasn't home. But I come up empty.

"How long has this been going on?" Gibbs demands.

River ignores him. "You sure you heard someone in her room?"

"Positive. It was at like three in the morning or something like that. Now, answer the question. How long has this been going on, Reese?"

"I…" I shake my head. "Who was in my room?"

Goosebumps break out along my skin as I look at River. Softly, he shakes his head. He's just as lost as I am.

"What's going on?" Gibbs demands.

Ignoring him, I race to my room and fling open the door. But there isn't a single thing out of place. The bed is still a mess of sheets and pillows. My dirty clothes are still in the hamper near the corner. A couple of pairs of shoes are scattered along the floor, but the familiar scene does nothing to erase my fear as I drop to the ground and look under my bed. Only dust bunnies greet me.

Who the hell was in my room? And why do I feel like I'm going to puke?

Pushing myself to my feet, I stride to the closet on shaky legs before ripping it open.

It's empty too.

"What's going on?" Gibbs murmurs from the doorway, the guitar hanging limply from his arm near his side.

"You sure you heard someone in here?" River demands beside him, but his eyes don't leave mine.

"I *know* I heard someone in here. But if it wasn't you, then who was it?"

Lips quivering, I look around my room and stutter, "I-I don't know."

But I do.

It was Ian. It had to be. But why? Why would he care? Why would he break into my room? Why can't he leave me alone? Why can't he let me go?

Striding over to me, River pulls me into his arms and hugs me tightly as my fear overwhelms me.

"Sh...," he croons. "It's okay."

My entire body is trembling like a leaf, but I don't know how to make it stop. I feel violated. Dirty. Like I need to scrub at my skin and disinfect every single inch of my room to erase the intruder who tainted it.

"It was Ian," I whisper. "It had to be."

"We don't know that."

"Who else would break into my room, River?" I cry. "What if I'd been home? What if I wasn't with you last night?"

"You were with River?" a deep voice interrupts from the entrance to my room. But it doesn't belong to Gibbs.

It's Jake's.

My head snaps toward the doorway of my room. Standing next to Gibbs is Jake. His usual calm and collected expression is absent, replaced with a rage so palpable I can almost taste it.

My lower lip quivers. "Jake--"

"Were you with River last night?" he accuses.

"I can explain--"

"Then you better start talking, Reese. Because it looks to me like you just stabbed your brother in the back."

Squirming out of River's grasp, I take a step toward Jake but stop when his eyes darken with disgust.

My nails bite into my palms as I squeeze my hands into fists. "I didn't––"

"Didn't what? Screw one of his best friends?"

"Back off, Jake," River growls, flanking my side. The tension rolls off him in waves, reminding me of a coiled snake that could strike at any second.

And he will strike if I can't get a handle on the situation.

"Don't get me started on you, asshole. Milo gave you one rule. *One.* And you broke it without batting an eye. I knew this would happen. I *knew* it," Jake seethes. "You can have any girl you want, you selfish bastard. Any fucking girl. Why her?"

Nostrils flaring, River steps forward, but I reach for his arm to hold him back. I feel like I'm going to be sick. Like I can't breathe. Like everything is spiraling out of control, and I don't know how to stop it.

With his feet planted between Jake and me, River throws a verbal punch instead of a physical one. And it almost breaks me.

"You know why I want her, Jake. I was just the only one who had the balls to take her. Don't be pissed at me because you didn't."

"You think this is about balls?" Jake laughs, though there isn't any humor in it. "This is about respect for a friend, you selfish bastard. Do you even know what that is? Or has your mother tainted you more than you'd like to admit?"

Ignoring the comment about his mom, even though I know it cuts River deeper than he'll ever admit, River spits, "You're not pissed that I slept with Milo's sister. You're pissed because you *didn't.*"

My chest heaves as I look between River and Jake, but neither of them denies it.

Deny it, Jake, I silently beg. *Tell Riv he's wrong. Tell him we're just friends. That you look at me like a little sister. That you're just trying to protect Milo. Say* something*! Anything!*

My skin feels too tight. Like I'm seconds from being torn into a thousand irreparable pieces. But I don't know how to take it back. This moment. All of my mistakes. Someone needs to backpedal and tell me they were kidding. Someone needs to break the silence I'm suffocating in because I can't do this. I can't be the reason their friendship falls apart. And I can't be the reason Jake looks like he's seconds from breaking. I can't.

"W-what are you talking about?" I whisper. Sure, River's joked about it before. But this is different. It can't be true.

Jake's jaw looks like it was chiseled from granite, but he doesn't say a word.

"Tell me," I demand.

He stays quiet, so River answers for him. "Jake's in love with you, Reese. I already told you this."

"You were just jealous," I argue, though I know it falls flat.

"Of course, I was jealous. I've wanted you since the moment I met you. And so has Jake. He's just pissed that he was too much of a coward to make a move. And now he's too late."

My heart breaks when I finally recognize the pain in my brother's best friend's eyes. The regret. The truth.

"Jake?" I whisper.

Talk to me, I silently plead.

He shakes his head. "If you don't tell Milo, I will. He deserves to know."

Then he storms back to his room. As he slams the door in fury, the house shakes, making me flinch.

"Jake!" I yell, storming after him.

Grabbing my wrist, River stops me. "Give him space."

"Let me go, Riv."

"Reese——"

I wrench my hand away from him. "I need to talk to him."

"You need to give him space."

Ignoring him, I race to Jake's room, then fling open the door and wrap my arms around his neck without waiting for permission.

I've ruined everything.

"**I**'m sorry," I cry. "I'm so sorry, Jake. I'm so freaking sorry. Please forgive me. Please don't hate me. Please don't push me away."

Jake's arms stay at his sides as I keep repeating the same words over and over again like a broken record. The tears roll freely down my cheeks, staining his dark red T-shirt before the frozen statue I'm holding onto finally melts to reveal the real Jake I know and love. With his arms snaked around my lower back, he drops his chin to his chest and breathes deep.

"Sh…," he consoles after a few minutes. "You're breaking my heart, Reese."

"You're breaking mine," I return with a sob. "I love you, Jake. You're one of my best friends. I can't lose you. You don't understand. You've been there for me since I was a little kid. You and Milo are my rocks. And seeing you look at me like you just did? Like I was dirty? I just… I can't let you look at me like that."

"Sh…," he repeats, rubbing his hand up and down my back in an attempt to soothe me. "You're not dirty."

"Was he right, Jake? Am I going to lose you because I look at you like an older brother? A protector? I-I can't lose you. Please don't leave me. I need you too much. And I need your support. I need your love. I need your texts and your friendship. I just... I can't. I can't live without you. I know you've been busy with school and with your thesis, and that's been fine. But I need to know we're okay."

"We're not okay, though, Reese," he murmurs. I tremble in his arms but refuse to look up at him. I can't. If I see resignation, or disappointment, or disgust, or anything that isn't acceptance and love, then I'll be obliterated.

Praying I've heard him wrong, I bite my lower lip to keep it from quivering.

"W-what?" I stammer.

"He was right, Reese. He was right. I've been in love with you since high school. The idea of you dating him?" His body tenses in my arms. "It...it makes me sick, Reese."

My heart leaps into my throat until I feel like I'm choking. But I don't know what to say. I don't know how to convince him that we're better off as friends. That he shouldn't want someone like me. He deserves so much more.

"Tell me something, Reese," he whispers. His breath tickles the top of my head as I continue clinging to him. "Did you know? Did you even have an inkling of an idea that I might look at you as more than my best friend's little sister?"

I shake my head but refuse to let him go because I'm afraid that if I do, it'll be the last time he lets me close.

"Did you ever see me as anything more than your brother's best friend?" he pushes, the defeat clear in his voice.

"I've always seen you as more than my brother's best friend." I squeeze my eyes shut and breathe him in, terrified it'll be for the last time. "I've seen you as one of mine too."

"But not romantically," he finishes for me. His shoulders

hunch and his arms fall to his sides. Like he's just been stabbed, and I was the one to deliver the final blow.

But he deserves the right to move on. To be happy. To find someone who makes him feel the way River makes me feel.

So, even though it breaks my heart, I choke out, "No. Not romantically."

He drops his head back and looks up at the ceiling, but I refuse to let him go. I can't.

"You deserve more than a girl like me, Jake," I tell him. "You deserve someone who looks at you like you hung the moon. You deserve someone who looks at you the way you look at me, even though I didn't want to see it. I'm so sorry, Jake, but I'm not that girl."

His arms return to my waist, punishing me with their iron grip for the last time before he lets me go and forces me to let him go too.

The absence kills me, but I fold my arms to keep from reaching for him again.

"Say something," I plead.

He rubs the light scruff along his jaw. "I know you're not that girl."

"I'm sorry––"

"I know," he repeats. There's a numbness in his tone that leaves me itching to hug him again. But I don't. Because it's what *I* need. Not him. And I can't be selfish anymore.

Wiping at my tear-stained cheeks, I choke out, "I'm so sorry, Jake."

"You need to tell Milo."

"I will," I promise.

"When?"

"Soon."

"When, Reese?" he presses.

"Soon."

He nods. "Okay."

"Are… Are we okay?" I whimper. "Because I really need us to be okay."

"I need time."

"And you can have time. As much as you need. I just… need to know that one day, we'll be okay."

Staying silent, his gaze bounces around my face, taking in my tear-stained cheeks and my swollen eyes before he finally caves. "I'll try, Reese."

"How? When? What can I do, Jake?"

"I"––he squeezes the back of his neck, the tips of his fingers turning white from the pressure––"I just need space, okay?"

And even though it kills me, I nod. "Okay. Whatever you need. But I'm here when you're ready."

"I know. And I'm here too."

But he isn't.

Not really.

Because I chose River instead.

I know it.

And so does Jake.

"I'm so sorry," I repeat for what feels like the thousandth time.

"Reese––"

The front door slams, making the windows in Jake's room rattle as both our heads snap toward its direction.

What the hell?

Everything happens in slow motion as we race toward the hallway, and heavy boots pound against the stairs. Milo is red with rage as I step out of Jake's room. Pointing at me, Milo spits, "You screwing Jake too?"

I freeze. "What?"

"Stay there," he seethes before bellowing at the top of his lungs, "River!"

He knows.

3 8

REESE

"**M**ilo!" I scream.

Storming toward River's room, my brother disregards my desperate plea and wrenches open the door like a freaking beast. Jake and I run toward him but dig our heels into the ground when we reach the threshold. It all happens so fast.

Ignoring River's hands raised in surrender, Milo grabs his collar, cocks his arm back, and hits him. Hard. I scream and cover my mouth as blood gushes from River's nose and down his chin, but he doesn't retaliate.

He simply stares back at Milo, waiting for the next blow to connect.

"Milo!" I shriek.

Keeping his voice deathly calm, Milo ignores me and flexes his hand at his side. "Did you touch her, River?"

River holds his gaze. "Yeah, man. I did."

Milo nods then hits him again. The crunch from River's nose breaking will haunt me for the rest of my life and spurs me into motion. Scrambling for my brother's right arm, I hold him back then wedge myself between them.

"Stop, Milo! I'm begging you to *please* stop!"

His haunted eyes turn to me, chilling me to the bone. "Go pack your shit. We're leaving."

"Milo––"

"Not the time, Reese. If you don't want me to kick the shit out of your boyfriend, then I suggest you back up."

"Milo, I'm sorry––"

"Too late for apologies." He digs into the back pocket of his jeans, then tosses 4x6 pieces of paper along the floor. As they scatter across the ground, I recognize them and cover my mouth in shock.

"W-where did you get these?"

"You lied to me," he seethes.

"Answer the question, Milo. Where did you get these? Were you in my room?"

Scoffing, he shakes his head in disgust. "Why the hell would I go into your room? I trusted you, remember?"

"Then where did they come from?"

His lips pull into a thin line as he debates whether or not he should deem my question worthy of a response. After a few seconds, he grits out, "Someone dropped them off at work."

"Who?" I plead. "Who dropped them off?"

"I don't know." Sensing my anxiety, his shoulders deflate, and he releases his hold on River's collar while the blood continues to soak his shirt. "They left them with the new receptionist."

Gibson flanks my side, staring at the pictures littered along the floor before muttering, "Were these in your room last night, Reese?"

"Y-yeah," I stutter, my fear choking me.

"What's going on?" Milo demands. Apparently, my panic is enough to distract him from the fact that I've been sleeping with one of his friends. For now, anyway. Ripping off his stained shirt, River presses it to his face to mop up a bit of the blood flowing freely from his broken nose. He looks terrible, and I close the distance between us to take a closer look.

"A-are you okay?" My guilt battles my fear until I can't focus on anything at all.

"Answer the question, Reese," Milo orders, his patience close to snapping a second time.

I squeeze my eyes shut and force out, "Someone broke into my room last night, stole those pictures, and delivered them to you."

"Ian," he surmises. It doesn't take long for him to come to the same conclusion I did.

"Yeah."

"How does he know where you live?"

"It's complicated," I tell him.

"Explain it to me."

"His friend, Rocky, moved out here a few months ago and happened to be my Uber driver. Small world, right?" I add sarcastically. My laugh is almost a sob.

"Too fuckin' small." Rubbing his hand across his face, Milo releases a deep breath but doesn't say anything. He's still reeling like the rest of us. But at least for the moment, he's not trying to kill River.

Jake clears his throat from the entrance of River's room, silently witnessing the entire blow-up and aftermath. Gritting his teeth, he looks around the room before his gaze lands on his best friend. "We need to go to the cops."

"Milo hates cops," I return. "You know that."

"Yeah, well, do you have any better ideas? This guy is stalking you, Reese. He's officially broken into your room. What if you'd been home? What if——"

"Stop," Milo growls, lifting his swollen hand to shut him up. "Jake's right. We gotta go to the cops."

"And what are they going to do?" I whisper, hating the way my voice trembles with fear. Growing up, the cops were called on more than one occasion to stop by our house for domestic disturbances. And even though they could see we weren't being taken care of, they left us there. With shitty parents and no food and all of the responsibility on a little boy's shoulders to take care of his baby sister and put up with a couple of abusive drunks.

But I guess I should be grateful. I've heard the horror stories about foster care. At least I got to stay with my brother. Still, it doesn't help our trust issues with law enforcement, and now, we're expected to report a stalker?

That sounds promising.

"They're gonna help us keep you safe. Come on. Let's get going. You"--Milo points at River with a deathly glare--"Stay here. We don't need you."

"What?" I interject. "Milo, you're being--"

"What am I being, Reese? Huh? Ridiculous? Petty? Callous?"

"Milo--"

"I'm trying to protect you from getting hurt again by another selfish asshole who's using you," he sneers. "But you sure as hell aren't making it easy on me."

My heart cracks at the look in his eyes. The disappointment. Disgust. And lack of trust. Folding my arms, I make myself small and let the tears flow freely from my eyes.

"I'm sorry," I mouth, my voice unable to make it past the lump of regret in my throat.

Without a word, Milo storms out of the room, and I'm left staring at his back before he disappears from view.

"What are we supposed to do?" I whisper to no one in particular. I've ruined everything.

"He's allowed to be pissed," Gibson mutters. "But we have

more important things to deal with right now. Come on. Let's get in the car."

With a deep sigh, Jake rubs his face roughly. "I'll talk to him, but Sonny's right. One shitstorm at a time. Let's go."

After three hours at the police station, we walk away with a little piece of paper and the promise that they'll call me as soon as they locate Ian and notify him of the restraining order.

Good luck with that.

But at least it's done, and I can focus on the next giant mess that needs to be cleaned up. River. Milo. And me.

I release a shuddered breath and fold my arms.

"How you doin'?" River asks as we walk through the parking lot. Gibson is texting on his phone, and Milo and Jake are hanging back a few feet, talking in low voices, though I have no idea what the subject is. And I don't really care, either.

All I want is a few minutes with my boyfriend to make sure he's okay. To make sure that I didn't ruin everything. That I didn't ruin *us*. The thought of losing him after the shitstorm this morning… It's unbearable. And his silence hasn't exactly been helping my nerves.

He's been quiet since this morning. But the bruising around his eyes combined with the swollen bridge of his nose is a sharp reminder that things are a little rocky right now.

Little *is a bit of an understatement.*

"I'm okay." I sigh and glance over at him. "How are you? You look like crap."

He laughs before wincing in pain. "Gee. Thanks. Are you sure you still wanna date me when I look like this?"

"You could look like Cookie Monster, and I'd still want to date you," I tease. "And you didn't answer my question. How are you feeling?"

His fingers brush along the bridge of his nose before he cringes and drops his hand to his side. "I'm fine."

"Liar."

"I'm fine, Reese," he repeats.

From the corner of my eye, I examine his injuries. Milo has quite the right hook. At least Gibson was able to set River's broken nose before we left for the police station. I'm just surprised the cops didn't question his swollen face when we came and told them about Ian breaking into our house.

"You don't look fine," I murmur.

"You've already mentioned that," he quips, gifting me with his sexy smirk. "But I thought you said you weren't one to care about looks, Floozy. You're starting to give me a complex."

"You? A complex about your looks?" I gasp and clutch at my chest. "I didn't think it was possible."

He scoffs. "Don't worry, Floozy. I'll be back to sexy in no time."

"I'm sure you will. But I need to know that I'm attracted to what's in here." As our pace slows, I press my hand to his chest, then motion to his bruised face. "Not just all of this. And I'm sorry if I hurt your feelings or made you feel otherwise."

"You didn't hurt my feelings," he returns with a tight

smile. But there's a vulnerability in his gaze that tells me I hit the nail on the head. It makes my chest ache with need.

A need to hold him.

To kiss him.

To tell him that he's perfect.

That, even after everything that's happened, I still choose us. And I'll always choose us. Even if he had a third eye or a snaggletooth, he'd still be the one for me.

Reaching for his hand, I brush my pinky against his but stop myself from tangling our fingers together the way I desperately want to. I can't. I've already fanned Milo's rage enough for one day. Still, the innocent touch causes a spark of electricity to race up my arm, begging me to burrow into River's chest and never let him go.

A swell of resignation blossoms in my lower gut before I fold my arms. "I *did* hurt your feelings because I made you question whether or not I like you for the *real* you instead of just the moneymaker."

A bark of laughter escapes River as we reach the car. "The moneymaker, huh?"

"Mm-hmm," I hum. "Speaking of which, Milo didn't even get on his knees before touching it. Doesn't he know the rules by now?"

"I guess it's fair since I broke his rule first." His usual cocky smirk falters.

"That's on me," I remind him. "Not you."

"Now who's the liar?" he jokes before his jaw tightens, and the playful River I've grown accustomed to is replaced by a much more serious man who knows he screwed up.

Who knows we *both* screwed up.

"We should've told him, Reese."

"We were going to--"

"We took too long. And it's a bullshit excuse. I feel like shit."

And it's all my fault.

"This isn't on you. You wanted to tell him. I'm the one who wanted to wait."

"I should've insisted––"

"And I should've listened." I take a deep breath. "We can't go back and change the past, Riv. But it'll be okay. He'll forgive us."

He has to.

Turning his helpless gaze on me, Riv shakes his head. "He'll forgive you because you're his sister."

"Riv––"

"He won't forgive me, Reese. But that's on me. I betrayed his trust. And we both know how hard that is to come by. Real friends don't do the shit I did."

The bite of pain keeps me grounded as I dig my teeth into the inside of my cheek to keep my tears at bay. I've ruined everything. This is all my fault. Yet River's the one who's going to truly pay for it.

Even though I'd give anything to argue the opposite, he's right. Milo's the most stubborn person I've ever met. It'll take a miracle for him to give me the support I'm craving. And it'll take an even bigger one for Milo to give River the second chance he needs to prove his loyalty to his best friend.

I'm the worst sister ever.

Sniffling, I glance over my shoulder at Milo. That same hard expression is painted across his face as he trails behind us.

"We'll figure it out," I whisper, though I'm not sure who I'm trying to convince.

"I guess we'll just have to wait and see. Do you have work tonight?"

"Yeah." I pull out my phone and check the time before cringing. "I have to go right now, actually. This restraining order crap took forever. I feel like I've ruined everyone's day."

"Stop blaming yourself, Reese."

"That's a little easier said than done," I point out.

"Which means you need a good distraction."

"Then I guess it's a good thing I have work, huh? Gibbs is working, too, and he offered to give me a ride."

"I'll follow behind you guys."

Confused, I ask, "What? Why?"

"Because your ex is stalking you."

I roll my eyes as we round the corner of his truck, then wrap my arms around River's waist as soon as we're out of Milo's sight. He returns it instantly, melting a few more of the reservations I have about our relationship before I remember what the hell we were talking about.

"Gibbs will be there," I remind him. "He can keep an eye on me and make sure I'm safe, okay? Not a big deal."

"It feels like a big deal."

"That's because all you boys are overbearing alpha protectors who want to keep me safe. And while it's adorable, it's unnecessary. I promise I'll be fine, Riv. Go get some rest and put some ice on that." I motion to his face. "It'll help with the swelling."

Shoes scuff along the asphalt, getting closer to us before I've had my fill of River's warmth, but we end our embrace anyway. River opens the passenger door to Gibson's car with a sigh and helps me climb into it. Milo had insisted he needed space, so he drove his motorcycle to the police station while Gibson, Jake, and I drove in Gibson's car. And even though Milo threatened to cut off River's balls, he trailed behind in his truck, then parked in the stall next to ours.

"Hold up," Milo calls, jogging closer to us before River has a chance to close my door. "What's the plan for tonight?"

"Me and Reese have work," Gibbs answers. "I'll keep an eye on her."

"I'll come and hang out at the bar," Jake adds, surprising me with his offer as he rounds the trunk of the car and slides into the backseat. For a guy who says he needs space, he's been pretty damn accommodating today. Maybe we'll be able to repair our relationship after all. I bite my lip and peek over at him, but he avoids my gaze.

Or maybe not.

"I'll cancel my appointment for tonight and come too," Milo replies.

"You already missed your entire day because of me," I argue, though the bastard won't look me in the eye, either. "Go to work, Milo. Gibbs and Jake will keep an eye on me tonight. I'll be fine."

"I'll be there too," River interjects, his tone brooking no argument.

I grimace.

Dammit, River! Keep your mouth shut.

Standing to his full height, my bear of a brother shakes his head and dares him to argue. "No, you won't."

"It's your sister's safety—"

"And like we discussed, Sonny and Jake will be there to keep an eye on her." He steps closer, crowding River against the still-open passenger door. "We don't need you. Go stick your dick somewhere else."

"What the hell is your problem, Milo? It's me, remember?" River snaps, slamming his hand against his chest to drive his point home. "We've been friends for years—"

"And yet you stabbed me in the back."

Dropping his head back in frustration, he mutters, "I didn't—"

Milo's scoff cuts him off. "Yeah, you did. I know how you treat women, Riv. It's the same way Sonny treats women.

322

The same way I do. Hell, even Jake isn't a saint, and he's *nothing* compared to you. Why the hell do you think I would *ever* want an asshole like you for my sister?"

"I might've been an asshole to other girls, but they've always known exactly what they were getting when they climbed into my bed."

"And that makes it okay for you to mess with Reese?" Milo's sneer makes my stomach churn with acid before he laughs darkly. "Not a chance in Hell."

"You guys––" I interrupt.

"Not now," they bark in unison.

Practically vibrating with anger, River refuses to back down and steps forward, getting right up in Milo's face and holding his piercing gaze with his own. He's already had the crap kicked out of him once today, and I'm terrified to watch him get hit again.

Because he won't fight back.

Not physically, anyway. Sure, he'll stand up for himself in an attempt to explain his point of view, but I think a small part of him believes he deserves the broken nose my brother gifted him with.

Trembling, I fold my arms as my focus bounces between the two most important men in my life while I pray this conversation won't end in more blows like it did this morning.

This is so messed up.

But I get what River's trying to do. He's trying to make Milo listen to him, no matter how hard it is. And I need Milo to listen too. I need him to understand that we weren't trying to hurt him. I need him to see that this is more than a fling to us. So much more.

Listen to him, Milo, I silently beg. But I don't waste my breath.

"You don't get it," River tells him, his voice bleeding

sincerity. "Reese isn't just some girl from SeaBird. Not to me."

"Bullshit––"

"Do you think I made my decision lightly when I hooked up with her?" Riv crowds Milo even more until their chests are almost touching. But my brother refuses to back down, his face still red with anger.

Careful, Riv.

"I didn't want her for a casual lay, Milo. Do you honestly think I care that little about her, let alone the years we've been friends?"

With a deathly calm voice, Milo murmurs, "Careful, River. I've already messed up your face once today, and we both know how much you care about your pretty boy appearance."

"I don't give a shit about my face, Milo. I screwed up, okay? I should've told you, and that's on me. But I care about her. She's it for me, and I'm going to spend the rest of my life treating Reese the way she deserves because after all the shit she's been through, she's earned it. And isn't that all you want for her?"

Chewing on the inside of my cheek, I turn to Milo. But it isn't my brother in front of me anymore. Stone cold expression. Fists tight. But a storm raging just beneath the surface.

And even though I know it would kill him if I ever voiced it aloud, he looks just like our father in this moment. Right before Milo would tell me to go to my room and lock the door. Right before I knew that I'd wake up to see his body bruised and broken. Right before I'd curl into a ball and cry for hours, wishing I was as strong as my older brother instead of his little sister, who needed protecting.

I pushed him here. I turned him into the monster he's loathed more than anything else in the world. And just like all those times when we were younger, I'm paralyzed. I can't find my voice. I can't move a freaking muscle. So I watch. And I wait. For the fallout. The yelling. And the moment when my brother steps into his father's shoes.

It's all my fault.

All my fault.

My *fault.*

"Milo," I whisper.

His Adam's apple bobs in his throat. Then his gaze slides from River to me, and the first spark of hope ignites inside of me.

Please, Milo, I silently beg. *Please forgive me. Forgive him. Give us a chance. Don't fight this with hate. And resentment. And every other toxic trait you were taught to embrace as a kid.*

"I'm going to work," he mutters, turning away from me. His keys glint in the dying sunlight as he dismisses us and strides toward his bike while simultaneously ending the conversation before it's barely even begun.

Grabbing his arm, River prevents Milo from escaping as he pleads, "What can I do to fix this?"

Milo's gaze slides down to where River is touching him. His jaw tightens, and his nostrils flare.

"Milo," I plead.

"Stay away from my sister," he breathes. "And don't step a foot inside SeaBird tonight."

And just like that, the tiny spark fizzles into a plume of smoke while the truth hits me square in the chest.

We'll never get his blessing.

River drops his hand to his side, releasing his hold on my brother and any hope we had that Milo would forgive us. No one moves a muscle as Milo stalks toward his bike then throws his leg over the side of it before the rumble of his engine shakes me to my core.

River and Gibson stay frozen in place. The silence is deafening before Jake's seat belt in the back of the car clicks into place and makes me jump.

"I'll talk to him," he mutters behind me.

My gaze stays glued to the windshield. "You don't have to."

With a sigh, he lifts his chin at Gibbs. "Let's get you guys to work."

I hesitate and turn to River as Gibson climbs behind the wheel. His hands are tucked into the front pockets of his jeans as he tilts his head toward his truck parked beside Gibson's beater. "I'll talk to you later, okay, Reese?"

Nodding, tears well in my eyes, but I blink them away. "Okay."

I love you.

My knee bounces up and down as we pull into SeaBird's parking lot a little while later. The sky is dark and angry, but only a few droplets of rain have fallen. For some reason, it seems to match my inner turmoil all too well.

"You okay?" Gibbs asks, turning off the ignition.

"Not really."

"Give him time," Jake tells me. Then he opens the back-door of Gibson's car and climbs out. Gibbs and I follow suit and head to the side entrance without another word when Jake pauses before stepping over the threshold.

Digging out his cell from his front pocket, Jake's brows furrow as he recognizes the caller. "I'll be there in a sec. It's my professor."

"No worries," I return. "I'll save you a booth."

The music is already pounding through the bar as we slip into the break room and put our stuff in our lockers.

"Hey!" Ashton calls as soon as he sees us. "Gibbs, will you grab some more Jameson and a case of the local stouts from the storage room? We're running low."

"Sure thing." He turns to me. "You gonna be okay?"

Rolling my eyes, I pat his shoulder. "I'll be out front. See you in a few."

"You sure?" he asks, stepping in front of me.

"I'm fine. Seriously. Now, let me go so I can find a booth for Jake to hang out in tonight, okay?"

The indecision is clear in his gaze before he releases a sigh and steps to the side of the dark hallway. "I'll be out in five."

"Yup. I know. And thank you for keeping an eye on me. You're a pretty good friend, Gibbs."

With a smirk, he challenges, "Only pretty good?"

"I mean, it would be nice if you did my laundry and didn't play the guitar at three in the morning. But hey, there's always room for improvement, right?"

He laughs. "Go find a booth for Jake, ya little shit. I'll see you in a sec."

I wiggle my fingers back and forth. "Bye."

Then I head to the front of the building. The place is pretty crowded as I grab a washcloth from behind the bar and scan the area for an open seat. A recently vacated booth catches my eye in the back.

Perfect.

I bob and weave between customers, then start wiping it down when a familiar voice chills me to the bone.

"Hey, baby," the voice slurs from behind me.

Flinching, I turn around. My pulse skyrockets as I look Ian up and down. "W-what the hell are you doing here?"

"Rocky said you like to hang out here." He casually examines the place while nodding his approval. "Ya know, I like it too. We should come here more often."

I wring the dirty rag in my hands and rise onto my tiptoes, desperate to find Gibbs. Or Jake. Or even Ashton.

It wouldn't take a genius to see I'm freaking out right now, right?

"Y-you shouldn't be here," I whisper.

"Why the hell not?"

"Because we're over, Ian."

"We're not over, babe. We were just taking a break. And you were right. I should've never let you go. I was being selfish. I swear I'll never be selfish again. I just need you. Come on. Let's get outta here."

Aaaand, he's officially lost it.

"Ian––"

Leaning closer, his pungent breath makes me gag as it fans across my face. "Look. My brother fired my ass. I'm lonely, and I miss you, and I just want to talk."

"We've already talked multiple times." My gaze darts over to the bar where Gibson is yet to be present.

"You cheated on me," he mumbles, looking more hurt than anything else as he reaches for my arm. Not roughly. More like I'm a precious artifact that could break if it isn't handled carefully.

I shy away from him and shake my head. "You cheated on *me*, Ian."

His shoulders hunch, but his hand drops back to his side. "She didn't mean anything."

"I didn't mean anything to you, either."

"Will you just listen to me?"

"Why did you deliver the pictures to my brother?" I ask.

He shakes his head back and forth. "What pictures? Reese, I'm here 'cause I love you. I want you back. You gotta understand––"

"Don't play stupid, Ian––"

"I'm not playing––"

A gasp escapes me as he's wrenched away like a ragdoll. I cover my mouth in surprise before my saviors come into view. With Gibbs on Ian's right and Jake on his left, they step between us, using their massive frames as a barrier before crossing their arms and giving me their backs.

"It's time for you to leave, Ian," Jake growls. "The cops are looking for you."

I peek around my protectors and watch the situation unfold like a damn train wreck in slow motion.

"W-what?" Ian's face drains of blood. "Wait, why?"

"Because you broke into her fucking house, moron," Gibbs spits. "She filed a restraining order a few hours ago. I suggest you turn around and get out of this bar before they find you on the premises."

"Dammit, Reese!" Ian seethes, his confusion morphing into anger.

The band stops playing, and the constant chatter surrounding us ceases, making my flesh prickle with awareness.

I can feel everyone's eyes on me. Their curiosity. Their confusion. Their pity. I can feel all of it, tainting my skin like a thick tar that I want to wash away. But I don't know how. I want to run. I want to hide. I want this night--hell, this entire day--to be over.

"You need to go, Ian," I whisper, choking back the need to curl into a ball and hide. My entire body is shaking like a freaking leaf, but I don't know how to make it stop.

A pair of giant bouncers sense the commotion and zigzag through the onlookers before their sausage hands dig into Ian's collarbones from both sides.

With a reddened face, he starts screaming my name over and over again. "Reese! Reese!"

My fingers dig into Jake's navy blue T-shirt as I squeeze my eyes shut and try to block out the sound, but it's no use. It's already etched into my memory.

"Hey, what's going on?" Dove squeaks.

I jump and clutch my chest. "Where the hell did you come

from? I thought you weren't working today."

"I wasn't, but my sister was particularly grouchy today, so I decided to give her some space and come listen to the band instead of tiptoeing around our apartment all night. I'm glad I did. Is everything okay? You look spooked."

"That's my ex. He's been…"

"Stalking her," Gibbs finishes for me. I can almost see the smoke coming from his ears as his face turns red with frustration. "He's been stalking her. But the cops can't arrest him for showing up in a bar when he hasn't been served the restraining order yet. Ashton just called them to let them know where Ian is, but other than that, there's not much we can do right now."

His phone buzzes in his pocket, and he takes it out before giving us his back. Then he answers it in a hushed voice.

Looking helpless--and like *my* Jake for the first time today--Jake asks, "What can I do, Reese? How can I help?"

"I just want to go home," I mutter under my breath, rubbing my hands along my bare arms.

I've been here for what? Ten minutes? But it's too much. First, Jake. Then, Milo. And now, Ian. What the hell am I supposed to do? And how did it spiral out of control so quickly? I'm so emotionally drained that I just want to curl into a ball and sleep for a week. Right now, there are too many stares and too many witnesses to the drama in my private life that should've never been aired out at work. It'll be a miracle if they let me keep my job.

Dove pulls me into a quick hug before I even register her arms around me. "I'll cover your shift."

"You don't have to do that," I whisper. My focus drifts to the concrete floor beneath my scuffed sneakers.

"I want to. Besides, I might as well get paid if I'm here to listen to the band, right? Go and get some rest. It looks like you need it."

I purse my lips. "Gee, thanks."

Her laughter lightens the somber blanket enveloping me as she gently nudges me toward the exit. "Seriously. Go."

"I'll take you." Jake's arm snakes around my shoulder, and I lean into his touch before Gibbs disconnects his call and turns to me.

The air whooshes from his lungs as if a thousand pounds are weighing him down.

"What's wrong?" I ask.

"River's outside."

"River?" I rasp.

A fresh wave of adrenaline courses through my veins as soon as his name slips past my lips. It's laced with a desperation that's so potent I'm afraid I might choke on it. I need to see him. To have him hold me and tell me that everything's going to be okay. That tomorrow will be better. And that we'll figure it out together.

"Yeah." Gibbs sighs. "He may have pissed off Ian when the bouncers threw him outside. Apparently, there weren't any fists thrown or anything, but he wanted to give us a heads-up that he's here."

"But...what's he doing here?" I ask. "Milo said––"

"That he couldn't step foot *inside* SeaBird. He didn't mention being outside," Gibbs clarifies with an amused smirk. "It's your call, though, Jake. If you want to take her instead of handing her off to Riv, you can use my car. But he sounded pretty distraught after seeing Ian get thrown out on his ass and would like to see Reese to make sure she's okay."

"River's never distraught," Jake mutters.

"Yeah, well, tonight he is. Might be good for him to spend a few minutes with Reese after everything that went down, don't you think?"

I can see what Gibson's doing. And even though it kind of pisses me off that he's letting Jake think he has a right to tell me what I can and can't do, I appreciate his effort. Because if Jake can give his blessing on the relationship, he might be able to convince Milo to do the same.

"Please, Jake?" I murmur.

He exhales and pinches the bridge of his nose, mulling it over as I wait with bated breath.

"Let me walk you out," he finally decides. The defeat is clear in his voice, but it manages to ease the ache in my chest.

"Thank you," I breathe out.

With his hand pressed to my lower back, Jake guides me through the crowded bar. The people are slowly snapping back to their own little realities and give us a wide berth as we sneak out the front.

As soon as the cold air kisses my cheeks beneath the awning, a set of strong hands tug me into a hard chest. I recognize who it belongs to instantly. And even though it's pouring outside and River is soaked to the bone, his warmth surrounds me. Comforting me in a way that I didn't even know was possible. He squeezes me tighter, and I breathe deep, committing to memory his familiar scent combined with the smell of fresh rain.

"You okay?" he murmurs. His breath brushes against the crown of my head as he leans closer. "I saw them throw Ian out and lost my shit."

"I'm fine," I mumble against him. "Promise."

Jake clears his throat and steps back to give us a bit of space. "Take care of her."

Riv nods. "I will."

Then Jake heads inside, taking a small piece of my heart with him.

"Let's get out of here," River murmurs before he lets me go and leads me into the parking lot. The rain has picked up from a slow drizzle to an angry thunderstorm. As the lightning sparks in the distance, we pick up our pace, racing to his truck that's only a few stalls away. I hunch my shoulders and cover my head, but it doesn't stop the water droplets from soaking me to the bone in a matter of seconds.

"Get in," Riv orders, cupping my ass before pushing me inside his truck.

My hair is a wet, tangled mess as I shove it away from my face and click the seat belt around me. Another clap of thunder booms in the distance. I flinch in the leather seat. Rounding the front of the truck, River hops inside, then turns the heat to full blast before pulling out of the parking lot.

"You sure you're okay?" The light bounces off his bruised face as he glances over at me before clutching the steering wheel with both hands. The water is pounding against the windshield in angry sheets, and River's brows furrow in concentration before he turns onto the main road.

"I'm fine. Are you okay?" I return.

He looks in the rearview mirror then mutters, "Yeah. Fine."

A few minutes tick by in silence, and I let myself melt into the leather seat as the day finally catches up with me. So much hate. So much commotion. So much animosity. I just want everything to slow down and let me breathe for a second. I close my eyes and rest my head against the cold window.

"Shit," River breathes. The curse is so quiet I'm surprised I hear it. Prying my eyelids open, I look over at him.

His forehead wrinkles before he rechecks the rearview mirror a few seconds later.

"What's wrong?" I ask.

He doesn't answer me but glances behind him as the windshield wipers continue flailing back and forth in time with my pulse.

Looking over my shoulder, a pair of headlights glare back at me.

"Who is that?" I ask.

"I don't know," he murmurs. "But I think they've been following us since we left SeaBird."

Our street slips by on my right, and I turn back to River in confusion.

"Our street's a dead end. I'm going to keep driving for a minute in case I'm not imagining things."

"W-what do you mean?" I stutter, twisting in my seat to find the car getting closer.

"It'll be fine, Reese."

"You sure about that?"

The headlights are blinding as they bounce off the rearview mirror, so I can't tell the model of the car to confirm my suspicion. "Is it Ian?"

"I don't know."

"Should I call the police?"

"I don't know," he repeats before glancing in his rearview mirror another time. Coming to a conclusion, he decides, "Yeah. It's better to be safe than sorry. Call the police. Tell them we're headed to the grocery store on Eighth Street."

Too anxious to talk on the phone, I send a quick group text to Jake, Gibbs, and Milo, telling them to make the call and meet us there as soon as they can.

River presses the brakes when the road curves, but his truck doesn't slow down the way it's supposed to. He tries again, pumping the brake pedal a few more times.

"Shit," he curses under his breath, his panic rising.

"What's wrong?"

Glancing behind him, his grip tightens around the steering wheel until his knuckles turn white. "Something's wrong with the brakes."

"Riv—"

"Hold on, Reese. I'm gonna have to take this corner a little sharp." The tail of his truck slips against the slick asphalt as I fumble with the 'oh shit' handle above the window before the truck regains its momentum, sending us careening down the road.

The stranger's car fades a little further into the distance but stays in our rearview mirror.

"One turn down. One to go," Riv mutters under his breath, though I'm not entirely sure who's he talking to. "Then there's a straight shot to the store. The big patch of grass and slight hill will slow us down. Just one more turn."

When another sharp corner approaches, my breath hitches, and I look at River to find his jaw tight with determination.

"Riv––"

"It's gonna be okay," he tells me as he pumps the useless brakes again. It does nothing to stall our momentum. Hurdling closer, the sharp turn mocks us, but I don't know what to do.

"River––"

"I love you––"

With a hard jerk, my shoulder jams into the window before my neck snaps forward and the seat belt tightens against my chest.

My mind scrambles to figure out what the hell is happening when it hits me like a ton of bricks.

We didn't make the turn.

And now, we're rolling.

Over and over again, we tumble down the hill as the crunch of metal tattoos itself in my memory. Broken glass bites at my face and the exposed skin along my arms, but I don't feel it as the world rushes around me in a blur of chaos. My limbs are floundering, making me feel like a rag doll as I wait for it all to just…stop.

41

REESE

With my heart in my throat, the truck lands on its roof and rocks back and forth a few more times before finally ceasing.

Vision blurry, I blink several times and wince at the sharp pain shooting down my spine as I find myself hanging upside down with only the seat belt to keep me in place.

"R-River?" I cough.

"Reese?" he grunts beside me. His voice barely makes it past the ringing in my ears. "You okay?"

"Yeah." *Cough. Cough.* "Yeah. I'm okay. W-what's that...?" I squeeze my eyes shut and try to focus, but my head is killing me, and my wrist feels like it's been snapped in two. Clutching it to my chest, I try again and ignore the way the blood is rushing into my skull. "W-what's that smell?"

"The truck's on fire, babe. Can you get out?"

In a daze, I try to comprehend his words, but it feels like my brain is in a thick, jumbled fog, and I can't concentrate.

"What?" I croak.

"The truck's on fire, Reese," he repeats, his voice deathly calm. "Can you get out?"

The truck. Is. On fire.

The truck is on fire.

The truck's on fire.

Shit.

We need to get out.

Bracing myself for impact, I unbuckle my seat belt then land on my hands and knees in a loud *oomph.* I wince as a piece of glass slices my palm but ignore it as the orange blaze starts spreading from the engine, licking its way toward the main cabin.

"River, come on, we gotta get out of here," I plead.

"My belt buckle is stuck," he grits out, jiggling it back and forth as he stays suspended in his seat.

The flames rise higher, burning my cheeks with their blistering heat as my weary focus bounces between the imminent danger and a trapped River.

"We gotta get you out of here," I tell him.

Jerking in his seat, he tries to force the buckle to release, but it's no use.

"River!" I scream, my anxiety overwhelming me. The flames claw closer, threatening to envelop the cab with their unforgiving heat.

"River! Come on. We gotta get you out of here!"

"Get out!" he yells back at me. "You need to get out!"

"I can't leave you!"

His tone is steady as he reaches for me and cups my cheek.

"Riv––" I cry.

"You have to calm down, Reese. You have to get out of the truck, and you have to get a safe distance away in case it explodes. Do you understand me?"

"I'm not leaving you––"

"You don't have a choice. I need you to be safe."

"But I need *you* to be safe," I choke out, leaning into his touch as if my life depends on it.

"Then get out and go get help. I love you, okay?"

The tears stream freely down my face before I reach for his strap and pull on it with all my might.

"Get out of the fucking truck, Reese!" he orders, losing his patience. "Now!"

"No--"

"Now!"

I drop my hurt hand to my side and whisper, "I love you, River. I love you so--"

"Get out!" he bellows. The fear in his eyes threatens to consume me before the sound of sirens echoes through the trees.

Help. I need to get help.

I scramble out of the car and run up the hill as fast as I can, waving my arms wide.

"We're here! Hurry! We're here!" I yell at the top of my lungs.

River's screams reach a new pitch as the flames finally spread to the cab of the truck, and a police car rounds the corner. It screeches to a halt at the top of the hill where we careened off it and is followed by an ambulance.

The rest goes by in a blur of chaos. One of the officers barrels toward the wreck with an extinguisher in hand, followed by a second officer who assists him in attempting to put out the fire.

Collapsing onto the wet grass, I cover my mouth and sob as they pull an unconscious body from the blaze.

This can't be happening.

This can't be happening.

This can't be happening.

With my knees pulled to my chest, I rock back and forth,

praying this is a dream while a voice inside of me is screaming that it's a nightmare.

And I'll never wake up from it.

42

REESE

BEEP. BEEP. BEEP.

The heart monitor drones on and on, but it's the only lullaby I need as my eyes flutter open.

White. So much white. There are a bunch of machines. An open curtain. A window to my left. And a small bouquet of dandelions that have my heart aching in under a second.

"Hey," a gritty voice calls.

"H-hi." My voice is rusty from lack of use and feels like I've been gargling broken glass for the last twenty-four hours.

"Do you like 'em? The flowers?" Milo asks.

A laugh that sounds more like a whimper is pulled out of me. "I love them. How did you remember?"

"I saw them outside. You used to pick them in the field by our house. Said they were the only flowers you ever needed because they managed to make…what was it again?"

"Beauty out of shitty circumstances," I finish for him.

"Yeah." Milo stands up from the uncomfortable-looking chair in the corner of the room and inches closer to me. "You scared us, sis."

My head is killing me as I try to piece together all the chaos, but it feels like trying to put a puzzle together in a pitch-black room.

Almost impossible.

"Where is everyone?"

"Sonny and Jake are waiting for an update on Riv in the waiting room."

River.

The tape on my IV tugs at my skin as I raise my hands to my face and cry into them. There's a cast on my left wrist, confirming the severity of the situation as the night replays itself like a bad movie. The storm. The headlights. The brakes. The sharp turn. The rolling. The heat. All of it. Each memory from the crash nearly breaks me, rising to the surface like a leaking oil drum in the ocean, tainting my soul in a way that's irreversible.

"W-where is he?" I choke out between sobs.

"He's alive."

"Where? Where is he? Is he okay? There was a fire——"

"Sh...," Milo croons. "We know about the fire. He's in surgery right now."

"Surgery? Wait, why? Why does he need surgery?"

His hand is warm as he places it on top of my own. The small gesture isn't so meaningless with him, and I hold my breath as a fresh wave of tears falls freely down my cheeks.

"Tell me," I plead.

"He was caught in the fire. They got him out as fast as they could but..." His eyes glaze over before he shakes his head back and forth.

"But, what?" I press.

"He got burned up pretty good. They have to, uh," he hesitates, rolling his shoulders while clenching his jaw tightly. "They have to remove a lot of the charred skin. We don't know the details because we're not blood, but his mom and dad are on their way."

"He hates his mom," I whisper. "You can't let her in there with him. You can't--"

"Sh... It's okay. I'll take care of it."

"It's *not* okay, though," I cry, my panic consuming me.

"It will be, Reese."

No, it won't, I want to argue, but the words get caught in my throat.

This can't be happening. My body wracks with sobs as I mourn the loss of...everything when a warm hand touches my shoulder.

"I'm sorry for the shit I said," Milo murmurs. "I'm an ass."

Pushing through the sharp pain in my head, I sit up and pull him into an embrace. One that we both desperately need. The guy is drowning in his own guilt when it's not his fault.

It's mine.

"I'm so sorry, Milo. I didn't mean to be the rift between you and River. I swear it. Please forgive him. I'm begging you. He needs you, Milo. I ruined everything when I came to you for help. I never meant to sleep with him. I never meant to fall in love with him. I never meant to lie to you. I never meant to hurt you. I never meant to bring Ian to your door. I just... I wrecked everything. And now your relationship is suffering for it. River is suffering for it. Ian is..." My dread rises. "Where is he? Where is he, Milo?"

"He wasn't on the scene. They found him passed out in his car in the parking lot."

"But..." I wipe roughly at my tear-stained cheeks. "Someone was following us, Milo. I know it."

"If someone was following you, it wasn't him."

"Then, who?"

"I don't know. But I need you to understand something."

"What is it?" I rasp, peeking up at him.

"We were wrecked long before you showed up, Reese. In our own ways, all of us were. *Are*," he corrects himself. "But I'll fix this. I promise."

Nodding, I rub my hand beneath my nose and squeeze my eyes shut. "When can I see him?"

"I don't know. The nurse isn't telling us much since we're not family, but I'll go see what I can find out."

"Thank you, Milo."

He drops a quick kiss to the crown of my head. "You love him?"

"Yeah." I bite my lip and let the tears flow freely from my red-rimmed eyes. "I really do."

With a jerky nod, he disappears around the curtain, leaving me alone.

With my pain.

My guilt.

And the knowledge that nothing will ever be the same again.

REESE

Milo's brash knock rouses me from a restless sleep a few hours later. I blink slowly as he strides over to me and sits on the side of the hospital bed.

"He got out of surgery about thirty minutes ago."

"Is he okay?"

"As good as he can be," he mutters before squeezing the back of his neck. "His dad is checking in with the nurse right now and is seeing if he can add us to the approved visitor's list or some shit."

"Can I see him?" I plead.

"I already asked your nurse if you could leave your room. She said if you're on the list and feel good enough to walk, then she can't make you stay in here."

Determination swells in my veins as I force myself to move.

Cringing, I sit up and swing my legs over the edge of the bed even though it feels like I'm being stabbed in the chest with every movement. Hell, I feel like I've just run a marathon with how labored my breathing is, but it doesn't matter. I need to see him. To make sure he's okay. To make sure he doesn't hate me for putting him in this mess.

Please don't hate me.

"Slow down," Milo orders, watching me struggle with a pained expression on his face. You'd think my discomfort was his own with the way he's looking at me.

"I need to see him."

"Then you need to wait until his dad gets you on that list."

"How long will that take?"

He rubs his hand over his tired face. "I don't know, but if you promise to keep your ass in this bed, then I'll find a wheelchair."

"I don't have time for a wheelchair. I need to see him."

His warm hand pushes me back. "His dad wants to meet you first."

"What? Why?"

Does he know? That this is all my fault? That because of me, River's hurt?

Reading my mind, Milo barks, "Cut the shit, Reese. It's not because he thinks any of this is your fault. River's just not exactly known for having a girlfriend, and he wants to see it for himself."

Oh.

My brows pinch in the center of my forehead as I push myself up a little further until I'm sitting more than lying down. "Is he nice? River's dad?"

"He's a good guy."

Coming from my brother––the same guy who was raised with an asshole for a father like me––that means a lot. I melt into the mattress a bit more.

"Okay," I breathe out. "Okay. I'll wait and meet him."

Another knock taps against the door, though it's much softer than Milo's. With a forced smile, I welcome Gibbs and Jake into my room.

"Hey," I murmur.

"Hey," Jake replies. "How're you feeling?"

I bite my tongue to keep from saying, *like shit,* and answer him with a shrug before wincing in discomfort. "I'm okay. Just a few bruised ribs, a cracked wrist, and a concussion."

It could be worse. So much worse.

They both come a little closer, their eyes scanning me from head to toe as they inspect my injuries when I want to scream at them for bothering to see me when they should be at River's side.

"Are we on the list yet?" I whisper, that same anxiety overwhelming me.

"Yeah. There was a change of plans. We're going to go see him right now," Gibbs informs me. "His dad wants to meet you, but he had to step outside when River's mom called. Apparently, she's bringing her entourage, and Ted is less than pleased about it. The hospital's only allowing two visitors in River's room at a time, so Ted suggested we get you over there before his mom shows up."

"We brought a wheelchair. Just in case," Jake adds. "It's in the hall."

With everyone's help, the guys guide me to Room 401 in the ICU then leave me alone, promising they're only a few yards away in case I need anything. I lick my lips and hold my breath before entering the quiet room. When I see him, my knees nearly buckle, but I force myself to take a step closer. One step. Then another. Each one more labored than the last.

He looks broken.

Battered.

Like he's been to Hell and back, and it's all my fault.

My IV trails beside me as I gingerly take a seat on the edge of the bed and try not to lose my shit.

River's entire left arm and shoulder are covered in white

bandages ending a few inches below his collarbone. There are so many tubes attached to him that I'm afraid if he moved a muscle, they'd get tangled instantly.

My teeth dig into the inside of my cheek as my guilt threatens to consume me before I give in and place my uninjured hand on top of his.

"I'm so sorry," I breathe, grateful for the privacy.

A soft knock from the doorway bursts the little bubble I'd found myself in as soon as I entered the room. Feeling like I've been caught doing something I shouldn't, I pull my hand into my own lap and look up at the stranger. He looks just like River, only thirty years older and with a bit of salt peppered into his dark hair.

My gut tightens.

"I assume you're the girlfriend?" the stranger asks.

Eyes watering, I try to keep the tears at bay, but it's no use. The cast scratches my cheek as I brush away a stray droplet of moisture before sniffling. "Um, hi. I'm, uh, I'm Reese. It's nice to meet you."

"I'm Ted," he replies before taking another hesitant step into the room. His gaze slides over to River, causing his shoulders to hunch in defeat. "My son and I, we don't talk much. Not because we have a bad relationship. We're just... guys, I guess. We don't have much to say unless there's something important to be said."

"Oh."

"He called me about you, though. A few weeks ago. Didn't tell me your name, just called you Floozy." He chuckles. "He's always had a warped sense of humor. But he wanted to fill me in about the girl who stole his heart. He didn't say it like that, but I was able to piece it together."

"Oh," I repeat, swallowing thickly. I drop my attention down to my hands in my lap, twisting the crisp cotton sheets like a toddler with a baby blanket.

I don't know what to say.

Closing the distance between us, he sighs then sits beside me. "He's going to feel different now. More insecure. Less sure of himself. I'd like to think I was able to erase his mother's hand in raising him, but I know he can be a bit superficial sometimes. I know how much he worries about landing his next job. Hell, he won't even eat a cupcake on his birthday. The only exception is——"

"Sugary cereal," I answer for him with a tight smile. "And s'mores. On occasion. I know."

Eyes glazing over, he pats my hand. "This is going to do a number on him, regardless of how much he tries to hide it."

"I know."

"Do you love him?"

I feel like my heart is cracking in two as I hold his gaze and whisper, "I do."

"Then you're gonna have to work extra hard to prove it to him. Do you think you can do that? Even if he pushes you away? Even if he thinks he's unloveable?"

"I'll make it right," I promise while attempting to push away the overwhelming helplessness that's clawing at my insides.

He shakes his head back and forth. "You don't need to make it right because that's not within your power. We can't change the past, Reese. We can only focus on the present and hope for a brighter future."

I glance down at the love of my life lying lifeless in the hospital bed. I feel like I stole his future. And his present. He's going to hate me.

My lower lip quivers as I turn back to Ted and ask, "So, what should I do?"

"You need to make him see himself the way you see him. The way his friends see him. And the way I see him."

"I'll…" I turn back to River and take in the dark blue bags

under his eyes, the swollen bridge of his nose from Milo's fist earlier, and the purple bruise along his jaw. "I'll do my best."

I just hope it's enough.

"I know you will. And I know it'll be enough because I know how much he cares about you. In fact, I'd be worried if it wasn't for you, Reese. But now that I've met you, I'm not so worried anymore."

The Darth Vader theme song cuts off our conversation. Ted scrubs his hand over his tired face before standing up and digging into his front pocket. "Riv's mother is here. I'll be back in a few."

He raises his phone to his ear and mutters something into the phone, then disappears down the hall, leaving me alone with Riv.

Riv's mother is here? The infamous Monet Cavier?

Lovely.

Hushed whispers echo near the entrance of River's ICU room, but there's an edge to them that makes my skin prickle with awareness. Unfortunately, I can only make out the higher-pitched comments, and they leave my molars aching from the strained pressure as I catch myself grinding them together.

"Get her out of this room."

Silence.

"He doesn't know what he wants."

More silence.

"You can't be serious. I'm his *mother*."

Shit.

"He craves the spotlight just as much as I do. If he were awake right now, he'd kill to cash in on this."

Finally snapping, the click-clack of heels ends the conversation as the most gorgeous woman I've ever seen enters the room like it's the red carpet. If Jennifer Aniston had an evil twin sister with less class and more vanity, this would be her. Long, caramel-colored hair, make-up on point, baby-smooth skin, big breasts, tiny waist, long lacquered nails, tall black heels, and a resting bitch face that says, *oh honey, I'm going to eat you for breakfast*, make up the infamous Monet Cavier.

A sour taste fills my mouth, but I swallow it back.

"Why, hello. I don't believe we've had an introduction, although my son has told me *so* much about you." *Ha! Liar.* "I'm Monet Cavier." She says her name like it's a gift from God but doesn't offer her hand for me to shake.

"Hi. I'm Reese. Reese Anders."

"Reese. That's a…"––she purses her lips––"*pretty* name. Perfect for a pretty girl."

Why doesn't that sound like a compliment?

"Uh…thank you?" I mutter. It takes everything inside of me not to cower under her attention, but I stay strong.

"You're lucky this happened to him, you know," she points out, waving her perfectly manicured hand toward her unconscious son.

What. The. Hell is wrong with this woman?

Seeing my disgusted shock, she grins before explaining, "Because now, he might actually be in your league."

"I'm sorry. What's your problem?" I snap.

"My problem is that my baby boy is lying in a hospital bed, and it's all because of you." Glancing over at an unconscious River, my blood starts to boil on his behalf.

I've been in his room for less than two minutes with this woman, and I can confidently say that it's two minutes too long. How the hell did someone as sweet, easy-going, and accepting of those around him come from genes this twisted? It's a freaking miracle.

"Now, my son might not admit it, but he craves my approval like a junkie."

I snort but bite my tongue as her catlike eyes narrow in annoyance before she defends, "Why do you think he became a model? Why do you think he auditioned for the B.T.

Henderson project? It's obvious he's looking for my approval."

Seems I'm not the only one with a crazy stalker, I think to myself before questioning her. "How did you know about the B.T. Henderson project?"

"Because I have connections. You know he's going to lose the role for this, don't you? That is unless we spin it in our favor. Heroic boyfriend sacrifices himself to save girl-next-door from her crazy stalker who cut the brakes in his truck. Has a nice ring to it, don't you think? It's a little long. I'll give you that. We'll have to cut it down. Make it a little...*snappier* perhaps, but I think it'll do quite nicely."

"Where's Ted?" My attention darts to the empty doorway. And how the hell does she know anything about Ian, let alone the cut brakes? Even *I* didn't piece together that little tidbit until now. That's why River couldn't stop. That's why he lost control.

But...how did she know?

"Only two visitors at a time, remember?" Monet answers while picking at her blood-red fingernails. "You've never dealt with the paparazzi, Miss Anders. You don't understand the importance of weaving a palatable story together before it gets twisted into something that's bad for business."

Nerves frazzled, I point out, "If you weren't here, there wouldn't be a story."

"But I'm his mother."

"You're a washed-up actress who's hoping to make the headlines because her son was in a car accident."

She scoffs. "Washed-up? I could have any role I want delivered to me on a silver platter."

"Unless B.T. Henderson is directing it. Tell me something, Miss Cavier," I ask, mimicking the same condescending tone she so eloquently delivers. "Were you jealous when you found out he was given the part? Were you hoping to milk your connection to him, but he wasn't interested in airing out his dirty laundry to the public? And when I say dirty laundry, I mean *you*. Is that why you're here?"

"He wouldn't be anyone without me."

"He's who he is in spite of you," I return, my words practically dripping acid. "How did you know about my ex? How did you know someone was following us tonight? And how, exactly, did you know about the cut brakes?"

"The, uh––" She hesitates before regaining her composure. "Ted. He told me all about it."

"Ted didn't know about the cut brakes."

"Then it must've been the police."

"But you said, Ted."

Waving her hand through the air, she argues, "Does it matter? The past twenty-four hours have been a bit chaotic. You'll have to forgive me for a minor slipup or two."

"How did you know about the audition? About the role River was given?"

"You're surprised? I know everything in this business."

"He went through a lot of work to keep the opportunity discreet."

She laughs. "And he thought I wouldn't be able to piece it together? I might be beautiful, Miss Anders, but I'm not stupid."

"No, you're more calculating than that," I answer, stroking her precious ego in hopes of her opening up a bit more. Something doesn't feel right.

Her botoxed smile curves up in the corners. "Maybe you aren't as dull as I'd initially assumed. I might've even underestimated you, and that's a rare occurrence."

"I'm flattered," I mock her.

"I'm sure you are. To answer your question, Henderson might not be a friend of mine, but he is a big influencer in the industry, and whenever there are whispers of a new film in the works, you can bet your life on Brett doing the heavy lifting for finding promising additions to the cast. And when Olivia was booked for a simple lingerie shoot with Brett and a no-name model, it was quite easy to piece it together."

"So, you knew he auditioned for the role. Big deal. I'm sure a lot of people auditioned."

"Yes, but not with the help of Brett," she counters while slowly pacing the room. "He's the key."

"Okay, so, you could assume this no-name actor––aka your estranged son––had gotten the part. Then what? You could've just leaked your relationship to the media."

"And have him air out his dirty laundry?" she counters with a quirked brow.

"So, this was…what, exactly? A PR stunt for you? Loving mother visits son in the hospital?"

"Don't be ridiculous," she scoffs.

Shrugging, I tap my finger against my chin as it all clicks into place. "I'm not a PR expert, but I can see the weight of a palatable story woven together like the one I just suggested. Especially when it's compared to a leaked birth certificate and a flimsy claim to a toxic relationship between an up-and-coming actor and a washed-up, deadbeat mother with a drug addiction."

"What, exactly, are you insinuating?" Her eyes narrow into tiny slits as she purses her lips and dares me to voice the truth. But if I'm wrong, it'll be catastrophic.

Still, I finally understand how my brother feels when he needs to protect me. How Gibson, Jake, and River felt when they found out about my past.

And now, I'm going to protect River.

"You cut the brakes," I accuse her.

"I was in LA."

"Then you paid someone to do it. It's obvious you keep tabs on people of interest, and once River was given the role in Henderson's movie, he became one to you. But you couldn't convince him to give you another chance, could you? The texts, the calls...all of them were an attempt to reconcile your relationship. Not because you're a good mom, but because you crave the spotlight even if you have to take it from your own son to steal another taste. And I'm sure that once you found out I had a possessive ex, the rest of your plan practically wrote itself. Are you the one that stole the pictures from my room, too, then dropped them off at my brother's work?"

"I don't know what you're talking about."

"Like you said...you're not dumb, Ms. Cavier," I seethe. "You know *exactly* what I'm talking about."

Running her hands along her perfectly coiffed hair, her eyelids flutter a few times as a fresh wave of anxiety rolls off her.

"Admit it," I push.

"You're grasping at straws––"

"Maybe. But if that's the case, then I'm sure you won't mind being interviewed by the police when I tell them my theory, right?"

Her spine straightens. "You'd be wasting their time."

"I think I'm willing to take the risk." Pushing the nurse call button on River's bed, I cross my arms and have an epic staredown with one of the most intimidating people I've ever met. She might be a pretty good actor, but I refuse to back down because I know I'm right.

Now, I need to figure out how to prove it to the police.

"Is there a problem?" the nurse asks. Her kind eyes bounce between an unconscious River, a thoroughly pissed off Monet, and me. The girl who's about to toss out an accusation that could be detrimental to everyone in this room.

"Hi," I greet her. "Is there any way I could speak with a police officer? I don't have my phone, and I don't feel comfortable leaving the patient alone with"--I look at River's mom--"her."

"Is there a problem?"

"Of course not," Monet starts at the same time I answer, "Yes."

Not moving a muscle, the nurse catches onto the precarious situation and calls out, "Bethany!"

Footsteps echo from the hall before a cute brunette pops her head into the room. "Yeah?"

"Can you call security for me?"

"You can't just go around accusing people of things like this," Monet tells me, her anxiety ratcheting up a few notches while completely ignoring the nurses. "Especially people like me. Don't you understand what this could do to my reputation? I will not allow you to make a silly allegation like this."

The first nurse stays quiet, watching the entire ordeal unfold around her while Bethany disappears down the hall to hopefully find a security guard to help us. Because Monet reeks of desperation, and desperate people are capable of anything.

With my hands raised in defense, I murmur, "They're just going to ask you a few questions."

"And what? Cart me away in handcuffs? Do you know what that will do to my reputation? The paparazzi are practically flooding the parking lot. Hell, I invited them here. I wanted them to cover the story, but I will *not* be made a spectacle. Do you hear me? Besides, everything is ruined. River won't be able to keep the role now. They wanted an attractive rockstar for the part, not a hideous beast. You ruined him."

"You ruined him," I spit. "You cut the brakes. You put him in this position. This is on *you*. Not me. And it's all because you wanted to ride your son's coattails, and he wouldn't let you."

"It was supposed to be a fender bender, not this!" she shrieks, tossing her hands into the air as her beautiful face becomes tainted with outrage.

"Yeah, well, sometimes we can't control the consequences of our decisions. And now, you're going to have to pay for it. And so will River." I clear my throat and blink back my tears. "Tell me, who did you hire to follow us? Because it sure as hell wasn't my ex. Was it whoever you paid to cut the brakes? Did they want to make sure they finished the job? Is that it?"

"Of course not!"

"Then who was it?"

"You don't understand––"

"Then why don't you explain it to me?" I demand.

"I've already told you!" she screams. "It was supposed to be a simple fender bender. Javier wasn't trying to run you off the road. He was there to take pictures of the damage and run an article on the situation, weaving the palatable story for the media that would help him with his big break."

I clench my hands at my sides to keep from slapping the bitch in the face.

She's lost her damn mind.

"Stop hiding behind that bullshit excuse for what you did," I snap. "You wrecked your son in a way that is almost irreparable. You used him. Then you broke him. The fact that you still consider yourself to be his mother is laughable. A mother doesn't do this. She doesn't use her child for her own personal gains. You mean nothing to him. And you never will."

Lips curling in disgust, she stalks closer to me, but I stand my ground.

With my head held high, I keep my voice calm and add, "Don't worry, though, Monet. He's picked himself up before, and he'll do it again with me by his side. And where do you think you'll be? Hmm?"

Her nostrils flare.

"I have one word for you. *Prison.*"

Hurried footsteps slap against the linoleum floors before a big, burly security guard enters the room without waiting for permission and cuts our conversation short.

The nurse breathes a sigh of relief when she sees him. "Hey, Len. Would you mind escorting this individual to one of the back offices, please?"

Her overly-inflated lips purse before she interrupts, "My name is Monet Cavier."

"Of course," Len replies diplomatically. "I apologize, Miss Cavier. If you could please come with me? I'd greatly appreciate it."

Her posture could rival a runway model's as Monet follows his suggestion and exits the room. I cover my mouth and heave out the pent-up oxygen I'd been holding hostage in my lungs for far too long as she retreats.

"Are you okay?" the nurse asks, rushing over to me as soon as we're alone.

I shake my head. "I didn't imagine that, right? She did it. She did this to her son––to me––all because of greed?"

A soft sigh escapes her before she rubs her hand up and down my back. "Yeah. I think she did."

"What if they can't prove it? What if she gets away scot-free? It'll be her word against mine. There's no way they'll believe me over her––"

"I heard it too. It'll be our word against hers. Don't worry. It'll be okay."

Looking over at River's broken body, a sob escapes me. His angry, raw skin peeking from beneath the white bandages. His bruised face. The IV attached to his arm dripping much-needed painkillers into his veins so that he can be at peace for a few more minutes before reality hits him harder than the truck ever could. The combination paints a picture of our future that's bleak at best. At least for a little while. And it's all because of his mother's greed.

"No, it won't," I rasp. "Because I'm not the one who's going to have to live with the repercussions. He is."

And it's not fair.

45

REESE

A soft groan from the bed rouses me from another restless sleep. My eyes are still swollen from crying as I pry my lids open and look at River.

He tosses his head back and forth, slowly coming out of the sedation with pinched brows and a slight frown. The combination manages to make him look twenty years older than he is while reminding me of a confused little boy at the same time. Like two opposites of the same coin, though neither one is *my* River.

"Sh...," I soothe. His skin is a little hot as I run my hand across his forehead in hopes of wiping away the wrinkles etched into it. "It's okay."

His eyelids flutter before he looks up at me and tries to focus.

"Reese?" he croaks.

"Hey."

"W-what happened?"

I bite the inside of my cheek and fuss with the crisp, white sheets surrounding his broken body. "You should get some rest."

"I feel like I've been sleeping for years."

With a laugh, my eyes well with a fresh set of tears. "I know."

"What's going on?"

"You've been out for a while. Your dad said you woke up while I was in my room getting released from the hospital, but you fell asleep again before I got back."

"My dad's here?" That same look of confusion is painted across his handsome face as he searches the empty hospital room.

"Yeah," I breathe out. "We've been taking turns hanging out with you."

His heavy eyelids fall, and his forehead wrinkles with concentration again. Like he's searching his memories for any hints about what the hell is going on.

After a few seconds, he looks up at me. "I remember seeing him. But it's...kinda fuzzy."

"That's probably the drugs," I inform him.

"What drugs? What happened, Reese?"

Steeling my courage, I breathe in a deep, unsteady breath and try to restrain my anguish. Because he doesn't need it right now. He needs my strength. My encouragement. My determination. And even though it feels impossible, I do my best to give it to him.

"We were in an accident," I explain carefully. "The truck rolled and caught on fire. They got you out but——"

Panicked, he reaches for me. "Are you okay? Babe, your wrist——"

"Is fine." I laugh again, but it gets caught on a sob before I choke it down and smile tightly.

How can he be so damn thoughtful right now?

"I'm fine," I clarify. "And you're going to be okay too. I promise."

Wincing, he raises my injured wrist closer to his face and

inspects the damage with the cutest, most concerned expression a guy could have. My eyes burn with unshed tears as he brushes his good hand along the rough surface of the bright pink cast while his injured side stays limp on the hospital bed. His concern only makes me love him more, and I hate that he might question it when he finds out the damage to his perfect body.

This isn't fair.

Satisfied I'll be all right, Riv lets me go and carefully sets his head back on the deflated pillow behind him.

"Why do I feel like shit?" he murmurs in a tired voice, closing his eyes again for just a second as the exhaustion threatens to pull him back under.

I stay quiet and bite my lower lip. They're pumping him full of painkillers right now, but his brows are still pinched with excruciating pain. Once he realizes the damage he's going to have to recover from, it'll break him.

"Tell me," he orders.

My breath hitches again. "Y-you got burned pretty bad, Riv. They were able to remove most of the damaged skin in surgery, but it's going to be rough for a little while. Now, you just get to take your time and recover, okay?"

He opens his mouth, then closes it before shaking his head slightly. Like he can't wrap his head around what I've revealed. And I don't blame him. I still can't believe it. Everything was perfect just a little while ago. Then it all fell apart. But I'm not going anywhere. We'll get through this.

We have to.

"Reese…?" His voice trails off as he searches my face. I wish I knew what he's looking for.

"Yeah?" I choke out.

"Is it bad?"

The tears I'd been holding back manage to slip past my barriers and glide down my cheeks. But I can't find my voice.

So, I nod. And confirm his greatest fear. That nothing will ever be the same for him again.

Squeezing his eyes shut, Riv grabs my uninjured hand, then tightens his hold as if I'm the only thing keeping him grounded while the truth seeps into his tired bones.

"I'm so sorry," I cry.

The intensity in his piercing green eyes pins me in place as the same determination I've fallen in love with rises to the surface.

"Don't you dare be sorry, Reese."

"Riv--"

"It's not your fault. Besides, you're okay. So, it's okay." He rubs his thumb along the back of my hand in an attempt to soothe me, but it only widens the chasm in my heart.

How the hell is he the one comforting me right now?

I feel so helpless. And it sucks.

"It's okay," he repeats.

No, it's not, I want to argue, but I swallow the toxic words and lean forward to brush my lips against his.

"I was so scared, Riv. I can still hear your screams. I can still smell the gas mixed with the rain. When I close my eyes, I can still see the flames. It terrifies me."

"Sh… Don't think about that."

"I can't help it," I tell him, blinking back tears. "But you're right. Right now, we need to focus on getting you better. You should get some rest."

"I don't want to sleep anymore. I need to know what happened. Did they catch Ian?"

I swallow and attempt to give him some space, but he keeps me close, clutching at the back of my neck until our foreheads are pressed together.

"They caught the culprit, yeah," I answer vaguely, avoiding his gaze.

"The culprit?"

"We'll talk about it later."

"Tell me."

The bite of pain grounds me as I dig my teeth into my lower lip. "I don't want to."

His chuckle turns into a cringe. "Tell me, Reese," he demands.

With another shaky breath, I grab his good hand from behind my neck and kiss the back of it, praying for the courage to tell him the truth.

"Please?" he begs.

Those same mesmerizing eyes that held me captive when we first met pull the truth out of me with ease. "Your mom paid someone to cut the brakes."

"What about Ian?" he asks, confused.

"He's an ass, but he wasn't the one following us. They found him passed out in his car at SeaBird. It was the guy your mom paid to cut the brakes. Javier."

"Her assistant?"

"I guess?" I confirm. "She was going to frame Ian and spin the story in your––and *her*––favor."

"How did she know about Ian?"

"I don't know."

I can almost see the wheels turning in his head as he mutters, "She probably hired a PI to follow me when I stopped answering her calls. She's done it in the past," he adds, looking up at me as the puzzle pieces click into place. "She probably asked him to dig into your history when she saw us together. But…why would my mom do that?"

"She didn't mean to hurt you like this––"

"Don't defend her," he spits. But I can't help myself. His pain is too much for me to witness. She really is a monster, but no one wants to hear that about their own flesh and blood.

"She just wanted it to cause a fender bender," I explain.

"Then she'd be able to use it as a publicity stunt to reconnect with you just in time for the big reveal about the movie."

He drops his head back and scoffs quietly. "Of course, this was about the movie. Has she been arrested yet?"

"They took her in for questioning, but I haven't received an official update."

"Have the press announced the accident?"

"I haven't been watching the news. I'll find out, though." I attempt to stand, but River's grasp tightens around my good hand, keeping me in place.

"Has Gina called?" he prods, appearing more and more lucid as the conversation goes on. Pretty sure the adrenaline pulsing through his veins is competing with the morphine and is clearly the victor.

"I don't know where your phone is," I admit.

"Can I use yours?"

Retrieving it from my back pocket, I see a text from Dove, but I don't bother to read it before handing my phone to him.

"What's the passcode?"

"0-0-2-3-5-1," I answer without hesitation.

He punches in the numbers, then dials Gina and puts the call on speaker.

It rings for a few seconds before a feminine voice filters through. "Hello?"

"Hey, Gina. It's me, River."

"River! I've been trying to call you for days! People are freaking out about the news. Are you okay? There are rumors that your mom showed up at the hospital but was escorted out like thirty minutes later. They won't let me see you since I'm not on your approved visitor's list or some shit. And since I haven't met your dad or any of your friends, they aren't exactly very trusting of me, either."

"Wait. Where are you?" River asks.

"I'm at home now, but I tried to come see you earlier. Like I said, they wouldn't let me in. Are you okay?"

His eyes shoot to mine. "I'll be fine."

"You sure?"

"Yeah."

"Henderson called. He wants an update. What should I tell him?"

He sighs and glances over at me. "I don't know. Can you stall him until I talk with a doctor?"

"Yeah, of course."

"Thanks, Gina. Call this number if you need to chat. It's my girlfriend's."

Girlfriend.

My stomach swells with butterflies, but I shove them aside and focus on the conversation at hand.

"Okay," Gina replies. "I'll keep you updated, and I expect you to do the same."

"Will do. Talk soon." Then he disconnects the call and hands my phone back to me. "Have you spoken to the doctors?"

I nod.

"And how bad is the damage?" he asks again. "You mentioned the surgery and that they removed the burnt skin, but what's the recovery time look like? I need you to be honest with me, Reese."

"Ya know, you're pretty lucid for a guy doped up on drugs."

"It's in the genes," he quips sarcastically. "How do you think my mom was able to film all those movies while slipping oxy between scenes and snorting coke in the bathrooms?"

Jaw dropping, I ask, "Seriously?"

"My childhood was no picnic, Reese. Now, I need you to

tell me the truth so we can figure out what to tell Henderson. Am I going to scar?"

My mouth feels like it's been filled with cotton as my attention drops down to his bandaged side.

"Tell me."

My gaze snaps back to his. "You got burned pretty bad, Riv."

The bandages are mainly on his left forearm, bicep, and shoulder, then trail up the side of his neck before ending at his jawline. My lower lip quivers as I take it in for the hundredth time and mourn for the confident man he once was. Because his dad is right. This might break him.

"Am I going to scar?" he asks. His tone is matter-of-fact, but his eyes tell a different story. They're filled with a fear that's so palpable I'm afraid I might choke on it.

This is his greatest fear. *This* is the one thing he's been terrified of losing. Not because he's that vain, but because his mom made him believe it's his only true worth. That if he isn't absolute perfection on the outside, then who would want him for what's on the inside? It's as if the repercussions from the accident are *finally* catching up with him, and he's truly starting to grasp the severity of his condition.

"Tell me," he pleads.

"Yeah," I rasp. "I think you'll scar. They mentioned skin grafts in the near future, but I don't know the details. You'll be okay, though. I promise––"

"You're lying, Reese. The entire left side of my body is covered in bandages and feels like an open sore that's been dipped in acid. Do I have any skin left?"

"I haven't seen you without the bandages," I hedge.

"Answer the question, Reese. How long of a recovery am I looking at?"

"I don't know. They didn't say."

With a jerky nod, he turns toward the window and

releases a pained sigh. The quiet sound is like a noose around my heart, squeezing it until I'm positive it'll never beat rhythmically again.

"What are you thinking?" I whisper. When he first woke up, and I told him about the accident, he seemed okay. Like he'd be able to get through this. Like we'd *both* be able to. But now that he knows the severity of the situation, I feel like my world has been flipped upside down just like I'd feared.

"I'm going to lose the part," he mutters.

"That's not true. We don't know--"

"It's true, Reese. They wanted a sex god for the role, not a guy who got burned up in a fire and needs skin grafts. Now, I'm nothing."

The words cut me like a knife. I cup his cheek and force him to look me in the eye.

"You're not nothing, River. You mean the world to me. You did before the accident, and you do now. You're a talented actor, and it's not just because you look pretty, okay? If it were all about looks, then your mom would've gotten that part all those years ago and would've worked with the infamous B.T. Henderson. But she didn't because Henderson doesn't care about looks alone, even though I still think you're the sexiest guy I've ever laid eyes on," I add with a smile. "He cares about raw talent, and you have it in spades. Gina sees it, Brett sees it, and so does Henderson. If this part slips through your fingers, there'll be another one to replace it down the road. I need you to know that," I plead. "But you need to get better before you can pursue any of those roles, and that means you need to stay strong and be the man you know you are. The man on the inside who fought tooth and nail to get away from his mom and stand on his own. Do you think you can do that?"

Closing his eyes, he leans into my touch and savors the

feel of my skin against his before returning to reality with a fresh look of determination.

"I need to ask you something, Reese, and I need you to promise me that you'll give me an honest answer. I won't hold it against you. I just need the truth."

"I promise," I whisper.

"Will you stick with me through this? Even after these bandages are removed? Even if my skin never looks the way it used to? Will you still love me? You don't have to stay because of guilt. I won't hold it against you––"

"Stop," I plead. "Please stop."

"I don't want you to feel obligated––"

"I could *never* feel obligated to be with you."

My heart cracks as I take in the vulnerable man beside me, making me want to climb into his hospital bed and pull him close, but I restrain myself. Instead, I carefully lean forward and press a gentle kiss against his lips. "I love you. *You.* Not your body. Not your muscles. *You.* You could look like an ogre, and I'd still love you, River."

"Promise? 'Cause ogre might be a pretty apt description after all of this."

His sense of humor brings a smile to my lips before I reprimand, "One, don't say that. It hurts me to hear that you'd think so low of yourself. And two, trust me. Even all busted up and in a hospital bed, I'd still jump your bones if I wasn't afraid it would hurt you."

And for the first time since he woke up, a genuine smile threatens to peek through his damaged façade. "Are you telling me that my cock survived the fire?"

I laugh and look at the thin hospital sheets covering his half-mast erection. "I assume? But if you'd like me to take a closer look, I'd be happy to oblige."

"Way to take one for the team, Floozy."

"I'm thoughtful like that," I quip.

As I scoot a little closer, he turns his head toward me then winces. "I, uh, I might have to take a rain check on that, though."

Forcing my pity aside, I reach for his good hand and squeeze it softly. "You okay?"

"Yeah. My neck is just..." His voice trails off before reality hits us both square in the chest. He has a long road to recovery, and it isn't going to be pretty. It's going to be painful, and overwhelming, and likely filled with a crippling loss that he'll have to learn to accept. But I'll be here for it.

All of it.

"Get some rest, Sex God/Master of Orgasms." I press another kiss to his forehead. "And remember, chicks dig scars, okay?"

"Is that right?"

"Uh-huh. We love 'em. Now, go to sleep. We'll chat with the doctor when you wake up."

"Love you, Floozy."

I close my eyes and commit the sound of his gritty voice to memory. For a minute, I was afraid I'd never hear it again. His words are a balm to my aching soul. And with all the guilt eating me alive, I was positive that even if he came out of surgery okay, his love for me would be tainted, and the potential for our future would've been burned up in his truck, leaving only mistakes to keep us warm at night.

And I've made so many mistakes. But now, I'm going to fix them. And I'm not going to take a single second with my Sex God/Master of Orgasms for granted. Because I now understand what it's like for them to be taken away in an instant.

"Love you too, Riv."

His lids flutter closed, then the worry lines framing his eyes soften, and he loses himself in sleep.

A few minutes later, there's a soft creak near the doorway, and I turn toward it.

"Oh. Hi," I greet River's dad. "Sorry, I didn't know you were standing there. He woke up and seemed pretty lucid, all things considered."

"I saw that," he notes. "I apologize for eavesdropping. I've been here for a few minutes, but I couldn't help it. I needed to hear his voice and make sure he was okay."

"I get it. I'm going to go stretch my legs for a minute. I'll be back in a few."

"Sounds good."

Pushing up from the chair, I walk toward the exit when he stops me.

"And Reese?"

"Yeah?"

"Thanks for being here for him."

"Trust me," I murmur before glancing back at a sleeping River. "I'm not going anywhere."

46

RIVER

The television in the corner of the room drowns out the silence. This bed is uncomfortable as shit, but I don't bother finding a better position. The constant ache that covers my left side has finally stopped throbbing for a minute. I'm sure as hell not going to risk it returning by shifting in the bed.

"Hey," a voice calls. Milo lifts his chin in greeting, hanging out near the doorway of the hospital room. It's been almost a week since the accident. Everyone has come to visit with one exception.

Milo.

Rumor has it that he's been hanging out in the waiting room. But I don't know for sure.

He looks like shit.

"Hey," I return.

"Can I come in?"

With an amused chuckle, I challenge, "Since when have you ever asked permission for anything?"

"Since I feel like shit from the last time we talked."

But the bastard doesn't bother to wait for my permission.

He just saunters over to the cushioned chair next to my hospital bed.

I hit the mute button on the remote.

Then I wait.

Resting his elbows on his knees, Milo sits there.

The silence is suffocating. But the bastard doesn't say a word.

"I don't need your pity, man," I mutter, voicing the only possible reason I can think of as to why he's here.

"I know."

"So, stop giving it to me."

His mouth ticks up on one side. "I'll work on it."

Silence.

Scratching the side of my jaw, I glance over at him. He's staring at the television.

"So, they've arrested her?" he asks, keeping his attention glued to it.

I slide my gaze toward the television. My mom's face flashes across the screen. Her hands are cuffed behind her back as they escort her to a police car surrounded by paparazzi. They're busy snapping pictures and video footage to document the scandal of the year. The news stations have been eating the story up ever since they questioned Javier, her assistant. Squealing like a pathetic little pig, he explained everything. The plot. The money. The botched story. All of it.

"Yeah," I answer Milo. "They arrested her a couple of hours ago."

"Have you talked to her?"

"Nah."

"Don't blame you," he consoles. "She gonna make bail?"

"I'm sure she will."

He turns to me. "Do you want her in prison?"

I shake my head. "She's already been hit where it hurts. Her image is ruined. Even if she gets away scot-free, she'll never get another role after this. So, honestly? I don't give a shit about what happens to her. As long as she stays away from Reese and me, I'll be happy."

He nods but doesn't comment.

More silence.

"Reese went home to shower," I offer after another minute. She hasn't left my side until today. I finally joked that she was starting to smell and needed a hot bath or something. Reluctantly, she gave in to my suggestion but promised to be back in a few hours.

Milo nods again. "I know. Figured we could use the privacy."

Ah, so that explains the timing.

"Why are you here, man?" I ask.

He rubs his hand over his face roughly. "Because we need to talk."

"Then you should probably start talking." I laugh.

Sighing, he clears his throat. "I'm sorry."

My eyes widen in surprise. "Excuse me?"

"I said, I'm sorry."

"What the hell do you have to be sorry for?"

"I was wrong."

"About what?" I question. Getting Milo to talk is always a feat, but when it's something serious that he doesn't want to talk about, it's like pulling teeth.

Holding my stare, he mutters, "You and Reese."

"You weren't wrong about me and Reese. You had every right to be pissed at me. You warned me to stay away––"

"Yeah. That's where I was wrong. I shouldn't have put you in a position where you felt like you had to sneak around. That's on me. I should've given you more credit. You might be a dick sometimes, but I know you well enough to know you'd never be a dick to her."

My chest tightens. "I love her."

"I know."

"I don't deserve her, though."

He laughs. "I was wrong about that too. You're gonna treat her right."

His confidence makes me pause as my insecurities rush over me. Will my love be enough to keep her happy? Will she be okay waking up to my sorry ass for the rest of her life? Not that I've proposed, but I'm in it for the long haul. If I wasn't, I would've never put my friendship with Milo at risk.

Unable to help myself, I voice my greatest fear. "How can you be so sure?"

"Because if you don't"––he shrugs––"I'll have to mess up your pretty face again."

Coming from Milo, this is the biggest blessing on our relationship that I could've asked for. Almost immediately, I feel the weight lifted from my shoulders. I feel like I can finally breathe again.

Tsking, I joke, "I've already told ya, Milo. If you want to touch my pretty face, then you gotta get on your knees first."

With a bark of amusement, he counters, "Nah. I think Jake was right about that one. If anyone's getting on their knees, it'll be you."

Chuckling, I shake my head back and forth. "Good point."

"But I have one rule with Reese," he adds.

"And what's that?"

"You keep your sex life private. I don't wanna hear it from down the hall or any shit like that. We clear?"

Another laugh escapes me. "Noted."

"Then I'm happy for you," he announces.

"Thanks. And thanks for…coming around. I know we screwed up and should've told you."

"Doesn't matter."

"I told you not to pity me," I remind him.

He sobers and pats my knee. "We're gonna get you through this."

"I know." So much has happened in the past week or so. I feel like I'm starring in a movie stuck in fast forward. But it's moments like this that remind me what's really important. And it's the family you keep. They might not be blood. But they're more important than anything.

"There's another good thing that came out of this, though," I mention.

"What's that?"

"Now, I can finally get that sleeve we've talked about."

Brow quirked, he scans my bandaged arm. "I thought tats were frowned upon in the movie industry."

"And so is messed up skin," I offer with a sardonic grin. "At least now, I won't be afraid of what other people think."

"So you're just gonna be you?"

"There a problem with that?" I challenge.

With a shrug, he jokes, "At least you kept your pretty face."

Throwing my head back, I laugh even harder before shoving him with my good arm. "Thanks, asshole."

His grin softens. Then he drops his gaze to my injured arm. "Let me know when you're ready to start."

"As soon as I'm all healed up and the doctor gives the okay, I'm good to go."

"All right. I'll be ready." An amused smile flickers across his face before he adds, "Is my sister's name gonna be on there?"

"Will she kill me if it is?"

"Nah. You make her happy. It's good to see her that way again."

"Thanks, Milo."

"Don't thank me. Without you, Reese wouldn't understand what she deserves. You've done a good job showing it to her."

"So have you," I reply. "She's lucky to have a brother who looks out for her the way you do."

With a ghost of a smile, he stands up and pats my good shoulder. "Get some rest."

Then he leaves.

And I feel at peace for the first time in months.

The next couple of months go by in a blur of chaos, bandage changing, doctor appointments, and healing. They transferred River to a rehabilitation center and have finally taught me how to change his bandages twice a day so we can go home.

Home.

Not gonna lie. It's been rough.

But SeaBird gave me some time off to help him, and I've loved witnessing how damn strong he is.

And stubborn. *So* stubborn.

As the doctor slides off her rubber gloves, she announces, "You're looking a lot better, River. Have you been keeping up with your physical therapy homework?"

"Yes, ma'am," he answers. "Four times a day."

"You're only required to do it twice."

"Yeah, well, apparently, I'm an overachiever." His shit-eating grin is contagious.

She laughs before turning to me. "Is he always this much of a go-getter?"

"Have you seen his abs?" I reply with a smirk. "The guy doesn't know the meaning of taking it easy."

Spending most of his time without a shirt to help the healing process, River has practically become a celebrity in the rehabilitation center, and it's been fanning his ego just fine.

"Good point," Dr. Ellis concedes. "As long as you keep up with changing his bandages the way we've discussed and make it to the weekly appointments, I think he's ready to go."

"Thank you, Dr. Ellis. I really appreciate it," River tells her.

"Anytime. It's been a pleasure to work with someone so positive and entertaining. I'll see you in a few days, okay?"

"Sure thing."

"Oh, and maybe put a shirt on before you leave," Dr. Ellis adds. "Wouldn't want the nurses to leave drool all over the floors as you're discharged, eh?"

With another bark of laughter, River counters, "Now, where's the fun in that?"

~

THE DRIVE HOME IS RELATIVELY QUIET. GLANCING OVER AT River sitting in the passenger seat, I ask, "How are you feeling?"

"I'm okay."

"Does it feel weird to be going home?"

"A little," he admits. "It's been a while."

"It has," I agree before shifting my gaze back to the road.

His gentle touch surprises me as he trails his fingers along my bare arm. "How're you holding up, Floozy?"

I snort. "You know I still hate that name, right?"

"Come on. It's endearing."

"Says the Sex God/Master of Orgasms," I quip. "I'm fine, by the way. Happy you're coming home."

"Me too."

"Have you heard anything from Gina?"

"She texted to let me know she'll be at the house when we get there." He shrugs as I turn onto our street.

Two big, black SUVs are parked in the driveway, along with a sleek blue convertible that belongs to his agent.

"Did she bring friends?" I inquire.

With another shrug, he slides his aviators a few inches down his nose to inspect the foreign cars closer. "No idea."

I park along the sidewalk, then switch off the ignition. "Do you need help getting out of the car?"

"I'm good. But if you could grab my bag from the back——"

"I got it." I open the driver's side door when his command stops me.

"Wait."

Turning toward him, I ask, "Yeah?"

"I love you."

My smile brightens. "I love you too."

"Thank you——"

"You've already thanked me a hundred times," I point out.

"And I'll thank you a thousand more."

Sliding closer to me, he carefully leans his forearm against the center console then presses a kiss against my lips. It's so soft and sweet I could get lost in it forever.

When he pulls away, I breathe out his name. "Riv..."

"I'm serious, Reese. I couldn't do this without you. I don't know where I'd be or how I would've recovered from the hell we've been through if it wasn't for you."

"And I don't know where I'd be if I didn't have a guy like you to make me understand what true love is. It's unconditional with you. And for a girl who's never truly experienced it like that––well, other than Milo, but he doesn't count––it means a lot to me. You're stuck with me, Riv."

"You're stuck with me too."

"Good. Now, will you let me get out of the car so we can go chat with your visitors?" I ask with pursed lips.

He grins. "So bossy."

"And don't you forget it. Chop, chop, mister."

After I grab his bag from the back of the truck, he takes it from my grasp in his good hand, and we walk side by side into the house.

Jake greets us at the door with a wide smile before pulling River into a hug while being careful of his bandaged arm.

"Hey, man. It's good to have you back."

"It's good to be back," River returns.

Releasing him from their embrace, Jake raises his chin toward the family room. "You have company."

"Thanks."

Then, in a quiet voice, Jake adds, "Good luck," and disappears into the kitchen.

Curious, River cocks his head to the side before dropping his bag onto the wooden floor. Once our fingers are tangled together, he tugs me with him into the family room.

"Hey!" Gina says as we come into view. Popping up from the couch, she strides closer and pulls us both into a careful hug. We've met a time or two since the accident, and she's actually a pretty awesome lady––leather skirt and all.

"Thanks for letting us stop by," she gushes. "I'm sure you're tired from the drive home and everything, so we'll get right to the point. River," she motions to the familiar photographer on the couch. "I'm sure you remember Brett."

"Hey," River greets him.

"What's up, man?" Brett pipes up.

"Not much. Just happy to be home."

"And this," Gina interjects, "is B.T. Henderson."

"Call me, Brooks. Nice to meet you." The stranger stands up and offers his hand to River. He reminds me of a suave Harrison Ford with thick salt and pepper hair and a confident smirk that's well deserved after his success in the film industry.

Shaking off his surprise, River takes it. "Nice to meet you too."

"And you must be Reese," Brooks surmises as he scans me up and down. "You're even prettier in person."

Somehow, he's able to make the compliment seem effortless and almost classy as if he's discussing a famous painting instead of commenting on a person's outward appearance. My cheeks heat, but I attempt to shrug it off. "Oh, thank you."

"I heard you were quite the trooper during River's audition."

I laugh before tossing a half-assed glare at Brett who's feet are resting on the coffee table like he doesn't have a care in the world.

"I see someone's a tattle-tale," I mention.

Brett's lazy grin is the only response he gives me before Brooks quips, "You'll have to cut him a little slack. He said you were both brilliant during the photoshoot. That you could cut the sexual tension with a knife."

"He's too kind," I deflect.

"I think he was spot-on. Now, as you both know, I'm working on an interesting project that I'm sure Gina has already told you about."

"The rockstar one?" I clarify.

"Yes. After a great deal of deliberation, I've decided to take a risk and turn it in a different direction than I'd initially anticipated. I'm an old man who craves a challenge and thinks it could be brilliant."

"And what direction is that?" River prods, his curiosity almost palpable.

"We're looking for something raw and beautifully painful that the audience can connect with. We want the story to feel gritty and real. And, while I thought the original script held a lot of promise, we had an epiphany that left me no choice but to implement a few new additions to it. For starters, we're looking for a completely fresh cast without any big-headed actors to steal the spotlight."

"I thought you already had a contract with Olivia Porter?" I interject before biting my tongue.

She's huge.

"We decided she wasn't the right fit before contracts were officially written. She's a brilliant actor, but we're hoping for a cast with a personal connection to the story who can hopefully portray it in a more meaningful way."

Scratching the scruff along his chiseled jaw, River asks, "I'm sorry... What are you trying to say here?"

"We want your story," Brooks declares, getting right to the point. "With a few minor tweaks, of course. We feel like it could be perfect for cinema. The forbidden relationship, the spiteful ex, the greedy mother, the crippling accident. All of it. I'd like to keep the rockstar aspect as well as the second-chance relationship portion to keep us from getting sued by your mother," he adds with an amused smirk, "but we can go over the details later. Would you be interested in going over the script I've pieced together?"

"Y-yeah," River answers as if he's still in shock. Brett stands up and hands each of us a copy of the script printed on a small stack of white papers.

After flipping through it for a few seconds, River looks over at me then back at Brooks. "And your investors are okay with you just switching the story like this?"

His arrogant grin brooks no argument. "I'm the *only*

investor for my projects, and I feel like this could be one of my best films to date. So my question is this: are you both in?"

"B-both?" I stutter, convinced I've heard him wrong.

"Like I said, we want your story, and we feel like you're the perfect candidates to portray it correctly."

"I'm not an actress," I point out.

"And you weren't a model either," Brett declares, clearly more entertained than I am.

Eyes wide, I turn to River and silently beg for him to pinch me or something because this...this is absolutely insane.

"River will be by your side the entire time," Brooks explains in an attempt to put me at ease. "He's a talented actor and can carry you through any scenes you're uncertain about. You'll also have a pretty damn good director to help you out when you need direction too."

The world feels like it's spinning as my eyelids flutter and tell him, "I... I don't know what to say."

"Just think about it. We'll be in touch."

Gina squeezes my arm in excitement as our guests grab their things then head out the door before murmuring to me, "We'll be in touch!"

Once everyone is gone, I push my hair away from my face and stare up at the ceiling. "This can't be happening."

River laughs. "This is definitely out of the ordinary. I'll give you that much. I knew Henderson was a bit eccentric and liked to mix things up, but..." His voice trails off as he steps in front of me. "You doin' okay?"

"I don't know what to think right now. I can't do this... Can I? I mean, obviously, you're a shoo-in, but..."

"But what, Reese?"

"But what if I'm terrible at it?"

"At being yourself?"

"I'm not entirely myself. I'm still technically Kristine."

He laughs. Again. "Toe-mae-toe, toe-mah-toe. I think you should give it a shot. You always dreamed of being an actress, remember?"

"Well, yeah. But those were just childish dreams––"

"Were they so childish?" he argues, tucking my hair behind my ear before forcing me to look up at him. "Or were you just so used to disappointment that you never bothered to get your hopes up and fight for what you wanted?"

"I don't..." I take a deep breath. "I guess I don't know."

With his mouth ticked up on one side, he points out, "For a girl who loves to tell me that I should fight for what I want, you sure do roll over easy when it comes to your own dreams. But I don't want to push you into doing this if it isn't what you really want."

"I can't act," I argue.

"You just had two very important people in the film industry tell you otherwise. What's your next excuse?"

"Milo––"

"Will be so damn proud of you for going after your dreams."

"And you?" I whisper. "Is this what you want? I feel like I'd be riding on your coattails––"

"Bullshit. Sure, I might've gotten you the audition in a roundabout way, but you got yourself the part. You. Reese Anders. And I'm just the lucky bastard who gets to cheer you on and see how bright you shine."

His confidence is contagious, though it doesn't stop my stomach from churning. Rocking back on my heels, I look up toward the ceiling before collapsing onto the couch.

"Am I really doing this?" I ask, my voice laced with disbelief.

The couch sinks under River's weight as he sits down next to me. "I sure as hell hope so. That way, we can travel together, work together, have sex in our trailers together." He bounces his eyebrows up and down. "You get the idea."

I roll my eyes. "Well, when you put it that way, how can I say no?"

His eyes widen in shock. Like he can't believe I said yes and is speechless.

"Is that a problem?" I joke, wringing my hands in my lap.

He grabs my wrist and stops me from fidgeting. "You serious?"

"Yeah." I take another deep breath and nod while ignoring the sudden onslaught of butterflies attacking my stomach. "I'm serious."

With a holler of excitement, he pulls me against his good side and kisses the ever-loving shit out of me. Like I'm his air. His other half. His everything.

"I love you, Floozy."

"I love you, too, Sex God/Master of Orgasms. And I think I'm gonna love all the adventures we have together."

"Damn straight?" he challenges.

I nod and blink back my tears of happiness. "Damn straight."

EPILOGUE

REESE

"This is insanity. You know that, right?" I mutter under my breath as the limo pulls up to the curb. Flashing lights threaten to blind me through the tinted glass, so I squeeze my eyes shut. Thankfully, there are a few limousines in front of us. I have a bit of time to breathe and get my anxiety in check before the hoard of cameras can document it firsthand.

With a gentleness I've come to expect, River rests his hand on my upper thigh. "Just breathe, Reese."

"Breathe? That's all you have to tell me? Dude. We're at a freaking red carpet event with paparazzi and cameras and news people and––"

"You're cute when you're stressed," he quips before planting a quick kiss against my forehead.

I roll my eyes. "And you're annoying when you're *not* stressed."

"Why are you stressed?" He laughs. "Gina told us about this months ago––"

"I know! But when it was just a blip on the calendar, it didn't seem like that big of a deal."

"And now?" he prods, brimming with amusement.

"Now, I'm freaking out! What if the critics or whatever don't like my dress? What if I trip over my feet and look like an idiot? What if I say the wrong thing and a bunch of news people catch it on camera?" My eyes widen in panic.

"Reese. Calm down."

"I don't know how to handle being in the spotlight," I whine.

"Then you probably should've considered that before you knocked it out of the park when you played Kristine."

I glare back at him. "Har, har. Besides, we aren't here to celebrate me and my acting skills, mister. We're here to celebrate your award nomination. So, maybe you should've done a shittier acting job, eh?"

Clutching his chest, he feigns offense. "Harsh, Floozy. Real harsh. And don't downplay your skills. Gina told us about you being in the running for best-supporting actress. Give yourself a little more credit. But I'll work on making my acting a little shittier for the sequel so that you don't have to come with me to these things. Mmmkay, pumpkin?" he teases, shrugging off my half-assed attempt at picking a fight. "Now, come on. Let's get out there and make all of the other guys jealous."

"And why would they be jealous?"

"'Cause they have to watch you cling to my arm instead of theirs."

Fighting off the urge to roll my eyes again, I rest my head against his shoulder and breathe in his familiar scent in hopes of it grounding me.

It works like a charm.

"Speaking of which," I start. "I'm proud of you."

"For what?"

"For that interview the other day where they went into depth about your experience recovering from the accident.

How you told them to stay strong, to be proud of your scars because they make you who you are, and that you promised to have them on full display for tonight's event." My eyes drop to his exposed arm. The sleeve of his fitted, white button-up shirt has been rolled up to his elbow and displays an intricate set of tattoos created by Milo. They're still relatively fresh since it took so long for the scar tissue to heal completely, but it doesn't fully camouflage the burns. In a way, the ink almost highlights them, making his forearm, bicep, and shoulder look like a badge of honor earned in a fiery pit of despair. And I kind of love it.

Running my fingers along my name woven throughout the flames near the inside of his wrist, I smile then press my lips to it.

"I'm just glad you're not pissed that I inked your name onto my skin," River points out.

"Why would that make me upset?"

"Because you're it for me."

"And that should make me upset?" I challenge with a grin.

He shrugs. "I didn't want to freak you out."

"Not possible. You're it for me, too, River. You know that." Lifting my chin, I wait for him to kiss me, and he does exactly that before the driver presses a button to get rid of the glass divider that separates the front of the limo from the back.

"Excuse me, sir," he calls, "but they're ready for you."

"Thank you," River replies before turning to me. "Let's get this party started, shall we?"

"Fiiiine."

After opening the passenger side door, an onslaught of flashing commences before microphones are shoved in our faces, and a chorus of questions are tossed our way. The next couple of hours go by in a blur until I find myself next to the man of my dreams in a sea of celebrities as we wait for them to announce the winner of the Best Up-And-Coming Actor.

River's fingers clasp mine and tighten as his name echoes through the speakers a few seconds later. My jaw drops before I cover my mouth and soak up the moment like a dry sponge.

He freaking did it!

The applause is so loud that my ears are ringing, but I don't even care. Standing with him, I pull River into a hug and squeeze him as tight as I possibly can before untangling myself from him so that he can claim his award. His steps are light and easy as he makes his way to the podium. Then he accepts the gold statue from the announcer and takes his place in front of the microphone like it's exactly where he was always meant to be.

Clearing his throat, he scans the audience while looking sexy as hell, like he's right in his element, being front and center. When his eyes land on me, he smiles. It's real. And genuine. And makes my heart race.

How the hell am I so lucky that I get to call him mine?

"Hey," he starts in his signature gritty voice. "I, uh, I'm not gonna lie. I'm in shock. When B.T. Henderson approached me and Reese about this project, we were blown away. I want to thank him for taking a chance on us and seeing the potential in not only the story but also in ourselves. He's incredible to work with, and I can't wait to dive into future projects with him."

The audience roars their agreement, and River patiently waits for them to calm down before continuing with his speech. "I want to thank the rest of the cast, as well as my agent, Gina, and Brett, the guy who was generous enough to connect me with Henderson in the first place. I'd also like to thank my roommates and best friends for their support. And for making sure I don't get too big of a head after this." The audience laughs while River smirks and shakes his head. "I would, uh... I would also like to thank Reese, my other half. Reese? Do you mind coming up here for a second?"

A spotlight finds me in the crowd before the audience goes wild. Clapping ensues mingled with whistling and a not-so-subtle nudge from Brooks as he motions to the stage.

"Better get up there, Reese. Wouldn't want to keep your man waiting, would you?" His chuckle acts like gasoline on an inferno of nerves licking at my insides, but I stop myself from smacking him in the arm and do as I'm told.

Digging my teeth into my inner cheek while silently cursing River under my breath, I stand up and wave to the cameras before grabbing my dress and walking up the stairs.

Please don't trip. Please don't trip, I silently chant as I make my way toward a very entertained River.

"I'd bet you fifty bucks she's cursing me in her head right now," he announces for everyone to hear. The audience cracks up, and I glare at the love of my life while trying to maintain a bit of decorum even though I know I'm failing miserably.

Pulling him into a quick hug, I whisper, "I'm going to kill you for this. You know that, right?"

He presses a quick kiss to my cheek but ignores my empty threat and continues with his little speech. "Reese, I love you. I can't tell you how many times I've had people comment about my arm, about the accident, about the recovery, about the burns, all of it. They act like I'm a saint because I faced my challenges head-on. But they don't understand something. You faced those challenges with me. Without you, I wouldn't have had the courage to survive any of it. Without you, I wouldn't have accomplished all of my dreams. I wouldn't have landed the role that led me here today. I wouldn't have met Henderson. I wouldn't have learned what's truly important in life. And I wouldn't have understood what true, unconditional love feels like." My smile softens as I take in the sincerity in his voice and the gentleness in his touch as he tangles our fingers together. Lifting my hand to his lips, he presses a gentle kiss to the back of it before taking a deep breath that holds so much promise my knees shake.

"And today, in front of all these people, I want you to show me what it feels like to be the luckiest man in the world. Because yeah, this award is pretty damn awesome, but guess what would make it even more incredible? If you said you'd marry me."

Trying to get a handle on my emotions, I cover my face and blink back a wave of happy tears that threaten to spill down my cheeks as the crowd goes wild.

Then my brows furrow, and I lean toward the microphone. "I'm sorry… Was that a question?"

The audience roars with laughter.

With a grin, River digs for something in his front pocket before dropping onto one knee. A little blue box rests in his hand as he offers it to me. "Will you, Reese Anders, love of my life and partner in crime, make me the luckiest bastard on Earth and marry me?"

My teeth dig into my lower lip as I stare at the most attractive man I've ever laid eyes on kneeling in front of me. And even though every ounce of him is oozing confidence right now, I can feel the vulnerability in his request. The fear of rejection that I have his mother to thank for instilling in him all those years ago. And the quiet desperation that lets me know I'm the luckiest girl in the world.

"Yes," I whisper.

"A little louder, please," he quips. "I gotta make sure your brother hears it."

Throwing my head back, I laugh even harder as I finally give in and let my tears of joy fall. "Yes! Yes, I'll marry you!"

His arms snake around my waist before he spins me around, and I tuck my face between his jaw and collarbone, soaking up the moment that is so surreal I'd think it was scripted if I didn't know any better.

But I know the truth.

River––the model, actor, master of orgasms––is all mine.

For real.

No matter what.

And I wouldn't have it any other way.

The End

FORBIDDEN LYRICS

Chapter One
Dove

A bead of sweat clings to my brow as I reach across the table and wipe it down with the damp rag when something grazes my bum. I jerk upright, my spine a steel rod, then twist around.

"Can I help you?" I squeak, unsure whether or not the creepy stranger hears me over the speakers. The bar I work at, SeaBird, isn't exactly the place you go to have a quiet chat, especially when Broken Vows is on stage. I don't recognize the song echoing through the bar, though, so they must be taking a break.

"Fender," the stranger returns. "Is he here?"

I peek around the guy's giant body in search of the band's lead singer, but find the stage empty. Then I shake my head. "I, uh, I'm not sure. Sorry. Can I get you something to drink?"

And will you stop staring at me like that?

"Only if you're on the menu." His mouth quirks up on one side as he scans me up and down, making my skin crawl.

"You're new," he notes.

"I started a little while ago," I hedge before side-stepping to my right. He follows the movement and inches closer.

With a gulp, I stutter, "A-are you sure you don't want a drink? I can go grab one for you..."

His massive frame crowds me against the table, its sharp edge digging into my lower back as I try to keep myself from cowering, but it feels impossible.

"When do you get off work?" he demands.

"I'm uh," I twist the rag in my hand. "I'm here all night."

"Maybe I'll stick around, then. Watching you bend over that table was the highlight of my evening."

Zeroing in on the peanut lying on the concrete floor beneath my feet, I try to ignore the way his gaze rolls over me like hot tar, like I've been burned.

"I'm uh, I'm not sure my boyfriend would appreciate that," I choke out.

"Boyfriend, huh? Who's the lucky bastard?"

My eyes widen with panic before the first name that comes to mind tumbles out of me. "Gibson. He works here. He's actually--"

"I know, Gibbs." He scans me up and down again as if I'm a piece of meat at the butcher's. "And I gotta give you props. You're rocking the whole innocent vanilla waitress like a champ."

"Excuse me?"

"If you and Gibbs are a thing, then that means you and Milo are, too."

Confused, my mouth opens then closes like a fish out of water.

What the heck is he talking about?

Milo and Gibson are friends, but I've never gotten the vibe they're anything else, and--unless my gay-dar is broken-- they're both *very* straight.

He chuckles, then toys with the ends of my hair, his knuckle brushing along the top of my breast, but I'm too frozen––too shocked–– to move.

What. Is. Happening?

"You into sharing, Babe?" he murmurs, his voice low and husky.

I shy away from his touch, and push my hair behind my shoulder. "I-if you don't want anything to drink, then I should probably get back to work––"

"You should give me your number."

"I have a boyfriend," I remind him, my voice shaky.

"One you'd be smart to stay away from."

My brows furrow as I pull my lips into a thin, white line.

He laughs, dryly, though I'm not sure what he finds so amusing. Personally, I'm about to vomit all over the floor if this conversation goes on much longer.

"He's dangerous," he informs me as if we're talking about the weather.

"Huh?"

"Your boyfriend. He's dangerous. You'd be smart to stay away from him."

I gulp, but stay quiet, praying he'll grow bored of our conversation and leave me alone, but I'm afraid that's wishful thinking.

"Do you know what happened to his last girlfriend? Em?" he asks, grabbing my chin and forcing me to look at him. "She disappeared. Vanished into thin air. I'd hate for that to happen to you too. I've always been a sucker for an innocent girl who likes kink."

"Hey, Dove!" Reese interrupts, her voice light and chipper, though her eyes are anything but. She's another waitress at SeaBird and is slowly turning out to be one of my good friends too, especially now that she just saved me from Mr. Creeper.

"Everything okay here?" she asks.

I gulp, again, and look up at the mystery man who can't be more than five or six years older than me, yet still makes me feel like a little kid.

"No problem," the stranger answers for me "Right, *Dove?*" He emphasizes my name like it's a secret password that gives him permission to speak with me, when all I want to do is run and hide. "I was just leaving."

He steps around me, but still manages to make me feel small and insignificant as he does so. Reese's upper lip curls in disgust as she watches him leave. But not before he gives me one last knowing look before he walks out the door.

Whoever he was...I hope I never see him again.

"You okay?" Reese asks once he's out of sight.

Blinking slowly, I try to wrangle in my emotions but it feels impossible.

"Uh, yes. Yes, I'm fine," I lie.

"What was that about?"

"Nothing."

"You sure?"

With a jerky nod, I wring the dishrag between my hands like it's a lifeline. "Yes. Yes, I'm fine."

"You don't look fine. What happened, Dove? Who was that?"

"I-I don't know. He was looking for Fender."

"And?"

"And I told him that I didn't know where he was."

"Okay?" She frowns. "Is that it?"

With a deep breath, I shake my head. "No. Then he started asking me how long I'd worked here and if I'd be interested in..."--I clear my throat, hating the way my cheeks heat-- "in hooking up later. I lied and told him I had a boyfriend, thinking maybe that would get him to back off."

Surprised, Reese points out, "That's a good idea, actually––"

"It didn't work. So, I told him that Gibson was my boyfriend and that he'd be back any minute, and wouldn't appreciate him talking to me. I know it's the furthest thing from the truth and that Gibson hates me, but it just popped into my head, and––"

"Seriously, Dove." She grabs my wrist to keep it from shaking. "I think that was a brilliant idea."

Again, I shake my head. "He knows him. Gibson. Supposedly, anyway."

"Oh."

"Yeah." I give her a tight smile. "That's not the part that was weird though."

"What do you mean?"

I hesitate, replaying the conversation in my head to confirm I didn't imagine the whole thing. But it happened so fast. Honestly, I'm not even sure anymore.

"He said that if Gibson and I were a thing, then I must be having...relations with his friend Milo, too," I admit.

"Oh." Reese's lips purse as if she's tasted something sour. "Yeah...I heard they're into sharing."

"That's a thing?" I squeak.

With an awkward laugh, she shrugs. "Supposedly. Is that why you're spooked? With your history and all, I'd get it. That probably sounds terrible. For two guys to––"

"That wasn't it," I mutter. Part of me hates the fact that she knows I'm a virgin and was raised in a crazy religious household with parents who never even uttered the s-word let alone gave us the talk of the birds and the bees. Not that I don't know what sex is, but still. That's not the point.

I shake off my inner monologue and continue. "I mean, it sounded weird, but who am I to judge? No. He…" I pause, again, and look over at the bar where a very oblivious

Gibson is mixing drinks. "H-he warned me about something."

"Huh?"

"He just said that if I was smart, I'd stay away from Gibbs. And Milo."

"Why?" Reese asks, just as confused as I am.

"Because their last girlfriend disappeared after they broke up, and it would be a shame if the same thing happened to me."

"He said, *what?*" Reese screeches.

"I know," I rush out. "It sounds crazy, right?"

"Definitely crazy. I know Gibson, Dove. And I know Milo," she adds. He's her older brother. "Whatever bullshit that guy was spewing...it was exactly that. *Bullshit.*"

"You're right. You're right," I repeat, though it does nothing to sooth my nerves. "It was just...the way he said, ya know? Like he knew something. But you're right. He was probably just being a jerk."

"I'm sure that's exactly what he was being––"

"Do you know anyone named Em?" I interrupt. "Emma? Emily? Something like that?"

With a frown, Reese shakes her head. "Sorry. I don't. But if it makes you feel better, you could always ask him."

With a dry laugh, I roll my eyes then tuck my hair behind my ear. "No, thank you. That would be...weird. He hates me, remember? But you're right. It doesn't matter. We aren't even dating," I remind myself. "He's my co-worker, I just made that up to get the guy to leave me alone. It's fine. Everything's fine."

"You sure?" Reese asks.

I nod. "Yes. Definitely."

"Okay," she mutters, though she doesn't look very convinced. "We still on for tomorrow night?"

"Yes. Definitely," I repeat, a little more sure this time. I'd give anything to get out of my stifling apartment and away from my grumpy pregnant sister for reasons other than work. The girl's night Reese suggested earlier tonight before our boss got mad at us for slacking sounds pretty dang perfect.

"Let's get back to work before we get yelled at again," I add. "And thanks for saving me."

"Anytime."

Order Forbidden Lyrics Here

Sophie

Marcus

Anthony

Skye

Saylor

Advantage Play Series

(Steamy Romantic Suspense/Mafia Series)

Wild Card

Little Bird

Bitter Queen

Black Jack

Royal Flush

Stand Alones

Fifty-Fifty

Drowning in Love (A Signature Sweethearts Spin-Off Novella)

Hired Hottie (A *Steamy* Signature Sweethearts Spin-Off)

Crush (A *Steamy* Signature Sweethearts Spin-Off)

Bartered Souls Duet

(Urban Fantasy Series)

Gambled Soul

Wager Won

Sign up for Kelsie's newsletter to receive exclusive content, including the first two chapters of every new book two weeks before its release date!

Dear Reader,

I want to thank you guys from the bottom of my heart for taking a chance on Model Behavior, and for giving me the opportunity to share this story with you. I couldn't do this without you!

I would also be very grateful if you could take the time to leave a review. It's amazing how such a little thing like a review can be such a huge help to an author!

Thank you so much!!!

-Kelsie

ABOUT THE AUTHOR

Kelsie is a sucker for a love story with all the feels. When she's not chasing words for her next book, you will probably find her reading or, more likely, hanging out with her husband and playing with her three kiddos who love to drive her crazy.

She adores photography, baking, her two pups, and her cat who thinks she's a dog. Now that she's actively pursuing her writing dreams, she's set her sights on someday finding the self-discipline to not binge-watch an entire series on Netflix in one sitting.

If you'd like to connect with Kelsie, follow her on Facebook, sign up for her newsletter, or join Kelsie Rae's Reader Group to stay up to date on new releases, exclusive content, give-aways, and her crazy publishing journey.

Printed in Great Britain
by Amazon

79373947R00234